SHENANDOAH

THE CIVIL WAR BATTLE SERIES
by James Reasoner

Manassas
Shiloh
Antietam
Chancellorsville
Vicksburg
Gettysburg
Chickamauga

SHENANDOAH

James Reasoner

CUMBERLAND HOUSE
NASHVILLE, TENNESSEE

Published by
CUMBERLAND HOUSE PUBLISHING, INC.
431 Harding Industrial Drive
Nashville, Tennessee 37211
www.cumberlandhouse.com

Cover design by Bob Bubkis, Nashville, Tennessee.

Library of Congress Cataloging-in-Publication Data

Reasoner, James.
  Shenandoah / James Reasoner.
    p.   cm. — (The Civil War battle series ; bk. 8)
    ISBN 1-58182-294-4 (alk. paper)
    1. Shenandoah River Valley (Va. and W. Va.)—History—Civil War, 1861–1865—Fiction. 2. Grant, Ulysses S. (Ulysses Simpson), 1822–1885—Fiction.
3. Spotsylvania Court House, Battle of, Va., 1864—Fiction. 4. Wilderness, Battle of the, Va., 1864—Fiction. 5. Mosby, John Singleton, 1833–1916—Fiction. 6. Cold Harbor, Battle of, Va., 1864—Fiction. 7. Culpeper County (Va.)—Fiction. I. Title.
PS3568.E2685 S54 2002
813'.54—dc21   2002012049

Printed in the United States of America.

1 2 3 4 5 6 7 8 9 10—05 04 03 02

This one is for all my friends
around the Campfire

SHENANDOAH

Chapter One

TITUS BRANNON COULDN'T DECIDE what was going to kill him. The way things were going, it was a pretty even race. He might cough his lungs out from the grippe, or he could simply freeze to death. One way or the other, he didn't much care. He'd had enough. He was ready to die.

An icy mist stung his face as he swayed back and forth on the wagon seat. He wondered if he would fall off before they got where they were going. Every so often the woman beside him put an arm around his shoulders to steady him, but most of the time she needed both hands on the reins. The mules were balky, and Louisa Abernathy had to keep slapping their rumps and yelling at them to make them move. Dumb brutes, Titus thought. Of course, the same could be said of him and Louisa, or else they wouldn't have been out on a night like this. Hell, the whole human race was a bunch of dumb brutes as far as Titus was concerned. He didn't give a fig for any of them. After everything he had endured, he didn't believe there was a lick of goodness in anybody.

Well, maybe in Louisa, he amended. After all, she had helped him to escape from that hellhole of a Yankee prison camp, and she had stayed with him and helped him all the way from Illinois back here to Virginia. At least he thought they were in Virginia. He hoped they were. Since he'd gotten sick, he had lost track of things such as where they were.

"Is this the right road?" Louisa asked, raising her voice to be heard over the frigid wind.

Titus didn't answer. His eyes were closed and his head was tipped forward, but he wasn't really asleep. Just resting his eyes. He opened them when she repeated the question.

"Wha—? What did you say?" A fit of coughing took him after that, and it was several moments before it subsided. Louisa

11

gathered the reins in her left hand and put her right arm around Titus. He huddled against her, seeking what meager warmth he could draw from her.

Finally, she asked for the third time if they were on the right road. Titus forced himself to concentrate. He couldn't see much, what with the fog and the mist. No light from the moon and stars penetrated the overcast. Blackness surrounded them. Titus couldn't even tell if they were on a road, let alone the right one. But he didn't want to stop, so he mumbled, "Yeah . . . right road. Shouldn't be . . . much farther now."

"I hope not," Louisa said. "I'm not sure how much more of this weather you can take."

Titus wasn't sure, either. But unlike Louisa, he didn't care.

They had come over the Blue Ridge in the stolen wagon several days earlier. He hadn't been quite so sick then, so he had been able to tell her which roads to follow. There had been Yankees between Port Republic and Brown's Gap, and several times they'd had to leave the road and take to the woods to avoid blue-clad cavalrymen. Stealth was their only chance. They couldn't outrun a patrol, nor could they put up much of a fight. Their only weapon was an old pistol, and they had only a few rounds for it. They'd had a carbine at one point in their journey from Illinois, but Titus was sort of fuzzy on what had happened to it. He thought Louisa might have traded it to a farmer for some food so that they wouldn't starve to death. Titus was grateful to Louisa for everything she'd done, but she wasn't much of a forager.

Badly armed or not, if they had run into any Yankees, Titus would have fought. He would have forced them to kill him, and he hoped that in a case like that, he would be able to send a few of them to hell ahead of him. The one thing that was strong enough inside him to withstand all the fatigue and illness and hunger of the journey was his determination not to be recaptured. They would send him back to a prison camp, either Camp Douglas or some other godforsaken place like that. He wasn't going to let that happen. He would die first.

A smile tugged at his thin, cracked, bleeding lips as that thought crossed his mind. He was pretty much convinced that he would die before this night was over, and the damned Yankees wouldn't have anything to do with it. His string had run out. That was all there was to it.

"I'm looking for lights," Louisa called out beside him. "We've come far enough. We should be at the farm by now."

The farm. That was right, Titus reminded himself. He was almost home. Back to the loving arms of his family. His mother, Abigail, who packed enough rigid, bitter self-righteousness in her birdlike body for half a dozen normal people. His older brothers, Will and Mac, who had never been shy about showing their disapproval of everything about him. His little sister, Cordelia, wasn't too bad, though, and his younger brother, Henry, was the only one who looked up to him, blundering around after him like a puppy. And Cory, of course, the smartest one in the family, who had gotten the hell out years before when he had the chance. Titus had wished more than once that he had gone west like Cory.

Too late now. Too late for everything. The damage had already been done.

He thought about Polly.

Beautiful Polly, with hair that shone like spun silver in the sun. The woman he had loved for so long and finally, against all odds, made his wife. But when push had come to shove, she had chosen her father, that old bastard, Duncan Ebersole, over him. Titus wondered what had happened to her after he'd joined the Confederate army and gone off to fight. She was probably at Mountain Laurel, the Ebersole plantation, he thought, waiting hand and foot on the old buzzard like always. She wouldn't be glad to see him, that was for sure. She hadn't cared when he left, and she wouldn't care that he was back.

Yet he found himself wanting to see her again. Aching inside for a glimpse of her face, maybe even a touch of her hand. As memories of Polly flooded his mind, he sat a little straighter on the wagon seat. Maybe he wasn't ready to give up after all. His hatred of the Yankees and his burning desire to kill more of them had sustained him during the dark days at Camp Douglas and during the long, arduous journey home as well. But there was more to life than hate and killing, Titus realized as the feverish haze inside his head cleared a little. He wanted to see Polly again, despite everything that had happened between them. He even wanted to see his family . . .

"There! Is that a light?" Louisa almost shouted.

Titus blinked and squinted through the mist. He thought he saw a faint yellow glow. "Could be. Better steer for it." Talking set off another round of coughing, and the violence of it made him double over on the seat. Between the wracking spasms, he laughed. Wouldn't it be just his luck to finally make it home and die just as he got there?

And on Christmas Day, at that. The memory came back to him of how, earlier in the day, Louisa had mentioned that it was Christmas. December 25, 1863. The day that marked the birth of Jesus Christ and the death of Titus Brannon.

His laughter continued until the coughing finally overwhelmed it.

Titus was only vaguely aware that the wagon had stopped. He felt himself falling, but then his feet hit the ground, and he realized she had hauled him down and caught him, holding him upright with all the deceptive strength in her slender body. She pulled him along, forcing him to take one staggering step after another. He stumbled on the steps leading up to the porch, but Louisa kept him on his feet. Consciousness threatened to slip away from him. His head hung forward, limp and swaying.

A pounding noise. She was knocking on the door. The wind howled, but over the sound of it, he heard a man's voice through the door.

"Who's there?"

"Is this the Brannon farm?" Desperation strained Louisa's voice. "Oh, please, help us!"

Titus heard the hinges creak as the door swung open. A gust of wind blew past the two miserable figures on the porch, and its icy blast made the man at the open door draw back a little.

"Thank God!" Louisa gasped. "I thought we would never get here. Help me get him inside. Please. He's so ill."

"Who in blazes—"

Something about the voice was familiar. Titus lifted his head. It was Henry, standing there big as life just inside the door, a shotgun in his hands. Titus managed to grin, and in a cracked voice that sounded as if it were coming from the grave, he said, "Hello, little brother."

That greeting took all the strength he had, and as blackness even darker than the night closed in around him, he toppled forward. He didn't know if Louisa caught him, or if Henry did, or if nobody did. He didn't know anything.

⟨∞⟩

HENRY WASN'T sure whether to curse or pray or just stare in mingled horror and amazement, so he did a little of all of it for a couple of heartbeats. Then instinct took over and he sprang forward, holding the shotgun in his left hand while he reached out to grasp the arm of the man passing out in front of him.

This couldn't be Titus, Henry thought as his fingers closed around the painfully thin arm of the man. Titus was dead, killed by the Yankees at Fredericksburg more than a year ago. This stranger might look like Titus, but that was all.

The redheaded woman had hold of the man's other arm, and together she and Henry kept him from pitching to the floor.

"Let's get him inside," Henry said. Over his shoulder, he added, "Ma, we've got a sick man here." He turned to help the stranger in, thinking that they would put him on the divan where Cordelia and Polly had been sitting, close to the fire so that he could warm up. The poor fellow had to be half-frozen on a night like this.

Then, as Henry turned and the women got a good look at the stranger, Abigail cried out, "Oh, my God!" Cordelia exclaimed, "Titus!" Polly just screamed, the shrill sound muffled by a hand she clapped over her mouth.

The reactions of the women made Henry look again at the stranger's face, and he felt his mind swimming in disbelief. A feeling of dizziness washed through him, as if the world were no longer spinning the way it should be. Henry's guts clenched.

He might not want to believe it. He *couldn't* believe it. This gaunt, wretched stranger was his brother Titus. Finally, Henry could deny it no longer.

He kicked the door shut as he and the woman half-carried Titus toward the divan. No matter how crazy the world had gotten all of a sudden, there was no point in letting any more cold air into the house. Henry clung to that practical notion, sensing that he had to carry on as if brothers came back from the grave every day; otherwise he might lose his mind entirely.

"Cordelia, get some quilts," Henry said. "We need to get him out of these wet clothes and warm him up, or he's liable to get even sicker." He glanced at the redheaded woman, who really *was* a stranger. "What's wrong with him?"

"The grippe, I think," she said. "He has a fever. And he was already awfully weak from all that had happened at the camp."

Henry didn't know what she was talking about, but he figured they could hash it all out later. He could tell that Titus had been through hell. His brother was just a shadow of his former self. Titus had always been the lean, muscular sort, but he had packed a normal amount of weight on his frame. Now he was wasted away to almost nothing.

Polly was silent now, still staring wide-eyed at Titus, her face twisted with disbelief and maybe fear. Fear of the dead coming back to haunt her, Henry thought. Like the rest of them, she had believed that Titus was dead.

Otherwise she never would have become Henry's wife. Never would have lain with him in the first place and gotten herself with child by him, the child that now lived inside her rounded belly . . .

Henry's head jerked as he shoved those thoughts out of his mind. Later, he told himself. Deal with all of it later. Right now, he could think only about getting Titus on the divan and keeping him from freezing to death.

Cordelia had hesitated when Henry told her to get some quilts, but she had shaken herself out of that daze and run upstairs. Now she hurried back down, her arms full of quilts. Henry said, "Spread one of them on the divan to keep it from getting too wet while we get him undressed."

Cordelia dropped all the quilts but one, shook it out, then spread it on the divan. Henry and the woman stranger lowered Titus onto it as gently as they could. Titus muttered something incoherent. His eyes were closed, and Henry knew he wasn't conscious. He started fumbling with the buttons of Titus's ragged garments.

"That's not my son," Abigail said, her voice shaking. "My son is dead. Dead and buried. That's not my son."

She was on the verge of hysterics, Henry knew. Maybe a chore would help her to control her emotions. "Ma, why don't you heat up some broth?"

For a second, Abigail didn't say anything. Then she nodded her head. "Yes, some warm broth might do that poor man some good. But he's *not* Titus. He's not my son."

With that, she headed for the kitchen. Henry didn't argue with her. He knew exactly how she felt. A large part of his brain was still shouting that this haggard stranger couldn't possibly be his brother.

Titus's face was flushed with fever, but the rest of his body was fish-belly white, so pale that he really did look like a corpse. Henry tried not to think about that as he undressed his brother. Titus was soaked to the skin. After Henry had removed his drenched clothes, he used a quilt to dry him as best he could, then lifted him while Cordelia pulled the wet quilt and the clothes off the divan. The strange woman seemed to be a straight thinker and had a dry quilt ready. They wrapped Titus in it and laid him down again.

"That can't be Titus," Polly said. "He's dead. He was killed at Fredericksburg."

The redheaded woman looked at her. "No, he was captured there and sent to a prison in Illinois. That's where I met him." She looked around at Henry, Polly, and Cordelia, her eyes widening as she lifted a hand to her lips. "Oh, dear Lord. You all believed he was dead. You had no idea he was alive."

Henry was still trying to wrap his mind around the whole thing. What the woman said made some sense. Will and Mac had come back to the farm after the battle at Fredericksburg and told them that Titus had been killed. They had been sincere; Henry was certain of that. But they could have been mistaken. That was how it had to be, because Titus was here, lying senseless and sick on the divan. Despite his illness, he wasn't dead. Henry knew he had to accept that.

He looked again at Polly. His wife . . .

His brother's wife.

Again he shook his head and told himself that he couldn't afford to think about that now. He looked at the redheaded woman. "We're obliged to you for bringing him home, Miss . . . ?"

"Louisa Abernathy," she said.

"Thank you, Miss Abernathy. You're Titus's . . . friend?"

"I helped him escape." She closed her eyes for a moment and pressed her fingertips to her forehead. When she looked up at Henry again, all she could say was, "It's a long story, and I'm awfully tired and cold . . ."

"Of course! Lord, I'm sorry, Miss Abernathy. You go on over by the fire and warm up." Henry pulled Abigail's rocker closer to the hearth. "Here. Please, sit down."

With a grateful, exhausted sigh, Louisa Abernathy sank into the rocking chair. Her eyes closed again. Henry figured if she were left alone, she would be asleep within minutes.

He turned back to the divan. Polly still stood there, staring down at Titus. "It can't be," she whispered as Henry moved closer to her. "It just can't be."

He put his hands on her shoulders and turned her toward him. "It's all right," he said quietly. "It'll be fine, Polly. Don't you worry about a thing."

"But he's *dead!* I mourned for him. I cried for days. He can't be alive."

Abigail came out of the kitchen with a cup of broth and a spoon. Tendrils of steam curled up from it. "Cordelia," Henry directed, "hold Titus's head up so Ma can give him some of that broth. That'll help thaw him out."

Gently, he also urged his wife away from the divan. "Come on, Polly. Let's get out of the way."

He led her to another chair on the other side of the room and got her to sit down. She had a stunned look on her face, but she didn't try to get up. Henry left her sitting there, her hands lying limp in her lap, while he went over to the fireplace and added some wood to the blaze. He looked at Louisa Abernathy and saw that she was asleep now, her head leaning back against the rocker's cushion.

Henry took a deep breath. He wasn't as dizzy now, and although he still had a hard time believing it, he was coming to accept the fact that Titus was alive and had somehow, against all reason, returned to the Brannon family farm.

He would have to let Will and Mac know about this. Mac was with General Stuart, the leader of the Confederate cavalry, at the winter headquarters of the Army of Northern Virginia, some twenty miles south of Culpeper at Orange Court House. Will was in a Richmond hospital, recovering from a terrible wound he had received at Gettysburg the previous summer, though the reports the family had received of his condition were promising enough that they hoped he would be able to return home soon to complete his recuperation. Both Will and Mac would want to know as soon as possible that Titus was alive.

Henry rubbed a hand over his face and felt a surge of anger inside him. How could Will and Mac have made such a mistake? They had claimed that Titus had received a proper burial, which meant they must have seen his body. Or what they *thought* was his body. Had the man who'd been laid to rest as Titus Brannon been so torn up by the battle that he wasn't recognizable? Henry supposed that was possible. But Will and Mac should have made sure. They should have been certain of the facts before they brought such awful news home!

Henry shook his head and turned away from the fireplace. He thought about Cory, who had received the news of Titus's supposed death while he was at Vicksburg, over in Mississippi. But then the Yankees had laid siege to Vicksburg and eventually captured it, and the family hadn't received any letters from Cory since then. Henry didn't know where Cory was or even if he was still alive. He didn't have any idea where to write to Cory with word of Titus's unexpected return.

All of this was one hell of a lot to drop onto his shoulders, he thought. But as the only one of the Brannon brothers still at home, it was up to him to handle things. Despite his relative youth, he wasn't a child anymore. He was a married man and soon would be a father.

He looked at Polly. She was still sitting in the chair where he had put her, staring across the room at Titus. Cordelia had sat down on the divan and gotten Titus's head in her lap, propping him up so that Abigail could spoon the broth into his mouth. Titus was coming around a little, but he wasn't conscious yet.

Louisa Abernathy sat up in the rocking chair with a gasp and a jerk. She must have been dreaming, and some nightmare had jolted her out of her slumber. From the few things she had said, Henry suspected that the woman had been through enough to justify plenty of bad dreams.

He knelt beside the rocking chair. "It's all right, Miss Abernathy. You're safe here."

"The . . . the Union soldiers . . . ?"

"None closer than Brandy Station. Their patrols come this way from time to time, but they won't be out in this weather. And it's Christmas to boot."

"Christmas," Louisa repeated in a half-whisper as she stared into the flames. "I brought you a rather unexpected Christmas present, didn't I, Mr. Brannon?"

"Henry. Call me Henry. That's my sister, Cordelia, over there, with Titus's head in her lap, and our mother, Abigail, who's giving him the broth." Henry hesitated then added, "And the other lady is Polly."

"Titus's wife?" Louisa frowned. "He's spoken of her, but only a little. I don't understand. How can she be—"

She stopped short, but Henry knew what she had been about to say. *How can Polly be pregnant when Titus has been gone for more than a year?* From the look in Louisa's eyes, Henry could tell that she had figured out the answer.

"Polly is my wife now," he said in a low voice, his hand resting on the arm of the rocker. "We all thought Titus was dead."

Louisa's teeth caught at her lower lip for a second then she nodded. "Of course. I understand."

Henry forced his mind back to practical matters. "You're almost frozen yourself, and you must be starving. Why don't you come into the kitchen with me, and you can have some of that broth. I'll bet I can rustle up a biscuit, too. I'm sorry, but there's not any ham left from our Christmas dinner."

"Whatever you have would be wonderful."

He took her arm and helped her to her feet. She wasn't quite as thin as Titus, but there was no extra meat on her bones, either. They must have been on short rations the whole trip. Unfortunately, they had come to a place where food was no longer in abundance, as it once had been. This region had been a land of milk and honey, just like in the Bible. But now all of northern Virginia had been stripped almost clean by war.

Henry paused as he and Louisa went past the divan. "I'm going to get Miss Abernathy something to eat," he said.

"All right," Abigail said as she dipped the spoon into the cup of broth. "The pan is still on the stove."

The fire in the big cast-iron stove had been banked earlier, but it still gave off enough heat so that the kitchen was warm. Louisa sat at the table while Henry ladled up a bowl of broth for her. She started on that while he got a biscuit from the breadbox. A few biscuits had been left at dinner, and Abigail had wrapped them in linen and stored them away for tomorrow.

Louisa would have liked to pick up the bowl of broth and drink it all down in one swallow, Henry thought, but she was forcing herself to use a spoon and take it slow and easy. If she ate too much too fast, it might make her sick. He put the biscuit on a saucer and set it in front of her. She smiled at him, tore off a small piece, and put it in her mouth.

Henry pulled out a chair and sat down on the other side of the table. Trying not to be too obvious about it, he studied Louisa Abernathy. She was older than him, probably in her late twenties. Her woolen shawl was around her shoulders now, leaving her head bare. She had thick, curly, dark red hair that fell in wings around her face. If she hadn't been so thin, she would have been pretty.

Her coat was ragged, and under it she wore a gray woolen dress that also showed the ravages of long, hard wear. Henry wasn't sure how either she or Titus had kept from freezing to death tonight. "My sister must have some clothes that will fit you. After you've eaten, Cordelia can take you upstairs and help you get changed. You need dry clothes as much as Titus does."

Louisa shook her head. "No, thank you. I'm fine. I'm not ill, like Titus is."

"How long has he been sick?"

"Almost a week. He's gotten worse every day. For a while, I . . . I wondered if we would make it here before . . ."

"I understand," Henry said as her voice broke with emotion and trailed away. "I can't tell you how much we appreciate what you've done. I reckon you saved Titus's life."

"Perhaps. It was the only thing I could do, once I'd seen how he was being treated in that awful prison camp."

"Tell me about it," Henry said. "That is, if you can."

Louisa took a deep breath then nodded. "I can. But once you've heard the story, you may wish you had never asked."

Chapter Two

IT WAS A HORRIBLE story, all right, as horrible as anything Henry had ever heard. His hands clenched into fists as he sat there and listened to Louisa Abernathy describe the torment Titus and the other Confederate captives had endured at the Yankee prison known as Camp Douglas, a sprawling compound on the outskirts of Chicago, Illinois.

"The men were given the worst food, and barely enough of it to keep them alive," Louisa explained. "There was no heat in their barracks, and they had only a few blankets that were so vermin-infested they should have been burned. After some of the men tried to dig a tunnel out of the camp so they could escape, the floors were torn out of the barracks. The prisoners had to sleep in the mud. Of course there were no . . . sanitary facilities, only a . . . a trench. And a similar trench in which the bodies of the poor men who died were thrown like they were so much garbage." Louisa's voice trembled. "Men died every day, of starvation or disease or from the beatings they received from the guards when they committed some trivial infraction of the rules. Many of them were shot for accidentally stepping over some imaginary line that marked the boundaries of where they were allowed to go. The dead line, the prisoners called it." She covered her face with her hands, and for a few moments she couldn't go on. When she finally spoke again, Henry almost wished she hadn't because her voice was filled with such pain. "I have seen men forced to stand at attention in freezing weather for so long that their bare feet froze to the ground. They couldn't move without ripping the skin and flesh away. I have seen them beaten with clubs and whipped until their backs were raw. Is it any wonder my heart went out to them?"

"It sounds mighty bad, all right, Miss Abernathy," Henry agreed. His voice was hoarse from what he was feeling inside as he thought about what Titus and the other prisoners had suffered through.

Louisa smiled, but her expression was grim. "I'm told that, in the South, slaves are treated in much the same fashion."

Henry's jaw clenched as he looked down at the table. He thought of the rumors he had heard about how badly Duncan Ebersole's overseers handled the slaves on Mountain Laurel in the days before the war. "I reckon some folks who hold slaves might do that," he admitted. "But they're wrong to do it. Just like those Yankees are wrong."

"Yes," Louisa said. "I'm a member of the Society of Friends. Some people call us Quakers. We don't believe that two wrongs make a right. No matter what the causes of this awful war, there is no excuse for such inhumane treatment of prisoners. That's why I had to do what I could to help. I would have freed all those prisoners if I could. But since I couldn't, I decided to help Titus and Nathan get away."

Henry frowned in confusion. "Who's Nathan?"

"Nathan Hatcher. I believe he was from this area, too."

A sudden crash of crockery startled both of them. Henry jerked around and saw his sister in the doorway, the pieces of a shattered cup scattered around her feet. Titus must have finished the broth, he surmised, because the cup seemed to have been empty.

"Oh my," Cordelia said. "Oh, my God. Nathan?"

Louisa nodded. "Yes, that's right. Did you know him?"

Cordelia stared at her, seemingly unable to speak. After a moment, Henry said, "Nathan and Cordelia were friends."

Finally, Cordelia found her voice. "That's not possible!" she exclaimed. "Nathan went to fight with the Yankees. He joined the Union army more than a year ago! He couldn't have been in one of their prison camps!"

"I'm afraid he was," Louisa explained. "I'm certain of it. He and Titus knew each other because they both were from these parts. I overheard them talking together on many occasions."

She shook her head. "But now you say he was in the Union army . . . I don't understand that. I can't explain it, Miss Brannon. But he was with us when we left Illinois. He and Titus both escaped with my help."

"What happened to him?" Henry asked.

"I . . . I don't know. I honestly don't. A Federal patrol trapped us in a barn where we were staying. There was some shooting and a fire . . . Titus and I got away on horseback, but I never saw Nathan come out of the barn. He was either recaptured . . . or he died there." Louisa looked at Cordelia. Shock and grief were etched on the younger woman's face. "I'm sorry, Miss Brannon, I truly am. I wish Nathan could have returned safely with us."

Cordelia put her hands over her face and began to sob. She turned and ran out of the kitchen. Henry called after her, but she didn't stop. He came halfway out of his chair then sat down again with a sigh.

"Nathan and your sister . . . were close?" Louisa asked.

"I'm pretty sure she was sweet on him for a while, and he felt the same way about her," Henry said. "But then he told her that he couldn't support the Confederacy because he was opposed to slavery, and they argued over that. I reckon Cordelia might have come around and accepted his decision sooner or later, but he got it in his head that he had to go off and fight for the Union. Nobody around here could accept that." He chuckled humorlessly. "I remember, back in the early days of the war, folks wanted to tar and feather Nathan because he hadn't joined up yet. They never bothered me, though, I guess because two of my brothers enlisted. And now here it is, two and a half years later, and I'm still not in the army. Nobody gives a damn anymore. It's too late. Too late . . ."

For a few moments, they sat in brooding silence at the table. Finally Louisa said, "I'm sorry about Nathan, but I'm glad I was able to help Titus get home. I . . . I suppose I should be going now . . ."

Henry lifted his head to look at her. "Going?" he repeated. "Where in blazes can you go? It's freezing out, the roads are bad, and there's no place in town for you to stay. We have plenty of room right here."

"For tonight, perhaps. Now that Titus is home, I can go back north—"

"You said you helped him and Nathan escape. Won't the Yankees be after you for that?"

"I don't know. It doesn't matter. I have to face the consequences of my actions."

"Don't be a damned fool," Henry said harshly. "I'm sorry, Miss Abernathy, but it's the plain truth that you can't go back now. The Yankees would think of you as a traitor. They'd send you to prison or maybe even hang you. Was anybody killed in that escape you set up?"

Louisa closed her eyes and jerked her head in a nod, obviously upset by the memory.

"There you go, then," Henry went on. "The only safe, sensible thing for you to do is to stay right here. On behalf of the family, I'm asking you." He hoped his mother would go along with that. Abigail didn't have any use for Yankees, and she could be stiff-necked about things when she wanted to. But Henry thought maybe she would make an exception for Louisa Abernathy, since she had returned a lost son to them.

"I suppose you're right," Louisa said. "I could stay for a while, anyway."

Henry reached across the table and patted her hand. "Good. You're doing the right thing."

Now, he thought, if he could just figure out what was the right thing for him to do about Polly . . .

6∞9

THE NEXT morning, Henry wasn't any closer to having an answer to that question. Polly was asleep beside him in the narrow bed, her back to him as she huddled under the covers. She hadn't said more than a dozen words to him since Titus and Louisa had arrived. What few words she had said were curt, distracted responses to Henry's questions. He hadn't pressed her to talk, knowing that she was so surprised by Titus's reappearance she couldn't think straight.

He wasn't sure he was thinking straight, either. He had tried not to think too much. After turning Louisa over to Cordelia to get the woman some dry clothes and settle her into one of the spare bedrooms, Henry had tended to Titus, carrying him upstairs and putting him to bed. If Titus had been packing his full weight, Henry wouldn't have been able to handle him so easily, but under the circumstances he had managed all right.

Then he'd gone back downstairs to find his mother sitting in the rocker again, her Bible open in her lap. She looked up from the Scriptures and said, "I never prayed for the Lord to bring him back."

"What?" Henry had asked.

"I never prayed for the Lord to bring back your brother Titus. I mourned his death, but I figured it was all part of God's plan. And I wouldn't dare to presume to think I knew better than the Lord and ask him to change His plan. I just prayed for Him to give me the wisdom and strength I needed to accept Titus's loss." Abigail looked into the flames of the fireplace. Her mouth worked soundlessly for a moment before she could get more words out. "But he wasn't lost," she finally said. "He was alive all along. I could have been praying for him, and I didn't."

"You didn't know, Ma," Henry had said gently. "None of us knew that he might be alive."

"I should have. He's one of my boys. I should have known."

Henry hadn't been able to argue with that feeling. He had looked around the room instead then asked, "Where's Polly?"

"Gone up to bed. That poor girl. That poor girl."

That was probably the first time Henry had ever heard his mother sound so sympathetic to Polly. She had been dead set against Titus's marrying Polly in the first place, and she hadn't been happy when it came out that Henry had gotten his brother's widow in a family way. Given the fact that there was a baby coming, Abigail hadn't objected to Henry and Polly's getting married, but she hadn't liked it, either. She and Polly had grown a little closer over the months, just as Polly and Cordelia had, but Henry was still surprised to hear his mother lamenting over what Polly was going through.

"We sure have some things to work out, don't we?" he'd said as he went upstairs.

"In the morning," Abigail had replied. "Tonight, we all need rest. And time to pray for the Lord's guidance."

Henry hadn't said a prayer before going to bed, but he sure wouldn't have minded some guidance. He didn't know what to do, but as he lay there and watched the dark room turn gray with the approach of dawn, he knew he would have to do *something*. A woman couldn't have two husbands any more than a man could have two wives, but that was the situation in which Polly Ebersole Brannon found herself now.

Henry swung his legs out of bed and shivered as his feet hit the cold floor. He reached for his socks, intending to pull them on before he did anything else.

A sudden scream from down the hall made him bolt from the bed, however, and run out of the room in only his nightshirt.

The screams came from Mac and Will's former room, which was where Henry had put Titus to bed the night before. Henry hurried down the dim hallway and threw the door open. Titus was sitting up in bed, tangled in the covers and thrashing around as he yelled.

Henry bent over him and caught hold of his shoulders. "Titus!" he shouted, his voice sharp enough to break the hold of whatever demons had Titus in their grip. "Titus, wake up! It's all right. You're home!"

"What's wrong?" Louisa asked from the doorway. She had been asleep in the bedroom across the hall. Her slumber must have been a deep one, Henry noted, because he had gotten to Titus's side first.

Henry laid a hand on Titus's forehead. Titus yelled and knocked it away, but not before Henry was able to tell that his brother's fever was even worse than it had been the night before. "He's burning up," he told Louisa.

"Is there a doctor close by?"

Henry nodded. "In town. I'll have to ride in and fetch him."

Abigail and Cordelia were in the hallway behind Louisa, looking past her into the room. As they watched, Titus slumped back down in the bed and began to whimper. It was a pitiful sight, but at least he wasn't screaming and fighting anymore. Abigail moved Louisa aside, not roughly but firmly.

"I'll tend to Titus," she said. "This isn't the first fever I've seen. Cordelia, get a wet cloth and wash your brother's face. Henry, get dressed and be ready to ride for the doctor."

"Yes ma'am," Henry said. He was more than happy to turn the job of caring for Titus over to his mother.

Polly hadn't come out of their bedroom, he noticed as he went into the hall. Surely she had heard the commotion. Titus's shouts and screams were loud enough to wake the dead two counties away.

When he came back into the room he shared with her, he saw that she was sitting up in the bed, the covers clutched around her. Her face was pale and drawn. "What's wrong?" she asked. "I heard some awful noises."

"Titus pitched a fit," Henry explained. "I don't know if he was having a nightmare from everything he's gone through, or if he was seeing things because of the fever. He's mighty sick."

"I . . . I should go help."

She was damned right she should, he thought, but he stopped himself before he put the sentiment into words. Still, Titus was her husband. She had a duty—

Henry reined back hard on those thoughts. Polly had been married to Titus once, but she was *his* wife now, not Titus's. The realization came to him without any conscious effort. In the eyes of the law, however, Polly's marriage to Titus might still be valid. Her union with Henry might be considered bigamous. Henry didn't care. They had all believed that Titus was dead, and he and Polly had fallen in love with each other. Their feelings for each other were real, and nothing could change that. In the only place that really mattered—in their hearts—he and Polly were husband and wife. What they had to do now was set things right with the law.

He pulled his nightshirt over his head and reached for his long underwear.

"What are you doing?" she asked.

"Getting ready to fetch the doctor. My mother thinks she can take care of Titus by herself, but if he takes a turn for the worse, I need to be ready."

"I hope he'll be all right," Polly said, her voice soft, almost a whisper.

"So do I," Henry said.

But even as he spoke the words, in the back of his mind, he wondered if he really meant them.

◇▨▨▨◇

THE DAY after Christmas 1863 was one of the longest in recent memory in the Brannon household. For the most part, Titus was quiet but fitful, only semiconscious. From time to time he was seized by another bout of screaming and fighting to get out of bed. Henry and Cordelia had to hold him down more than once. His skin was hot to the touch and seemed to be drawn even tighter than before over his bones. Henry thought he looked almost bad enough to have come back from the grave literally as well as figuratively.

But Abigail was encouraged by the way she was able to get more broth down him. She kept a pan of water on the bedside table and used it to dampen a cloth she sponged almost constantly over his face. "He'll be all right," she said to Henry. "You'll see. Once the fever breaks, Titus will be fine."

Henry wasn't sure if she was trying to convince him or herself, but he kept quiet about that doubt. Abigail already felt guilty enough about Titus, though as far as Henry could see, she really didn't have anything to blame herself for.

Only once did Polly come to Titus's room, and then she stopped just inside the door and looked from there. Henry happened to be there as well. He watched her, trying to see if he could discern what she might be thinking and feeling. Such auguring was impossible, because Polly was under such rigid self-control that no expression showed on her features. She may as well have been looking at a tree or a rock instead of the man who had once been her husband. After a few moments, she turned and left the room without saying anything.

Louisa Abernathy was a different story. She relieved Abigail every now and then at the task of bathing Titus's face, and she didn't seem to want to leave the room. She was still exhausted, though, and Abigail persuaded her to spend much of the day lying down and trying to get her own strength back, instead of worrying about Titus. After all she had been through, however, first saving him from the prison camp and then accompanying him on the long, perilous journey from Illinois to Virginia, it was difficult for her to let go and rest.

Late in the day, after seeing to the few chores still necessary to the running of the farm, Henry went upstairs to check on Titus. He found Abigail sitting in a straight-backed chair beside the bed, as she had been before, but now her head was tilted forward and she was sound asleep. The long day finally had taken its toll on her. Quietly, so as not to disturb her, Henry moved closer to the bed and looked down at Titus. The day was overcast again, the curtains were drawn, and it was almost as dark as night in the room. The single lamp was turned down very low. But the glow it gave off was enough for Henry to see the huge drops of sweat beaded all over Titus's face and soaking the pillow under his head. Henry's heart gave a jump. He knew what that hard sweating meant. The fever had broken at last. Titus was going to be all right.

Henry touched his mother's shoulder lightly. "Ma," he coached her, "wake up."

With a gasp, she came awake and looked around the room for a second, wild-eyed as if she didn't know where she was or what was going on.

"Look at Titus, Ma," Henry said and pointed to his brother.

Abigail stared at Titus's sweat-slick face for a moment then breathed a sigh. "Thank God. Oh, thank the Lord! The fever's broken!"

"That's right, Ma," Henry added, squeezing her shoulder. "He'll need a lot of rest and some good food, but I reckon he'll be all right now."

Abigail clasped her hands in front of her and her lips moved in a silent prayer of thanksgiving. Then she dipped the cloth in the basin to wet it and washed away some of the perspiration from Titus's face. "When he's done sweating it out, we'll likely need to change the bedclothes."

"I can handle that. Right now, though, I'm going to tell Cordelia and Polly and Miss Abernathy the good news."

"Yes. I'm sure they'll want to know."

Henry left the room, closing the door behind him but pausing momentarily in the hallway. *Good news*, he repeated to himself. Was it really good news? Had this illness claimed Titus's life, Polly would now be his widow. Nothing would have to be done concerning the legality of the marriage between her and Henry. Oh, just to make things proper, they might want to have another wedding ceremony, he thought, but that could be handled quietly and discreetly.

Henry grimaced as a wave of self-loathing went through him. What was he thinking? How could he let himself believe, even for a second, that things would be better if Titus were dead? He scrubbed a hand over his face and tried to banish such thoughts.

He should be happy that his brother was going to be all right, and for the most part, he was. He had been thrilled when he realized that Titus's fever had broken. Sure, it complicated things, but that didn't matter. Everything could be worked out. What was important was that Titus was alive, and it looked like he was going to recover from the sickness that had almost killed him.

Henry drew in a deep breath and went down the hall to the room he shared with Polly. When he opened the door, he saw that the chamber was empty. He checked the room Louisa was using, and she wasn't there, either. Probably both of them were downstairs with Cordelia, he decided. Abigail had put her daughter to work baking more biscuits and cooking the last of the beans they had hoarded. They were going to have to come up with some more supplies from somewhere, Henry thought as he went downstairs. That problem could wait, though. Right now, he had good news to deliver.

And the news really *was* good, he repeated to himself.

He found the three women in the kitchen. Cordelia was at the stove, stirring the water in the pot where the beans were boiling. Polly and Louisa sat at the table. As Henry entered the room, he thought that the two of them were eyeing each other suspiciously, like a couple of cats who were maybe after the same mouse. That might have been his imagination, though.

All three of the women turned to look at him as he smiled. "Titus's fever has broken. Looks like he's going to be all right."

Cordelia's hand went to her mouth. "Oh, thank God!" she almost cried.

Louisa closed her eyes and took a deep breath. When she opened them, she said, "That's wonderful news. I was afraid that he would only get back home to . . . to . . ." She couldn't finish the thought. Her hands knotted together, and she looked down at the table and sobbed in relief.

Polly commented emotionlessly, "That's good."

Cordelia removed her apron and started away from the stove. "I'm going up to see him."

Henry held out a hand to stop her. "He's not awake. At least he wasn't when I left up there. But he seemed to be sleeping good for a change. Better just let him rest."

Cordelia looked like she wanted to argue, but after a moment she nodded. "You're right. I'll go up later. Ma's with him now?"

"She's not going to leave him anytime soon," Henry said. "I don't reckon you could pry her away."

And that was funny in a way, he thought, because back in the days before Titus had joined the army, no one had been more disapproving of him and his habits than his mother. Titus had been too fond of whiskey and bad companions, and Abigail had threatened more than once to throw him out of the house. But all of that was forgotten now. There was a lot of truth to that old Bible story about the prodigal son, Henry thought.

Louisa started to get to her feet. "Perhaps I should go help your mother."

"No," Polly said, her voice sharp. "You've done enough."

Louisa sat back in the chair, a look of surprise and a little hurt on her face.

Henry frowned. "Polly, there's no call to talk to Miss Abernathy like that. We owe her a lot. She brought Titus back to us."

Polly's face was like stone. "You're right," she said. "We owe her a great deal." The legs of her chair scraped on the floor. "I'll go up to him. After all, he is my husband."

She went toward the kitchen door. Henry thought about trying to stop her, but he didn't. He stepped aside and let her go. When he turned to look at Cordelia and Louisa, both of them were watching him with concerned expressions.

"You can't blame her for being upset, Henry," Cordelia said. "She doesn't know what to make of all this. None of us do."

"The situation certainly is . . . complicated," Louisa added.

Henry sighed. "That ain't the half of it." He gave a little shake of his head. "Now that it looks like Titus is going to be all right, we have to let Mac and Will know that he's back. Mac can probably get leave to visit for a spell, and he can get word to Will faster than we can. I'll ride down to Orange Court House tomorrow and find him."

Cordelia nodded. "That sounds like a good idea."

"Maybe he'll know what to do about . . . well, about everything." Right now, he needed some sage advice, Henry thought, and it would be mighty nice to dump this whole mess in the lap of one of his older brothers. It would be even better if Will could come home, too, but that was out of their control. It was up to the doctors in Richmond to decide when Capt. Will Brannon was fit to travel.

Suddenly weary, Henry sat down in the chair Polly had vacated. To his surprise, Louisa reached across the table and clasped his hand in both of hers. "I'm certain everything will be all right," she said. "The Lord has a purpose for everything. I'm sure He would not have allowed Titus and me to reach this place safely if things weren't going to work out."

"I hope you're right," Henry said.

But in his heart, it was getting harder and harder to believe that was true.

Chapter Three

THE SPIRITED PLINKING OF banjo music floated through the chilly December air, countering to an extent the gloom of the overcast sky that hung over the cavalry's winter camp near Orange Court House. Gen. Jeb Stuart had christened the place Wigwam. The camp was full of visitors. The general's wife, Flora, had her own tent, which she shared with their three-and-a-half-year-old son, Jimmy. A correspondent from the *Illustrated London News*, Frank Vizetelly, was in camp, along with a visiting British officer, Fitzgerald Ross. There was still talk that the British might come into the war on the side of the Confederacy, so the Englishmen were treated as special guests, just as Col. Arthur Fremantle had been when he accompanied Robert E. Lee to Gettysburg the previous summer.

Though the Union army under Gen. George Gordon Meade was camped no more than fifty miles away, things were quiet. There had been no skirmishes since November. Both sides in the great conflict were content to sit and lick their wounds during the long chill of winter. When spring came, the rival armies would once again begin their bloodstained waltz. Time enough then for more killing.

Unless some miracle occurred and an agreement was struck that would end the fighting. Capt. MacBeth Brannon thought about that as he stood beside his tent and brushed the silver gray stallion that had carried him into battle countless times during the past two and a half years. In the early days of the war, rumors had abounded that a peace treaty would be worked out soon. The Yankees would see that they couldn't whip the Confederacy, and they would withdraw their armies from the hallowed ground of the South.

Nobody talked about that much anymore. The hallowed ground had soaked up too much blood, Union and Confederate alike, for anyone to believe that a negotiated peace was still possible. Bolstered by victories at Gettysburg and Chattanooga and the surrender of the besieged city of Vicksburg, the Yankees now believed they could win. Perhaps more important, many of the Confederates no longer were convinced that they could never be defeated.

So here at Wigwam, banjo strings were plucked and voices were raised in song, as they always were whenever Stuart's cavalry was at rest. In Mac's ears, however, the revelry had a hollow sound. It reminded him a little of a small boy whistling a merry tune as he hurried past a graveyard, trying not to admit the reality and inevitability of death.

The clattering of hoof beats was a welcome distraction. Mac shook himself out of his reverie and turned to see who was coming. To his surprise, he recognized Henry riding one of the few horses left on the Brannon farm.

"Henry!" Mac called out as he set the stallion's brush to one side. He moved into the open while his brother reined his horse to a halt and deftly swung down from the saddle. The two clasped hands at first, then Mac drew him into an exuberant bear hug and slapped him hard on the back. It had been only a few days since they had seen each other, but in time of war—even during a lull such as this one—brothers were always glad to see each other.

Mac took a step back and rested his hands on Henry's shoulders. "What are you doing here?"

"I've got news, Mac," Henry said. His face was solemn under the floppy-brimmed hat he wore. "You might ought to brace yourself."

Dread washed through Mac at the tone of Henry's voice. "What is it? Has something happened to Ma? Cordelia?" He hesitated, recalling that his older brother was still in a hospital in Richmond. In a whisper, he said, "Will?"

Henry shook his head. "It's not bad news, Mac, just mighty unexpected. Titus is home."

For a moment, Mac stared at him, unable to comprehend. Titus was dead, killed at Fredericksburg over a year earlier. Mac had heard all about how Titus had led a group of men out from the Confederate lines at the base of Marye's Heights to finish off a bunch of pinned-down Yankees, only to be trapped themselves. They had been wiped out.

At least, that was what he and Will had been told by men who had been there. They had seen the bloody, broken bodies for themselves.

But they hadn't seen Titus, not really. To spare their mother's feelings, Mac and Will had lied about Titus's being laid to rest with a decent burial. Those chopped-up pieces of meat that had once been men had been dumped into a mass grave, and Mac honestly had believed that Titus was among them.

Mac's hands tightened fiercely on Henry's shoulders. "What are you saying?" he rasped. "Titus is *alive?*"

"We couldn't believe it at first, either. He showed up night before last, on Christmas. He'd been in a Yankee prison camp in Illinois until he escaped and finally managed to get home."

Mac felt dizzy. He let go of Henry and sat down on a three-legged stool in front of his tent. "My God." He looked up. "It's really Titus?"

"I reckon I know our brother. It's him, all right. He was mighty sick when he got there, but he's getting a little better now. I think he's going to be all right."

"This is just too much. It's amazing. Will and I were told he was dead—"

"You didn't see his body for yourself?" An angry edge crept into Henry's voice as he asked the question.

Mac frowned. "You don't know what it was like there at Fredericksburg, Henry. You've never been in a battle."

"That hasn't been entirely my choice," Henry snapped. "With Cory gone, with you and Will and Titus all off fighting the war, somebody had to stay home and help Ma and Cordelia look after the place."

Mac waved a hand. "I'm sorry. I didn't mean that the way it sounded. I just meant that it was so bad . . . that the rifle fire and the artillery had torn up the men so much that you couldn't tell . . . well, sometimes you couldn't tell where one body stopped and another started. It was like something out of hell, Henry. Like something straight out of hell." He gave a hollow laugh. "And we *won* that fight."

"Sorry, Mac. I reckon I understand."

"Will and I talked it over. We decided we didn't want to tell Ma and Cordelia what it was really like. We wanted to spare them the awful truth of it. So we said that Titus had had a proper burial. We were convinced he had been slaughtered along with the rest of his bunch."

Henry hunkered next to the stool where Mac sat. "He made it out alive somehow, and the Yankees hauled him off to that prison camp. Not only that, but Nathan Hatcher was with him."

Mac frowned in confusion again. "Nathan? He went off to fight for the Yankees, the last I heard of him."

"I don't know how to explain it," Henry said with a shake of his head. "But I'm pretty sure it was him. Miss Abernathy's convinced of it."

"Who?"

"Louisa Abernathy. She's a Quaker lady who went out to inspect that camp. Somehow she wound up helping Titus and Nathan get away, and she stayed with Titus all the way back home. I still don't understand the whole story, but I reckon he really would be dead now if not for her."

"Lord. I never dreamed Titus was still alive."

"None of us did," Henry said, and something about his voice made Mac look at him. After a second, Mac's eyes widened with understanding.

"Polly," he said.

"Yeah," Henry agreed. "Polly . . . my wife. The mother of my child."

"But if Titus is still alive . . ."

"A fine mess, ain't it? Still, you got to be happy about Titus. I know I am."

"Sure. It's wonderful news." Mac stood, and Henry straightened as well. "I'll tell General Lee. I'm sure, given these circumstances, he'll allow me to ride on out to the farm with you and stay for a while."

They walked across the camp toward divisional headquarters, leaving Henry's horse tethered at the tent along with Mac's stallion. Mac noticed that Henry looked around at everything, eyes wide with interest. This was the largest group of soldiers Henry had ever seen, having never been in an army camp before. The youngest Brannon brother had not been happy about not being able to enlist, Mac knew. Joining up was the only honorable thing for a young Southern man to do, and many who were not so young had gone off to the army as well. Nearly every able-bodied male in Virginia had fought for the Confederacy at one time or another. Not enlisting must have been a badge of shame to Henry, but he had borne it well, with few complaints, putting the needs of his family ahead of his personal desires. Mac admired his little brother for that.

He felt less admiration for the manner in which Henry had gotten involved with his brother's widow, but Mac supposed that was none of his business. He had never been an expert on affairs of the heart. He had admired quite a few young ladies in Culpeper County and had danced with plenty of them at various balls—taking care to see that his mother didn't find out about it, since Abigail Brannon was just about the staunchest Baptist in all of creation and didn't hold with dancing—but as far as real romance went, Mac had always been more comfortable tramping around the woods and talking to animals than he was trying to court a girl. He knew considerable about the physical act of mating, having been raised on a farm, but what went on in the hearts and minds of a man and a woman in love was uncharted territory to Mac. Nobody had ever carried out a topographical survey in those regions, at least not that Mac knew of.

"You're sure it's Titus?" he asked again then waved off Henry's words before he could answer. "Of course it is. I'm just being foolish."

"No, you're just shocked as hell that he's alive, like the rest of us," Henry said. "And I don't blame you a bit, Mac."

"And Nathan Hatcher was with him?"

"Only at first. Nathan didn't make it back with Titus and Miss Abernathy."

"I'm sorry to hear that. He was a stubborn fool, but I liked him. I know Cordelia did, too."

"He may not be dead," Henry said warily. "They were separated one night while they were trying to get away from a Yankee patrol. He might have been killed, but he might have been captured again."

Mac grunted. "From what I've heard, being locked up in some of those Yankee prisons is worse than being dead."

"That's the truth. Some of the things Miss Abernathy told me about Camp Douglas . . ." Henry shook his head. "Well, I had a hard time believing 'em. I hate to think fellas who are human could do such things to other fellas."

They reached the large tent that housed the headquarters of the Second Division, First Virginia Cavalry. A young private in ragged butternut trousers, a gray tunic, and a round-brimmed brown hat stood stiffly on guard duty by the entrance. He recognized Mac, nodded and grinned. "Howdy, Cap'n. Y'all come to see Gen'ral Lee?"

"That's right. Is he here?"

"Sure thing." The sentry turned and opened the tent flap a few inches. "Cap'n Brannon to see you, Gen'ral. He's got a civilian with him."

"Mac? Send him in," came the enthusiastic response from inside the tent.

The guard held the flap back, and Mac and Henry ducked their heads a little to enter. The inside of the tent was partitioned so there were two rooms, one larger and one smaller. The smaller section served as personal quarters for Fitzhugh Lee, nephew of Robert E. Lee and commander of the Second Cavalry Division. The bigger room accommodated several folding tables, surrounded by camp chairs. Maps were spread out and pinned down to the tables. When it came time to plan a campaign, Lee and his brigade commanders would hover over these maps, and Lee would lay out the strategy devised by General Stuart, the overall commander of the cavalry.

At the moment, however, Fitz Lee was alone in the tent, seated on a camp chair in his shirtsleeves, his legs stretched out in front of him and crossed at the ankles. A cigar was clamped between his teeth and a newspaper was spread open in his lap. He grinned around the cigar. "That bastard in the *Whig* is at it again, printing more scurrilous lies about how Beauty is no longer fit to command."

Lee was not only Mac's commanding officer, but since the first summer of the war he had also been a friend and mentor. He spoke freely with Mac, especially if none of the more stiff-necked junior officers were around. Mac knew what Lee was talking about. For the past couple of months, a war of words had been going on in the Richmond newspapers, principally between the *Whig* and the *Enquirer.* An anonymous writer who called himself the Investigator had published a series of columns in the *Whig* that were highly unfavorable to General Stuart, whom Fitz Lee had known so long that he often called him by his West Point nickname, Beauty. Supporters of Stuart had fired verbal salvos in return in the pages of the *Enquirer.* Mac didn't foresee an end to the hostilities anytime soon. Stuart had such a vibrant, forceful personality that he usually provoked one of two responses—devoted admiration or blind hatred.

Recent events had forced Mac into something of a middle ground. He had witnessed most of the stunning triumphs orchestrated by Stuart, but in the past six months he had seen as well the indecision that had begun to plague the general. In the past, Stuart seemed to have a genius for doing the right thing at

the right time. Beginning with an ill-advised foray far to the east
and north when he was supposed to be screening the Confederate column during the invasion of Maryland and Pennsylvania
that had ended at Gettysburg, his luck had deserted him. He
had fought the Yankees to a draw on a couple of occasions, but
that was the best he could do. Battles that should have resulted
in victories had ended either inconclusively or with the Confederate cavalry in retreat. It was an unpleasant feeling for men
accustomed to winning.

With a rattle of paper, Fitz Lee closed the *Whig* and looked at
Henry. "Who's this, Mac?" he asked then held up a hand. "No,
wait a minute, I recall now." He came to his feet and extended
his hand. "Henry, isn't it? I remember you from my visit to the
farm awhile back."

"Yes sir," Henry said as he shook Lee's hand. "I remember
you, too. I reckon you'd be hard to forget."

Lee laughed. "I'll take that as a compliment."

"That's how I meant it, sir," Henry said hurriedly.

"Well, what are you doing here at Wigwam? Paying your
brother a visit? Or have you come to join the cavalry as well? We
can always use another good man, and I know all of you Brannons fit that description."

Mac answered the question instead of Henry. "No sir,
Henry's brought me some important news from home."

Lee frowned. "Nothing bad, I hope. Your mother and the
rest of your family are well?"

"Yes sir. Better than we knew, in fact. You see, my brother
Titus is alive. He's come home from a Yankee prison camp."

"Titus? I thought he fell at, where was it, Chancellorsville?"

"Fredericksburg," Mac said. "But he wasn't killed, just captured by the Federals. We didn't know that until a couple of
days ago."

Lee tugged on his full, dark beard. "Well, I'll swan. That *is*
good news, mighty good news. I reckon you want to ride up and
see him?"

"Yes sir, I was hoping to, if that's all right."

"Of course, of course."

"I realize I had several days' leave not that long ago—"

"I've already said it was all right, Captain," Lee interrupted with a grin. "Now you'd better go on and get out of here before I change my mind."

"Yes sir. I was also wondering if you could help me to get word of this to my brother Will. He's still recuperating in a hospital in Richmond."

Lee nodded. "Write a note to your brother and leave it with me before you go. I'll see that it goes out with this afternoon's dispatches to Richmond."

"Thank you, General. I truly appreciate it."

Mac turned to go, but Henry said, "General, there's one more thing . . ."

Mac wondered what Henry wanted of Lee. Henry hadn't said anything to him about asking the general anything.

"What is it, son?" Lee asked, his tone still pleasant.

"Supplies are running awful short around our part of the country. I was wondering if you might be able to spare a little flour and maybe some beans."

Mac was surprised by the question. The army had been on short rations for months. In fact, the need to replenish their stores was one reason they had marched north the previous summer. Of course, that hadn't worked out so well, and the situation was still bad. And yet Henry was begging food from a general. Mac felt a wave of embarrassment go through him.

"Sorry, General," he said quickly as he took Henry's arm and started to steer him toward the front of the tent. "We'll be on our way—"

"Hold on, Mac," Lee said sharply.

Mac stopped, gave Henry a dark look, and turned to face Lee. "Yes sir?"

The general didn't seem to be upset by Henry's audacity. "There's nothing wrong with your brother's question, Captain, if that's what you're thinking. The good people of Virginia have supported us to the utmost of their ability for the past two and a half years. Naturally their own supplies have run short. Nearly everything has gone to the cause." Lee looked at Henry and went on, "I'm sorry. I'd send a whole wagonload of goods with you if I could, Henry. But we've none to spare. This winter has got a long ways to run yet, and we can't have our boys starving before it's over, not if we want to be able to fight the Yankees again come spring."

Henry nodded. "Of course, General. I understand. I meant no offense."

"And none was taken," Lee assured him goodheartedly. "Best of luck to you, son, and I'm glad that lost brother of yours came home safely."

"Yes sir. Thank you."

A moment later, they were outside the tent, and Henry said anxiously, "I didn't mean any harm, Mac—"

"No, that's all right, Henry. What General Lee said is true. I sometimes think the war has been harder on the ones who stayed home than on the ones who've been fighting it."

"That's crazy. Nobody's been shooting at us."

"Sometimes there are worse things than being shot at." Mac shook his head. "Come on. I'll get my gear together and saddle the stallion. I reckon we can get a little grain and water for your horse, at least. Let's go home." He smiled. "I'm ready to see that long-lost brother of ours."

◌〰〰◌

TITUS WASN'T sure where he was. At first he wasn't even sure he was still alive. But once he thought about it, he knew he couldn't be dead, because he was cold, not hot. If he'd been dead, he would have been feeling the flames of Hades about now. He wasn't sure he believed in heaven, but he was damned sure there was a hell and that was where he was bound.

So he was alive, and the coldness he felt was a normal winter chill, not the alternating freezing and burning of fever. He was alive, and despite the weakness that enveloped him, he sensed that the grippe was gone. It had almost killed him, but he'd beaten it. He laughed softly. The hate inside him was too strong for some mere sickness to put him six feet under.

"Titus?"

It was a woman's voice. Memories came flooding back to him. Louisa Abernathy. Red hair. Milky skin. She had come to him out of loneliness and desperation, and he supposed he had felt much the same. But it didn't matter why. Whatever the reason, they had turned to each other, and the passion he'd awakened in her had surprised them both. Good little Quaker gals weren't supposed to like their lovin' that much.

But good little Quaker gals didn't help Johnny Rebs escape from Yankee prison camps, either.

"Titus, are you awake?"

The woman's voice again. Titus tried to open his eyes so that he could look at her, but his eyelids were heavy, so heavy. And something was different about the voice, too. Different but still familiar somehow. Not Louisa's. Confused, he forced his eyes open at last.

He was lying on his back in a soft bed, and she was leaning over him, an anxious expression on her face. Red curls tumbled to her shoulders, but a more fiery red, not the coppery hue of Louisa's hair. Titus swallowed and his dry, cracked lips moved, but it was a few seconds before he could get the words out.

"Cor . . . Cordelia? Is that . . . you?"

A big smile came onto her face, and she leaned over to put her arms around him. "We thought you'd never wake up!" she said as she hugged him.

Titus tried to push himself out of her grip as she lifted him half out of bed in her enthusiasm. He was too weak, though, as weak as a kitten. Cordelia finally lowered him to the pillow again and kissed his forehead.

"We knew the fever had broken, but you still didn't wake up for a while," she said. "We were all terribly worried. Thank God you're all right!"

Titus wouldn't have described himself as all right, not by a long shot, but at least he was better than he had been. More memories were creeping back into his brain. He remembered shooting a son-of-a-bitch Yankee sergeant in a cemetery in Chicago, where Titus and Nathan were supposed to be burying a couple of alleged Masonic brothers. That had been a ruse, of course, to get them out of camp, and it had worked. They had gotten away, taking Louisa with them. She had smuggled guns to them and set up the whole thing. She said that she'd done it because she was so horrified by the treatment he and Nathan had been receiving at the hands of the Yankees, but Titus figured she had wanted him, even then. She just hadn't been aware of it yet. That realization had required the time they spent together on the road, dodging Yankees and trying to get to Virginia.

They had made it at last, though Nathan had been lost along the way. Titus recalled the cold, mist-cloaked night as they drove up to the Brannon farm in a wagon they had stolen in the Shenandoah Valley. That was the last thing he remembered. He wondered how long he had been unconscious since then.

"Quit fussin' over me, Cordelia." His voice was so weak it wasn't much more than a whisper. "You're gonna suffocate me if you don't give me a little room to breathe."

She straightened. "You're right. I'll fetch the others. I know they'll want to see you. Mac's here, too."

Titus grunted. He supposed that after all he'd been through, all he had endured to get home, even dour old Mac would look pretty good.

Cordelia hurried out of the room. Titus looked around. He thought this was the room Will and Mac had shared before the war. Mac was all right; Cordelia had said he was here. Titus wondered about Will. Where was he these days? Was he even still alive, or had the Yankees killed him?

Titus felt sleepy and could have dozed again if given the chance, but footsteps in the hall told him that wasn't going to happen. Mac appeared in the doorway, dressed in a hard-worn but neatly kept uniform. Smiling, he came across the room and stood beside the bed to put a hand on his brother's shoulder.

"Hello, Titus," Mac said. "It's mighty good to see you."

"Good to be . . . home," Titus said. "How you . . . doin'?"

"Fine, just fine. Better now that you're back."

More people crowded into the room. Abigail came up on the other side of the bed and leaned over to put her arms around Titus. "My boy, my boy," she murmured. "Praise God you're all right. He's brought you back to us."

Titus wanted to say that he didn't recall God's standing there in that cemetery shooting at the Yankees with him, but he kept the thought to himself. No point in setting his mother off on one of her hellfire-and-brimstone rants. Besides, he had to admit that it *was* good to see her.

Cordelia was there again, standing at the foot of the bed with Henry beside her. Titus summoned up a grin. "Howdy, little brother." He was beginning to feel a little stronger. He didn't know if it was from the rest he had gotten or the fact that he was surrounded by his family at last.

"Hello, Titus," Henry said. "Like Mac said, it's mighty good to see you."

"Yeah. Good to . . . see you, too." Titus looked around at them, at the solemn expressions on their faces as they stared at him, and he frowned. "What's the matter . . . with y'all? You look like . . . you've seen a ghost . . . or somethin'."

Mac spoke for everyone. "We all thought you were dead, Titus. We believed you'd been killed at Fredericksburg."

It took a moment for that to soak into Titus's brain, but when it did, he grinned and began to laugh.

Abigail was sitting on the edge of the bed next to him, holding his left hand in both of hers, and her fingers squeezed his. "What's wrong, son?"

"Ain't nothin' . . . wrong," Titus managed to say between chuckles. "Y'all should've known . . . this ol' bad penny would . . . turn up again."

"You're not a bad penny, Titus," Cordelia said. "You're our brother, and we're all so glad that you're all right, that you've come home to us."

"I'll bet . . . ever'body ain't glad. Has anybody got word . . . to my lovin' wife yet?" Titus heard the bitterness in his voice and didn't care. If his own family had given up on him, what more could he expect from Polly?

"I'm here, Titus," a voice said, and the sound of it was like a bayonet in his bowels. His eyes swung to the doorway as she appeared there, her fair hair long and shining and beautiful, her pale features as lovely as ever, just the way he remembered them. In fact, she hadn't changed a bit in the year and more he'd been gone.

Except for the rounded belly where another man's bastard was growing.

Chapter Four

POLLY CAUGHT HER BREATH as Titus stared at her. Henry started to step toward her, anxious to comfort her. Seeing the glower that Titus cast toward her and the faint shake of her head, he stopped, unsure what to do. Despite the fact that she was obviously uncomfortable, Polly wore an expression of determination on her face. She wanted to have it out with Titus, to see this unpleasantness through and get it over with. Henry supposed he couldn't blame her for feeling that way.

Polly stepped closer to the bed. Henry and Cordelia moved one way and Mac moved the other to give her more room. She reached up and took hold of one of the carved posts at the foot of the bed. "I'm glad you're alive, Titus."

His mouth twisted. "That's nothin' but a goddamned lie."

"Titus!" Abigail said as she let go of his hand and pulled away from him. "I don't care how sick you've been, I won't have that sort of language in my house."

Titus seemed unable to take his eyes off Polly. He didn't look at his mother as he said, "You don't like cussin', but you don't seem to mind havin' this whore under your roof!" A moment earlier, he had seemed so weak he could barely acknowledge the presence of visitors in the room. Now, the emotions coursing through him had galvanized him so that he looked like he wanted to leap out of the bed. He still lacked the strength to do so, but the desire was there.

But Titus wasn't the only one who was furious. Henry could no longer hold his anger in. "Blast it, Titus, you can't talk to her like that!"

"Shut up, little brother," Titus said. "This ain't none of your concern. It's between me and my wife."

"She's *my* wife!" Henry burst out, ignoring the warning looks sent toward him by his mother, Mac, and Cordelia.

Titus lifted himself on his elbows. Now, stunned at the revelation of Henry and Polly's marriage, he slumped back on the pillow and stared.

"It never entered your mind that maybe Polly and me got married, did it?" Henry demanded hotly. "You still think of me as just a kid. But I'm not. I'm a man now, and Polly's my wife. She's the mother of my child!"

"You son of a bitch," Titus whispered. "You dirty, rotten, backstabbin'—"

"Oh, hush, Titus!" Polly said. "We all thought you were dead. Do you hear me? *We all thought you were dead.* You can't hold what happened against me or Henry or anybody else."

"Polly's telling you the truth, Titus," Mac interrupted. "Will and I were told you were killed along with a bunch of men who were wiped out at Fredericksburg when you went after those Yankees. We didn't know it wasn't true."

Slowly, Titus's hollow-eyed gaze moved to Mac. "Did you look for me?" he asked. "Did you try to find my body?"

"It didn't seem like there was any need—"

Titus looked away. Mac's hands clenched into fists. He and Will had made a mistake by not making sure that Titus was dead, and he knew it. Henry could tell by looking at Mac how guilt was eating on him. And that wasn't fair, just like the way Titus was acting toward Polly wasn't fair.

"What could they have done?" Henry asked. "You'd already been taken prisoner. There was no way Will and Mac could have helped you, Titus."

"They didn't have to give up on me." Titus glared around the room. "All of you were probably happy when you heard that I'd been killed."

"That's not true!" Cordelia cried. "It was awful. We all grieved for you, Titus. We grieved for months."

Titus's eyes flashed toward the roundness of Polly's belly. "Yeah, I can see how some of you grieved for me. Probably every damn chance you got."

"That's enough," Abigail said. "This isn't doing anyone any good. Let's leave Titus alone, and maybe he'll start to see things a little clearer."

"I see things just fine, Ma." Titus lifted a trembling hand and waved it toward Polly. "A belly pokin' out like that is sort of hard to miss, ain't it?"

Polly just shook her head. "You've got it all wrong, Titus," she said softly. "All wrong." She turned and walked slowly out of the room.

Titus lifted himself from the bed again. He shook with rage. "Bitch! Whore!" he shouted after her. "Get out of here with your bastard!"

Mac grabbed Henry's arm and practically dragged him out of the room before he could attack Titus. Cordelia and Abigail followed. Abigail was the last one out, and she looked back at her son with a sorrowful expression. Titus slumped down on the pillow and closed his eyes.

In the hallway, Henry hurried after his wife, who was heading toward their room. "Polly!" he said as he caught up to her and took hold of her shoulder. "Polly, he's crazy. He's got no right to say those things—"

"The way he sees it, he has every right to say whatever he pleases," she said as she turned a bleak face toward Henry. "In the eyes of the law—and in the eyes of God—he's just telling the truth. I'm his wife, not yours."

"No!"

"Yes, Henry." Polly's voice was pitched low. The words came out flat and dull, echoing with defeat. "This child I'm carrying *is* a bastard."

"Damn it, no! I won't have you say that!"

"Whether you like it or not, it's true."

"He abandoned you! That's got to count for something."

"As far as the law is concerned, Titus enlisted in the army and went off to fight Yankees. How many others did the same thing. No court is going to consider that abandoning a wife."

"Well, then, I'm not talking about courts. I'm talking about what's right!"

Polly shook her head. "It's too late for that. It's been too late for a long time. I hoped maybe things could change. I hoped they could get better." A tear rolled down her cheek. "But they're not going to, are they? The way the world is now, things never get better. They just get worse."

Henry put his arms around her, but she stood there stiff and unresponsive. "It doesn't have to be like that," he said, choking back a sob. "Titus will come around. You'll see. It'll be all right."

But he knew, even as he spoke the words, how hollow they sounded. Neither of them believed what he was saying.

He held on to her until she finally pulled away from him and went on into their room, closing the door behind her.

⚙

TITUS LAY there for a long time, his pulse hammering inside his skull, his chest rising and falling rapidly as his breath rasped in his throat. He was filled with such rage that he was shaking. His wife and his brother—*his own brother!*—rutting together like barnyard animals. He groaned as the images filled his head.

No matter what excuses they made about believing he was dead, they had been wrong. And it didn't matter, either, that the only reason he'd joined the army and gone off to fight in the first place was because he had thought that his marriage was over. Polly had chosen her father over him, and if that was the way she wanted it, then he wanted no part of her. He hadn't even been able to remain in the same county as she had. Those memories lurked in the back of his mind, but he ignored them, concentrating instead on the fresh pain that had been dealt to him from the most unexpected source of all: his own family.

And yet it shouldn't have been unexpected. When had any of them ever done anything except disapprove of him? Always after him to stop drinking, they were, and to stop spending time with Israel Quinn and the other no-accounts like him. His mother was the worst of the bunch, but Will and Mac and prissy little Cordelia were almost as bad. Only Henry had seemed to really like him. Only Henry . . .

And he had turned out to be the biggest viper of them all.

The faint creaking of door hinges made him look up. The door was open about a foot, and Louisa Abernathy peered in, a worried look on her face.

"Titus?" she half-whispered.

"What is it?" Even he noted the bitterness and weariness in his voice.

"Are you all right?"

He laughed coldly. "Oh, I'm fine. Damned fine. Couldn't you tell?"

Louisa opened the door wider and came a step into the room. "They told me earlier that you were awake, but I didn't want to intrude. I thought you'd want to see your family first."

"Yeah, my family." Titus looked away, unable to meet her eyes for a moment. "My lovin' family."

Louisa eased the door shut behind her and moved closer to the bed. "I know what's wrong. I'm sorry, Titus. For what it's worth, I really do believe that your brother and Polly thought that you were . . . gone forever."

"You mean dead, don't you? Lyin' in the cold, cold ground with the worms eatin' me?"

Louisa's face was pale and drawn. She looked like she wanted to turn and run away, but something held her here. Titus knew what that something was. She was still sweet on him. Even after she had seen him kill men and never bat an eye, even though every bit of her Quaker upbringing must have been telling her to stay away from this evil, evil man, she couldn't deny what she felt for him.

It would serve Polly right if he took Louisa right in front of her. He would need to get some of his strength back first, though, so he could do it good and proper.

"I don't blame you for being upset," she said, "but you have to forgive those who have wronged you. The Friends call it turning the other cheek. It's the only way, Titus. Otherwise the hatred and anger you feel now will consume you."

"They told you I was mad, did they?"

"They didn't have to tell me. I knew from their faces when they came downstairs that something was terribly wrong."

"What's wrong is that my brother and my wife betrayed me!" he bit out. "Hell, even if I had been dead, what they did was wrong."

Louisa nodded. "Yes, it probably was."

"No prob'ly about it. A fella just don't go out and lay with his brother's wife, not even if his brother is dead and gone. It just ain't proper."

And then he laughed at the very idea that he, Titus Brannon, the black sheep of the whole family, was worried about whether or not something was proper. It suddenly struck him as hilarious, and he laughed until weakness seized him and left him shaking and panting for breath.

Louisa hurried over to him and bent to put a hand on his shoulder. "What can I do for you, Titus?" she asked anxiously.

He reached up and grabbed her arm, his fingers digging into the flesh so hard that she gasped. "Kill me!" he said in a hoarse whisper. "Get a gun and put a bullet through my brain! It'd be the kindest thing anybody could do for me now."

Louisa looked horrified and tried to pull away. "You don't mean that!"

"The hell I don't." He paused, drew a couple of ragged breaths, then went on. "All the time we were comin' back here, I thought the thing that was keepin' me goin' was how much I wanted to kill me some more Yankees. I even dreamed about how the blood and the brains would go flyin' out of their heads when I shot 'em."

Louisa let out a moan at his vivid description of the violence he so desired.

"But that wasn't really it," he continued. "Not all of it, anyway. I guess a fella can't live just on hate. I wanted to see my family again, and . . . and I wanted to see Polly. That's what kept me goin'." His hand tightened even more on her arm, forcing tears from her eyes. "But it was all for nothin'. *Nothin'!* I never knew it, but there wasn't anything here for me to come back to. That's why I want you to kill me, Louisa. They all wish I'd stayed dead, anyway."

She shook her head. "That's not true, Titus," she said. "I know it's not. I've talked to your mother and sister a great deal these past two days. They were both so happy to know that you were alive after all."

"What about Henry? What about Polly?"

Louisa didn't say anything. She looked like she wanted to, but no words would come from her mouth.

Titus finally let go of her arm, giving her a little shove as he did so. "I thought as much. Henry and Polly got their own life now. Last thing they need is to have me around messin' things up. Better kill me. Make everybody happy."

Louisa's face was wet with tears. "Not me," she said. "I could never be happy with you dead, Titus."

"Well, then, you're a bigger fool than I thought you were," he said, his tone deliberately brutal.

After a moment of strained silence, Louisa said, "I don't care what you call me. I know I've turned my back on my religion, on everything I believe in. Because I believe in *you* . . . Titus. I believe that you're a better man than you know."

His lips drew back from his teeth in a grimace. "Believe this," he said in a low, intense voice. "If I live, the time will come when I kill them who betrayed me. I'll kill 'em both."

Louisa turned and practically ran out of the room, unable to stand it anymore.

Titus let his head sag back against the pillow. It had been a long day, and he had only been awake for a little of it. But that had been long enough. He wished he could go back to sleep and when he woke up everything would be all right. Polly would still love him and want to be with him. Henry would be the hero-worshiping little brother all over again. The world would be back like it was supposed to be—except for the war, of course.

He had been right all along, he realized. Killing was all that was left for him. Killing Yankees . . . and anybody else who deserved it.

⚬⟭⟭⟭⟭⟬⟬⟬⟬⚬

OVER THE next few days, the Brannon household settled into an uneasy routine. Henry and Mac tended to the chores. Abigail and Cordelia took care of the house. And Louisa saw to Titus's needs. She was the only one he would tolerate near him. As for Polly, she spent most of her time in the room she shared with Henry, sitting in a rocking chair and brooding. Henry wished there was something he could do to help her, but she would barely speak to him. At least she was taking care of herself, eating to keep up her strength for her and the baby, though food was getting perilously scarce on the farm. They were living on greens and the occasional squirrel or possum that Mac was able to kill in the woods. With the bond he felt toward animals, Mac had never cared for hunting—in earlier days, that chore had fallen mostly to Titus, who was a crack shot—but now there was no choice. Abigail still had a little flour for biscuits, but she planned to bake some only once a week, to make the supply last as long as possible.

Only a couple of days were left in 1863 when Titus came downstairs one evening, wrapped in a thick robe and helped by Louisa. She kept a firm grip on his arm while they were on the stairs. When they reached the bottom, he tried to shrug off her hand, but she stayed stubbornly beside him.

Titus was still pale and gaunt, but Louisa had trimmed his hair and beard and a little color had come back into his face. He looked much better than he had on Christmas night, when he had shown up on the brink of death. Now vitality burned in his eyes, but it wasn't a healthy glow. His body might not be wracked with fever anymore, but his mind burned with a different sort of zeal.

With supper over, the family sat in the parlor, huddled close to the fireplace. Abigail and Cordelia were on the divan, Mac and Henry in the armchairs that flanked the hearth. The reddish-yellow glow of the flames painted the faces that turned toward Titus and Louisa.

"Evening, Titus," Mac said. "You're starting to look a lot better. Glad you could come down to join us."

"I didn't come down to join nobody," Titus said. He looked around the room. "Where's Polly?"

"She's already turned in," Henry said. "She's pretty worn out these days."

"Carryin' a baby is hard work, I reckon." Titus's lips curled in a sneer that made Henry clutch the arms of his chair in anger. "Go up and get her."

"You don't give any orders around here," Henry snapped. "I'm not going to bother her—"

"Get her," Titus said. "It's time we had this out."

"If you're just going to argue," Abigail said from the divan, "maybe it would be best if you went back upstairs."

He shook his head. "No, Ma. We got to settle this, and you know it." His baleful gaze swept the others in the room. "You all know it."

"I tried to convince him not to do this—" Louisa began.

Titus finally jerked his arm out of her grip. "You can go upstairs if you want," he said coldly. "This is family business."

Louisa caught her breath, plainly hurt by his tone. But even though she backed off a couple of steps, she said, "I'll stay. You might need help to get back to bed."

"Suit yourself," Titus grunted. He looked at Henry. "Are you goin' to get your *wife*, or do I have to climb back up there and fetch her myself?"

Henry pushed himself to his feet. "You just won't let this go, will you?"

"Not hardly. It's gone on long enough. Too long."

"Yeah, I reckon you may be right about that." Cautiously he headed for the stairs, swinging wide to keep plenty of distance between himself and Titus as he passed.

"Henry," Abigail called after him, "I don't think this is a good idea."

Henry ignored her and went up the stairs. Cordelia clutched Abigail's hand, and Mac's teeth clamped down harder on the stem of his pipe. The air in the room seemed heavy, like a thunderstorm was about to break.

Henry hoped that Polly was already asleep. If she was, he had a legitimate excuse for refusing to wake her. She needed her rest. At the same time, he was tired of having this whole thing hanging over their heads. Maybe Titus really *was* right about getting it over with.

Polly was awake, sitting up in bed with a lamp, its wick turned low, burning on the side table.

As soon as Henry came into the room, she asked, "What is it? What's wrong?"

He wondered how she had sensed that something was wrong. "Titus is downstairs."

"That's good," she commented. "He must be getting some of his strength back."

"I'm not so sure it's good. He wants to have a showdown . . . about us. He wants you to come downstairs."

Polly pushed back the covers so that she could swing her legs out of bed. She was wearing a thick flannel nightgown, and she reached for a robe of the same fabric that was even thicker and heavier. "All right. Whatever he wants."

Henry stepped closer to her. "You don't have to do this. I'll go back down there and tell him to go to hell, if you want."

She shook her head. "No. He's already been to hell." She paused then added almost inaudibly, "And so have I."

Henry didn't know what to say to that. He stood there while she put on her robe and slippers then went to her and took her arm. He knew it would infuriate Titus that much more to see the two of them coming downstairs arm in arm, but he didn't care. Truth be told, he sort of looked forward to it a little.

When they reached the top of the staircase, Henry paused for a second. He couldn't hear any talking coming from the parlor, but the silence itself had a tense, strained quality to it. They started down.

Titus was standing in the doorway to the parlor, and his scowl darkened even more when he saw them, as Henry expected. He drew some slight satisfaction from that, but at the same time he realized he was being petty. He kept his expression carefully neutral as he led Polly into the room.

"All right, Titus, we're here," Henry said. "Say whatever you've got to say."

Titus's gaunt face creased in an ugly smile. "It ain't goin' to be that easy, little brother. You got a lot to answer for."

"I haven't done anything to you."

Titus leered. "No, but you done it to my wife. Your own brother's wife."

Henry felt his face growing warm but didn't know if the reaction was from embarrassment, anger, or both. "You got no call to talk like that."

Titus pointed. "That baby growin' in Polly's belly says I do. You want me to get to it, I'll get to it." He took a deep breath. "Polly is my wife. Mine. Your marriage to her don't mean nothin', little brother. Not in the eyes of the law or anybody else. And since she's my wife, that baby is mine, too, whether I want the little bastard or not. So you get away from her, and you stay away from her. I don't want you touchin' her or even talkin' to her ever again." Titus crossed his arms over his chest. "There. I've said it, and that's the way it's gonna be."

"Go to hell!" The words exploded out of Henry. He had held in his rage as long as he could. He let go of Polly's arm, and a long step put him in Titus's face, only inches separating them. "Polly's my wife now! You'll never have her again!"

"Henry!" Abigail said as she came up off the divan. "Titus! You two boys stop this!"

Mac and Cordelia were on their feet, too, watching the confrontation with anxious expressions on their faces.

Ignoring all of them, Titus stared into Henry's eyes and laughed. "You think things are gonna be that way just 'cause you say so? You're wrong, boy. You're bad wrong."

"Leave us alone," Henry pleaded. "Things have changed, Titus. They can't go back to the way they were."

"Maybe not, but you can't have her. I'll see you in hell first!"

With that, Titus's hands shot out and fastened around Henry's neck.

Considering how sick he had been only days before, Titus moved with shocking speed and surprising strength. Henry didn't even have a chance to draw a breath before Titus's fingers closed over his windpipe. A wave of dizziness went through him. A red haze shot through with black streaks dropped over his eyes. He heard shouts, but they seemed to be coming from far away. He struck out blindly, instinctively, slamming a punch into Titus's midsection.

Titus's attack was fueled by a bottomless fury, but his body was still weak. Henry's blow knocked his grip loose and sent him stumbling backward. Gasping for breath, Henry hesitated only a second then launched himself in a flying tackle that smashed Titus to the floor in front of the hearth.

Titus fought back, lifting his knee into Henry's groin, but the blow was a feeble one and slow enough so that Henry was able to twist aside from it. Titus's knee caught him on the thigh instead and did no damage. Henry jabbed a short, wicked punch into Titus's face. The blow bounced Titus's head off the floor.

Before Henry could strike again, strong hands caught hold of him and hauled him up. "Stop it!" Mac shouted. "Stop it, you fool! You'll kill him!"

"He deserves to die!" Henry raged. "He should've stayed dead in the first place!"

From the floor, Titus lashed out with a foot, aiming the kick at Henry's groin again. This time it landed, and Henry cried out in pain, doubling over in Mac's grasp. That grip was the only thing that kept Henry from crumpling to the floor.

Titus scrambled up onto his knees and tried to throw another punch, but Louisa caught hold of his arm. Cordelia moved in and grabbed his other arm. Together, the two young women were able to hold him back as he surged to his feet and spewed curses at Henry. Spittle flew through the air along with the obscenities.

Abigail stepped up and slapped Titus, her palm cracking sharply against his face. "Stop that!" she cried. "I won't have a son of mine talking like that!"

Titus's chest heaved with emotion, but he gulped down some air and regained a little control of himself. He glowered at Henry, who was starting to straighten up with Mac's help. "You're a piece o' work, Ma," he said.

"You keep a civil tongue in your head, young man!"

Titus's breath rasped through his clenched teeth. "Yeah, you're a God-fearin' woman. Won't allow no cussin' in your house. But I said it before and I'll say it again—you don't seem to mind Henry ruttin' with his brother's wife!"

"Stop it!" The words were half-shrieked. They came from Polly, taking everyone by surprise. "Damn you, Titus Brannon! You never were a real husband to me! You turned your back on me when I needed you the most, and then you . . . you slept with this woman!" Her finger stabbed in accusation at Louisa. "At least I had the decency to marry Henry! The two of you are nothing but adulterers!"

She put her hands over her face and started to sob.

Polly's sudden tirade left everyone staring at her in stunned silence. A moment later Henry glanced toward Louisa and saw the hurt and humiliation on her face. He could tell that Polly's accusation was true. He had suspected as much himself, knowing his brother and knowing that Titus and Louisa had been traveling together for a long time. But now Louisa's stricken look and the fact that she wasn't denying the allegation confirmed Henry's suspicion.

Titus recovered his wits first. "That don't have nothin' to do with nothin'," he said. "It sure as hell don't change what you did." He looked over at Cordelia and Louisa. "Let go of me."

"I don't want any more fighting," Abigail said.

"I'm done fightin'." Titus looked around at the others, his expression scornful. "All of you believe in the law, don't you? Well, we'll let the law settle this. Bring Judge Darden out here. See what he's got to say."

"There's no need—" Henry began.

"What's the matter, little brother?" Titus sneered. "Afraid to put it to the test? Afraid the judge'll say that Polly's still married to me?"

Polly shook her head. "It doesn't matter what the judge says. I'll never be your wife again, Titus. Never."

"We'll see about that." Cordelia and Louisa still had hold of his arms, but when he jerked free, this time they let him go. "We'll just see."

He walked shakily to the stairs, shrugging off Louisa's attempts to help him. At the bottom of the stairs, she turned to look at the Brannons, but after a moment it became obvious there was nothing for her to say. She just shook her head and followed Titus upstairs.

The pain in Henry's groin was subsiding. Titus's kick had caught him only a glancing blow. He was able to stand up without Mac's help now, so he stepped over to Polly and put a hand on her shoulder. He could feel her trembling. She had held her reaction to Titus's return inside her for so long that when it finally came out, it left her shaken to her core.

"It'll be all right," he said yet again, knowing that he had given her the same reassurance several times over the past few days, and it hadn't come true yet. But what else could he say? "I won't let Titus bother you or the baby."

"I'll never be his wife," Polly whispered. "No matter what the law says. He left me . . . he left me there . . ."

Henry wasn't sure what she was talking about, but right now he didn't care. He put his arms around Polly and held her, hoping his touch could accomplish what his words could not.

Chapter Five

ONCE MAC GOT AN idea in his head, it was hard to talk him out of it.

"What the judge says doesn't necessarily have to have any effect on what we do," he said the next morning as he and Henry sat in the kitchen. "But like it or not, Titus is right about one thing. We need to find out exactly what the law is pertaining to something like this."

"So you're going to ride into Culpeper and fetch Judge Darden, like Titus wants?" Henry asked in astonishment from the other side of the table. "You're going to give in to that crazy son of a bitch?"

They were alone in the kitchen, or Henry wouldn't have spoken in such blunt terms. Abigail had come downstairs earlier and started the coffee boiling. It wasn't real coffee, of course, only roasted grain, but it was the best they could do these days. She was back upstairs now, getting dressed. None of the others were up yet.

"It's not giving in to Titus," Mac said. "It's just trying to be reasonable. Maybe Judge Darden will side with you. Did you ever think about that? If he does, then surely Titus will see that he's wrong to be causing such a ruckus."

Henry frowned down at the table. He didn't believe Titus was ever going to admit to being wrong about anything. There was too much hate and bitterness in him for that.

It had been a long night. Henry had tossed and turned, unable to sleep, and finally he had gotten up and spent the rest of the night in a chair so that he wouldn't disturb Polly. Even so, he wasn't sure if she slept any, either.

Mac was also bleary-eyed this morning, a testament to his own restless night. Titus had thrown the whole household into an uproar, that was for sure.

"All right, if you're bound and determined to do it. Be sure and tell the judge how you and Will were convinced Titus was dead, though."

Mac nodded. "I'll see that he gets the whole story. I'd just go into town and talk to him, but I know Titus wouldn't be satisfied with that. He'll want to tell his own side of it."

"He doesn't have a side to take," Henry muttered. "He's dead wrong."

"We'll see," Mac said.

He drank a cup of the grain coffee then went out to the barn to saddle the stallion. He wasn't going to wait for breakfast.

"Where's your brother?" Abigail asked when she came back into the kitchen a short time later.

"Getting ready to ride into town," Henry told her. "He thinks it'll be best to bring Judge Darden out here and let him sort through the mess."

Abigail shook her head, a doubtful expression on her face. "I hope this doesn't just make things worse."

"You and me both, Ma. You and me both."

Later, Henry took a tray up to Polly, but for once she would not eat, claiming that she was too upset to do so. Henry didn't try to force her. The Brannons weren't the only family with stubbornness in their blood. The Ebersoles could be just as muleheaded when they wanted to be, he thought.

He wondered if Duncan Ebersole knew yet that Titus had returned. For a while there, Titus had been Ebersole's least favorite person in the whole world. The plantation owner could not have been more opposed to his daughter's romance with Titus. Henry supposed he might have gotten a little more tolerant while Titus and Polly were living at Mountain Laurel after their wedding, but Henry couldn't be sure about that since he hadn't been there and Polly didn't like to talk about those days. Later, after Polly had turned up pregnant, Henry had come in for his own share of Ebersole's hatred and anger. The old man hadn't gotten over it, either. From the rumors Henry had heard,

Ebersole stayed drunk most of the time these days, guzzling down the corn liquor that Israel Quinn brewed at his cabin in the foothills of the Blue Ridge.

Like Polly, Titus stayed in his room that morning. Louisa came down for breakfast looking pale and hollow-eyed, and Henry wondered if everybody in the house had spent a sleepless night. It was beginning to look like it. Louisa offered to help with the chores, but Abigail said, "Nonsense. You're a guest in this house, Miss Abernathy." Her tone became crisp as she added, "You Yankees *will* allow us to retain our Southern hospitality, won't you?"

"The Friends take no side in the conflict, Mrs. Brannon, other than to declare war to be evil and a sin."

Abigail could only sniff at that. For the moment, she might be caught up in the problems of her own family, but she would never forget—nor allow anyone else to forget—that she was a staunch supporter of the Confederacy.

Henry was in the barn later that morning, putting out a little grain for the family's lone remaining cow, when he heard hoof beats and the rattle of wheels. He stepped out into the weak sunshine and chilly air, pulling his coat tighter around him, and saw that Mac had returned. The judge was with him, climbing down from a buggy in front of the house.

The heavy-set, florid-faced attorney wasn't actually a judge anymore, though he had been one in the past and everyone still called him by the title. He was now the most prominent lawyer in Culpeper County, but of course that didn't mean much in a land scourged and wracked by war. Still, there was no more astute legal mind in the area. If anybody could set them straight on what the law had to say about husbands who were supposed to be dead and wives who married other men, it was the judge.

"Hello, Henry," Darden said as Henry hurried across the yard between barn and house. "Mac tells me you have yourself a legal dilemma."

"Did he give you all the details?"

"All of them," Mac said. "The whole story."

Darden chuckled. "Took most of the ride out here, too. Why don't we go inside and discuss it? This cold winter air's bad for my rheumatism."

The three of them went into the house and found Abigail waiting for them. "I sent Cordelia up to tell Titus and Polly that you're here, Judge," she said.

Darden took off his black plug hat. "You're looking as lovely as ever, Mrs. Brannon," he said, evidently unwilling to get down to business without at least a few pleasantries.

"Thank you. Would you like something to drink? We have some fresh buttermilk . . ."

"That would be fine."

Henry knew the judge would have liked that buttermilk spiked with a shot of whiskey, but that was unlikely, if not downright impossible, in Abigail Brannon's house. The judge took off his hat and overcoat, and Mac hung them in the foyer.

Titus came downstairs with Louisa behind him. He had dressed in one of his old black suits that he'd left behind when he joined the army. Henry was surprised at how dignified Titus appeared, despite being so thin and pale. When he looked at Titus, he felt a little ashamed of the work clothes he wore.

"Well, my boy, I surely didn't expect to ever see you again," Darden greeted Titus. "I heard a little about the ordeal you suffered at the hands of those damnable Yankees. You're lookin' mighty well, considerin'."

"Thanks, Judge," Titus said. He glanced at Mac. "I suppose my big brother has poisoned your mind against me already?"

"The law deals only with facts, Titus, not feelin's. I'm here to talk about the facts."

Titus looked around. "Where's Polly?"

"I'm here," she answered from the top of the stairs. Cordelia was with her and held her hand as they came down. Polly wore a dark blue dress, and Henry thought she looked beautiful despite the strain that showed on her face.

Abigail brought a cup of buttermilk from the kitchen and handed it to the judge, then Mac ushered the small group into the parlor. Befitting his role as interpreter of the law, Darden stood next to the fireplace where he would be the center of attention as the others took their seats around the room. He sipped the buttermilk, set the cup on the mantel, and waved a pudgy hand. "Ask me anything you'd like," he said, "and I'll give you my best legal opinion."

"Is it legal for a treacherous skunk to lay with his brother's wife?" Titus said before anyone else could speak.

Henry shot to his feet. "By God, I won't stand for—"

Mac's hand fell heavily on his shoulder, silencing him. "Sit down, Henry. We've already had one brawl about this, and it didn't settle anything. Let's let the judge do his job."

Titus's smirk made Henry want to smash a fist in the middle of his face, but with an effort he controlled himself and sank back down on his chair.

Judge Darden didn't seem bothered by the brief outburst of anger. As a lawyer, he was accustomed to emotions running high whenever he was called into a case. He said, "I've heard from Mac already. You tell me what you have to say about all this, Titus, but without the inflammatory language."

"All right, Judge. I'm legally married to Polly Ebersole. You know that. You were there for the wedding at Mountain Laurel."

Darden inclined his head. "Indeed I was."

"The Yankees captured me at Fredericksburg, and I spent nearly a year in one of their prisons, at Camp Douglas in Illinois. Seemed more like ten years."

"I expect it did," Darden murmured.

"Nathan Hatcher was there, too. I believe he used to clerk for you."

The judge nodded solemnly. "He did. He was a fine boy until he decided that he was a Yankee at heart and had to go off and fight for 'em. You got to tell me sometime how he came to be in one of their prison camps."

"I will, Judge," Titus promised with a nod. "Anyway, I got out of there, and I came home to find that my wife up and married another man while I was gone—my own brother Henry. Not only that, she got herself pregnant by him."

"You weren't just *gone*," Polly said. "You were dead. We all thought so."

"Thinkin' don't make it so," Titus snapped.

Darden held up a hand to halt the exchange. "I'll hear from you momentarily, Miss Polly. Right now I'm listenin' to Titus. Go ahead, son."

Titus shrugged. "That's all there is to tell. I say Polly is still my wife, and her marriage to Henry might as well have never happened as far as the law's concerned."

Darden nodded. "All right. Henry? Polly? What've you got to say for yourselves?"

Henry felt his spirits sinking as he looked at the judge. Everything the man had said so far made it sound as if he had already made up his mind that Titus was in the right. And maybe that's how it might go in a law court. But he wasn't going to give up without a fight, Henry told himself.

"Judge, you yourself believed that Titus was dead, killed in combat, didn't you?"

"Well, sure. Will and Mac said that he was, and I know those boys tell the truth. That was the way they was raised, wasn't it, Mrs. Brannon?"

"It certainly was," Abigail said matter-of-factly.

"Polly and me, we believed it, too," Henry went on. "And both of us mourned for Titus."

Titus gave a brittle laugh but didn't say anything.

"We mourned for Titus," Henry repeated, "but there came a time when we were ready to move on with our lives as best we could with this war going on."

Judge Darden nodded.

"We fell in love with each other." Henry said it as plain as he could. "We fell in love and we got married, the same as folks do all over the country. There's nothing wrong with what we felt, and there's nothing wrong with what we did."

"Polly was already with child at the time of the ceremony, I believe," Titus drawled.

Henry's head jerked around to face him. "If you're going to condemn us for that, you might as well condemn half the people in Virginia, you self-righteous—"

"Polly came to *our* weddin' night a virgin," Titus said.

Polly started to laugh.

They all swung around to look at her, and as she continued to laugh, Titus's face grew red. "Stop that!" he snapped. "You stop it right now, woman!"

"We're not here to dig up the past," Judge Darden said in his growling tones. "We're here to figure out what the law says. And it seems pretty clear to me."

That declaration made Polly stop laughing. She looked at the judge with an expectant expression, as did everyone else in the room.

Darden clasped his hands together behind his back. "Titus was assumed to be dead by one and all," he began, "but like he said, thinkin' something don't make it so. Mac, on the way out here, I asked you if there was ever a petition filed with the court to have Titus declared legally dead. What did you tell me?"

Mac shook his head. "No, we never did that, Judge. There didn't seem to be any need."

"I wrote it in the family Bible," Abigail said. "That's all the record we ever had of most births and deaths, Judge."

"That's all well and good, Mrs. Brannon, but it ain't official. So it don't really matter what anybody thought. Titus was still alive, and as such, his marriage to Miss Polly was still legal and binding. Still is, as far as I can tell."

Polly let out a low moan as her head sunk to her chest, and Henry's hands clenched into fists.

"That means the marriage between Miss Polly and Henry here is bigamous," Darden continued. "Now, I don't reckon anybody would ever file charges against the two of you, because clearly there wasn't no fraud or deception involved, just a terrible mistake. But I'm certain that if it came down to it, any court of law in this great Confederacy of ours would set aside your marriage and declare it null and void."

"You're sure, Judge?" Mac asked.

"This ain't a legal rulin', you understand, since I'm no longer on the bench, but it is my considered opinion, yes. And my record shows that the laws of the Commonwealth of Virginia agree with my opinions ninety-nine times out of a hundred."

Henry hesitated to grasp at that straw, but he couldn't help himself. "Then you could be wrong, Judge?"

Darden gave him a hard look. "I wouldn't bet the farm on it, son—or anything else."

"I knew it!" Titus said. He grinned at Polly. "I knew you were still my wife."

"Under the circumstances, my suggestion would be that divorce proceedin's be started," Darden said, "so that Henry and Miss Polly can get married again, legally this time. Then this whole unfortunate situation can go away."

"No," Titus said, almost before the words were out of the judge's mouth. "There won't be no divorce."

"My God, Titus!" Polly burst out. "You've got to see that's the only thing we can do."

Titus shook his head. "No divorce," he repeated. "I'm the one who's been wronged here. It was my wife who committed adultery. If I want to forgive her and take her back, that's my right. Ain't it, Judge?"

Darden hesitated, hemming and hawing a couple of times before he said reluctantly, "I don't reckon there's any way to force a fella to file for divorce."

"What about me?" Polly asked. "Can't I divorce him?"

"You'd have to have grounds for that—"

"He committed adultery, too!" Polly pointed at Louisa Abernathy. "With that woman."

"Do you have any evidence of that?"

Titus cackled and nodded at Polly's belly. "Not nearly as good evidence as I got, Judge!"

Despite the late December chill, Darden was sweating. He pulled a handkerchief from his pocket and mopped his face. The judge looked like he was sickened by what he had seen and heard here today. "I've given you folks my legal opinion. That's all I can do. Reckon I'll be headin' back to Culpeper now."

Mac stepped over to him and shook his hand. "Thanks, Judge. I . . . I can't pay you now, but after the war . . ."

Darden patted him on the arm. "Don't you worry about my fee, son. For one of Jeb Stuart's glorious cavalry, well, I'll be more than happy to postpone the payin' of it." He looked around and nodded to Abigail, Cordelia, Polly, and Louisa. "Ladies. Good day to you."

It was far from a good day, Henry thought. Mighty far.

But at least there was a glimmer of hope. Somehow, they had to persuade Titus to divorce Polly. That was the only way any of them could get on with their lives.

When Judge Darden was gone, Titus put his hands on his knees and pushed himself to his feet, a satisfied look on his face. He grinned at Polly. "You heard what the judge said. You're still my wife, gal. So you better just move out of that room where you been stayin' and move in with me."

Polly regarded him with the same revulsion she would have felt if a snake had crawled up her dress. "I'll never stay with you again, Titus," she said. "The law may say that I'm your wife, but that doesn't mean I have to act like one."

Titus's grin vanished, and he scowled at her. "That's where you're wrong. I got my husbandly rights—"

"You touch her and I'll kill you," Henry said.

Mac moved to get between his brothers. He turned a hard gaze on Titus. "I wouldn't push this if I were you," he said. "The law may be on your side, but that's the only friend you've got, Titus."

"That ain't true," Titus said with a defiant jut of his chin. He turned to look at the woman who had engineered his escape, brought him back to Virginia, back to his family. "You're still my friend, ain't you, Louisa?"

"Please, Titus," she pleaded wearily, not answering his question, "why don't you just go back upstairs and rest in your room? You still have a lot of your strength to regain, now that you're getting well again."

"Yeah, I reckon you're right." He raised his hand and pointed a finger at Polly. "But it ain't over between us. You'll see. It ain't over by a long shot."

He left the room and went upstairs. Louisa followed him, a shamed look on her face. Despite all the emotional turmoil Henry was experiencing, he felt sorry for her. Considering all she had done for Titus, he was treating her badly.

But he was threatening to do even worse to Polly. "There isn't any way he can force Polly to live as his wife, is there?" Henry asked Mac.

"I don't know. Seems to me there are some things the law just can't control, and the way people feel is one of them. But with Titus . . ." Mac shook his head. "I honestly don't know what he's capable of anymore."

"I won't go to him," Polly said. "No matter what he does to me, I won't. I'll kill him first."

Cordelia put her arm around Polly's shoulders. "Don't talk like that, Polly. Nobody's going to make you do anything you don't want to do."

Polly gave a low laugh. "If they don't, it'll be the first time in my life."

Henry didn't know what she meant by that, but they could talk about it later. He took her hand. "Come on upstairs. Maybe you'll feel better if you lie down for a little while."

Polly started to shake her head, but then she gasped and caught her breath. Her hand went to her stomach. "Oh, my," she said, her eyes wide.

Instantly, Henry was afraid. "What is it?" he asked. "Is something wrong with the baby?"

"No, it just . . ." Henry still had hold of her hand, so she took his hand and placed it on her belly. "Wait," she said.

Henry wasn't sure what he was waiting for, but then, a couple of seconds later, he felt the movement under his hand. His eyes widened in amazement. "Is that . . . ?"

Polly nodded. "That's right. The baby just kicked."

The other members of the family gathered around, smiling and offering their congratulations. Polly accepted them graciously, but Henry thought he saw a shadow of some sort lurking in her eyes, as if she wasn't as happy about this development as the rest of them were. Of course, he wasn't the one carrying the baby, he reminded himself. He didn't know how he would react if the situation were reversed.

Right now, though, even after everything that had happened this morning, he couldn't help but be pleased. The little kick came again against his hand, and he thought that that was his son or daughter in there, growing and moving around and waiting to come out into the world. It was a world torn apart by war and suffering at the moment, Henry thought, but it wouldn't always be that way. Sooner or later, the great conflict between North and South would be over. He was no longer sure what the outcome would be, but a part of him was beginning to accept that whatever it was, it would be better than all the killing and devastation. The war probably wouldn't be over by the time this baby was born, but before it grew up, things would be different. Folks would care about each other again, and they would work together to make the world a better place. His son or daughter would be right there with them, he vowed, doing whatever he or she could to improve the way people lived.

The possibilities, he realized as he stood there with new life stirring under his touch, were endless.

Chapter Six

NEW YEAR'S DAY CAME and went, and 1863, the worst year yet for the Confederacy, was finally over. Mac could only hope that the new year would be better . . . but he had no great confidence that it would be. The wide-eyed innocence and optimism of the first days of the war were long gone.

Abigail had been saving some black-eyed peas she'd put up the previous summer, since tradition said that eating black-eyed peas on New Year's Day would bring good luck. Unfortunately, the Confederacy was going to need more luck than some peas could bring.

Mac didn't know if Louisa Abernathy had had a talk with Titus or not, but something had persuaded him to back off a little. Most of the time he stayed in what had become his room, not coming out even for meals. He refused to discuss the possibility of giving Polly the divorce she needed so that she and Henry could marry legally, but at least he was no longer pressing her to leave Henry and move into his room.

Polly was pale and worried-looking all the time now, and Henry was afraid her mental state would hurt the baby. He had confided that concern to Mac, but Mac hadn't known what to tell him. Pregnancy was something he knew very little about. It made sense, though, that worrying all the time couldn't be good for anybody, let alone a woman with a new life growing inside her body.

A couple of days after the New Year, the family was gathered around the table in the kitchen for the midday meal. Louisa had already taken a tray upstairs for Titus and herself. The day was a bit warmer, the sun a little brighter. Spring was still a long way off, though, and that was all right with Mac. Good weather would mean that the war was back on. Wildflowers blooming would signal a fresh start for the killing.

The family's old hound bayed from the porch, and a second later Mac heard hoof beats. With things the way they were, there wasn't much telling who the visitor might be. A neighbor, maybe, or someone from town. It could even be a Yankee patrol. The Union lines actually were closer to the farm than the Confederate lines were.

Mac and Henry exchanged a glance. The unknown always held a possibility of trouble these days, so Mac said to his mother and Cordelia and Polly, "You three stay here. Henry and I will see who it is."

"Be careful," Abigail said as her sons got to their feet.

Mac was wearing farm clothes instead of his uniform, but his holstered pistol hung in the parlor as well as his saber in its brass scabbard. On the way to the front door, he stepped into the parlor and retrieved the pistol, checking the cylinder before placing his hand on the door knob.

Henry joined him, picking up the shotgun leaning against the wall next to the door. They heard heavy footsteps on the porch, then someone slammed a fist against the door.

"Open up! Open up, damn it! I come t' see my daughter!"

Mac and Henry glanced at each other, both of them recognizing the voice of Duncan Ebersole. The planter hadn't been on the Brannon farm since Henry and Polly had gotten married. No one had missed him, either. It was all right with the Brannons if Ebersole just stayed at Mountain Laurel, stewing in his own bitterness.

Ebersole continued to beat on the door. "Let me in, I say!"

"He sounds drunk," Henry said in a low voice.

"Yes, but he doesn't sound like he's going away." Mac stepped to the door and grasped the knob in his left hand. His right was wrapped around the butt of the pistol. He jerked the door open, evidently catching Ebersole a little by surprise as he was about to knock again. He stumbled forward a half step before catching himself. Henry's guess about his father-in-law's drunken state was correct. Mac could smell whiskey on the man's breath. More than likely, the planter was Quinn's best customer these days, since Yancy Lattimer had killed himself.

Mac didn't waste any breath on a polite greeting. "What do you want, Ebersole?"

The older man blinked owlishly at him. Ebersole looked even worse than he had the last time Mac had seen him. His long, reddish-gray hair was matted and tangled, and his normally close-cropped beard had grown out in ragged tufts. The man's face was haggard. His nose was red from drink, but the rest of his skin had an unhealthy pallor to it. His suit was stained and rumpled. And he swayed a little as he tried to pull himself upright and regain some dignity.

His Scots accent was even thicker than usual as he demanded more than stated, "I've come t' see my daughter. Come t' see my lil' Polly."

"I'll ask her if she wants to talk to you," Mac said. "Wait here, Mr. Ebersole."

"Not even goin' to invite me in the house? Not very hospitable, are ye, Brannon?"

"Not to some folks," Mac said tersely.

Ebersole turned his bleary-eyed gaze to Henry. "Ah, my son-in-law! How are you, boy?"

"Fine," Henry said.

"Although . . . ," Ebersole leered. "From wha' I hear, ye ain't my son-in-law at all, are ye? Yer brother Titus is back, and ye ain't nothin' t' me anymore 'cept the son of a bitch who planted a bastard in my lil' girl's belly."

Henry's face was taut with anger. He started to step forward with the shotgun clutched tightly in his hands. Mac put out an arm to stop him. "Hold on, Henry." To Ebersole, he said, "If you're going to talk like that, you might as well get back on your horse and go home. I won't fetch Polly unless you promise to treat her decent."

Ebersole's lips drew back from his teeth as he glared at Mac. "How I treat that gal's none o' yer damn business, Brannon. I never heard her complain none, though. She's my flesh an' blood, so ye better get her out here."

Mac drew a deep breath and thought about kicking Ebersole off the place. He and Henry wouldn't have any trouble putting him on his horse and starting it away from the house at a gallop. If Ebersole was too drunk to stay in the saddle and fell off and broke his neck, it would be his own fault.

Before anything else could happen, Polly asked from behind them, "What do you want, Father?"

"There she is!" Ebersole exclaimed, craning his neck to look past Mac and Henry. "There's my precious lil' girl!"

Polly came forward into the foyer, and Mac and Henry moved apart a little so she could confront Ebersole. "What do you want?" she asked again.

"Why, I want ye t' come home to Mountain Laurel, o' course." An odd expression came over Ebersole's face, and it took Mac a couple of seconds to realize that the plantation owner was trying to look contrite. "I'm mighty sorry for all the trouble I give ye, and it'd sure gladden the heart o' this old man if ye'd come home, girl."

Polly shook her head. "This is my home now, with Henry."

"Haw!" The harsh laugh burst out of Ebersole's mouth and his sorrowful expression vanished, to be replaced by a look of scorn. "This little piss-ant ain't even yer real husband! Yer still married t' that bastard Titus!"

From the staircase, Titus's voice lashed out. "I'll thank you to keep your filthy tongue off my name, Ebersole."

The old planter leaned back, looked up, then dramatically continued. "There he is! Back from the dead! I heard about it in Culpeper, but I didn't believe it at first. We all figured ye was worm food, boy." He chuckled. "Me, I was hopin' an' prayin' ye really was dead. You're the one took my girl away from me in the first place."

"No one took me away from you," Polly snapped. "You drove me away."

Ebersole grinned at her. "But when ye had t' choose, ye finally come back to yer ol' pa, didn't ye? Ye knew who always treated you better'n anybody else."

"Get out of here," Polly hissed between clenched teeth. "My God, if you don't get out of here, I'll—"

"Ye won't do nothin'! And neither will any o' these white trash Brannons you're so fond of."

"That's enough," Mac said sharply. "You've talked to Polly. Now get out."

"Ye don't give me orders, boy. Not me. I'm the biggest land-holder in this whole damned county—"

"You don't hold this land," Mac said as he lifted the pistol. "It's Brannon land, and it has been for a long time. And if you don't get off of it, I may have to shoot you for trespassing."

"Ye wouldn't dare!"

"Don't try me," Mac warned.

At that moment, he wasn't sure what he would do if Ebersole refused to leave. All he knew was that the whole family was miserable and had been for over a week now, and there didn't seem to be anything he could do to fix it. Mac had always thought of himself as a peaceable man, but his frustration had grown to the point that it had turned into anger, and he was ready to unleash that anger. Duncan Ebersole would be a mighty handy target . . .

"I'll leave ye today," Ebersole said, his speech and manner still haughty, "but I got one more thing to say." He looked at Polly. "Ye got to stop livin' in sin wi' this boy. Go on back to yer legal husband, ye hear? Bad enough ye'll be givin' birth to a bas-tard and dishonorin' the Ebersole name. Don't make it no worse than it has to be."

Henry turned his head to glare up the stairs at Titus. "Did you put him up to this?" he demanded.

Titus gave a curt shake of his head. "Lord knows I never thought I'd be agreein' with anything Ebersole ever had to say, but he's right. I didn't have anything to do with it, though."

Polly looked back and forth between her father and her first—and allegedly legal—husband. "Both of you can go to hell," she said.

Ebersole let out a cry, as if she had wounded him physically. "How sharper is the serpent's tooth—" he started to blubber.

Mac stopped him by stepping forward, grabbing his arm, and propelling him toward the edge of the porch. "Get out of here, Ebersole. Now!"

At the same time, Henry moved to get between Polly and Titus. The barrels of the shotgun were pointed toward the floor, but it was evident from every tense line of Henry's body that he wanted to aim the weapon at Titus.

"Go on back upstairs," Henry said to him in a low, barely controlled voice.

"Or what, little brother? You'll blow my guts out with that scattergun?" Titus shook his head. "I don't think so. You say she's your woman now, but you wouldn't kill for her."

"Don't be so sure of that."

Polly clutched at Henry's arm. "Leave him be, Henry. Let's all just leave him alone with his own miserable self."

Grudgingly, Henry went with her down the hall toward the kitchen. Titus's mocking laughter followed them.

Outside on the porch, Duncan Ebersole jerked his arm out of Mac's grip. "I'll have the law on ye for assaultin' me!" he said.

"Try it," Mac told him. "Anything that'll get you off the place is fine with me."

Ebersole wagged a finger in Mac's face. "One o' these days, all you Brannons'll get yer comeuppance. Mark my words. You're worse'n a bunch o' damned uppity darkies. Ye need some o' the same treatment. A touch o' the lash'd teach you to mind yer manners around your betters!"

"If I believed for one second that you were better than me, Ebersole, I think I'd blow my own brains out. I really believe I would." Mac lifted the pistol again, and this time he thumbed back the hammer. "But today I think it'd be your brains I'd be

ing off this porch if you don't get the hell out of here right
minute."

For a heartbeat, Ebersole's eyes glared into Mac's, then the
nter looked away. "I'm goin', I'm goin'," he muttered. "But I
on't forget this, Brannon."

"Neither will I," Mac said.

Ebersole backed away, almost fell when he reached the steps
that led down to the ground, and stumbled out to his horse,
which stood waiting with reins dangling on the ground. Awkwardly, Ebersole climbed into the saddle then cruelly jerked his
mount's head around. Mac almost shot him then and there when
he saw the pain in the horse's eyes, but he managed to suppress
the impulse. Ebersole kicked his heels into the horse's flanks
and rode off, shouting curses over his shoulder.

Mac stood there on the porch and watched him go. As he
looked along the lane that led from the road to the farm, he saw
a buggy on the road. It reached the turnoff for the lane at the
same time that Ebersole got there, and the driver had to haul
back on the team's reins to avoid a collision. Ebersole leaned
over and yelled at whoever was in the buggy as he rode by.

Mac expected the buggy to drive on past the lane once
Ebersole was out of the way, but to his surprise, it turned in and
rolled toward the house instead. He didn't recognize the vehicle
and didn't have any idea who else would be visiting the Brannon
farm today. As the buggy came closer, he saw that a young black
man was handling the reins. Something about him was familiar.
The young man lifted a hand in greeting and grinned, and suddenly Mac knew him. "Roman!" he exclaimed. The slave that
Will had inherited from his friend Yancy Lattimer . . .

And if Roman was driving that buggy, more than likely
meant—

"Will!" Mac shouted. "Ma! Cordelia! Come quick! Her
Titus! Will's here!"

As he leaped off the porch and ran out to meet the bu
the thought crossed Mac's mind that he was going to feel av

foolish if Capt. William Shakespeare Bran␣␣␣
in that vehicle.

⟨ formatting ornament ⟩

WILL BRANNON wondered what Duncan Ebersole␣
doing at the farm. Ebersole had been a thorn in the sid␣
Brannons for years. If the planter had greeted them civill␣
might have thought that Ebersole had come to the farm to ␣
his daughter, Polly. But Ebersole had cursed at Roman for ge␣
ting the buggy in his way then galloped off after peering through
the windows of the vehicle. Ebersole had looked drunk, and
Will wasn't sure if the man had recognized him or not. He didn't
particularly care. He had as little use for Ebersole as any of the
Brannons did.

Ebersole wouldn't have recognized the buggy, that was for
sure. It belonged to Dorothy Chamberlain. Actually, it had
belonged to her late husband, but now it was hers, along with
the rest of the family estate.

Dorothy laid a hand on Will's arm. "Who is that awful man?"
she asked.

He looked over at her and gave her a grim smile. "An awful
man, just like you said. Name's Duncan Ebersole. He owns a big
plantation not far from here."

"He's your sister-in-law's father," Dorothy guessed.

Will nodded. "That's right." One way or another, Polly was
still his sister-in-law, whether she actually was married to Titus
or Henry. Will wondered if they had gotten that mess straightened out yet.

The shock he'd felt when he read Mac's note had been
enough to make the pain shoot through Will's chest. Most of the
time, he felt only a dull ache deep inside, but whenever he got
upset about something, the pain grew sharper, like the stab of a
saber. The Yankee bullet that had knocked him off his horse at
Gettysburg had torn him up inside something fierce, and even

though the doctors at the hospital in Richmond said that he was all right now, he had his doubts. They claimed all he needed was plenty of rest, and maybe they were right. He hoped so. At any rate, he had stopped complaining about the pain, figuring there was no point in doing so. The surgeons had done all they could for him; from here on out, he would just have to take his chances and see what happened.

Pretty much the way he had lived his whole life.

At first Dorothy had tried to talk him out of it when he said he was going back to Culpeper County, back to the family farm. "You're not well enough to be traveling," she had insisted.

"The doctors have already said that they'll release me anytime I'm ready to go," he'd said. "Well, I'm ready. I thought my brother Titus was dead, and now I find out he isn't. I have to see him, Dorothy. You ought to be able to understand that."

He hadn't liked talking to her in such a blunt fashion. She had been good to him, mighty good. When they had first met, she was volunteering at the hospital, doing what she could to assist the overworked doctors and nurses. She was doing it to honor the memory of her husband, a Confederate officer who had fallen at Chancellorsville. Will had been just another patient to her.

That had changed over the course of the months he had spent in Richmond. She had spent more and more time with him, and he got to where he expected to see her pretty face and her shining blonde hair every day. The days she couldn't come to see him were bleak and depressing. She read to him, she wrote letters for him, and the day came when she took his hand and held it tightly and he knew that what had grown between them was more than just a friendship between a hospital patient and a volunteer. He could tell from the look in her eyes that she knew it, too.

So when he insisted on going home, it came as no great surprise to him that at first she resisted the idea then declared that if he was going, she was coming with him. "I have a perfectly good buggy and team," she had said, "and you might as well make use of them."

By that time, Roman had shown up in Richmond, looking for the man he called Cap'n Will. If not for the young slave, Will would have died more than once, first at Gettysburg and then during the hazardous journey back to Virginia from the Pennsylvania countryside where that disastrous battle had taken place. Neither Will nor any of the Brannons had ever owned a slave until Yancy Lattimer put it in his will that Roman was to go to him. And Will didn't intend to own Roman for a single day longer than was necessary. He had promised that Roman would have his manumission papers, making him a free man, and that was another reason Will wanted to go home. Those papers would have to be filed in Culpeper County. Will figured Judge Darden could take care of it.

Roman and Will had gotten separated after the retreating army crossed the Potomac into Virginia, and it had taken awhile for the young man to walk to Richmond and search out his owner. Now that they had been reunited, Roman insisted that he wasn't going to let Will out of his sight. "I'll drive you back to Culpeper, Cap'n Will," he had said. "That is, if Miss Dorothy don't mind."

"Of course that's all right," Dorothy had said. "I know how devoted you are to Will, Roman."

But she didn't fully understand, Will thought. In her eyes, Roman might be a highly favored slave, but he was still a slave. To Will, he was a friend, a good friend that law and custom said was something else, something less than that.

Will Brannon didn't give a damn about that. He believed in the Confederacy and in the right of those states to secede from the Union and form their own nation. That it was legal to do such a thing was spelled out right there in the Constitution. And the Yankees had started the fight by refusing to leave Fort Sumter, which stood on ground belonging to the sovereign state of South Carolina.

But just because he had no qualms about fighting the Yankees, that didn't mean he had to support everything the Confederacy did. It would be just fine with him if they did away with slavery, and he knew plenty of other Southerners who felt the same way. Some of the politicians from the Southern states had been working toward that for years before the war ever started. For all Will knew, there might have been Yankees who felt the same way. But firebrands on both sides had turned it into an all-or-nothing battle. They were damned idiots as far as Will was concerned. He couldn't free all the slaves, but by God, he could free Roman, and that was just what he intended to do.

So, prompted by the startling news that Titus was still alive, Will had decided to come home, and now they were within sight of the farm. He felt a different sort of pain in his chest as he gazed at the whitewashed house and the surrounding trees, barns, pens, and fields. This was a good pain. No battles had been fought here. The fields hadn't been trampled by the armies or cut up by the wheels of artillery caissons, nor were they pockmarked with shell holes. The place looked a little run down, true, because the whole family wasn't there to take care of it anymore. But it was still beautiful to Will. It was home and always would be.

In a voice thick with emotion, he said, "Let's go, Roman."

The young man grinned over his shoulder and flicked the reins to get the team moving again. As the buggy rolled down the lane toward the farm, Will saw a familiar figure coming out to meet them. Mac! Mac was home from the war.

By the time the buggy came to a stop in front of the house, several more people had hurried out. Will saw Abigail, Cordelia, and Henry, who had his arm around Polly, who looked a little tired and drawn but still pretty. Will supposed it was true what folks said about ladies who were in a family way having a glow about them.

"Hello, old-timer!" Mac said as he reached up to grasp Will's hand. "Let me help you—"

"It's mighty good to see you, Mac," Will said, "but I reckon I can climb down from here all right." It was prideful, he knew, but he wanted his first step back on Brannon land to be unassisted.

Mac seemed to understand. He moved back to give him some room.

Dorothy, however, leaned forward anxiously. "You should let me help you, Will. Or let Roman."

Roman turned his head and saw the look in Will's eyes, understanding it as well as Mac did. "I reckon the cap'n's fine, ma'am," he said.

"All right," Dorothy sighed. "But be careful, Will."

"Always am," he lied and grasped the side of the buggy and swung down. There was a slight twinge of pain, but nothing so bad that he couldn't ignore it. "It's mighty good to be home," he said once his feet were on the ground.

Everyone gathered around him. Mac and Henry pumping his hand, his mother and Cordelia hugging him around his neck. Even Polly hugged him, and Will sensed that she was more a member of the family now than she had ever been when he was around before. When she had been married to Titus . . .

That thought led him to ask, "Where's Titus? I couldn't hardly believe it when I got your note, Mac."

"He's around, all right," Mac said, and the grim tone that came into his voice told Will that something was wrong.

"Well, where is he?"

"In the house, I reckon."

"No, I'm here, big brother," Titus called from the front door. He stepped out onto the porch, thin and pale and carrying himself as if he were somehow brittle and terribly fragile, pretty much the way Will appeared to himself whenever he glanced at a mirror. Both of them bore mute testimony to the hardships they had endured.

A redheaded woman came onto the porch behind his brother. Will didn't know her, but from the way she hovered near him, a hand lifted as if she were ready to reach out and steady him if need be, he knew there had to be some kind of connection between them. Will walked slowly to the porch. Titus came down the steps so that they met at the bottom of them. Will extended his hand. Titus hesitated a second before taking it, but then the brothers shook. Will pulled Titus closer and clapped him on the back.

"Lord, but it's good to see you," he said hoarsely. "Mac and I were sure you were dead."

"I know. Reckon you were wrong."

"Yeah. And I'm mighty glad of it."

Abigail moved closer to the buggy and held up a hand to Dorothy. "You must be Mrs. Chamberlain," she said. "You wrote all those letters for Will. Thank you for everything you've done for my boy."

"I was glad to, Mrs. Brannon," Dorothy said as she took Abigail's hand and stepped down from the buggy. "Your son is one of the finest men I've ever met. It's been my honor to assist him in his recovery."

"We appreciate your bringing him out here. You'll stay the night?"

Will turned his head toward them. "Dorothy's staying as long as I do, Ma. She wouldn't have it any other way, even after I assured her that you and Cordelia would fuss over me just fine by yourselves."

"Will Brannon, you speak respectfully to your mother," Abigail snapped, but the smile she gave Dorothy took any sting out of the words. "Come along inside, Mrs. Chamberlain. I'm sure you must be mighty tired after your trip."

"It was a bit wearying," Dorothy agreed. "I'd like to meet the rest of your family first, though."

Will performed the introductions. Everyone greeted her warmly except for Titus, who still seemed reserved. That was because of everything he had gone through, Will told himself. Titus would come around. Give him a little more time, and he would be the same as he always was.

He wondered how things regarding Titus's marriage to Polly had been resolved. Obviously, she still considered herself Henry's wife. He would ask Mac about it later, he decided. He didn't want to cast a pall on his homecoming. For the same reason, he didn't ask what Duncan Ebersole had been doing at the farm. He didn't figure it could have been anything good.

But everything would be all right, he told himself. All the Brannons were home now except for Cory. With the family mostly together and the war in a winter lull, things were going to be just fine.

Chapter Seven

HE DID *what?*" Will said, astonishment and anger mingling in his voice.

"Refused to give her a divorce," Mac said again.

"He says that she should leave me and go back to him," Henry added.

The three of them were seated around the kitchen table. Abigail, Cordelia, and Polly were in the parlor with Dorothy, making her feel welcome. Titus had gone back upstairs with the redheaded woman. Will knew her name now and that she had helped Titus and Nathan escape from a Yankee prison camp. Like everyone else, he wasn't exactly clear on how Nathan had come to be in the camp with Titus, but that didn't really matter right now. What was important was the bitter rift that had developed within the Brannon family.

Mac and Henry told him everything that had happened since Titus's shocking return on Christmas night.

Will was still trying to sort it all out in his mind. "I don't reckon I blame Titus for being upset at first," he said slowly. "But by now he should be able to see how things stand."

"Oh, he sees how they stand, all right," Henry said. "He's just bound and determined not to let them be that way."

"And you know how stubborn Titus can be," Mac put in. "Shoot, he never would have courted and married Polly in the first place if he hadn't been the most mule-headed son of a gun in this part of the country."

"True enough," Will agreed. "But stubborn or not, he's got to come to his senses and do the right thing. Henry and Polly are expecting a baby, for God's sake!"

Mac nodded. "Maybe you can talk some sense into his head. We don't seem able to. And the law is on his side, too. Judge Darden said so."

"I'll talk to the judge," Will announced, determined. "I've got to see him anyway regarding manumission papers for Roman."

"You still plan to free him?" Mac asked. On their way back from Gettysburg, Mac had promised he would take care of that if Will didn't make it.

"Don't you think it's the right thing to do?"

"Of course I do. That's why I promised to handle it for you if you couldn't. But I don't know how well it'll sit with folks around here."

A short bark of laughter came from Will. "You think I give a damn? Anybody who thinks I don't support the Confederacy because I choose to free a slave can take a look at my battle scars. Hell, I still limp from that wound in my leg, especially when the weather is wet."

Mac reached over and squeezed Will's arm. "I know," he said. "And I don't care what they think, either."

"Brannons have always gone their own way," Henry said. "That's what Pa taught us."

That was the truth, Will thought. John Brannon had looked at things differently than most. He had been willing to go along and not argue with folks as long as they extended him the same courtesy. But when he had been challenged, he had bristled and dug in his heels and fought for what he believed was right. His sons and daughter had been raised the same way.

Which was one reason this situation with Titus was so frustrating. Titus probably felt that he was doing the right thing, that Polly really and truly belonged with him. But it couldn't be that way anymore, and Titus had to accept that. After all, Will recalled, their marriage had been pretty much over when Titus went off to war. Getting away from Polly had been Titus's main motive for enlisting. Well, that and having the chance to kill Yankees, Will amended.

"I'll have a talk with Titus," he said again. "Worst comes to worst, I may have to pound some sense into his head. I'm his big brother, and I got that right."

But even as he said it, he knew it was probably too late for that. Things had gone too far, the divisions within the family were too deep and bitterly felt. But he had to try to make things right. He was the oldest, and it was his duty.

He just wished that the pain in his chest wasn't quite so insistent . . .

𝒪𝕀𝕀𝕀𝕀𝒪

WILL DECIDED to go into Culpeper to see Judge Darden, but before he could do that, the judge showed up at the farm the next day, pulling his buggy to a stop in front of the house. Will was sitting on the front porch with his mother and Dorothy. It was a warm day for January, the chilly overcast having departed for the time being, and the fresh air smelled good to Will. He had been cooped up in the hospital for so long that just being outside was a treat for him.

Will got to his feet as Darden climbed down from the buggy. "Hello, Judge," he welcomed him. "I was planning on visiting you in a day or two."

"Well, then, I beat you to it," the judge said with a grin as he came up the steps to the porch. "Mighty glad to see you, son. You're lookin' well."

"He still needs a lot of rest before he's fully recovered," Abigail put in.

"Yes ma'am, and I expect you'll see to that." The judge took off his hat and smiled at Dorothy. "I don't believe I've had the pleasure, ma'am."

"This is Mrs. Dorothy Chamberlain, Judge," Will said. "Dorothy, Judge Darden."

She offered the judge her hand, and for a second Will thought the portly old attorney was going to bend over and kiss the back of it. Darden settled for shaking it instead then turned back to Will. "You said you were comin' to see me, Will. Was it on a legal matter?"

"You recall Yancy Lattimer's boy Roman?"

"Don't you mean your boy? Yancy left him to you."

"I know," Will said with a nod, "and I want to do something about that. I want you to draw up manumission papers for him. I'm granting him his freedom."

Darden rubbed his heavy jaw. "Are you sure that's a good idea, Will? Folks around here are still pretty hot under the collar about that god—dadblasted Emancipation Proclamation last year." He nodded to Abigail. "Beggin' your pardon for my language, ma'am."

"That's all right, Judge," she said. "I'm sure you could have expressed yourself in a more blunt fashion if you had chosen to do so."

"You're right about that, ma'am."

Will didn't want to get into an argument about slavery or how the citizens of Culpeper County would react if he freed Roman. As far as he was concerned, it was none of their business. "Will you draw up the papers or not, Judge?"

"If that's what you want, I'll draw 'em up, never you fear," Darden said. "I'll make sure everything's done legal and proper. That darky o' yours will be a free man soon's I can get the papers filed." He paused then went on, "Like I said, I'm mighty glad to see you, Will, but I really come out here for another reason. Is Henry around?"

"You've changed your mind about his marriage to Polly?" Abigail asked.

The judge sighed. "No, I'm afraid the law is pretty clear on that. I want to see him concernin' another matter."

"I believe he's out in the barn with Mac. I'll call Cordelia to fetch him—"

"Never you mind, ma'am. That won't be necessary. With your permission, I'll just take a stroll out there and talk to him."

"It's all right with me, if that's what you want to do, Judge."

"Thank you, Mrs. Brannon." Darden nodded to Dorothy. "Nice meetin' you, ma'am."

As Darden started down off the porch, Will fell in step beside him. "I'll walk out there with you, Judge."

"Fine by me. Might be a good idea, at that. The question I got to ask Henry is indirectly related to you, too, Will."

The judge was being overly mysterious about the errand that had brought him to the farm, Will thought. He couldn't figure out what business Darden could have with Henry if it didn't concern the marital mess that he and Polly and Titus found themselves in with Titus's return. Only one way to find out, though, Will told himself.

On the way to the barn, the judge asked, "How are you doin', Will, really?"

"Fair to middlin', Judge."

"I heard that wound you got at Gettysburg was a bad one."

Will chuckled. "Bad enough. Any worse and I reckon they would have buried me up there."

"Along with tens of thousands of other good Southern boys who fell."

"Yes," Will said with a nod. "Along with all those boys." He drew in a breath. "But they took good care of me at the hospital in Richmond, and I figure I'll be back with the army before the spring is over."

"Just in time for more fightin', eh?"

"Yeah. Just in time for the war to start all over again."

Mac and Henry were forking down hay from the loft as Will and the judge came into the barn. Mac stopped and leaned on his pitchfork handle. "I thought I heard a buggy drive up," he called. "Howdy, Judge."

"Howdy yourself," Darden replied with a grin. "Henry, get yourself down here. I got to ask you a question."

Mac and Henry placed their pitchforks aside and climbed down the ladder from the loft.

Henry wore a puzzled frown as he reached the ground and turned to face Darden. "What is it, Judge?" he asked. "Is this about Titus and Polly?"

"Nope. That's still a problem you'll have to work out amongst yourselves. I'm here because this blasted war has played hob with county government."

The three Brannon brothers stared at him. "Judge, what in blazes are you talking about?" Will finally asked.

"Most o' the able-bodied men in the county have gone off to war," Darden said. "A few have mustered out and come home when their first enlistment was up, but most signed the papers again and are still in the army. Then, too, a lot of the boys who've come back were shot up pretty bad and can't do too much anymore."

Henry's face was beginning to flush with anger. "Judge, if this is your way of saying that I've been shirking my duty—"

"Not at all, not at all," Darden said quickly. "Everybody around these parts knows you Brannons are some o' the fightin'est boys in the county. What with Will in the Stonewall Brigade and Mac ridin' with Jeb Stuart, folks understood that you had to stay home and take care of the place, Henry. But the fact o' the matter is, we ain't had a decent sheriff in Culpeper County since your brother Will, here, left the job. Fact is, the office is empty right now. We'd like you to take it, Henry."

The offer was so unexpected that all the three brothers could do for several seconds was stare at the judge. Mac found his voice first. "You want *Henry* to be sheriff?"

Darden nodded. "That's right. I've talked to all the town leaders, and we're agreed. Jasper had to quit because of his rheumatism. If you won't take the job, I don't know what we'll do. It ain't fittin' for the county to be without a sheriff."

"That's an elected position," Will pointed out.

"In normal times, that's true. But this is wartime, boys, and we figure we can appoint Henry to the job and have it be legal enough until the war's over. Then, if he wants to stay on, he can run for election just like you did."

Henry finally found his own voice. "Judge, this is crazy! I'm no lawman!"

Darden looked solemnly at him. "Henry, I've known you all your life. You're just like your pa and your brothers. Personally, I know you to be a decent, honest, brave young fella. You know how to handle a gun, and you can hold your own in a fight. You ain't the ring-tailed terror your big brother was back when he wore the badge . . ." The judge grinned at Will. "But you're the most qualified candidate for the job in the whole blasted county. Usin' the word candidate loosely, of course, since there ain't goin' to be an election for a while." He paused again. "Well, what do you say?"

"I . . . I don't know what to say." Henry looked at his brothers. "Will? Mac? What do you think?"

Mac shook his head. "This has thrown me for a loop as much as it has you. You'll have to make up your own mind, Henry."

"I agree with Mac," Will said. "It's your decision."

"But the farm . . ."

"It ain't like the sheriff has a lot to do these days," the judge said. "Hell, you might almost say the job's more for show than anything else. You won't have to spend much time at it. But we want somebody wearin' the badge, just in case any trouble crops up that ain't got anything to do with the war."

Slowly, Henry shook his head. "I honestly don't know what to say, sir."

"It'd sure be a help to the citizens of the county if you said yes, son."

"Well . . . if you put it like that . . ." Henry still looked a little stunned, but he was nodding now. "I guess I can give it a try. If folks really want me to be sheriff, I'll take the job and do the best I can."

Darden slapped a hand on Henry's shoulder. "I'm mighty glad to hear you say that, Henry. Mighty glad!"

Henry looked at his brothers again, and Will felt a little sorry for him. It was Henry's decision, as Will had said, but he believed Henry didn't truly understand what he was letting himself in for.

And he sure as hell hadn't thought about what his mother was going to say when she heard about this.

☾〰〰〰☽

"I ABSOLUTELY forbid it," Abigail declared as she stood in the kitchen, wiping her hands on her apron. "No son of mine will ever wear a lawman's badge again."

"But, Ma—" Henry began.

She shook her head and cut him off. "Surely you remember what happened with your brother and those awful Fogarty boys. They almost killed you, boy, to get back at him!"

Will certainly remembered. Plain as day, in fact. He would never forget how he'd been forced to gun down Joe Fogarty in Michael Davis's emporium in Culpeper, nor would he forget how Joe's brothers had come after him seeking vengeance. The fact that Joe had been a murdering outlaw didn't make any difference to them. He was blood kin and had to be avenged.

The feud had put the whole Brannon family in danger and led to Abigail practically disowning Will in an effort to protect the rest of her children. Then the war had come along and Will had left town, and the deaths of Ranse and George Fogarty at Manassas finally put an end to the whole thing. The Fogartys had some cousins in the county, including Israel Quinn, but they weren't inclined to continue the feud.

Like Will, though, Abigail had not forgotten, and neither had Henry. "This isn't the same thing," he insisted. "Judge Darden said it's more for show than anything else."

Abigail sniffed. "If it's just for show, then let the judge pin on that badge."

"He can't be sheriff. He's too old!"

Abigail just shook her head.

Henry's face flushed with anger. He slapped a hand down on the table. "I don't care what you say! I'm a grown man and I'll do what I think is right!"

"Henry . . . ," Will said in a warning tone, not wanting this discussion to turn ugly.

It was too late for that, though. "What are you going to do about it?" Henry asked his mother. "Kick me out of the family like you did Will?"

Abigail drew in her breath sharply, and Will winced. He and his mother had mended their fences after the battle of Antietam, when he and Mac had come home for a short visit. That was the first time Will had returned to the farm after enlisting in the Confederate army, and Abigail had welcomed him. Henry shouldn't have brought that up. At this late date, all it could do was cause unnecessary pain.

"Boy, you need to learn how to rein in that mouth of yours," he said.

Abigail lifted a hand. "No, he's right." The words took Will by surprise. She looked at him and went on, "I shouldn't have treated you like I did."

That statement was even more shocking. Will had never known his mother to admit that she was wrong about anything; it just wasn't in her nature.

"Nothing is worth breaking a family apart," Abigail said. "If you're determined to do this, I suppose I'll have to accept it. But I don't have to like it."

The look of anger on Henry's face faded, replaced by a grin. "It'll be all right, Ma. You'll see. And after the war's over, this'll give me a real start on being something."

"You're already something," Abigail said. "You're a Brannon. And that's good enough."

"Yes ma'am," Henry said, a little abashed. But Will could tell that he was pleased by his success at winning his mother over to his side, even though he'd had to do it by reminding her of such a painful time in all their lives. In fact, as soon as the two of them left the kitchen, Henry shot a grin over at his brother.

"Looks like I get to pin on that badge after all," he said in a low voice that Abigail wouldn't overhear back in the kitchen.

"I just hope it doesn't wind up weighing you down as much as it did me," Will said.

⚬〜〜〜〜⚬

HENRY WAS sworn in as the sheriff of Culpeper County in a ceremony at the courthouse two days later. His heart was thudding in excitement as he lifted his hand and took the oath. For the first time in his life, he felt like he was more than just the little brother of the Brannon family. Now he was someone important in his own right.

Will, Mac, Polly, and Dorothy attended the ceremony. Abigail had begged off, pleading a headache, and Cordelia had stayed home to see to her mother's needs. Knowing her opposition to Henry taking the job, no one was surprised that Abigail didn't ride into town with the others. Nor was Titus's absence any shock, and Louisa always stayed close to Titus. Similarly, Dorothy kept an eye on Will, insisting that she accompany the group into Culpeper. Polly, of course, was glad for the company of another woman. She and Dorothy had gotten along well so far.

When the ceremony was over, Judge Darden asked the three Brannon brothers to come back to his office for a celebratory drink. Will and Mac agreed, but Henry looked at Polly to see what she wanted him to do. She smiled and waved a gloved hand at him. "Go ahead," she told him. "I'll show Mrs. Chamberlain around town—what there is of it to see."

Henry kissed her cheek. "I'll see you in a little while."

The men trooped off down the street. Polly watched them go, her eyes lingering on Henry, and Dorothy surprised her by saying, "You're really proud of him, aren't you?"

"What? Oh, you mean Henry. Of course I'm proud of him. What woman wouldn't be proud of her husb—I mean, her . . . well . . . you know what I mean."

"You started to say husband, and that's what he is to you," Dorothy said in a kind voice. "Of course that's the way you feel.

I was married for quite a while, Polly, and I can see the same sort of bond between you and Henry that my husband and I had."

"The law says different."

"Oh, pshaw. The law doesn't have anything to do with the human heart."

Polly smiled sadly. "I wish Titus understood that."

"Perhaps he does. Perhaps he loves you so much that he can't stand the thought of you loving his brother instead of him. So he's using the law to try to force you to come back to him."

"That will never happen," Polly declared. "I love Henry."

"Did you love Titus when you married him?" Dorothy laid a hand on Polly's arm. "I'm sorry! That's no business of mine. You don't have to answer."

"No, that's all right," Polly said as she started to stroll down the main street. Dorothy fell in step beside her. "I know you're just trying to help, Mrs. Chamberlain."

"Please, Polly, call me Dorothy. I'm not *that* much older than you, dear."

"All right, Dorothy. You are most kind." Polly hesitated for a moment before answering the question. "Yes, I suppose I did love Titus when we got married."

"You suppose?"

"It was . . . different. He was so stubborn to try to court me in the first place, and my father hated him so much . . ."

"That made him even more attractive to you, I imagine."

"I hate to admit it, but yes. I found the fact that he would stand up to my father appealing. Even after Father had his overseers hand Titus a beating, he wouldn't give up. He just kept coming back, defying anyone to stop him."

No one who hadn't been there could understand what that had been like, Polly thought. Before Titus had come along, defying Duncan Ebersole was something unheard of in her experience. No one dared to say no to him or to tell him that he couldn't have what he wanted, no matter how wrong he was. But Titus was willing to stand up to him—and had stood up to him at a great cost. Polly had dared to hope that if she were married to Titus, things would change.

But of course, they hadn't. Nothing changed. In the end, Duncan Ebersole had still gotten his way, just like he always had. She had married Titus not solely out of love, Polly now realized, but also so that he would be her champion, her protector. And he had failed her miserably at that. But was that all his fault? Not entirely. In the end, it had taken her own determination not to let her father bully her, along with her love for Henry, to free her.

Dorothy touched her arm again. "I'm sorry," the older woman said. "I didn't mean to stir up bad memories."

"They're not all bad," Polly said with a shake of her head. "Most of them, perhaps. But not all." She smiled at Dorothy and they turned to walk on.

After only a couple of steps, Dorothy stopped short. "My lands, who's that? And what's wrong with him?"

Polly stopped, too, and looked along the street. Coming toward them, a couple of blocks away, was a familiar figure. His gait was a shambling walk, and from time to time he lurched to one side or the other.

She knew right away what was wrong with him: He was drunk. Polly had seen her father in that condition too many times not to recognize it.

"That's my father," she said quietly to Dorothy. "Duncan Ebersole. The wealthiest man in Culpeper County."

Right now, Ebersole looked more like a tenant farmer than a plantation owner. His clothes were rumpled and dirty, and he wasn't wearing a hat. He gazed along the street with a fixed glare, and Polly felt his eyes boring directly into her. As Ebersole passed a parked wagon, a man on the vehicle's seat hopped down and spoke to him, holding out a hand as if to stop him. Ebersole brushed past with a snarled curse, clearly unwilling to let anything deter him from whatever goal he had in mind. He ignored the bystander, who looked after him angrily.

"I recognize him now," Dorothy said. "He spoke to us when we were arriving at the farm the other day. Actually, he shouted at Roman and was rather abusive."

"That's my father," Polly said.

Sizing up the situation and an impending confrontation, Dorothy suggested, "Perhaps we should go back to the judge's office and rejoin the men."

"You go ahead," Polly told her. "I'm tired of running from him." Her chin came up defiantly. "I'm not going to back down from him anymore."

"Well, in that case . . . I believe I'll stay with you."

Duncan Ebersole drew himself up a little straighter as he approached the two women and recognized his daughter. His leaden steps became more controlled and determined.

His efforts did not go unnoticed. Polly realized that he was trying to fight off the effects of the whiskey he had consumed.

He came to a stop in front of her and said stiffly, "Good day t' ye," as if he were an acquaintance rather than her father. "Would ye do me th' favor o' havin' a word wi' me?"

"Say whatever you have to say," Polly told him.

Ebersole glanced at Dorothy. "An' good day t' ye, too, ma'am. I dinna believe we've met . . ."

"This is Mrs. Chamberlain from Richmond," Polly said tersely. "She's Will Brannon's friend. Dorothy, my father, Duncan Ebersole."

Dorothy managed a smile. "Hello, Mr. Ebersole. I'm told you own a fine plantation—"

"Mountain Laurel," Ebersole interrupted. "Ye'd be welcome there anytime, ma'am. Th' place would be brightened considerably by th' presence of a beautiful woman. Ain't none been there since my lil' gal here ran off."

"I didn't run off," Polly said. "I got married and went to live with my husband, like a normal woman."

"Normal!" Ebersole echoed. "Now, that's one thing ye'll ne'er be, gal."

With an effort, Polly held in her anger. "What do you want?"

"A word. Just a word, girl." Ebersole glanced at Dorothy. "In private, if ye please, madam."

Anything to get rid of him, Polly decided. "All right." She turned to Dorothy. "Do you think you can find your way to Judge Darden's office? I'll be all right."

"Of course," Dorothy said. "But are you sure—"

"I'll be fine," Polly assured her. "Tell Henry I'll be there in just a few minutes, please."

Dorothy nodded. "All right. If you're sure." She moved off down the street, but not without casting a few apprehensive glances over her shoulder.

Polly faced her father again. "I don't have much time. What do you want?"

"Th' same thing I've always wanted. I want ye t' come home, girl."

"You know that will never happen. You're just wasting your time—"

Ebersole's hand shot out in a flash and grasped her arm tightly. Surprised, Polly gasped in sudden fear as he leaned in closer to her and pulled her to him. All the old dreads and horrors came flooding back to her as she smelled his foul, whiskey-laden breath.

"Listen t' me, gal," he hissed. "I've put up wi' yer defiance for as long as I'm gonna. If ye dinna want me t' tell those dear husbands o' yers—both of them—the truth about you, ye'd better give some serious thought t' goin' along with what I'm tellin' ye to do."

"You're crazy!" Polly gasped. "Let go of me. Henry's the sheriff now—"

"Oh, he is, is he? And how long d'ye think that would last if the good citizens o' Culpeper County found out what his wife is really like?"

She shook her head and tried to push away from him. "I don't know what you're talking about!"

"I think ye do. I been doin' some countin' up in my head. I never had much schoolin', ya kin, but I can cipher all right. An' I know the truth, lassie."

He released her arm and stepped back. "I'll give ye three days. Come t' Mountain Laurel before that time's up, an' we'll hash it all out. Past time we did that. If ye don't, the whole county will know what sort o' gal ye really are."

"You wouldn't dare," Polly whispered.

"Don't bet on that, gal." He turned away but threw a mocking laugh over his shoulder as he stumbled off down the street. "Remember. Ye've got three days . . . ."

Polly was still standing there several minutes later when Henry hurried up to her. She was looking down at the ground, and her hands were clenched into such tight fists that her nails were digging into her palms. She didn't notice the pain.

"Polly!" Henry said. "Are you all right? Polly?"

The second time he said her name, she finally lifted her head and looked around. He stood there, a worried, angry expression on his face. Will and Mac were coming along the street behind him, along with Dorothy Chamberlain. Obviously, Henry had run on ahead of them.

Polly took a deep breath. "I'm fine."

"Mrs. Chamberlain said your father was bothering you."

She shook her head. "No. He was just being arrogant and obnoxious, as usual. It's nothing to worry about, Henry."

"You're sure?"

She smiled at him and touched his arm. "I'm certain. But you're sweet for worrying about me. Now, if it's all right I think I'd like to go back to the farm. I'm a little tired."

"Sure. I'll get the buggy, and we'll go right now."

"Thank you, Henry." Her hand tightened briefly on his arm. "Thank you for everything."

He looked like he wasn't sure what she meant by that, but he hurried off to fetch Dorothy's buggy, which they had used to come into town, the women riding in the vehicle while Henry drove and Will and Mac rode horses. Polly made small talk with the others, deliberately ignoring their curiosity about her confrontation with her father. It was really no one else's business.

But in the back of her mind, his words echoed ominously. *Three days . . . the truth . . . three days . . .*

Chapter Eight

POLLY WAS IN A daze for the next forty-eight hours. Even her sleep was disturbed by the hangover from the unpleasant scene with her father. In her dreams, she saw Duncan Ebersole's face looming huge and hideous in front of her, heard his harsh laughter, smelled the whiskey and tobacco on him. She was a little surprised that she didn't wake up screaming.

But she didn't, and even though she was sure Henry knew something was bothering her, he didn't press her for the details. He probably figured that she was just upset about seeing her father in Culpeper. That was true, of course, but he didn't know the real extent of it. He didn't know everything that had happened . . .

And he never could. She couldn't allow that to happen.

That realization came to her on the third day, and with it the knowledge that she would have to go to Mountain Laurel, as her father had demanded. Once again, Duncan Ebersole was going to get what he wanted. But she swore this would be the last time. After this, never again would she set foot on the plantation where she had grown up. Her home was with Henry now, no matter what her father said, no matter what Titus said. She would deal with her father, then she would deal with Titus, and it would be over. Nothing would be in front of her except Henry and the baby and a long, happy life.

But first she had to get away from the farm without anyone's seeing her, because she was sure that if Henry or any of the others knew what she was planning, they wouldn't allow her to go through with it.

She waited until midmorning. Henry had ridden into town to pay a visit to the sheriff's office in the courthouse. This was becoming his routine, as he checked to see that no one needed his services as the county's law enforcement officer. If there wasn't any trouble brewing in Culpeper, he would be back on the farm a little after noon. Abigail and Cordelia were in the kitchen, Will and Mac were out walking through the fields, and Titus was upstairs, holed up in his room as usual, like a badger in its den. Polly supposed Louisa was up there, too. The woman was growing more and more pale. She was like a ghost, seldom seen or heard, attached to Titus by some mysterious bond. Polly wasn't sure where Dorothy was. She would be careful as she left, in hopes that no one would see her.

Clouds had moved back in, bringing with them a cold wind. Polly put on her coat, and as she buttoned it around her, her fingers pressed against her swollen belly for a moment. She felt the new life there stirring under her touch. Her eyes threatened to fill with tears, but she blinked them away. There was no time for sentiment now. She had things to do; things that would ensure the baby grew up to enjoy a decent life without the threat of humiliation and degradation always hanging over it.

She pulled on a bonnet, tied it under her chin. Then she went downstairs quickly and slipped out the front door. As she headed for the barn, the hard weight in the pocket of her coat bumped against her side.

She had brought the little pistol with her from Mountain Laurel, never telling Henry that she had it and keeping it hidden all this time. Now she was taking it with her, back to the plantation. She had never fired it, but she knew how. It was just a matter of cocking it, pointing it, and pulling the trigger . . .

The little buggy she always used was kept in the barn. Polly hitched the mare to it and led the horse out through the doors at the rear of the barn, so that she was less likely to be seen from the house. Then she climbed onto the seat, took up the reins, and got the horse moving. She drove around the barn then down the lane toward the road. A glance over her shoulder told her that no one was coming after her. She couldn't see Will and Mac anywhere; unable to sit still for too long, they were off in the far fields, probably talking about the war. Even though it was winter and no campaigns were going on at the moment, the clash between North and South was never far from the minds of most people.

Polly had a much more basic clash to worry about. Her father had won all the battles so far, but it remained to be seen which of them was going to win the war.

Because, like all wars, ultimately it could end only with blood and death.

⚬〰〰⚬

"THAT'S ODD," Louisa said as she stood by the window, looking out at the gray, overcast day.

"What is?" Titus muttered from the rocking chair where he sat with a blanket wrapped around him. He got chilled easily these days, especially when the sun wasn't shining. Maybe that was a lingering effect of the illness that had almost killed him, he thought.

"Polly is driving off in a buggy."

Titus frowned. "What?"

"Polly," Louisa said. "I saw her go out to the barn a few minutes ago, and now she's driving down the lane in a buggy."

Titus stood up, clutching the blanket more tightly around his shoulders. He seemed to feel the air getting colder as he moved closer to the window. That might be his imagination, he told himself. But on the other hand, it might not be.

He leaned closer to the glass and pushed the curtain aside. As he peered toward the road, he could see the buggy itself, but the vehicle blocked any view of its driver. "Are you sure it was Polly?" he asked.

"Well . . . not completely. I think it was, but she was wearing a bonnet, so I couldn't see her hair."

Titus knew what she meant. Polly was the only woman on the Brannon farm whose hair was so pale and fair. Dorothy Chamberlain's hair was a darker blonde, more like spun gold.

Cordelia had the fiery red hair she had inherited from their father. And Abigail Brannon's hair was mostly gray with only a little brown left in it.

Titus watched the buggy until it reached the intersection of the lane and the main road. It swung to the left onto the road. He turned away from the window, his frown dark and puzzled.

"She was by herself?"

"Yes, as far as I could tell," Louisa said.

Where the hell was Polly going by herself? That wasn't like her at all. She always had to cling to some man, first her father, then Titus, and finally Henry.

Mountain Laurel was in the direction the buggy had gone. But surely she wouldn't be going there. Surely . . .

Titus had heard of how Ebersole had accosted Polly in Culpeper a few days earlier. Dorothy had mentioned it to Louisa, and Louisa had told him. Titus had been angry when he heard about the incident. It was true that most of what he felt toward Polly these days was resentment and outrage at her betrayal of him, but his hatred for Duncan Ebersole was even stronger. He would never forget how Ebersole had ordered him beaten that night in the gardens at Mountain Laurel, after Titus had danced with Polly and kissed her . . .

He should have killed Ebersole a long time ago, he had told himself when he heard what had happened in Culpeper. That was the way to deal with problems. You couldn't talk to a Yankee, couldn't make him listen to reason. All you could do was put a bullet through him or rip his guts out with a bayonet. The same thing would work on Duncan Ebersole. If he were dead, Ebersole would never bother anyone again. But as long as he lived, there was no telling what he would do, no way of knowing how much pain he would inflict on innocent people. Or on not-so-innocent ones like Polly, who still didn't deserve to be plagued by Ebersole no matter how much she had wronged her husband.

That thought stirred him to action. He tossed the blanket on the bed and reached for his coat.

"Titus," Louisa said anxiously, "what are you doing?"

"I better go see what that woman's up to. She's liable to get herself in trouble if I don't."

Louisa caught hold of his arm as he tried to shrug into his coat. "Titus, no! It's cold and raw out, and you're still not strong enough to go gallivanting all over the countryside. Not for *her.*"

"She's my wife," he growled, and as the words left his mouth, he saw the flare of pain in her eyes.

Louisa was jealous, he thought. Jealous of the way he still felt toward Polly. Titus supposed he could understand that. She had risked her life helping him and Nathan escape. To her way of thinking, she had risked her very soul by turning away from her religion, all because of him.

But he hadn't asked her to do any of that. He was damned glad she had, because otherwise he would be either dead or still festering in that Yankee hellhole of a prison camp. He didn't owe her anything but his thanks, though, and he had given her those. The longer she stayed around now, the more of an annoyance she became.

Louisa clutched at his sleeve. "Titus, please—"

He jerked away from her. "Let go of me, woman! Can't you see I got things to do?" He turned his back and stalked toward the door.

Louisa lunged after him and caught hold of him again, and Titus let his instincts take over. He whipped around, and his palm cracked sharply across Louisa's face. She let out a brittle cry and slumped to her knees, her hand going to her cheek, which reddened from the force of the slap.

"Sorry," Titus muttered. "But you got to learn to stay out of my way."

He put on his hat and stalked out of the room, closing the door firmly behind him.

He didn't think anyone saw him as he slipped out of the house and went to the barn. It had been quite a while since he'd saddled a horse, but he managed without much trouble. The chore wore him out, though, and he had to lean against the animal for a moment, breathing hard, before he felt strong enough to swing up into the saddle. Then he rode out through the still open doors in the back of the barn. The cold wind whistled and whined as it blew through the building.

Titus put the horse into a fast trot. It felt good to be riding again. He was a little lightheaded but steady enough so that he knew he wouldn't fall off the horse or lose control of it. If Polly was headed for Mountain Laurel, she probably would reach the plantation before he could catch up to her, but he told himself that he wouldn't be too far behind her. He would get there before she could get herself in too much of a mess.

Once before, when forced to choose between her husband and her father, she had picked Ebersole. Titus had good reason to remember that. The bitterness he felt over Polly's decision would never go away. This time, however, the idea that she might be leaving Henry to go back home to her father didn't even occur to Titus. He had seen with his own eyes how she felt about Henry. He didn't like it, but he had seen it. Finally, Polly had broken away from Duncan Ebersole.

So why was she going back now? It had to have something to do with the incident in Culpeper, and her motives couldn't be anything good. Maybe she was going to have a showdown with her bully of a father at last.

Maybe she wasn't even going to Mountain Laurel, Titus thought. If that was the case, he was going to look pretty foolish riding up to the place like one of those old-fashioned storybook knights out to storm a castle and rescue a pretty damsel in a gauzy dress and pointy hat. But he couldn't figure out where else Polly would go, especially by herself like that.

Titus rode on through the overcast day, unease growing inside him.

6️⃣〰️9️⃣

THE WEATHER matched her mood, Polly thought: gray and gloomy. She was ready for some sunshine, ready for spring. But spring was a long time off, and her father's evil still cast a pall over her.

Not for much longer, though, she told herself as she guided the buggy into the curving drive at Mountain Laurel. Not for much longer.

The drive was lined with the trees that gave the plantation its name, their branches bare now in midwinter. To Polly's eyes, those branches clawed at the iron sky like skeletal fingers. She gave a little shake of her head, seeking to rid herself of that notion. The drive circled in front of the house, and she brought the buggy to a halt before the entrance.

In normal times, one of the stable boys would have run out to take care of the horse and buggy, but these were far from normal times. Some of Mountain Laurel's slaves were still on the plantation, but many others had slipped away, knowing that no one would be coming after them if they ran off. The overseers had all gone off to the war, and two of the slaves themselves were now in charge of all the work on the plantation, their loyalty bought by Ebersole with added privileges and a promise that eventually they would be free. Polly suspected her father had no intention of keeping that promise, but so far it had proven effective.

Most of the time these days, Ebersole was alone in the big house. A woman came in to cook for him, whenever he didn't run her off in a drunken rage. The white-haired old butler who had run the household for years, however, had been banished to the slave quarters with the field hands. In the winter like this, not much work would be going on. All the slaves would be huddled in their squalid cabins a half-mile behind the house, trying to keep warm.

Would they hear a shot from the house? Polly didn't know, but even if they did, they might not come to investigate. At the very least, it would take them awhile to get up here. She would have plenty of time.

She climbed down from the buggy and tied the horse's reins to an iron ring set atop a post for that purpose. Then she went to the front door and tried the knob. It was unlocked, just as she expected. People in this part of the country never locked their doors, even in wartime.

Polly entered, easing the door shut behind her. She stood there in the richly paneled foyer, listening for any noise. But the house was eerily quiet, ominously silent. The lack of life almost compelled her to turn around and bolt out of there. Moreover, it was unseasonably cold, too. Her breath fogged in front of her face. Were there no fires lit anywhere in the house? There were fireplaces in almost every room.

She took a few quiet, careful steps forward. She thought about calling out, but for some reason she hated to break into that looming silence.

Then something crashed in one of the rooms along the main hall, and Polly jumped. It was all she could do not to scream, but she muffled that reaction before it could escape.

The loud noise had come from her father's library, she decided. He had knocked over something in there. Either that, or he was so drunk he had fallen on the floor. That was possible, too. Polly started toward the library door. Her heart hammered wildly, and her pulse beat so loudly in her head that she was surprised her father didn't hear it and come out of the library.

She paused outside the door. Something scraped in there, like it was being dragged across the floor. What was he doing?

Polly took a deep breath. There was no point in delaying this. It had to be done. She thought about Henry and the baby. What she was about to do was for them. And yes, for her as well, she admitted. God, yes, it was for her, too.

She grasped the knob, swung the door open, and stepped into the room.

⚭

HE CAME out of the blackness not knowing where he was or what had happened. For a few seconds, he wasn't even sure of who he was. But then that much came back to him, at least, and he remembered that he was Duncan Ebersole, by God, the biggest, most important man in Culpeper County.

He felt something cold and wet at his crotch and knew he must have pissed himself. A groan welled out of him as he tried to lift his head. His stomach lurched. Muscles that had refused to work only seconds earlier now responded to his urgent need. He rolled onto his side as the contents of his belly exploded up his throat. The vomit puddled around him, reeking of whiskey.

Yes, he was the very picture of genteel wealth at this moment, he thought, and crazed laughter echoed in his head. It took him a few seconds to realize that he really was laughing, and when he did, he fell silent, choking off the ugly sound.

He pushed himself to his hands and knees then staggered to his feet. His eyes were open now, but he still couldn't see much of anything. Gray shadows surrounded him. Where in blazes was he? He stumbled a few steps and ran into something, fetching up hard against it. He grunted in pain as he caught his balance before he could fall again. His hand reached out, touched smooth, polished wood.

A carriage door. That was what it was, he decided. He had run into the fancy carriage in which he rode around Culpeper County. His county. No one else could lay claim to it.

So he was in the carriage house, next to the stables. He sniffed the air, smelled dung, horseflesh, and straw, and knew his guess was correct. There were no windows in the carriage house, which explained why it was so dark. But what was he doing out here? It was cold, and he needed a drink. There was a bottle in the house, he recalled. Israel Quinn had dropped it off the day before.

Ebersole took a step away from the carriage. His foot hit something that rolled across the hard-packed dirt floor. The thing struck one of the carriage wheels with a dull clink and came to a stop. Holding tightly to the wheel, Ebersole bent and picked up the thing he had kicked. It was a bottle; empty, of course. He sniffed at the neck of it and caught a faint, tantalizing whiff of whiskey.

He threw the bottle away. It wasn't any good to him empty. He hoped that wasn't the one he'd been thinking about. If he got back in the house and couldn't find a drink, he didn't know what he would do. He let out a little whimper at the thought.

The disheveled man stumbled to the door of the carriage house and shoved it open then recoiled as the light struck him. Not that it was very bright outside; thick gray clouds hung in the sky, obscuring the sun, but after being in the darkened carriage house, even the faint light of an overcast, misty afternoon was hard on his eyes.

His vision adjusted, and he began walking toward the plantation house. It was a hundred yards away, and those hundred yards seemed much longer to Ebersole. When he finally reached the back of the house, he was exhausted and out of breath. A drink would brace him up, he told himself. He jerked the door open and went in, his ragged footsteps echoing hollowly against the high ceilings.

Where had he left that bottle? Probably in the library. He spent a lot of time there; not reading, of course, but drinking and staring broodingly at the exquisite portrait of his wife that hung over the fireplace.

Polly looked so much like her, so much . . .

That resemblance was what had caused all the trouble, Ebersole told himself. If the two of them just hadn't looked so damned much alike . . .

He stumbled and caught himself against the library door. The knob gave him a little trouble, but after a few moments his clumsy fingers managed to turn it. The door opened and he stepped inside.

Blood was the first thing he saw. His eyes followed the thin red trail across the floor. It twisted its way into a spray of pale blonde hair, and for a second Ebersole couldn't quite comprehend that the hair was his daughter's and that Polly lay on the floor in front of the fireplace, her face turned toward him and her blue eyes staring sightlessly, lifelessly—at him.

Then he began to scream in horror, his drunken stupor vanishing in a single terrible instant of knowing that she was dead. He rushed toward her only to trip over something.

He fell hard enough to knock the wind out of his lungs when he landed on the once lush carpet. As he lay there gasping for breath he turned his head and saw that he had stumbled over the outstretched legs of Titus Brannon, who was also lying on the floor, face down.

Brannon was alive, though. His back was rising and falling as his breath rasped in his throat. To Ebersole's eyes he seemed to have passed out.

The planter stared at one of his sons-in-law, his horrified gaze following the line of Titus's outflung arm to his hand, the fingers of which were curled loosely around the handle of a fireplace poker.

He didn't want to look anymore, but his eyes were drawn inexorably toward the end of that poker. He saw the red stain there, as well as the two long strands of fine, pale hair that had wrapped around the poker when it struck and then were jerked free when it was pulled back from the killing blow.

Ebersole stared and wept, and the need for vengeance began to burn within him. He could take the poker, he thought, and smash it down on Brannon's head just as Brannon had used it to kill poor Polly. In his mind's eye, Ebersole could see the poker rising and falling in his grip until there was nothing left of Titus Brannon's head except a smashed, ruined mess that didn't even look human.

But that wouldn't be enough, he realized with a wrenching sob. Brannon had to pay more than that. The whole filthy lot of them had to pay. None of them should have ever come near his daughter, his beautiful, precious little girl . . .

Ebersole crawled across the floor toward her and, reaching her, pulled her head, her broken head, into his lap and cradled it there, stroking the fair, bloodstained hair and wailing to the heavens as he thought of what he would do to avenge her.

HENRY REALIZED something was wrong as he rode down the lane toward the house and saw Will and Mac hurrying out of the barn, leading their saddled horses. His brothers were going somewhere, and there was an unmistakable sense of urgency to their movements. Henry dug his heels into his horse's flanks and sent the animal galloping along the lane.

In Culpeper that morning, he had stopped at the courthouse and then dropped by Judge Darden's office for a brief visit. So far he hadn't had to do a thing in his new position as sheriff, not break up a fight or arrest a drunk or even shoo a dog off the street. As far as Henry could see, Culpeper County didn't really *need* a sheriff.

His family might need him, though. Will and Mac turned grim faces toward him as he rode up and reined his horse to a halt. Something was wrong, no doubt about it. Bad wrong.

"Keep your saddle, Henry," Mac called to him. "We have to ride over to Mountain Laurel."

"What is it?" Henry asked, feeling something like dread growing inside him. He realized it was a fear unlike any he had ever known before.

"There's been some trouble," Will said. "One of Ebersole's slaves rode over here to tell us about it. Ebersole told him we were to fetch you, since you're the sheriff now, and bring you over there."

Henry relaxed a little. "So Ebersole's got some sort of complaint, does he? Well, he's a citizen of the county, so I reckon I've got to listen to him, but he'd better not expect any special treatment just because he's my father-in-law."

That sounded to him just like something Ebersole would do—rant and rave about his daughter marrying a poor farmer, then turn around and curry favor when that farmer became someone more important.

Will shook his head. "That's not it, Henry."

"Well, then, what—" He stopped short and leaned forward in the saddle, that awful fear blossoming in his belly again. "Where's Polly?" he asked.

"It looks like she took her buggy and went over there this morning," Mac explained. "We don't really know the straight of it, Henry. It was hard getting any details from the boy who brought word."

"Where is he?" Henry demanded. "I want to talk to him."

"Already started back to Mountain Laurel." Will swung up into the saddle, moving stiffly because of his wound. "That's where we'd better get going, too."

"Is she all right? Is Polly all right?" Henry could hear his voice shaking, could sense the hysteria creeping into his tone.

Mac mounted up as well. "Let's just get over there, Henry," he said gently, and the pain and sorrow in his eyes were plain to see now. Mac never had been the sort of man who could hide his feelings. The expression on his brother's face told Henry all he needed to know.

"No!" he cried as he slumped forward in the saddle. "I don't believe it!"

"Come on, Henry," Will said. There was a tone of command in his voice, and numbly, Henry responded to it. He turned his horse and brought it alongside the other two.

"Titus," Henry said brokenly. "Should we fetch Titus along with us?"

"He's already over there," Mac said.

The situation was growing more confusing by the second, but none of the details really mattered right now, Henry thought. All that was important was that Polly was over at Mountain Laurel, and something had happened to her. Something terrible.

Something so bad that Will and Mac could barely bring themselves to talk about it or even look at him.

Suddenly Henry jammed his heels into his horse's flanks again, and with an incoherent shout, he sent the animal lunging forward. In a matter of seconds, he was riding at a breakneck pace along the lane. He didn't look back, didn't care if his brothers would be able to keep up with him or not. He had to get to Polly. He couldn't waste any more time.

Later, Henry recalled very few details of that frantic ride to Mountain Laurel. He knew the roads well, and he was able to follow them without thinking. He was vaguely aware that Mac pulled up alongside him on the big silver gray stallion, catching him easily. Mac didn't try to stop him. He just rode along with him, never leaving Henry's side. Will brought up the rear, traveling at a slower pace because of his injury.

The plantation house had a deserted look to it when Henry galloped up and brought his horse to a sliding stop. He was out of the saddle before the animal stopped moving. He ran to the front door, jerked it open, and pounded inside. "Polly!" he screamed. "Polly, where are you?"

Mac was still with him, gripping his arm now and saying, "In the library, the boy said. I'm not sure I remember where it is. Along this hall somewhere, I think . . ."

"Polly!" Henry called again. A part of him already knew that she would never answer him, but he couldn't stop himself from shouting her name. It was like he thought that if he called loud enough, she would be able to hear him and would answer him from wherever she was.

And wherever she was, Henry knew, their baby was there, too . . .

Mac opened a door and said, "In here."

Henry's blood roared like a mighty river in his veins and thundered inside his skull. He stumbled forward and then stopped to stare at the most awful scene that had ever met his eyes. The room was in a shambles; not as if thieves had ransacked it searching for valuables, but more like someone had tried to tear it apart out of sheer rage and spite. That was far from the worst of it, though. Polly—his wife, his beautiful, beautiful Polly—lay on the floor in front of the fireplace, her head in her father's lap. It lolled lifelessly on her slender neck. Blood was bright in her hair, and Henry could see the place where her skull had been crushed by a vicious, brutal blow. She was dead. Polly was dead.

One of Ebersole's hands stroked his daughter's hair. The other held a pistol that was pointed at the man who sat huddled on the floor a few feet away, his back against Ebersole's desk and his face covered by his hands. Henry didn't need to see the man's face to recognize his own brother.

"Arrest him, sheriff," Ebersole said in a voice that shook with rage and grief. "Arrest yer brother Titus for killin' this poor, poor girl."

Chapter Nine

I ... I DIDN'T DO IT."

Titus had to swallow a couple of times before he could force more words from his throat through his dry, foul-tasting mouth. "I didn't hurt Polly. I would never hurt Polly."

"You son of a bitch." Henry took a step toward him, fists clenched. "You lying bastard."

Titus thought his younger brother was going to take a swing at him. If that was what Henry wanted to do, Titus wouldn't even try to stop him. But Henry had to realize that wasn't going to change a thing. Polly would still be dead.

Henry didn't try to throw a punch. Instead he reached for the pistol on his hip, and as the gun started to rise, he thumbed back the hammer.

Go ahead, Titus thought. *Put a bullet through my head. I just don't give a damn anymore.*

Mac sprang forward, grabbed Henry's wrist, and forced the barrel of the gun toward the floor. "Stop it!" Mac said. "Have you gone crazy, Henry? You can't just shoot your own brother like that!"

"He killed Polly. He killed m-my baby ...," Henry choked.

Mac took the gun out of his hand. Henry didn't fight him. Will stepped up and rested a hand on their little brother's shoulder, squeezing it in sympathy. Mac put a hand on Henry's back.

Neither of them was going to waste any sympathy on *him,* Titus realized. Why should they? In their eyes, he was an insane murderer, no better than a mad dog.

The four Brannon brothers were in the parlor of the plantation house at Mountain Laurel. On the other side of the room, Duncan Ebersole was slumped in a wing chair, a shawl wrapped around his shoulders, his head hanging forward as he muttered incoherently. The man was out of his mind with grief.

143

Or was he? Strange thoughts were stirring around in the back of Titus's brain, like maggots in a piece of rotten meat.

Polly's body was still in the library, mercifully covered now with a quilt. Some of the house slaves were supposed to tend to her as soon as the undertaker, who was also the county coroner, got there and said they could. They would take her up to her old room and clean her, clothe her in a dress that didn't have splatters of blood on it like the one she was wearing. In the meantime, Will and Mac had sort of taken over, since Henry was too grief-stricken to think clearly. They had herded everybody out of the library and down the hall to the parlor. Now Henry had recovered enough of his wits to remember that he was the sheriff, and he was trying to carry out an investigation. As far as Titus could see, there really wasn't any point. They had all judged him and found him guilty already.

"I come in an' found the two of 'em like that," Ebersole had said before he fell into his stupor. "Polly wi' her head smashed in like a broken doll, an' Titus a-layin' there wi' the poker in his hand that done the foul deed. I dinna kin how he come t' be laid out like that. Polly could'a fought back and hit him hard enough to make him pass out after he'd killed her. An' he's stinkin' drunk, too. Ye can smell it all over him. Maybe he just passed out from th' whiskey."

As far as Titus could tell, Ebersole was the only one who was stinking drunk, or at least he had been very recently. He reeked of whiskey and puke. Surely Will and Mac—even Henry— could see that.

"I got my gun from my desk, just in case he come to before anyone could get here," Ebersole had gone on. "That's how it was when th' three o' ye came in. Ye saw wi' yer own eyes what he'd done."

They had believed the old man, too. Titus could tell that from the way they looked at him. His own brothers had jumped at the chance to believe that he would take a poker and smash in the head of the woman he loved.

Because he *had* loved her, still. There was no doubt of that in Titus's mind. Sure, he had been furious with her for choosing Henry over him, but in the end, that hadn't mattered. The sight of her lying there like that, so pitiful and broken, had gone into his heart like a knife, and in that instant he had known that he still loved her and perhaps always would love her, even though she was gone. He never would have hurt her. Never. He could never hurt her.

"I didn't do it," he said again as Henry stood there sobbing and being comforted by Will and Mac. Titus's voice was stronger now. "I swear, boys, I didn't hurt Polly."

Will looked at him. "Then who did? Do you deny that Ebersole found you like he said he did?"

Titus grimaced and rubbed at his bearded jaw. He was leaning against the back of a divan because he was still pretty shaky. "When I woke up, he was there, all right. And Polly was . . . like she was. But that doesn't mean I did it." He reached up and touched the side of his head a couple of inches above his right ear. "Hell, I've got a goose egg on my head where somebody clouted me. It had to be whoever killed Polly."

"Or like Ebersole said, she hit you, but you didn't pass out until you'd had a chance to swing that poker at her."

"Will, do you really believe I'd do that? You can't!"

Will shook his head slowly. "These days, I don't know what to believe about you, Titus. I had a hard enough time just believing that you were still alive when I'd been mourning you for over a year."

"I'll bet now you wish I really had been dead, don't you?" Titus knew the bitter challenge wouldn't help his case any, but he couldn't stop himself from flinging it at Will.

"Take it easy," Mac said. "That's not going to help anything. If you want us to believe you, Titus, you're going to have to tell us what happened."

"All right." Titus scrubbed his hands over his face. Henry was beginning to regain his composure and was watching him with a hate-filled but curious expression. He wanted to hear the story, too. Titus took a deep breath.

"Polly drove over here in that buggy of hers," he began.

"We know that," Will said. "We saw it parked outside."

Titus nodded. "Louisa saw her leaving the farm and told me about it in time for me to get a look at her, too. She came in this direction, and I couldn't figure out where else she would be going except here. I'd heard that she had a run-in with him in Culpeper a few days ago, and I thought she might be figuring on having it out with him. They hadn't gotten along too good for a long time."

"So you came after her," Mac said.

"I got worried." Titus pushed himself away from the divan and stood up straight. His nerves were stretched too taut to stay still, and he began to pace behind the piece of furniture. "I knew if she stood up to Ebersole, there was no telling what he might do. He's half-crazy to start with, and he's even worse when somebody defies him."

Titus stopped and looked hard at Ebersole. If the plantation owner heard what was being said, he gave no sign of it. But the more Titus thought about it, the more things made sense. He could imagine Ebersole pitching a fit if Polly dared to argue with him. In his drunken state, he might have reached out and grabbed a poker from the stand beside the fireplace in the library, swung it through the air without really thinking about what he was doing . . .

"Ebersole was out in the carriage house," Will said. "That's what he told us, anyway. He didn't even know Polly was here until he came in and found her body. And you."

"*He* was drunk!" Titus burst out. "Go over there and smell him. He probably had so much rotgut whiskey in him he doesn't remember where he was or what he was doing."

Henry spoke up for the first time in several minutes. "What about you, Titus?" he asked. His voice was cold and hard now, somehow more disquieting than it had been earlier when he was raging. "If that's the truth, what else do you remember? What happened here?"

"I . . . I got here to the house. I knocked but nobody came to the door. So I let myself in. It wasn't locked. Nobody was around when I came in." Titus shivered a little as he recalled the eerie emptiness that had seemed to grip the entire house. "I called Polly's name, but there was no answer. I knew Ebersole spends a lot of time in the library. I remembered where it was from when we . . . from when Polly and I lived here . . . so I went down the hall and opened the door. I remember . . . I remember . . ." His thoughts were getting more confused, everything jumbling together in his mind. He tried to force them back into coherent patterns and visualize the terrible scene that had met his eyes as he stepped into the library. "The place was all torn up, just like it was when you boys came in. Books all over the floor with their pages ripped out, furniture turned over, the curtains shredded like somebody took a knife to them . . . it was a mess. But I barely noticed all that, because I saw Polly lyin' there with blood around her head, and she wasn't movin' at all, and I knew . . . Lord, I knew . . ."

With a shuddering sigh, Titus's voice trailed away.

After a few heartbeats of silence, Will asked quietly, "What then, Titus? What happened after you saw Polly?"

All he could do was shake his head in misery. "I don't know," he choked out, his voice threatening to fail him again. "I swear I don't know. Seein' Polly, that's the last thing I remember until I woke up with that poker in my hand and found Ebersole pointin' a gun at me. Somebody must've been layin' for me, though. I've got this goose egg—"

"Shut up about your goddamned goose egg!" Henry shouted at him. "Polly gave you that before you killed her!"

Titus shook his head. "No. I didn't do it."

Henry stepped forward, away from Will and Mac and toward Titus. Despite his outburst, he was under control, and while Will and Mac watched him, they didn't try to stop him this time.

Henry stopped in front of Titus, facing him from only a couple of feet away. His features were as hard and unyielding as stone.

"Titus Brannon," he said, "I'm placing you under arrest for the murder of Polly Ebersole Brannon."

⟨⟨⟨⟩⟩⟩

NOBODY HAD been locked up in the Culpeper County jail for a long time. It was a small cellblock in the basement of the courthouse. Since the beginning of the war, only the occasional thief or boisterous drunk had occupied the jail. But now Titus sat on the iron-framed bunk in one of the cells, leaning forward, his hands over his face. Mac thought it was one of the most pathetic sights he had ever seen.

"Don't worry about him," Henry said almost emotionlessly from the foot of the stairs leading up to the sheriff's office. "Don't waste your pity on him."

A single lamp burned at the base of the stairs, casting only a dim glow into the cells. It was disgraceful for a man to be locked up in a hole like this, Mac thought. He knew that Titus had endured much worse in that Yankee prison camp, but still . . .

With a shake of his head, Mac went to the stairs and followed Henry up to the office. Will was there already, straddling a straight-backed chair that he had turned around in front of the sheriff's desk. That had been his desk once, and as Mac looked at his older brother, he could tell that Will was remembering those days. He wondered if things would have been different if Will were still the sheriff. Probably not, Mac decided. Will had been a good lawman, devoted to his duty and doing what was right. Given the same set of circumstances, Will would have arrested Titus, too, just as Henry had. All the evidence indicated that Titus had killed Polly in a fit of rage, more than likely over the fact that she had refused to go back to him as his wife. And of course there was the baby to consider, too. Titus had to be enraged that Polly was carrying another man's child.

Pile on top of that Duncan Ebersole's testimony about finding Polly's body with an unconscious Titus lying nearby holding the murder weapon, and no jury in the world would hesitate to convict Titus of murder. He would be sentenced to hang, too. Mac had no doubt of that.

Henry sat down behind the desk. "Reckon Polly is at the undertaker's by now," he said. Mac could tell that Henry was keeping a tight rein on his emotions. "I'll have to go down there and make the arrangements."

"Later," Will said. "There'll be time for that later, Henry."

Henry nodded, but he didn't really seem to see or hear Will. "She'll need a better gown for the funeral. I'll get Cordelia to go through her things and find something appropriate. You'll bring it into town for her, won't you, Mac?"

"Sure, Henry," Mac said quietly. "I reckon the best thing you could do right now might be to go on home yourself and get some rest."

"I'm not tired." Henry shook his head. "Why, I'm not a bit tired. And somebody has to stay here and guard the prisoner."

He didn't call Titus by name, Mac noted. *The prisoner.* That was all Titus was to Henry now.

"Mac and I'll stay," Will said. "We don't mind, do we, Mac?"

"Nope, not at all."

"Then you could bring in the gown that Cordelia picks out," Will went on. "Could be you might even help her."

"I guess I could . . ." Henry rubbed his jaw in thought. As he did so, tears rolled silently down his face. He leaned forward and put his hands palms down on the desk and cried without making a sound, and the silence somehow made everything even more awful. Mac didn't know what to do, and when he looked at his older brother, Will just shook his head, equally helpless.

Finally, Will got to his feet and went over to the desk. He took hold of Henry's arm. "Come on, Henry. Let's take you home." He looked at Mac and went on, "I don't reckon Henry needs to be by himself right now. I'll be back in a little while."

"Take however long you need," Mac told him.

Henry didn't argue or try to fight as Will urged him to his feet and led him out of the office. When they were gone, Mac sat down behind the desk and sighed. He hadn't had a chance until now to think about what *he* was feeling. All of his thoughts had been for Henry and Polly and their poor unborn babe—and even for Titus. Now he realized that he felt a sharp pain inside himself, a pain made up of grief and anger and disbelief. He and Titus had never been as close as he and Will were; the two of them were just too different, Titus the hunter and Mac the one who tramped through the woods talking to the animals instead of shooting them. But they were still brothers, still family. The thought that Titus, whom he had seen grow from an infant to a boy to a man, might be a murderer was almost too much for Mac to bear. He had endured the pain of losing Titus once already. Could he go through that again?

And there was Polly to consider. Mac hadn't known her well, hadn't cared much for her at first when she'd married Titus, thinking her merely a spoiled planter's daughter. But she had grown some in his estimation over the years, especially during the time she had been married to Henry. At first he'd had doubts about that union, just like everybody else. But Polly had turned out to be a good wife to Henry. She had loved him. Mac had no doubts of *that*.

Polly was gone now, ripped away from all of them so suddenly and unexpectedly that all Mac could think of was the Scripture about not knowing the day nor the hour when the end would come.

He thought about going down to the cellblock to talk to Titus, but he didn't know what he would say. So he just sat there while the afternoon dragged past and the light outside the office's single window, gray to start with because of the overcast, became even dimmer with the approach of dusk.

When the door opened, it was so shocking that Mac jumped a little in his chair. He looked up, expecting to see that Will had returned, but instead Judge Darden stood there, a worried expression on his beefy face.

"Howdy, Mac," the judge said. "I heard about what happened. I'm mighty sorry."

"Thanks, Judge."

"Did Titus . . . well, did he really do it? Did he kill Polly?"

"He says he didn't." Mac shook his head. "I truly don't know, Judge."

Darden took the chair Will had been using earlier, but he turned it back around and sat down normally, rather than straddling it. The judge was no horseman and would never be comfortable sitting in that way.

"I've known you and your family for a long time, my boy," he said. "If anyone had asked me before today if any of the Brannon boys could commit heartless, cold-blooded murder, I'd have said no."

"If Titus killed her, it wasn't in cold blood. It would have been because he was furious, enraged even, and didn't know what he was doing."

Darden inclined his head. "An important distinction. Have you ever considered studyin' the law after this infernal war is over, Mac?"

"Me, a lawyer?" The idea was so ludicrous Mac couldn't stop himself from chuckling. "I don't think so, Judge."

"You might give it some thought," Darden said, either not noticing or not caring about the implied insult in Mac's reaction. "At any rate, a man caught up in the throes of passion might find himself committin' a crime. That passion might also save your brother from the gallows."

Mac leaned forward and frowned. "How do you figure that?"

Darden spread his pudgy hands. "What they call mitigatin' circumstances, my boy. In fact, given the circumstances—technically, Polly *was* engaged in an adulterous relationship with Henry, and was with child by him to boot—a jury might decide that Titus was justified in his actions, accordin' to the unwritten laws that govern our society with much the same force as the ones legally enacted by the legislature of this great sovereign state of Virginia."

Mac just stared at the judge for a long moment then said, "You're telling me he might be found not guilty?"

"It's a possibility. Even if Titus were to be convicted of the crime, there's an even better chance he would not be sentenced to hang but rather would be sent to prison for the rest of his life."

"My God," Mac muttered. "Titus would probably rather hang than have that happen."

"That's as it may be. I'm just advisin' you of the situation as I see it from the prospect of the law. Out of respect for your family, I might add. No fee is due."

Mac chuckled at that, a dry, almost humorless sound. "Thanks, Judge. Don't think I don't appreciate the advice. I surely do."

"In that case, here's a bit more." Darden leaned forward in his chair, wheezing a little as he did so. "Duncan Ebersole rode into town not long after you and Will and Henry brought Titus in. There's still one tavern in business in Culpeper, as you may know, and Ebersole has been there all afternoon, buyin' drinks for the patrons and talkin' about his daughter. He's inflamin' their passions against Titus."

"Why would he do that?"

"Perhaps because he fears the outcome of a trial might not be sufficient for his wants. He may try to deal with the situation himself, he and his cronies."

"You're talking about a lynch mob," Mac breathed.

"Indeed." Darden put his hands on his knees and pushed himself to his feet. "I'll be goin' now, Mac. I just thought you should be apprised of both the facts and the potentialities, so that you can deal with 'em accordin'ly. Good luck to you."

The judge left, and Mac didn't try to stop him. Instead he sat there for several minutes thinking about what Darden had said. Maybe the judge was right. Maybe Titus could get away with killing Polly. If Darden knew that, Duncan Ebersole could have figured it out, too. Ebersole wouldn't stand for it. He would try to deal out justice of his own to Titus . . .

Even through the closed window and the thick stone walls of the courthouse, Mac heard the commotion that started quietly and grew louder as it approached. The sound was a low muttering at first that turned into angry shouts.

He had no doubt where the men who were doing that shouting were headed. They were en route to the courthouse, probably with Ebersole at their head, and their intent would be nothing less than lynching Titus, hanging him from the nearest tree that was tall enough and sturdy enough to do the job.

Mac looked around the sheriff's office. He was in civilian clothes without either his pistol or his saber. His carbine was back at the farm, too. But a shotgun hung from pegs on the office wall, and when Mac jerked open the desk drawer, he found a dozen shells rolling around inside it. That was where Will had always kept extra shells for the shotgun when he occupied this office, and Mac was glad this was one thing that hadn't changed. He stood up, shoving the shells into his pocket except for a couple of them. Those two he slid into the barrels of the shotgun when he took it down from the wall and opened its breach. He closed the weapon with a sharp snap.

Will would have known what to do. Mac had no idea. He had never dealt with a lynch mob. He thought about going out to confront them on the front porch of the courthouse but discarded the idea when he realized that someone could come in the back way and get to the sheriff's office. He stepped out into the hallway and pulled the door closed behind him. The corridor was narrow. A charge of buckshot would spread from one wall to the other, sweeping everything before it.

Could he do that? These weren't Yankees, members of an invading army. They were his countrymen, people he had grown up with. Could he cut them down if he had to, even with his brother's life on the line?

The front doors of the courthouse slammed open. The yelling was louder. Men came around the corner into the long hallway and stopped short at the sight of Mac standing in front of the sheriff's office door, shotgun cradled in his hands.

Somewhat to Mac's surprise, Duncan Ebersole wasn't in the forefront of the mob. In fact, Mac didn't see him anywhere. Instead, the group of angry citizens was led by several men Mac recognized as layabouts who frequented Culpeper's only remaining tavern. Ebersole had talked them into doing his dirty work for him. One of the leaders wore the ragged vestiges of a Confederate infantry uniform. He scowled at Mac.

"Get out of the way, Brannon. We're goin' in there and takin' that murderin' brother of yours."

Mac shook his head. "Turn around and go home, Caswell. You'll feel better after you sleep off all the whiskey Ebersole bought for you."

"No sir," Caswell said stubbornly. "Murder's been done, and it's got to be avenged."

"Not by you! That's the job of the law."

"Law won't get the job done, an' you know it. Now step aside, Brannon."

Caswell started down the hall, followed by the other men.

Mac raised the shotgun. "I'll fire if I have to," he warned.

"You can't kill all of us," Caswell responded with a laugh. He wouldn't have been so cavalier about facing a scattergun if he hadn't been drunk. Ebersole had filled him and the others with bottled courage—and foolhardiness.

"Maybe not," Mac said, trying to get through to him. "But *you'll* be dead, Caswell, and that's a stone-cold certainty. Take another step, and I'll blow you in half."

He would do it, too. Mac was sure of that. He knew he would pull the trigger.

"Get back, damn you!" a new voice bellowed. "Step aside!"

Mac felt a surge of relief as he recognized Will's voice. After two years' commanding a company in the Stonewall Brigade,

Will knew how to make men follow his orders. Even this drunken mob responded to the words he barked out. The cluster of men parted like the Red Sea for Moses. Will strode through the path they made. He had a pistol in his hand. When he reached Mac, he swung around and stood shoulder to shoulder with him.

"This is no place for you men. Go on home. Let the law deal with this."

"You ain't the law," Caswell said. "Not no more. You're just a murderer's brother, tryin' to protect him."

"You know me, Caswell. You know I was sheriff of Culpeper County for a long time. I'll see that justice is done. You've got my word on that."

Caswell laughed. "Your word ain't worth—"

He stopped short as Will raised the pistol. The hammer was back, and the barrel was lined on Caswell's head.

"If you want to insult my word, you just made this personal, mister. I'll see you out in the street."

Caswell swallowed a couple of times then shook his head. Even full of liquor, he knew he was staring death in the face. "Nah, I didn't mean that," he mumbled after a moment. "I know your word's good, Will."

"Then get out of here, and take your friends with you. If you want, go tell Ebersole you decided you didn't want to die for him after all."

Caswell hesitated. "I still say you can't kill all of us."

"Mac has two barrels loaded with buckshot in that scattergun. I've got two pistols. I think we'd stand a damn good chance of it."

That cool confidence was all it took to shatter the last of the group's resolve. They weren't a lynch mob anymore, just a bunch of men who wished they were somewhere else. They turned and filed out of the courthouse, muttering curses.

Mac heaved a sigh. "I'm mighty glad you got back when you did, big brother."

Will holstered his pistol and snapped the flap shut over it. "You were doing just fine. They wouldn't have charged you. They didn't have the guts."

"Still, I was sure happy to see—"

Suddenly, Will slumped against the wall, holding himself up with a braced shoulder. His face was gray with strain.

"Will!" Mac cried, "What's wrong?"

"Nothing," he managed to say. "I guess I'm just not all the way back on my feet. Got a mite tired all of a sudden."

"Come on in the office and sit down."

"I reckon that'd be a good idea."

Mac put a hand under Will's elbow to support him as they returned to the office. Will looked a little better already. Color was seeping back into his face.

Mac knew now his older brother wasn't well after all, not by a long shot. That was one more thing to worry about.

As if the Brannons didn't have enough worries right now . . .

Chapter Ten

SLEEP WAS SUPPOSED TO knit up the raveled sleeve of care. Balm of hurt minds, great nature's second course, chief nourisher in life's feast. That was what Shakespeare had called it, anyway, in *MacBeth*. Henry had heard his father quote the lines many times over the years.

Ol' Willie was full of horse droppings, Henry thought.

He had slept and woke up and slept and woke up, and Polly was still dead. Today was the day they would put her in a box and put her under the ground, her and the baby both. Henry would never see her again, never feel the warmth of her touch or hear the music of her laugh, music he had heard all too seldom in their time together. Of the babe he had nothing, no feel of tiny, fragile life held in his hands, no memories at all except the faint stirrings he had felt in Polly's belly. Where was the comfort in that?

Henry buried his face in the pillow and cried. Perhaps one day the tears would run out, but not yet. Lord, not yet.

⊙〰〰〰⊙

THE FUNERAL was at the Congregationalist Church in Culpeper, where Duncan Ebersole was a member even though he had not attended services there in a long time. A large crowd was in attendance, as both the Brannons and the Ebersoles were well known in the county, and the Brannons, at least, were well liked for the most part. Judge Darden was there as well as the Reverend Benjamin Spanner from the First Baptist Church. Both men shook hands with Henry, though he was barely aware of it. They pointedly avoided speaking to Ebersole. In fact, Ebersole stood by himself in a black suit, his head uncovered, with a small space around him in the crowd as if no one wanted to get too

159

close. If that bothered him, he gave no sign of it. His face was like stone.

Will and Mac wore dress uniforms and stood at attention as Polly's coffin was lowered into the grave. Abigail and Cordelia, their faces covered with dark veils, stood with Dorothy Chamberlain. Not far behind the family, Roman waited next to the wagon that had brought them into town, his hat in his hands and his eyes downcast in prayer.

Titus, of course, remained in his cell in the jail. Jasper Strawn, who had been acting sheriff before rheumatism got the better of him, still served occasionally as a part-time deputy and sat out front with a shotgun, just in case anybody got more ideas about a lynching.

Thick gray clouds clogged the sky, but there were gaps through which the sun shone at times. The light came and went, playing over the faces of the mourners as the minister's prayer droned on. Finally it was over, and Henry stepped forward.

At the same moment, Duncan Ebersole moved toward the grave.

Both men stopped short and looked at each other. After an interval of strained silence that seemed much longer than it really was, Ebersole stepped back. Henry made no acknowledgment of the gesture other than to go on with what he had started to do. He bent and picked up a handful of dirt from the mound next to the gaping hole in the ground. He held out his hand and opened it, letting the dirt spill onto the closed lid of the coffin. The larger clods thudded against the wood.

He turned and went back to his family. Ebersole came forward then and did as Henry had done, dropping the ceremonial handful of dirt on the coffin. When he was finished and had returned to his place, the minister launched into a final prayer then, thankfully, it was over. The mourners filed away, many of them stopping to shake hands one more time with the Brannons.

Ebersole went to his carriage, where the old butler from Mountain Laurel waited on the driver's seat, tears coursing down his cheeks. He had watched Polly grow up, had seen the troubles that had plagued her as a young woman, had sympathized but had been unable to do anything to help her. Now he cried for her, when it was too late for anything else.

"Stop that blubberin', Lige," Ebersole snapped as he started to climb up into the carriage. "I want t' get home."

A man came around the rear of the carriage before Ebersole could enter the vehicle. "Duncan," he said, "I'm right sorry for your loss."

Ebersole stopped with one foot on the step and looked at the newcomer, a tall, rawboned man in rough clothes and a felt hat with a broad, floppy brim.

"Quinn," Ebersole said. "What d'ye want?"

"Didn't you hear me?" the moonshiner said. "I'm offerin' my condolences."

"I don't want 'em. I dinna want anythin' more t' do wi' ye, Quinn. If I had not been drunk on yer whiskey, my little girl might still be alive t'day."

Quinn leaned closer to him. "Well, you see, Duncan, I sort of wanted to talk to you about that."

Ebersole's lip curled in a sneer. "I dinna recall givin' ye leave t' address me by my Christian name."

"Well, now, maybe it's time you and me got a mite closer. You see . . ." Quinn's voice dropped to little more than a whisper. "I know what happened out yonder at Mountain Laurel that day. 'Deed I do. And I don't think you want me talkin' about it. Not to Henry Brannon, that's for sure. *Sheriff* Henry Brannon."

Ebersole stiffened, his eyes blazing with hatred. His hand shot out and grabbed Quinn's arm.

"What are ye sayin'?" he demanded.

Quinn jerked free. "We've had our differences, you and me, but we got to put that behind us now. You and me workin' together, hell, we could wind up ownin' this whole county."

"Me, partner up wi' the likes o' you?" Ebersole shook his head. "I'm not thinkin' that's likely t' happen."

"Maybe you better think on it again. I know about you, Ebersole. I *know*."

Sickness roiled in Ebersole's belly. He couldn't think straight or bring himself to consider what Quinn was saying. But he knew blackmail when he heard it. In the past, he had not been above using such tactics himself when the situation called for them. Maybe Quinn *did* know something about what had happened. If so, that was more than Ebersole himself could say.

Because, though he had convinced himself that Titus Brannon was guilty, he didn't know that for a fact. To tell the truth, he wasn't sure what had happened when Polly arrived at Mountain Laurel. The thought that perhaps she had died some other way . . . at the hands of someone else . . . had haunted him for days now.

"Come to the house this evenin'," he rasped. "We'll talk."

Quinn nodded. "Now you're bein' smart, sensible. I'll see you tonight."

Ebersole climbed into the carriage and shouted, "Go! Go on, damn you!" to the driver. He didn't look back as the carriage rolled away, leaving Quinn behind.

⚬〜〜〜⚬

DOROTHY CHAMBERLAIN placed a hand on Will's arm. "Who's that?" she asked.

He turned and looked. "Who are you talking about?"

"Over there by that carriage, talking to Polly's father."

Will's eyes narrowed as he saw Ebersole and Quinn engaged in an intense discussion. After a few moments, Ebersole climbed into the carriage and it drove away. Quinn watched it go then went to his horse, mounted, and rode away.

"He's a fella named Quinn," Will explained. "Pretty much no good. Has a cabin up in the foothills of the Blue Ridge where he brews whiskey and sells it to folks around here. From what I hear, Ebersole's one of his best customers."

"They didn't seem too friendly the other day."

Will's frown deepened as he looked at Dorothy. "What do you mean?"

"The day Henry was sworn in as sheriff, Polly and I went for a walk, and that's when she ran into her father. But before that, I saw a man stop Ebersole and try to talk to him. Ebersole brushed him off and made him angry. I'd swear that man was the one he was just talking to."

Will thought it over then shrugged. "I suppose it could've been Quinn. Like I said, Ebersole's one of his customers. Anyway, I don't reckon it means anything."

"No," Dorothy said. "I suppose not."

⟨⟩

TITUS HEARD the footsteps on the stairs. They reached the bottom and came along the corridor in the center of the cellblock. He didn't look up, even when the steps stopped right outside his cell.

"It's over," Henry said solemnly. "She's buried now. Her and the baby."

"I don't want to hear about the baby." Titus kept his eyes on the damp stone floor as he spoke.

The barred door rattled as Henry gripped it and shook it in his rage. "Well, by God, you're going to hear! You took them away from me, both of them!"

"No, I didn't. You can believe me or not, I don't give a damn anymore, but I didn't kill her, Henry. You just go blame somebody else for that, 'cause it ain't me who done it."

Titus looked up at last. He saw the tears running down Henry's face.

"I've lost everything," he whispered. "Everything."

Titus shook his head. "No, you've still got the rest of the family. That's more'n I've got, little brother. You've all turned on me. You've all convicted me, without even a trial." Anger welled up inside him. "Lord! I'm your own flesh and blood. Don't I deserve a fair hearin', anyway?"

Henry used the back of his hand to paw away some of the wetness on his face. "All right. If you didn't do it, who did?"

"Ebersole! I been tellin' you right along that he's a lot more likely to have hurt Polly than I am. You know how crazy he is. Damn, you saw it for yourself! Cordelia told me about how he came over to the farm and nearly rode you down in the fields when he found out Polly was pregnant. And then he would have whipped you to death if Ma hadn't come up with a shotgun. Ebersole's the one you ought to have locked up in here, not me!"

Henry looked at him but didn't say anything. Titus felt a surge of hope. Maybe Henry was considering what he'd said.

"You got to admit it could've happened that way," Titus went on, pressing his case. "Ebersole could have hit Polly with that poker, then used it or something else to lay me out when I came in. All he had to do was put the poker in my hand and pretend to find us like that. You can see that it could have been like that."

"Maybe," Henry said. The word came out of him as if it had taken a crowbar to pry it loose.

"Look at it this way. You owe it to Polly to find out the truth. Because if I'm not lyin' to you—and I'm not, Henry—the person who killed her is walkin' around free. You don't want that, and neither do I."

"I'll think about it," Henry said. "That's all I can promise."

Titus slumped back on the bunk, his shoulders resting against the stone wall of the cell. "While you're thinkin' about it, are you goin' to keep those lynch mobs off of me? You weren't even here the other day when that bunch showed up. Will and Mac had to run 'em off."

"There won't be any lynchings," Henry said. "Not in Culpeper County. Not while I'm sheriff."

Titus chuckled. "Damned if you don't sound like you mean it. You said that just like a real lawman, little brother."

"You'd better be glad that's what I am."

Henry went away. Titus shook his head as he listened to the footsteps fade. He didn't know if he had really gotten through to Henry or not. Even if he had, what could Henry do about it? All the evidence pointed to Titus as the killer. The theory he'd laid out about Ebersole was just that—a theory. Without proof it didn't mean a thing.

Titus shivered. It was cold in this jail. He wondered if he would ever be warm again . . . this side of hell.

✺

TITUS'S TRIAL was set for the next week. In a way, that seemed to Henry like too long to wait, but Judge Wells, who would preside, and the county attorney, Herman Wilbarger, advised him that rushing things wouldn't look good.

"Your brother already has a certain modicum of sympathy on his side," Wilbarger explained. "To some people, he seems to be the wronged party in this affair."

"The wronged party?" Henry choked on the words. "How can that be?"

Wilbarger shrugged his shoulders. "He *was* legally married to Miss Polly. A husband has rights . . . Well, you understand, Henry. The unwritten law, and all that."

Mac had told Henry what Judge Darden had said on that subject, and now Wilbarger spouted the same nonsense. Yet Henry knew there was something in what he said. A jury might believe that Titus had killed Polly and at the same time find him innocent of murder because of the way fate had twisted their lives.

When Wells and Wilbarger were gone, Henry sat behind the sheriff's desk and asked himself the question he hadn't wanted to: Did *he* believe that Titus was guilty? He still hated his brother for all the misery he'd put Polly through when he came back, but he had to admit there was doubt in the back of his mind. Titus was capable of a lot of things; he'd been a drunkard and a troublemaker for most of his life. But even in a rage, could he have

166 · James Reasoner

swung that poker and crushed the life out of a woman he claimed to love?

Henry didn't know the answer to that question, but the mere fact that he could ask it of himself meant that he wasn't convinced. Lord help him, as much as he wanted to blame Titus for everything that had happened, he couldn't. Not without more proof than the word of Duncan Ebersole.

The door of the office opened and Will and Mac came in. Mac was in uniform. Henry managed a smile. "Looks like you're heading back to Wigwam."

Mac pulled up a chair and sat down, as did Will. "That's right. I'll have to get back pretty soon, even though I sent word to General Lee about . . . well, about what happened."

"You mean Polly being killed," Henry said.

"Yeah. I'm not leaving for a day or two, though, and we got to wondering about something."

"What's that?" Henry said, not really all that interested.

"What does Duncan Ebersole have to do with Israel Quinn?" Will asked.

Henry sat up straighter. "What? Ebersole buys whiskey from Quinn, I reckon. A lot of folks do."

Will ran a thumbnail along the line of his jaw. "Mrs. Chamberlain saw Quinn talking to Ebersole just before Ebersole had that run-in with Polly. Quinn wasn't happy. Then, later, at the funeral, Quinn was talking to Ebersole again. They were pretty serious about something. And Ebersole didn't look happy about it. I saw that with my own eyes."

"His daughter was being buried," Henry said bluntly. "How happy could he be?"

Will shook his head. "I know. I said that badly. What I meant was that Ebersole and Quinn looked like they were about to have an argument over something. Then Ebersole gave in."

"I don't understand what this has to do with anything."

"Probably nothing," Mac said. "Will and I were just curious, that's all. But Ebersole's in town right now, over at the bank.

Likely he'll be there for a while. I thought maybe you'd like to take a ride out to Mountain Laurel with me and ask some of Ebersole's people a few questions about Quinn."

Henry shook his head. "Ebersole's slaves won't talk to us. They wouldn't dare risk making him mad."

"I don't know. That old butler of his—what's his name, Elijah?—he looked mighty upset at the funeral. He knew Polly all her life, I reckon. He was probably pretty fond of her."

Henry gripped the edge of the desk as a thought occurred to him. "Titus has said all along that Ebersole must be the one who killed Polly." The words almost choked him, but he got them out. "If that was true, and if Quinn knew about it somehow . . ."

"He'd get Ebersole to pay him off," Mac said with a nod. "I reckon that's the idea we had in the back of our minds, too."

"Son of a bitch!" Henry shot to his feet. "That would mean Titus is telling the truth."

"That's right. We figure the chance is worth a ride out to Mountain Laurel."

Henry reached for his hat. "Let's go."

"I'll stay here and keep an eye on things," Will offered. He glanced around the office. "It'll be sort of like old times, and nobody will be able to get to Titus."

Henry and Mac left the courthouse and rode toward the edge of town. Before they got there, Henry reined in sharply. "Wait a minute," he said to Mac. He swung down from the saddle and walked over to a man who was ambling along the side of the road. "Caswell, I want to talk to you."

The ragged veteran stopped and looked at Henry with a mixture of fear and anger. "What do you want, Brannon? You ain't gonna arrest me for bein' in that bunch that came to the courthouse the other day, are you? We didn't do nothin'."

Henry had heard all about that incident from Will and Mac. He used it now as he said, "You were the ringleader, from what I'm told. Charges could be brought against you."

"The hell you say! It was all Ebersole's idea. That bastard."

"You know Israel Quinn, don't you?"

The question took Caswell by surprise. He drew the back of his hand across his mouth as he frowned in thought. "Sure, I know Quinn. I know all the Fogartys and Paynters and the rest of that bunch."

"Quinn and Ebersole are friends, too, aren't they?"

Caswell gave a short, unpleasant bark of laughter. "Those two? Friends? Not hardly. Ebersole thinks he's too good to be seen with the likes o' Quinn—or me. He just uses us whenever he sees fit. Like how he tried to get us to take your brother out of jail and string him up. The boys and me never would've done that if Ebersole hadn't been eggin' us on, buyin' us drinks and tellin' us all about how his poor little girl had been murdered and the skunk who done it was gonna get away with it . . ." He broke off with a shake of his head. "Sorry, Brannon. I don't mean to be goin' on and on about it."

Henry forced the pain deep inside him. He would never forget it was there, but he was able to ignore it. "So Quinn and Ebersole aren't friends?"

"No. Fact is, Quinn's had his back up about something Ebersole did awhile back." Caswell shook his head. "Don't bother askin' me about it, 'cause I don't know. But they ain't friends, that's for sure."

"Thanks," Henry muttered and started to turn away.

"That's all you wanted?" Caswell sounded like he couldn't believe it. "I ain't in trouble?"

"Not this time. Next time Ebersole starts buying drinks, I wouldn't listen to him if I were you."

Caswell snorted. "Probably won't be no next time."

"What did you find out?" Mac asked as Henry mounted his horse again.

Henry heeled his horse into a trot. Mac's stallion matched the pace easily. "From the sound of it, there was bad blood between Ebersole and Quinn. I don't think Quinn would hesitate to blackmail him."

They didn't say anything else on their way out to Mountain Laurel, but each man's mind was full of its own thoughts, chief among them the possibility that Titus hadn't killed Polly after all. If Quinn was holding something over Ebersole's head, there was only one thing it could be.

Ebersole had murdered his own daughter.

It was a horrible thing to contemplate, but no more horrible than the idea that his brother could be a murderer, Henry told himself. He could never feel the same way about Titus as he had when they were younger, but what Titus had said there was true: The worst thing of all would be for Polly's real killer to get away with his crime.

A cold wind blew as they reached Mountain Laurel. They rode up the drive and reined in. No one came out to take their horses. Mac held the reins while Henry hammered a fist on the door. There was no response from the house.

"Nobody's here," Mac said.

"Somebody's got to be here. We'll go around back to the slave quarters."

They rode around the plantation house and along a winding trail past the carriage house, the barns, the smokehouse, and the smithy to a cluster of squalid huts just inside the edge of the woods. An old man with white hair and a pinched face looked up at them from a stool outside one of the cabins. "Massa Henry, Massa MacBeth," he greeted them. "What y'all doin' here?"

"Hello, Elijah," Henry said as he dismounted.

The old man grimaced. "Elijah was the butler in the big house. I's a field han' now, when I ain't laid up with the rheumatiz like today. Call me Lige."

"Listen, *Elijah*," Henry said, "we need to talk to you. It's about Polly."

Tears shone in the bleary old eyes. "That poor, sweet gal. It weren't her fault. 'Twas all Massa Duncan's doin'—"

Henry's pulse leaped. "You mean Ebersole killed her? You know this for a fact?"

"What?" Elijah looked confused. He shook his head. "Naw. Naw, suh, that ain't it. Don't pay no 'tention to me. I's just an old man, muddled in my head."

Henry didn't believe that. Elijah knew something; he was sure of it. If he pressed the old man, though, chances were Elijah would sull up and refuse to say anything else. Now was the time to take things slowly and carefully . . .

"You may not be working in the big house anymore, but I'll bet you still see just about everything that goes on around here, don't you?"

"Yes suh, I 'spect I do."

"Has Israel Quinn been out here lately?"

Elijah made a face, leaned over, and spat. "That Quinn, he worse'n any slave I ever seen. He just pure trash, that man."

"I can't argue with you there. But has he been here?"

Elijah nodded. "Yes suh. He come out here on the night o' Miss Polly's services. Massa Duncan, he had me in the house that night, on account of I was still wearin' my suit from drivin' him to the church. He had me bring drinks to him and that Quinn fella."

Henry kept a tight rein on his emotions. "Did you hear what they talked about?"

"Naw suh, not really. But I know Massa Duncan was mad 'bout somethin'. Prob'ly the money he give to that Quinn."

"He gave Quinn money?"

"I seen him hand over a poke to that man. It jingled like it had coins in it." Elijah frowned. "Massa Henry, why you askin' me all these questions? If Massa Duncan was here, he'd whip the hide off my poor ol' bones for talkin' to you. Onliest reason I'm doin' it is 'cause you was married to Miss Polly, and I know you treated her decent."

"I tried to," Henry said. "I surely tried to. But in the end I reckon it didn't do any good."

Elijah put out a hand. "Naw, don't say that, Massa Henry. I seen her a time or two after you was married to her. She was happy, she surely was. Wasn't many times in her life she could say that. Never after her mama passed on and it was just her and Massa Duncan there in the house . . ."

The old man looked down at the ground and shook his head in sorrow.

Henry waited a moment as he struggled to bring his emotions under control. Then he said, "So Quinn came here when he wasn't delivering whiskey to Ebersole?"

"Yes suh, the night o' the services. And that other day."

"What other day?"

"That terrible, terrible day. When Miss Polly was . . . when Miss Polly was killed."

Henry stiffened and half-turned to glance at Mac, who was still mounted on the stallion. Mac looked just as surprised and intrigued as Henry felt. Henry swung back toward the old man. "Quinn was here that day?"

"Yes suh. He come up lookin' for Massa Duncan. I told him Massa Duncan wasn't here, but that was a lie. I know a darky ain't 'sposed to lie to white folks, but I figured that Quinn, he don't hardly count as white."

"Where was Ebersole?"

"In the carriage house." Elijah waved a hand toward the building. "He'd had too much whiskey. He was sleepin'. I knowed he wouldn't want to be disturbed."

My God, Henry thought. That much of Duncan Ebersole's story was true.

"What did Quinn do? Did he leave?"

"Yes suh, I reckon. I don't rightly know, 'cause I didn't see him after he went in the house."

"The big house? Quinn went in there?"

"Yes suh. He told me not to say nothin' about it, said he'd come back and skin me if'n I did." Elijah drew himself up straighter. "But I ain't afraid o' that Quinn."

Henry fought the urge to grab Elijah's shoulders and shake more information out of him. His thoughts were running rampant now, considering possibilities that had never occurred to him before. "Did Quinn leave before Polly got here?"

Elijah just shook his head. "I don't rightly know," he said again. "I had to go down to the fields. Didn't know anything else was goin' on until we heard Massa Duncan yellin' and screamin' from inside the house, after he done found Miss Polly."

"Henry," Mac said, "this changes things. We've got to think about this."

"You think about it," Henry snapped. He rested a hand on Elijah's shoulder for a second. "Thank you. You did the right thing by talking to me."

"I ain't goin' to get in trouble?"

"Not if I can help it." Henry turned back to the horses and took his mount's reins from Mac. "I'm deputizing you, Mac. Go find Ebersole and put him under arrest if you have to. Bring him to Quinn's place. That's where I'm headed."

"Damn it, Henry—" Mac began.

Henry swung up into the saddle and silenced him with a look unlike any Mac had ever seen from him before. "This isn't your little brother giving you orders, Mac. It's the sheriff of Culpeper County. Sorry it has to be that way."

With that, he kicked his horse into a gallop and rode away from Mountain Laurel, leaving behind a worried-looking Mac.

Chapter Eleven

HENRY'S MIND WAS A swirling maelstrom as he rode toward Israel Quinn's cabin. He felt like three people crammed into one. He was Polly's grieving husband determined to see his wife's killer brought to justice. He was Titus's brother, and regardless of how he might feel about Titus, he couldn't allow his brother to face a hangman's noose for a crime he hadn't committed. And he was the county sheriff charged with apprehending anyone who had broken the law. For all three reasons, he had to get to the bottom of this matter.

He wasn't sure what had happened at Mountain Laurel on that dreadful day. He knew now, though, that Quinn had been there. If Ebersole had killed Polly, Quinn was a possible witness to the crime.

On the other hand, if Quinn had been carrying some sort of grudge against Ebersole, as it appeared he had, and he had been in the house when Polly got there . . . well, it was possible he had killed her to get back at her father. Henry hadn't considered that angle until today, but the things he had learned from Caswell and Elijah made it sound possible.

Something was going on between Ebersole and Quinn. And it was time to bring them together and confront them about it.

Henry's hand wrapped around the butt of his gun as he rode. He had to force himself to relax his grip around it and not clutch it tightly.

He had seen Quinn's ramshackle cabin in the foothills once, several years before the war, when he and Will and Titus had been on their way to the Blue Ridge on a hunting trip. He wasn't sure he remembered how to get there, but his instincts led him along the right trails. It was late afternoon when he came within sight of the cabin. Clouds scudded across the sky. There hadn't been a clear, warm day since Polly was killed, Henry thought. It was like the world itself was mourning her. He knew that was impossible, that the lives and deaths of those who inhabited the earth meant little or nothing to the world. It followed its pre-ordained path through the heavens with no regard for what puny humanity did. But if it made him feel better for a moment to think that the mists that fell from the sky were tears of grief, then so be it.

Henry forced his thoughts back on what was facing him. Smoke rose from the cabin's chimney. Quinn's horse was out back in a split-rail pen. Another pen contained several loudly grunting hogs. Chickens scratched around the yard. A toddler in ragged clothes sat on the porch, pulling the ears of a sad-faced, tolerant old hound. The dog seemed half-asleep, but it lifted its head and bayed when it caught sight of Henry. Several more youngsters came out of the cabin and stared at him as he rode up.

Henry brought his horse to a stop. "Where's your pa?" he asked the children.

The oldest, a boy of perhaps twelve years, jerked a thumb over his shoulder. "He's in the cabin, a-pesterin' Ma. Said for us to tell whoever was out here to clear the hell out, else he'd take a gun to 'em."

Henry's eyes narrowed. "Well, son, you go back in there and tell him the sheriff is out here, and I'm not clearing out until I've talked to him."

"No sir. He'll wallop me if'n I do that."

Henry fought back his irritation and frustration. "All right. Take your brothers and sisters around back, why don't you?"

"There gonna be trouble?"

"Could be," Henry said.

The boy nodded. "All right." He didn't seem bothered by the fact that the law was looking for his father, nor did the prospect of trouble worry him. He seemed not to care at all, one way or the other.

If Quinn was his father, Henry thought, he might feel the same way.

When the boy had herded his siblings behind the cabin, out of harm's way, Henry raised his voice in a shout. "Quinn! Israel Quinn! Step out here! This is Sheriff Brannon!"

He had held the office for only a little more than a week, but already it sounded right to him when he said that. He had thought that he would never be anything more than a farmer, either on the family farm or elsewhere. Maybe he had found himself a career.

But he would have traded it all to have Polly back. He caught his breath as the pain of loss surged up. He tamped it down as best he could and concentrated on watching the cabin.

"Come on, Quinn!" he shouted again. "Get out here!"

The door flew open, but Quinn didn't come out. Instead, the barrel of an old flintlock rifle thrust out of the darkness inside the cabin. Henry tensed, ready to fling himself out of the saddle, but Quinn didn't fire.

"Git! You got no business here! Get off my land, Brannon!"

Henry stayed where he was. "Come on out, Quinn. I want to talk to you."

"I got nothin' to say!"

"You either talk to me now, or I'll come back with a posse and root you out. That'll be worse for you."

Quinn let out a cackle of laughter. "A posse? Where in hell are you goin' to find a posse, Sheriff? Ain't enough able-bodied men left in Culpeper for you to swear 'em in."

That might well be true, Henry thought. He decided to change tacks.

"Look, Quinn, there's been some charges brought against you. All I want to do is get your side of the story. I'm just trying to be fair."

"Charges?" Quinn echoed. "Who in Hades brought charges agin me?"

"Duncan Ebersole," Henry said. "He says you stole a poke of money from him. Told me to come out here and search your place for it."

Quinn's voice escalated to an angry screech. "Ebersole! That lyin' bastard!"

"So, you're saying you don't have a poke of money that belongs to him?"

"It's my money! He gave it to me!" Quinn finally came onto the porch, poking the rifle out in front of him. It wasn't pointed straight at Henry, but it was aimed in his general direction enough to make him nervous. The barrel shook a little as Quinn went on, "Double-crossin' son of a bitch! He better be careful I don't start tellin' stories on him!"

"You know stories on Ebersole, do you?"

"Damn right I do! I know what he done to that girl o' his."

With a huge effort, Henry forced himself to stay calm. "What do you know, Quinn? Tell me and I'll do what I can to keep you from going to jail."

A cunning expression appeared on Quinn's face. "What's it worth to you?"

"It's worth your freedom," Henry said, his voice hard. "Otherwise, I'll have to arrest you for stealing that poke."

"I didn't steal that money! He gave it to me, I tell you!"

"For keeping quiet about what happened up at Mountain Laurel a few days ago?"

"You know what happened?" Quinn shot back at him.

"Maybe." Henry seized the initiative, realizing that it was time to tighten the screws a little more. "I know what Ebersole says happened. And he says that *you* killed Polly." That ought to be enough to make the moonshiner blurt out the truth, Henry thought. He waited for Quinn to admit that he had witnessed Ebersole's murder of Polly.

Instead, Quinn jerked the rifle to his shoulder and fired.

Taken by surprise, Henry didn't have time to dodge. But Quinn had hurried his shot, and the heavy lead ball only clipped Henry's upper right arm. Still, the impact was enough to make him rock back in the saddle and lose his balance. His horse danced skittishly aside, and Henry pitched to the ground.

The breath was knocked out of him and his arm was numb. He couldn't reach for the pistol on his hip. All he could do was lie there and gasp for air as Quinn threw the empty rifle aside and charged toward him. The man reached behind his back and pulled a knife. He dropped to a knee beside Henry and pressed the blade to his neck.

"Tell me," Quinn hissed as he leaned over Henry. "How'd he know? I thought he was so drunk he didn't know what happened." Quinn's face was so distorted by hate that it barely looked human. He didn't give Henry a chance to answer the question. Instead, he babbled on, "That son of a bitch thought he could fool me, didn't he? Thought I was just a dumb ridge runner! He played along when I told him I seen him wallop the gal with that poker and gave me the money just so he could turn me in later. Well, it won't work! He can't prove a damned thing! He was drunk out back in the carriage house when it happened. He said so hisself!"

Henry was groggy from pain and confusion. He'd had a lot of practice in recent days at pushing aside mental and emotional pain. Now he had to do the same with the physical pain of being shot. He had to keep Quinn talking.

"So it's true then," he said between clenched teeth. "You killed her!"

"I never meant to!" The knife blade scraped Henry's neck as Quinn's hand trembled. "I was gonna tear up the place, maybe even burn it down. Ebersole deserved that much! He owed me for all the whiskey I'd brought him for months, but he kept puttin' me off. Said he didn't have the money. And him the richest man in the county!"

"Maybe he didn't," Henry rasped. "Folks are cash poor now, because of the war. Even Ebersole."

"He had the money! He just thought that he didn't have to pay me 'cause I'm trash! Hell, he's done worse things than I ever did. He may not have killed that gal, but I could tell you some things . . ."

Quinn stopped talking and wailed. After a couple of seconds, he announced, "I'm gonna have to kill you now."

"Like you did Polly?"

"I tell you, I didn't mean to! I was just tearin' up the place. But then she came in and started yellin' and screamin', and it made me crazy, I guess. I grabbed that poker . . ." Spittle drooled from the corner of his mouth. "When I seen what I done, I knew I'd have to burn the place down. I would have, too, if that damn brother o' yours hadn't come in."

"Titus?" Henry whispered.

"Yeah, Titus! That brother of your'n. I heard him comin' and laid for him behind the door. Walloped him a good 'un, too. Figured I'd killed him. But when I seen that I didn't, I got an idea. I put the poker in his hand so he'd get the blame for killin' the girl. Figured losin' her was enough punishment for Ebersole, at least for a while. Then afterwards, when Titus said he didn't do it and Ebersole admitted he was too drunk to know what happened, I got to thinkin' that if I hinted to him that he had killed her, he'd pay me what he owed me, and a bunch more besides. I don't know how in the hell he ever figured out it was really me what done it." Quinn grinned down at Henry. "Well, Sheriff, I'm gonna cut your throat now. I told you all that 'cause I wanted you to know I ain't as stupid as ever'body thinks I am. Once you're dead, ain't nobody can prove anything agin me. If Ebersole wants to, just let him try. I'll tell the world about everything *he's* done, and he knows it."

Quinn leaned over and bunched his shoulders, ready to rake the razor-sharp blade across Henry's throat. Before he could move, a rifle cracked in the woods nearby. Quinn was flung backward, arms and legs flying out to the sides as he sprawled in the dirt. The knife flew a dozen feet away and slid across the ground when it landed.

Henry rolled onto his side and pushed himself up and into a sitting position. His neck stung like fire suddenly. He raised his good hand to it and found a trickle of blood from a small cut.

Quinn's knife had left that little wound when the bullet jerked him away from Henry.

Mac came out of the woods leading the stallion. His other hand carried his cavalry carbine. Smoke still curled from the barrel. A whey-faced Duncan Ebersole followed Mac.

"I never used this carbine to kill anybody except the enemy in battle," Mac said as he stood over Quinn's body. "I reckon most of those Yankees didn't deserve a bullet nearly as much as Quinn did."

Ebersole swallowed hard. "We heard ever'thing th' bastard had t' say."

"Almost everything," Mac corrected. "He was already kneeling over you with the knife when we came up. We'd heard the shot a minute or two before."

"Then you know that he killed Polly," Henry said.

Mac nodded. "We heard that, all right. And all about how he put the poker in Titus's hand. All because he wanted to get back at Ebersole. Because he hadn't paid him for whiskey."

The shamed old man looked at the ground. "I dinna have the money—"

"You had the money to pay his blackmail." Mac's voice shook with anger. "My God, you must have believed it was possible you killed Polly, or you wouldn't have given Quinn his blood money! You really didn't know what happened out there at Mountain Laurel, did you? But that didn't stop you from accusing Titus of murder!"

Ebersole put his hands to his head. "I didn't know . . . Can't ye have some pity on a poor man who's lost his only child?"

Mac looked like he wanted to put his fist in the middle of Ebersole's face. Henry certainly understood that feeling, because he shared it. But right now, there were more important things than giving in to anger.

"Give me a hand, Mac," he said. "We've got to get back to town and Titus."

"You need a doctor," Mac began.

"I'll be all right. Tear a strip of cloth off my shirt and tie it around that scratch. That'll hold me for a while. The first thing we've got to do is release Titus."

Mac nodded. "Quinn's confession clears him, all right. And since Ebersole heard it, too, and will testify to what he heard, folks will believe it more than if just you and I said that Quinn was guilty." Mac looked at Ebersole. "You *will* testify to what you heard?"

"Aye," Ebersole said, his voice barely audible. "I've no use for yer brother, but if he's innocent, he ought t' go free."

"Let's go, then," Henry said.

Mac tied the makeshift bandage around Henry's arm, and the three men mounted and rode off. As the sound of hoof beats died away, a woman emerged from the cabin, came over to stand beside Quinn's sprawled body, and stared down at it expressionlessly. Slowly, the children emerged from behind the cabin and surrounded the body as well. They looked at it curiously.

But no one cried. Not a tear fell.

⊙∭⊙

Titus paused on the front porch of the courthouse and drew in a deep breath. The night air was cold and raw and made him cough. Still, it smelled good. It smelled a lot better than the air in that cell. That was because it was free air, he thought.

He was glad he'd had to spend only a few nights in jail. His sleep had been haunted on each of those nights by dreams about Camp Douglas. Everything that had happened at that Yankee prison camp, all the pain and humiliation, came back to him in those nightmares, and he woke up trembling and sweating despite the dank chill.

No matter what, he vowed to himself, he would never be locked up again. Anyone who tried to take him prisoner would have to kill him instead, because he would fight to the death rather than be captured.

Mac stepped up beside him and rested a hand on his shoulder. "Feels pretty good to be out, doesn't it?"

Titus shrugged off his brother's hand. "I never should've been locked up in the first place. Wouldn't have been if my own brother, the sheriff, had a lick of sense."

"Henry's the one who uncovered the evidence that freed you," Mac said. "You ought to be grateful to him."

"I'll get around to it . . . about the time hell freezes over."

Mac shook his head. "You never have been one to let go of anything."

Anger flared inside Titus, and he swung sharply toward Mac. "Let go?" he repeated. "You expect me to let go of the fact that he stole my wife away from me and then threw me in jail for something I didn't do?"

"Seems to me you'd be a little glad that Polly's real killer was brought to justice."

"You ever stop to think that she might not have been there, might not have got killed, if it wasn't for Henry?" Mac had told Titus the whole story of Quinn's confession when he came to unlock the jail cell and let him out, repeating it as close to word for word as he could. On the way into town, Henry had gotten faint from loss of blood and had stopped at the doctor's office to have his wounded arm patched up.

Mac frowned at Titus. "What in blazes are you talking about? How can you blame Henry for what happened to Polly?"

"We still don't know why she went to Mountain Laurel that day. Maybe it had something to do with the mess she was in with me and Henry."

"There wouldn't have been a mess," Mac snapped, "if you'd done the decent thing and divorced her so that she and Henry could get married proper."

"Why the hell would I want to do that? She was my wife. I loved her."

"You didn't love her," Mac said. "You were just determined that if you couldn't have her, nobody else could, either."

Instantly Titus's hands balled into fists as he turned toward Mac. He wanted to throw a punch, wanted it so bad he was shaking inside. But he knew he was still weak from everything he had gone through. Mac was slow to anger, but he would defend himself if attacked. Judging by the look in his eyes, he was mad enough to beat the hell out of Titus if given enough of an excuse.

Titus stepped back and laughed. "You don't know what the hell you're talkin' about."

"I know, and so do you. You stopped loving Polly a long time ago. You just *wanted* her, like a spoiled child wants a toy."

"Shut up," Titus growled as he turned away. "I don't have to listen to this."

"No, I don't suppose you do." Mac started down the steps from the porch. "There's your horse at the hitch rack. You know the way home. Just don't talk to me when you get there."

"Maybe I don't want to go home!" Titus called after him.

"Then don't. Go crawl in a hole with a whiskey bottle, for all I care." Mac stalked over to his stallion, jerked the horse's reins free, and swung into the saddle. He turned the stallion and heeled it into a trot that carried him down the street toward the doctor's office. Titus figured Mac intended to stop there and check on Henry.

Fine. Let him do that. The two of them could sit around and congratulate themselves for the way they had found Polly's killer. The way Titus saw it, they didn't have much reason to pat themselves on the back. The whole thing had sounded to him like pure dumb luck as much as anything else.

He stood there for a long moment, the cold wind blowing in his face, then lifted his hand and dragged the back of it across his mouth. Having a drink sounded like a good idea. After being locked up in jail, he was dry. Bone dry . . .

ᏩᏳᏳᎠ

TITUS REINED his horse to a stop then tried to dismount, but his head was spinning too much. He lost his balance as he swung his right leg over the animal's back and tumbled to the ground. Drunk and uncoordinated as he was, he still had the sense to kick his left foot free of the stirrup so that he wouldn't be dragged in case the horse bolted.

The horse danced a few nervous steps to the side but didn't run. Titus lay there on the ground nearby, trying to catch his breath. He realized he had dropped the bottle when he fell. He pawed around on the ground until he found it. The cork was still in the neck, keeping the remaining whiskey from spilling. Thank the Lord for small favors, he thought.

After a while he was able to sit up without feeling too sick. He reached out, caught hold of the stirrup, and used it to pull himself to his feet. The horse shied away again. Titus almost fell. He managed to stay upright. When he was a little steadier on his feet, he pulled the cork with his teeth, spat it out, and tilted the bottle to his mouth. The last few swallows gurgled down his throat. When the bottle was empty, he tossed it aside.

Swaying a little, he turned and squinted into the darkness. He saw some floating blobs of yellow and started toward them. After a few steps, the blobs resolved themselves into lighted windows in a house. When he came still closer, he could make out the white columns of the portico and the balcony that over-hung it. His feet rasped in the gravel of the drive that circled in front of the house.

He had come back to Mountain Laurel.

His first stop after leaving the courthouse had been the tavern in Culpeper. Word had gotten around town already that he had been exonerated of Polly's murder. When he came into the tavern, he had been greeted warmly by many of the patrons. At one time they had been his cronies, and they seemed to have forgotten that only a few days earlier they had been in the mob that came to the jail, intent on hanging him. Now they were ready to be his friends again. Plenty of backslapping went on, along with drunken declarations that they had known all along he was innocent, and Titus's hand was never without a drink for very long.

He took the drinks but wasn't fooled by the camaraderie. All these bastards had been eager to condemn him when they thought he was guilty; not a one of them had given him the benefit of the doubt. To hell with all of them, he thought. And to hell with him, too.

The bottle had been a gift from the tavern owner as Titus staggered out of the place. He hadn't known for sure where he was going when he rode off. Mac had said that he could come back home, but that didn't sound very appealing at the moment. Louisa was the only one there who seemed to care what happened to him. The rest of them would find some way to blame Polly's death on him, even though Quinn had admitted that he had killed her. Mac had started to blame him already, saying that the murder might not have happened if he had just gone along with what Polly and Henry wanted.

So he had turned his horse toward Mountain Laurel instead. Duncan Ebersole was a son of a bitch, and Titus hated Ebersole as much as Ebersole hated him. But now they had something in common. They both hated the Brannon family.

Titus tripped and went sprawling in a flower bed as he approached the house. Since it was winter, the flower bed was empty. He scrabbled in the dirt for a minute before he found enough purchase to push himself back to his feet. Then he stumbled on toward the lighted windows, skirting the portico and staggering along the side of the house.

He wasn't sure, but he thought those windows were in the library. The room where Polly had died so needlessly. Titus wasn't sure he could stand to look in there. He wasn't sure if he wanted to talk to Ebersole. It might be enough just to stand outside the window and look in at the scene of the tragedy. Whatever compulsion had drawn him here might be satisfied by that self-torture.

Titus came up to the closest lighted window and peered through the glass, resting his splayed hands against the wall on either side of it. The drapes were drawn back so that he could see clearly into the illuminated room. It was the library, just as he had thought. Ebersole's elaborate desk was to the left, the fireplace straight ahead. From his vantage point, Titus couldn't see behind the desk. He didn't know if Ebersole was somewhere in the room. He didn't care. His eyes were drawn to the grand portrait that hung above the fireplace. The details of the image were blurry, either because of the glass or his own diminished eyesight, but after a moment his vision seemed to clear. The portrait was a new one.

It was a painting of Polly!

His heart broke as he looked at the perfect rendering of her fair-haired beauty. Tears sprang to his eyes and rolled down his cheeks, and his vision blurred again. He pawed away the tears and looked again and saw to his shock that the portrait had changed. It wasn't Polly at all. The painting was of her mother, Ebersole's wife, and Titus had seen it many times before when he lived here on the plantation. Before his horrified eyes, it changed again, and once more he was staring at Polly. Then again . . . He had been aware that there was a strong resemblance between Polly and her mother, but he had never known the woman and hadn't realized they had looked so much alike. Of course, they hadn't when Polly's mother died, because Polly had been just a child. But as she grew, the resemblance became stronger and stronger . . . until now, as he stared at the portrait, Titus wasn't sure who he was looking at.

Then, from the corner of his eye, he saw Ebersole stumbling toward the fireplace. The planter must have been at the desk, but now he had gotten up to approach the portrait. Judging by his unsteady gait, he was as drunk as Titus. They were a fine pair, Titus thought, and it was all he could do not to laugh out loud. Yes, he and Duncan Ebersole were just alike, spreading misery everywhere they went.

As Titus watched, Ebersole fell to his knees in front of the fireplace. He lifted his arms as if he were reaching up to the woman in the portrait, whoever she was. "My God, my God, I'm so sorry!" he wailed the words so loud that Titus could understand them outside. "I never meant t' hurt ye, my darlin', I swear! I never meant for any of it t' happen!" Then he collapsed on the hearth and lay there sobbing.

Titus backed away from the window, sickness in his belly. He didn't know if the sickness was caused by the whiskey or the revulsion he felt toward Ebersole . . . or the revulsion he felt toward himself. All he knew was that he had to get away from here, away from this . . . unclean . . . place. There was nothing here for him anymore.

In truth, there never had been. But like everything else in his life, he hadn't known that until it was too late . . .

Chapter Twelve

SPRING RETURNED TO VIRGINIA as it did each year, bringing with it blue, sunny skies and warm winds that dried the roads, made buds pop out on the trees, and called the shoots of flowers up from the ground. The lifeblood of the earth, dormant since the previous autumn, began to flow again, and in its vitality, Virginia seemed to be born anew.

Along with the flowers, Gen. Ulysses S. Grant came to Virginia in the spring of 1864. Following his victories at Vicksburg and Chattanooga, in March Grant was elevated by President Abraham Lincoln to overall command of all the Union armies. Gen. George Gordon Meade, who had defeated Lee at Gettysburg but failed to follow up on that victory, remained in command of the Army of the Potomac in its winter quarters at Brandy Station, Virginia, but from now on, Meade would be directed by Grant in the field, an arrangement to which the normally irritable Meade was surprisingly agreeable.

All winter, the great beast that was the Army of the Potomac, more than one hundred thousand men strong, had hibernated in its lair north of the Rapidan River. Now the beast was stirring. Supply wagons were brought up and parked in the rear of the winter camp, ready to follow the army when it renewed the advance toward Richmond. Pontoon boats were hammered together by engineers; when the time came for the army to cross the Rapidan, these boats would support the planks of the temporary bridges needed to ford the river. It was obvious to the interested observers on the southern side of the river that the Yankees were getting ready to move. Exactly where and exactly when remained open questions.

On the Brannon farm, life had returned somewhat to normal following the death of Israel Quinn. Henry had shouldered his grief over losing Polly and their child and worked long hours on the farm, getting the fields ready for the spring planting even though the crop was expected to be poor. His job as sheriff took little of his time, as Judge Darden had promised. Abigail and Cordelia prepared to plant a vegetable garden near the house; the garden would have to feed the family, because there would be little else. Louisa Abernathy, who came from a farming family in Illinois, pitched in to help. She had nothing else to occupy her days. Titus showed up at the farm from time to time, but his visits were like those of a skulking animal: fleeting and usually at night. The family heard about Titus, even though they rarely saw him. He drank heavily at the tavern in Culpeper, sometimes passing out there, and he had been involved in more than one brawl with some of the other veterans who had returned from the war maimed in body, spirit, or both.

Mac had returned to Wigwam, the camp in which Stuart's cavalry spent the winter months resting men and horses, putting on reviews, and even staging elaborate pageants to keep the general and his entourage of admiring lady friends entertained. Stuart's flirtations were strictly platonic, but he constantly surrounded himself with highborn Southern belles, a fact that had to be annoying to his wife, Flora, who also spent much of the winter at the cavalry camp.

Will Brannon, still recuperating from his wound, remained on the farm, as did his lady friend, Dorothy Chamberlain, though he had told her that she could return to Richmond anytime she wanted. Dorothy insisted on remaining with him until he no longer needed her. To tell the truth, Will was glad she ignored his suggestion. He greatly enjoyed her company and even suspected that he had fallen in love with her. He wanted to spend as much time with her as he could.

But their time together was running out, as he knew even if she did not.

Finally, a nagging sense of honor compelled him to discuss the situation with her. They took Dorothy's buggy and drove over to Dobie's Run, an idyllic little creek that meandered through the Brannon property. Will handled the reins himself, telling Roman to stay behind at the farmhouse.

"You forget, Cap'n, I'm a free man now," Roman said with a grin. "You can't order me around no more."

"I most certainly can," Will insisted. "You were carried on the rolls of the Thirty-third Virginia as my civilian aide, remember? As such, you're still under my command even though I'm temporarily detached from the regiment." Will returned the young man's grin. "And my orders to you are to stay here and help spade up that garden patch."

"Yes sir," Roman said with a sigh. "I might've known you'd be stubborn about this."

Will clapped a hand on his shoulder. "We'll have a game of chess when I get back, all right?"

"Yes sir!"

Dorothy was surprised when she came out onto the porch and found Will at the reins. "Where's Roman?" she asked.

"He's needed here more," Will said as he hopped down from the driver's seat. "I can handle this horse just fine."

"Are you sure you're strong enough?"

Will grinned again and thumped a fist against his chest. "What do you mean? I'm as strong as an ox. I ought to be, the way you've been taking care of me for the past eight months."

"All right," Dorothy conceded, sounding a little doubtful. "But when you asked me to go for a ride with you, I thought Roman would be coming along. Can I trust an unchaperoned Capt. William Shakespeare Brannon?"

"I'm the very soul of propriety, ma'am."

"I'll hold you to that . . . maybe," she relied with a laugh and climbed into the buggy with Will's assistance.

As he stepped up onto the seat, he told himself that he hadn't lied to her. He *was* stronger. Maybe not as strong as before, but he had gained back most of the weight he'd lost during his convalescence, he slept well most nights, and the pains in his chest, though they still came from time to time, weren't as intense as they had been. He was no doctor, but he knew his own capabilities, and in his opinion, he was fit for duty again.

That was what he had to tell Dorothy today, and he was dreading it more than he had many of the battles he had faced.

The path that led to Dobie's Run was barely wide enough for the buggy. As he drove along it, Will remembered all the times he had tramped over this same ground with a fishing pole on his shoulder and a bucket of worms in his hand. He had hooked many a fish out of the creek since he'd first gone there as a small boy with his father. He remembered sitting on the grassy bank and dangling his bare toes in the slowly moving water while his father recited lines from the bard's plays.

"'A man may fish with the worm that hath eat of a king, and eat of the fish that hath fed of that worm.' That's from Hamlet, lad."

"Yeah, Pa, I know, but don't it scare the fish off when you talk too much?"

Even now, Will seemed to hear John Brannon's hearty laughter echoing on the wind.

As time passed, he had gone fishing in the creek with his brothers, first Mac then Titus and Cory and Henry, each joining in their turn. Mac, bless his heart, had a hard time not throwing back the fish he caught. He would have let them all go if it was up to him. Titus had taken to it just like he had taken to hunting, though he never was as good a fisherman as he was a hunter. Will thought it had something to do with patience or the lack thereof. Titus didn't mind hunkering in the brush for hours on end, a rifle in his hands, waiting for just the right shot, but drowsing on a creek bank waiting for a tug on his line was just too peaceful for him. When the fish were biting, Titus could set a hook with a natural jerk of his wrist better than any of his brothers; once a fish was on his line, it hardly ever got away. But when it was slow, Titus generally got bored and left. Cory got bored and impatient easily, too, testimony to his restless nature. Henry had been happy to be around his big brothers and didn't really care whether he caught any fish or not.

Cordelia, now . . . Cordelia had begged to come along, but Titus had flatly refused. He wasn't gonna go fishin' if he had to be saddled with some ol' *girl*. Will smiled as he remembered the way Cordelia had said, "Oh!" and stomped her foot. Cory felt the same way, and Henry went along with them, of course. But later, when the other boys weren't around, Will and Mac had taken Cordelia to the creek and had shown her how to bait a hook and toss it into the water. Will halfway expected her to decide she didn't want to fish after all when it came time to put the worm on the hook, but Cordelia had stuck her tongue out and screwed up her eight-year-old face with determination and jabbed her hook right through the fat, wriggling earthworm. Then she had looked up at Will.

"Do you reckon it hurts him?"

"Maybe some. I don't rightly know what a worm feels or doesn't feel. But I know one reason the good Lord put worms in the earth is so a fish will come along and bite them and get caught by a redheaded little girl."

"Why else did the good Lord put worms in the earth, Will?"

To eat the bodies of the dead.

He hadn't told her that, of course, but even now he recollected that thought meandering through his head when she had asked her innocent question. The worms had had themselves a goddamned feast the past few years, hadn't they? War was good for the worms . . .

"My God, Will, what's wrong?" Dorothy laid a hand on his arm as she spoke. Her face wore an anxious expression. "Are you in pain?"

Will drew a deep breath. Hell, yes, he was in pain, he thought, but for once it wasn't physical. For a time, a very brief time, he had retreated into his memories, and the good ones had been so poignant, had touched such a nerve deep inside him, that the sensations they created were almost too much for him. Then had come thoughts of war, not poignant but horrifying, and again deep inside him something had moved, like the plucking of a string. More like the breaking of a string, because he felt that something had come loose and was slipping away from him and he would never see it, never hold it in his hands again. The sense of loss battered him like an artillery barrage.

"It's nothing," he said. "I'm fine, fine. Just thinking about how, a long time ago, I used to come down here and fish with my father and with my brothers."

"Oh. We're not going fishing today, are we?"

He managed to laugh. "You needn't worry. I didn't bring my pole, or even any bait."

"That's good." She looked around at the trees. Sunlight slanted through branches that were beginning to put on leaves. "It's a lovely day, isn't it?"

"Not half as pretty as you."

She laughed, and he could tell she was pleased. "Why, Captain Brannon, aren't you the gallant today! Please do continue, and you might become as big a flirt as all the papers say General Stuart is."

"Not much of a chance of that. From what Mac tells me, General Stuart is almost always surrounded by beautiful women except when he goes into battle."

"And you're *not* surrounded by beautiful women?"

"Well, there's you . . ."

"Thank you. But what about your mother and sister?"

"Shoot, they don't count."

Dorothy laughed lightly again. "You should be glad that I won't tell them you said that. But you needn't forget your other houseguest, Louisa."

Will frowned. "I reckon these days she's too worried about Titus to even think about being pretty. Although I've noticed that at least she's put on a little weight lately. For a while there she looked like she was going to waste away to nothing."

"It's really not polite to discuss a lady's weight, Captain Brannon," she corrected him.

"I'll try to remember that, Mrs. Chamberlain. I'm just a poor dumb soldier, though. I ain't too awful bright."

Dorothy leaned her head against his shoulder, still laughing. To Will the gesture felt so good that he wished the moment would never end.

A few minutes later, they came to the creek. Dobie's Run twisted along between wooded banks about eight feet high. The stream was ten to fifteen feet wide and in most places no more than five feet deep. A few good swimming holes existed where the depth increased to ten or twelve feet. At one time, Will had known where all of them were. He might be able to find one now if he had to, but those particular memories had faded a bit. He had never liked swimming nearly as much as he did fishing. Anyway, it was still much too cool even to be thinking about jumping into a swimming hole, and besides, he didn't figure Dorothy Chamberlain was the sort of gal who'd go skinny-dipping with a fella who wasn't her husband.

Although that thought, and the images it conjured up, were mighty appealing . . .

Will brought the buggy to a halt and cleared his throat. "Well, here we are."

"What a beautiful spot!" Dorothy exclaimed. "I can see why you love it here, Will."

He stepped to the ground then turned to help her down from the seat. "We can walk along the bank for a ways. There's a path yonder."

Even at this time of year, when many of the branches were still bare, the growth was thick enough to create sun-dappled shade along the banks. Will started to link his arm with Dorothy's as they strolled beside the creek, but she moved somehow so that his hand found hers instead. Their fingers intertwined. That was even better than walking arm in arm, he thought. He squeezed her hand, and she squeezed back. It was amazing how nice a simple thing like that could be.

The stream twisted and turned, and in a few moments, they were out of sight of the buggy. In fact, from where they were when they paused, nothing man-made was visible. The scene was one of pristine beauty. They might as well have been the first two human beings to ever stand here and watch the creek flow gently on its way.

Will turned so that he was facing her and looked down into her eyes. He whispered her name. "Dorothy . . ."

"Yes, Will," she whispered back. He leaned over and brought his lips to hers.

At first it was a chaste kiss, almost one of friendship more than passion. But as the seconds passed, it grew more urgent and their lips worked against each other with growing need. Their hands were still clasped. Will put his other hand on her shoulder and drew her closer to him. When the kiss finally ended, she rested her head against his chest.

"I reckon you shouldn't have trusted me without a chaperone after all," he said when he could talk again. It had taken him a moment to get his breath.

"Perhaps you shouldn't be so trusting of me," she said with a little laugh. "I've become quite fond of you, Captain Brannon. My affections bid fair to get the better of me."

"And me," he murmured.

In the back of his mind, a voice cursed. As pleasurable as this interlude was, he hadn't intended for it to happen. He had brought Dorothy out here to talk to her, not kiss her. In the end, this was just going to make things more difficult . . .

Postponing the bad news would just make it worse, too. He took a deep breath. "Dorothy, we need to talk."

She tipped her head back to look up at him. "I thought that's what we were doing."

"No . . . I mean it. There are some things you have to understand about me."

Dorothy moved back a little, and her hand slipped out of his. He felt a pang of regret as she let go of him. "What are you talking about, Will?"

"Well . . . you know I've been waiting until I was better . . . before I went back to the army . . ."

Her eyes widened in understanding. "No! You're not ready!"

"As ready as I'm going to be," he said. "Like I told you, you've done a good job of helping me recover. I've got my strength back—"

"That's not enough," Dorothy broke in. "You're still in pain. I know it. I've seen the way you sometimes stop what you're doing and wait for it to pass. I've seen you turn pale from the pain, Will. Don't deny that."

He gave a little shrug. "I've never tried to deny anything with you, Dorothy . . . except maybe the way I feel about you. For a long time, I didn't want to admit that, even to myself."

"Will Brannon," she said in a low, dangerous voice, "don't you dare tell me that you're leaving then turn right around and tell me that you love me. You couldn't be that cruel!"

"I never meant to be cruel. Lord, I'd never hurt you—"

"What do you think you're doing right now?"

Will stepped back and turned away from her, unable to meet the look in her eyes. He would have sooner charged the whole damned Yankee army by himself. "I've heard the talk about how the Yankees are getting ready to move across the Rapidan, and when they do, General Lee will have to move to stop them. General Longstreet's corps is in Tennessee, so that leaves Lee with just Generals Ewell and Hill. He's going to need all his officers and every man he can find."

"Stop it!" Dorothy cried. "Don't talk tactics and generals with me, Will. I don't care about any of that."

His voice hardened instinctively. "You don't care about what happens to the Confederacy?"

Her hand came up so fast he couldn't have stopped it even if he had wanted to. It cracked across his face in a slap. "Don't you *ever* accuse me of not caring about the Confederacy!" she said. "My husband *died* for the Confederacy. It hasn't even been a year yet since he fell at Chancellorsville. You were there. Did you see him, Will? Did you see his blood running out and staining the ground?"

"I saw a lot of blood those days. I saw a lot of good men fall. And I've always sympathized with your loss, Dorothy. Surely you know that."

"Then you know why I can't bear to go through it again." The anger left her face abruptly as she reached up to touch his cheek with her fingertips. It was red where she had slapped him. "Oh, Will, I'm sorry."

He caught hold of her hand, pressed it to his lips. "No need to be sorry. I understand. But that doesn't change anything. I have to go back."

"Then please take me back to the farm. I'll be returning to Richmond directly."

"You could stay with the folks here, if you want." He didn't hesitate to make the offer. He knew his mother and the rest of the family liked Dorothy. None of them would mind if she remained on the farm and waited for him.

Dorothy shook her head. "No. I'll go back to the hospital. I can do some good there."

Will forced a smile onto his face. "You'll meet some other wounded, dashing young officer and—"

"No." The word was flat, emphatic. "I'll volunteer and do what I can to help. But what was between us . . . I won't allow that to happen again."

Will took a deep breath. "I'm sorry."

"Don't be. You're doing what you think you have to do." Dorothy looked around, studying the creek and the trees and the grassy banks as if she wanted to memorize them, burn the image into her mind and never forget them. "This is a beautiful spot, and we had a beautiful moment here. That's more than some people get in their entire lives, I suppose."

"I wish it could have been more."

"So do I," she said with a sad smile. "So do I."

HENRY WAS waiting for them when they got back to the house. As soon as Will saw the expression on his face, he knew that something was wrong. He brought the buggy horse to a stop and dropped from the seat to the ground.

"What is it?" Will asked.

"Grant's in Culpeper."

The tone of disbelief and dread in Henry's voice made it plain how much the news had affected him. "In *Culpeper!* You know this for a fact, Henry?" his brother asked.

"I saw the son of a—I saw him for myself. I was in the courthouse this morning when I heard some commotion outside. Men running and yelling in the street. I stepped out onto the porch in time to see Federal troops marching into town. No one could miss those blue uniforms."

Will's face was grim. "What else did you see."

Henry shrugged. "I leaned back into the doorway so they wouldn't notice me. That's when I saw Grant himself ride in with all his staff around him. They stopped at one of the houses and went inside like they owned the place." Henry paused then went on bitterly, "I reckon they do now. It was pretty plain they were going to commandeer the house, probably use it as headquarters for Grant."

Will was shaken by the news, but he tried to keep his head clear and think about what it might mean. "I suppose the troops went on and occupied the rest of the town."

Henry nodded. "I suppose. I can't say for sure because I slipped out the back door of the courthouse and got out of there as fast as I could. I didn't want them taking me prisoner, like they did Titus."

"They wouldn't have taken you prisoner," Will said with a shake of his head. "You're a civilian. They would have just confiscated your gun and made you sign a parole."

"It's a good thing they didn't try it." Henry sighed. "Well, so much for being sheriff. I reckon Culpeper's under martial law now. Federal martial law."

Will nodded. "That's right. I'll have to steer clear of there while I'm still here."

Henry looked sharply at him. "While you're still here? What's that mean?"

Dorothy answered the question before Will could. "Your brother is going back to the war, Henry."

"Yeah? This time you'll be taking me with you, Will."

Will shook his head again. "No, Henry. Somebody's got to stay here—"

"Damn it, Will!" Henry glanced at Dorothy and added, "Beg your pardon, Mrs. Chamberlain," then hurried on before Will could interrupt him. "You've been using that argument on me for three years now. Somebody's got to stay and take care of Ma and Cordelia and the farm. Well, why can't it be you this time?"

Will didn't say anything, and after a moment Dorothy asked, "Yes, Will, why not? You've given enough to the cause."

"The cause your husband died for," Will said. He saw the flare of pain in Dorothy's eyes and regretted it, but the words had to be said.

"Then perhaps *I've* given enough," Dorothy said. "You could look at it that way."

Will shook his head, his stubborn nature coming to the fore. "I'm an officer in the Army of Northern Virginia. I have a duty to my men and my country." He looked at Henry. "And you have a duty to your family."

"My family's not all here, remember? My wife and my child are gone." Henry's voice shook. "There's nothing to hold me here anymore. Not enough, anyway."

Anger welled up inside Will, and his hands shot out and gripped Henry's shoulders. He was a couple of inches taller than his brother. His eyes were blazing as he looked down at Henry.

"Don't you say that! I'm sorry as hell for what you lost, Henry. You know that. But Ma's still here, and Cordelia's still here, and by God, the Brannon land is still here! If that's not enough to stay and take care of, then . . . then stay for Dobie's Run!"

Henry stared at him, utterly confused now. "What?"

Will tilted his head in the direction of the creek. "Stay here because once upon a time a bunch of boys meandered down yonder and went fishing. And because of the times we took a watermelon out of the field and went down to the creek and busted it open and ate the whole thing. And because we chased fireflies in the fields between here and there on a bunch of summer nights, just before it got good and dark. And because this is our home, Henry, and somebody's got to take care of it and Ma and Cordelia . . ." Will's voice choked off, and he became aware that his cheeks were wet. He was crying. How about that, he thought. He was crying.

His hands were still on Henry's shoulders. Will didn't resist as Henry pushed them aside. Then Henry stepped forward and put his arms around Will and held on to him. "All right," Henry said, his own voice thick with emotion. "I'll stay. I can't fight the whole blamed Yankee army by myself, but I can see to it that Ma and Cordelia are safe."

Will nodded. "Thank you. Thank you, Henry."

A hand touched him gently on the shoulder. He stepped back from Henry and turned to see that Dorothy had climbed down from the buggy and come up behind him.

"Will," she said. "You could stay and help Henry take care of your family and the farm."

He shook his head. "For all the reasons I told him he had to stay . . . those are the reasons I have to go."

She leaned closer to him, and the smell of her hair touched his nose. "But can you win?" she asked in a whisper. "Is there even any hope anymore?"

"There's always hope," Will told her. "And even if there's not, it doesn't really matter anymore. We can't give up."

Not as long as there were fireflies and watermelons and fish that jumped in the creek, sending droplets of water shimmering in the air before plunging below the surface once more.

Chapter Thirteen

By THE END OF April 1864 everyone on both sides of the conflict knew it was only a matter of time before the Yankees began to move. The Army of Northern Virginia had not yet fully recovered from its staggering defeat at Gettysburg the previous summer. Indeed, there was every likelihood it would never regain its full strength. Depleted in manpower and supplies, the only thing the Confederates still had in full measure was spirit. Though some of the men might harbor the belief that the army had suffered a blow from which it could not bounce back, most were still devoted to the cause and to Robert E. Lee. They might be outnumbered, outgunned, and outprovisioned, but Marse Robert would find a way to whip those dastardly Yankees anyway.

Back with his company in the Thirty-third Virginia, Will Brannon wanted to believe that was true. Wanting to and actually believing it, though, were two different things.

Will's men had greeted his return with cheers. A lieutenant named Harrison had commanded the company during Will's absence and had kept the men in good order, but he didn't mind turning them back over to Will. One of the corporals, Lloyd Grady, had been promoted to sergeant to take the place of Darcy Bennett, who had been killed during the fighting on the second day at Gettysburg. Will knew that Harrison and Grady were competent men, so the company had been in capable hands while he was gone. Still, it felt good to be back—most of the time, anyway. He found himself haunted by memories of the look on Dorothy Chamberlain's face as she rode off in her buggy with Roman at the reins. Roman had seen to it that she got back safely to Richmond, then he returned to the Brannon farm and accompanied Will to army headquarters at Orange Court House. There was no way Will was going back to the Thirty-third Virginia without his civilian aide, Roman declared, and Will didn't waste time and energy arguing with him.

Will was disappointed as well that Mac was nowhere around. Gen. Fitzhugh Lee had taken his division of cavalry, including Mac, and set off toward Fredericksburg on a foraging expedition. The long winter had left supplies dangerously low, especially grain for the horses. The cavalry would be on the move nearly all the time once hostilities commenced again, so there would be no time for leisurely grazing.

Nerves grew more taut as the first week of May arrived and still there was no movement from the Union army. Confederate scouts kept an eye on the Rapidan at all times from their signal posts on Clark's Mountain. On the morning of May 2, Gen. Robert E. Lee and his field commanders met at the station, where Lee declared his belief that the Yankees would soon move across the river at Germanna Ford, Ely's Ford, or both places. Two days later, on May 4, Lee's prediction came true. Confederate observers signaled to Orange Court House that the Yankees were moving up their artillery and supply trains at both fords. That was a sure sign Grant was ready to move at last.

Along with the other junior officers, Will had been filled in on the plan devised by General Lee. Grant's objective was believed to be Richmond itself. In addition to the advance across the Rapidan, additional Federal forces under the command of Gen. Benjamin F. Butler were on the James River peninsula southeast of the capital city, and it was thought that Grant and Butler might try to carry out a pincer movement, menacing Richmond from two sides at once. Butler's force, however, was too small to pose any serious threat by itself, so if Grant could be stopped, the Union plan would be thwarted.

To reach Richmond, the Army of the Potomac would have to move both south and east. This route would take the Yankees through an area known as the Wilderness.

Running for some fifteen miles east and west and ten miles from north to south, the Wilderness more than lived up to its name. It was an area of thick forest and tangled undergrowth. The trees grew so close together that in places a man could scarcely pass between the trunks. Not only that, but what gaps there were between the trees were clogged with brush and thronged with thorny vines that clung and clawed at anyone who attempted to push through them. Three east-west roads had been cut through the Wilderness, but only one major road ran north and south. And that was the road the Federal troops would have to take. None of these roads would ever be mistaken for major thoroughfares. They were narrow, twisting, and so over-hung with trees that much of the sunlight was blocked and a state of perpetual twilight existed along them.

Will was familiar with the Wilderness. A year earlier, the Yankee army, then commanded by Gen. Joseph Hooker, had tried to advance through the area. Lee had taken the risk of dividing his army to counter Hooker's advance. Stonewall Jackson's corps—Will and the Thirty-third Virginia among them—had swung around and fallen upon Hooker's flank in the battle of Chancellorsville, which had resulted in a smashing Confederate victory. That triumph had been tempered by the bitter loss of Jackson himself, shot down by his own men who mistook him and his companions for Yankee cavalry during a nighttime reconnoiter. Will and Mac had been there when the general was wounded. Many times since then, Will had thought of how different things might have been if Jackson had lived. Jackson had seemed to bring out the best and the most daring in Lee, and if old Stonewall had been at Gettysburg, everything might have been different, including the outcome.

Such speculation was futile, though, and Will well knew that. The Army of Northern Virginia had to deal with things as they were, and that meant stopping Grant from advancing on Richmond. Grant knew how strongly entrenched the Confederates were along the Rapidan. He had tried to overwhelm such defenses before, at Vicksburg, but the attempt had failed and he had been forced to starve the city into submission. Here there was no such option. Grant had to bottle up the Confederates, and he expected to do that by moving on Richmond. If Lee did as Grant expected, the Army of Northern Virginia would have to move south as well and try to get between the Federals and Confederate capital. Then the fight would be on ground more of Grant's choosing.

Lee, however, still had within him the capacity for doing the unexpected. He decided not to wait but to attack the Union army while it was making its way through the Wilderness. Lee would dash east, not south, and strike the Federal right flank.

It seemed like a sound plan to Will. The Yankees would be thinking of the Wilderness merely as an obstacle in their path and would be trying to get through it as fast as possible so they could push on toward Richmond. They wouldn't be expecting trouble just yet. To their way of thinking, no sane man would try to fight a battle in that tangle of brush.

They would soon learn how wrong they were.

THE HORSE Will had ridden during the first couple of years of the war, a sturdy lineback dun, was long gone, lost in the chaos of Gettysburg after his rider had been shot off his back. Will's mount now was a chestnut gelding, a better-looking horse than the dun perhaps, but Will sensed that it was skittish and lacked the stamina of the other horse. Still, he was lucky to have a mount, and he knew it. Good horseflesh was yet one more thing the Confederate army found in short supply.

Late in the morning of May 4, he mounted up and called for Sergeant Grady to have the company fall in. When the men were arrayed in their usual ranks, Will rode past and carried out a perfunctory review, looking them over, noting familiar faces as well as a few new ones. The men were skinny, many to the point of gauntness, and only the most charitable could call their mismatched clothing uniforms. Many were barefoot. But their rifles were well cared for, and in their eyes shone an eagerness for battle. Gettysburg had not broken their spirit.

"Move out!" Will commanded when the orders shot down the line. These men who had marched under Stonewall Jackson, known in their own time as the general's foot cavalry, stepped off smartly. Will stifled a proud grin; officers had to maintain a certain demeanor. But that sense of detachment was hard to come by when one was going into battle with such magnificent fighting men as these, veterans proven in the Shenandoah and at Manassas, the Seven Days', Antietam, Fredericksburg, Chancellorsville, and ultimately Gettysburg.

Their route lay along the Orange Turnpike, which ran from Orange Court House, site of the winter camp, eastward through the Wilderness to Chancellorsville and eventually to Fredericksburg on the Rappahannock. The Germanna Plank Road, which ran down from Germanna Ford on the Rapidan, crossed the turnpike near a tiny settlement called Wilderness Tavern. The Yankees were reported to be crossing the river at Germanna and Ely's Fords. Their supply trains were visible to Confederate observers south of the Rapidan, and they ran for miles and miles in the rear of the Yankee columns until they vanished in the distance. It was possibly the largest army that ever marched on the North American continent.

The mutual advance of the armies would become a race, Will thought as he rode alongside his briskly marching company. They had to hit the Federals while the Yankees were still in the Wilderness. The intersection of the turnpike and the Germanna Plank Road would be a good spot to do just that.

Gen. Richard Ewell's Second Corps followed the turnpike while Third Corps, under Gen. A. P. Hill—and accompanied by Robert E. Lee himself—proceeded east along the Orange Plank Road, which looped to the south but still ran roughly parallel to the turnpike across most of the Wilderness before eventually rejoining it. James Longstreet's First Corps, now returned from Tennessee and reunited with the Army of Northern Virginia, had been camped at Gordonsville, a good distance to the southwest. Lee had sent word to Longstreet—Old Pete, as he was fondly known—to come up with all speed and join the Confederate maneuver.

Longstreet remained Lee's most trusted subordinate despite their disagreement over tactics at Gettysburg. Longstreet's desire to flank Meade's line, once they were dug in atop Cemetery Ridge, had gone unheeded by Lee. In the end, there was a theoretical probability that Longstreet's proposal would have been a more successful tactic than Lee's stubborn insistence on a frontal attack; at least, Longstreet's idea could not have been any more disastrous than Lee's had been. Then Longstreet had applied the strategy to his attack on Knoxville and seen for himself that it would have made little difference in Pennsylvania. Meanwhile, the two men still respected and trusted each other, and Lee did not want to open this battle with the Yankees until Longstreet's men were in position to take part.

So on this day in early May, there were five large groups in motion, all converging on the Wilderness: three corps of Confederates and two separate columns of Federals that had crossed the Rapidan and were following the Germanna Plank Road and the Brock Road, respectively. The Yankee column on the Germanna Plank Road was the larger of the two, but most of the supply wagons were with the smaller column to the east.

Will didn't know the details of the Union army's movements. He knew only that his men were moving along the turnpike at a good pace. During the afternoon, they left the rolling fields behind and entered the tangle of the Wilderness itself. Thickets closed in on both sides of the road, bringing an atmosphere of gloom and menace. The officers kept the men moving briskly, but some of the jauntiness, the eagerness for battle, had gone out of their step. That was the inevitable effect of the Wilderness. After a mile or two, the men began to feel hemmed in, as if at any second, the briars and brambles would reach out and grab them, pulling them into the dark maw of the woods to be devoured. Will knew the men had to feel that way, because he experienced those sensations himself.

In addition to that feeling of pride, he was doing pretty well physically. He had felt only a few minor twinges of pain during the past few days. For a moment he had wished that Dorothy could see him now so that she would realize he was all right. Then he changed his mind, knowing that he wouldn't have wanted Dorothy anywhere near here. She was better off in Richmond, though the city might find itself in danger sooner or later if the Yankees penetrated Lee's line.

All the more reason to stop them here and now, he thought.

But not on this day. Orders came along the line to halt and make camp for the night. A part of Will had hoped that they would run into the Yankees today and get it over with. Waiting to fight was in some ways harder than the battles themselves. The longer the fighting was postponed, the more chance the army's readiness for battle might drain away.

Men camped in the road itself and along its edges. Some of them made their way a short distance into the woods and settled down there. Will found a tiny open space just at the edge of the forest and was about to unsaddle his horse when Roman came hurrying up.

"Let me do that for you, Cap'n Will," the young man offered.

Will nodded and stepped back. As his aide, one of Roman's duties was to care for his horse. Other officers had slaves doing the same sort of thing for them. Will was glad no one could accuse him of that. Roman was a free man and was here because he wanted to be.

Once the horse had been tended to, Roman built a tiny fire and put a pot of grain coffee on to boil. Will had some hardtack and salted meat in his saddlebags. That would be their supper.

While Roman prepared the meal, Will walked up and down the road and checked on the men of his company. When he was satisfied that all of them had found suitable campsites for the night, he returned to the fire where Roman had the coffee ready.

Roman broke out the chessboard when the meal was over and he had cleaned their utensils. He had carved the board himself, along with the chess pieces he set out after balancing the board on the remains of a small stump. Both men filled their pipes and smoked as they resumed their game.

This contest had been going on for several days. They were evenly matched. Both Will and Roman recalled how the board had been arranged when they suspended play the day before, so it was easy to resume the match again. Will had the next move. He considered the situation for a few minutes then moved his only remaining knight. He had lost the other one a couple of days earlier.

"You're a brave man, Cap'n," Roman said with a grin, and Will knew he had made a bad play. That was confirmed a second later when Roman made a sweeping move with a rook and took the knight. Will looked for a way to take Roman's rook in turn, so that it would look like he had planned the whole thing, but that was impossible. All he could do was shift a pawn to forestall Roman's next move, which would have threatened Will's queen.

The evening passed pleasantly, and Will barely was aware of the ache in his chest. It was slight enough that he was able to ignore it. The chessboard and pieces had to be put away with the game still unresolved when word came that all officers were being summoned to a meeting with Brig. Gen. James A. Walker, the commander of the Stonewall Brigade.

Walker reported that because of the thickness of the vegetation, the scouts weren't exactly sure where the Yankees were. It was certain, though, that the Federals were still somewhere ahead, that they had not gotten out of the Wilderness before the Confederates could attack. "With all this blasted brush around us," Walker complained, "there's blessed little the cavalry can do about finding the enemy. Stuart was to be our eyes, but those eyes are blinded temporarily."

No mention was made of waiting to give the scouts more time to discover the Yankees. There was no time. Any delay might let the Union army slip away, and if that happened, Grant would have an open road to Richmond.

⟨≈≈≈⟩

WHEN WILL awoke the next morning, he was tired and short of breath, but a hurried breakfast made him feel a little better. He was back in the saddle not long after sunup, leading his men along the Orange Turnpike.

Roman strode along easily beside Will's horse. He began to whistle, and the tune was soon taken up by the men nearest to him in the ranks. From them it spread to others until it seemed as if the whole company were whistling. Will gave up trying not to grin as he looked out over his men. Some of them waved at him, and he waved back. His own aches and pains were forgotten. These boys had suffered through a hard winter, and spring had brought little if any relief. Yet they were in fine spirits this morning and looked like they could march all day and still kick Ulysses S. Grant clear back to Illinois, where he had come from.

A sudden rattle of rifle fire interrupted the whistling, and Will jerked his head toward the front. Skirmishers were in action up there, and not far ahead, either. No orders came to halt the march, so Will waved the company ahead. "Keep going, boys, until somebody tells you to stop," he called out.

He rode ahead to get some sense of what was going on. They had to be close to the Germanna Road, Will knew, which meant that the front of the Confederate column might have collided smack-dab into the right flank of the Union column. That would account for the gunfire.

The turnpike had been clogged with men to start with, and the crowding got worse as Will advanced. He saw men spreading out into the woods on both sides of the road as well. Their progress was slow because of the thickness of the vegetation. Men were bloodied without even coming under fire as the briars clawed and scratched at them.

He came upon a conference at the edge of the road between General Walker and the colonels who commanded the five regiments of the Stonewall Brigade. He sat his horse and listened intently as Walker explained that skirmishers had encountered Yankee skirmishers, just as Will had thought to be the case.

"General Ewell immediately sent word of the encounter to General Lee," Walker said, "and General Lee's orders were to establish our position here and hold it, advancing only when we heard the sounds of battle drawing even with us on the Orange Plank Road."

Will understood what Walker meant. General Lee wanted the two corps on the Orange Turnpike and the Orange Plank Road to advance in tandem. He also knew that Lee wanted to wait for Longstreet's corps to be in position before engaging in battle with the Yankees.

Lee might not have the chance to proceed so deliberately, however. Walker's briefing continued: "That was all well and good, but then the blasted Yankees turned and attacked *us!*"

That took Will by surprise. He had supposed the Federals would make a run to the south when they were attacked, trying to get out of the Wilderness without having to fight a battle. Instead, the Yankees were bringing the fight to them. The sounds of firing increased. Now they were only a couple of hundred yards away. The turnpike went around a bend up ahead, so Will couldn't see the action from where he was, but he could imagine knots of struggling men filling the road and spilling off into the woods on either side.

"Move your men up as fast as you can," Walker snapped to his officers. "They've already pushed us back some. We have to stiffen our lines."

Will didn't wait for the order to pass through the chain of command, since he had heard it for himself. He wheeled the chestnut and galloped back to his company.

The old familiar excitement coursed through him. Ten months had passed since he had last gone into battle, but the feeling was the same, a mixture of fear, anticipation, and anger. As he came in sight of his men, he waved them ahead.

"Forward, boys, forward! As fast as you can! Go through the trees if you have to, but get to the front and hold the Yankees!"

Roman was waiting at the side of the road. Will swung down from the saddle and pressed the reins into the young man's hand. A battle like this couldn't be fought from horseback.

"Stay back and hang on to the horse," Will told him, pulling his saber from its brass scabbard and then drawing his pistol.

"Cap'n, you best stay back, too—" Roman began, but he stopped short when he saw the look on Will's face. Nothing was going to keep Will Brannon out of this fight.

He paused long enough, though, to give Roman a smile and a reassuring nod. "Don't worry. I'll be fine."

With that, he turned and plunged toward the front lines along with his men.

He hadn't gone ten yards before the press of soldiers in the road forced him toward the forest. The thickets came almost to the edge of the roadway. Will stayed out of the trees as much as he could, but after a while he had to hack his way through the underbrush. Thorns snagged on his coat and trousers, and some of them penetrated the cloth to stab into his flesh. It was annoying as hell, not to mention painful, but the worst part was the way the brush slowed him down. He could hear the fighting just ahead of him; at least it sounded that close. But he couldn't seem to reach it. The undergrowth fought him like a thing alive. He slashed at the vines and brambles with his saber, making the blade sticky with the juices of the plants, rather than the blood of the enemy.

Suddenly, no more than ten feet in front of him, a bizarrely garbed figure burst into view. The man's uniform included baggy, bright blue trousers, an ornate blue jacket, a brilliant red sash, and a garish red cap. His jacket was decorated with gold stitching that glistened even in the thick gloom under the trees. Will had seen Zouave getups like this before. This Yankee soldier was from one of the volunteer brigades of New York and Pennsylvania that had adopted the outlandish uniforms styled after those worn by native North African troops who had fought for the French several decades ago. The stylish clothing didn't mean the Zouaves weren't good fighting men, though. Will knew they had acquitted themselves well in numerous battles.

So he didn't waste any time dealing with this one. Only a split second passed, just long enough for Will to recognize the man as a Yankee, before the pistol in Will's hand roared.

The Zouave was lifting his rifle. He never finished the move. Will's bullet smashed into his chest and knocked him backward. He bounced off the slender trunk of a tree then pitched forward. The man's red cap landed in a bush, caught there by the briars.

Will stepped past the fallen man. He could hear noises in the brush all around him, but he couldn't see anyone. An eerie feeling washed over him. He was in the middle of a battle. Tens of thousands of men were crowded into these woods. And yet it was as if he were alone.

Not for long, however. Another Yankee came out of the brush to his left, this one in a regular army uniform. The man lunged forward, aiming his bayonet at Will's midsection. Will swung his saber, steel clashing against steel. His wrist was strong enough that he parried the bayonet thrust, turning it aside as the Yankee's momentum carried him forward and brought him within reach of Will's other hand. Will smashed the pistol against the man's nose, pulping it. Blood spurted over the lower half of the Yankee's face. He stumbled and fell, stunned. Will thrust his sword into the man's back, shoving the blade all the way through his body into the loamy earth before jerking it free again.

Screams and shouts and gunfire filled the air. Bullets whistled past Will's head and clipped branches from the trees. There was no way of knowing if that lead was Federal or Confederate—not that it made a difference. A man laid low by one of those bullets died no matter who had fired it.

Will pushed on, cutting a path through the brambles. He broke out unexpectedly into a small clearing and found three Yankees bayoneting a lone Confederate soldier. Will caught a glimpse of the man's face and recognized the lieutenant who had commanded the company during his absence. Harrison's young face contorted in agony. Blood gushed out of his mouth as he was shoved back and forth, impaled on all three bayonets.

Those Yankees were damn fools, Will thought fleetingly as he leaped to the attack. One bayonet would have been enough to kill Harrison. This way, all three men were occupied and couldn't turn to meet the new threat fast enough.

Will's saber slashed into one man's neck, biting so deep that the blade hit the upper part of the Yankee's spine. At the same time, a shot from Will's pistol blasted another man's skull and sent brains and bone fragments flying into the air. That left the third man, and he reacted to the attack by shoving the dying Lieutenant Harrison into Will's path. Will stumbled as Harrison sagged against him. He tried desperately to push the dying man aside, but before he could do so, the Yankee had pulled his bayonet free and jerked the rifle up. He fired over Harrison's shoulder, almost point-blank in Will's face.

The report was both blinding and deafening. Something tore at Will's ear. The pain made him realize that the Yankee's shot had missed, just grazing his ear instead of blowing his brains out as the man had intended. A laugh pealed from Will's throat as he finally succeeded in hauling Harrison out of the way. The Yankee was trying frantically to reload as Will chopped at his throat with the saber. The man got the barrel of his rifle in the way just in time, knocking the blade aside at the last instant. Will shot him in the chest in the next second, knocking the man back off his feet. Cold steel would have been more satisfying, but hot lead did just as well.

Will hesitated before charging on through the brush. He dropped to a knee beside Harrison. The lieutenant was still breathing raggedly, but a grotesque rattle in his throat as Will knelt beside him signaled his final breath. His widely staring eyes turned glassy.

"Sorry, son," Will muttered. He got to his feet and went on, looking for more of the enemy to kill. His heart thundered in his chest, and blood roared in his head like a mighty river.

Chapter Fourteen

O H, MY LORD, Cap'n Will!" Roman exclaimed when he saw the blood covering Will's face. "What happened to you? How bad you hurt?"

"Don't worry, Roman," Will replied. "Some of this blood isn't mine. The part that is came from scratches, nothing more."

In truth, Will looked like he had tangled with a mountain lion. His face was covered with scratches and scrapes and gashes from the undergrowth that gave the Wilderness its name. His ear still bled from where the bullet had grazed it, but other than that, he was uninjured.

Firing was still going on at midday, but at a much more desultory rate than earlier in the morning. The Confederates had given ground before the Yankees' initial rush down the turn-pike, but their counterassault had regained—at length and at great cost—what had been lost so quickly early on. Now the Confederate front line was dug in along the eastern edge of a clearing that straddled the turnpike. The field was covered with brambles, and large sections of it had burned during the fighting as fires that had caught in the woods from exploding powder spread to the clearing as well.

The harsh tang of wood smoke still stung Will's nose. More fires burned in the thickets. It was a common thing during a battle to hear the screams of wounded men, sometimes so many and so loud that they practically drowned out the rattle of mus-ketry and the roar of artillery. Today the wounded were scream-ing not only from pain but from a mortal terror of being burned alive. Will wished he could help every one of them, but that was impossible. He tried to ignore the gut-wrenching cries instead.

That was damned near impossible, too.

He had rounded up as much of his company as he could find, herded them into position along the Confederate front line, and

ordered them to dig in and not give an inch. They found whatever cover they could behind trees, fallen logs, clumps of brush,
and the occasional rock. There they waited, firing occasionally
whenever Yankee lead came clawing through the brush at them
from the Federal positions a couple of hundred yards away. Will
had been standing there, in a relatively open spot, when Roman
found him.

After assuring the young man that he wasn't badly wounded,
Will said, "I told you to stay in the rear and look after my horse."

"That horse ain't goin' nowhere, Cap'n," Roman said, a look
of regret on his face. "An artillery shell burst right beside it,
killed it before anybody could do anything."

Will frowned. "Are you all right? That shell must have been
close to you, too."

"I couldn't hear too well for a while," Roman admitted. "But
my ears are workin' just fine again now. I was a little ways off
when it hit, fillin' up a canteen in one of those little creeks that
run through these backwoods. I swear, Cap'n, I never saw such a
place as this. Even the little animals that live here must have a
hard time gettin' through all this brush."

Will nodded. There wouldn't be very many animals in the
Wilderness right now, he thought. Any creature with any natural
instincts at all would have lit out as soon as it realized that man
was coming.

"I managed to find your saddlebags though," Roman went
on. "They were torn up a little, not too bad. I got some pone
here from 'em."

Will took the piece of rocklike cornpone and gnawed off a
bite. It was tasteless in his mouth. He didn't have any appetite
to start with, but he knew he ought to eat. He had to keep his
strength up. This fight was far from over.

In fact, judging by the sounds he heard in the distance, it
was heating up again to the south, along the Orange Plank Road.
There had been fighting down there all morning, too. Will wondered if Longstreet had arrived to give Hill's corps a hand, or if

the Yankees had attacked and forced Hill to go it alone, as they had done here along the turnpike.

General Lee was down there, too. Rumors had been going around that A. P. Hill was too sick to command. Hill, who had been born in Culpeper, was a fierce fighter and often wore a red shirt into battle, as if trying to make a better target of himself, but his health was notoriously bad. If Hill were incapacitated, Lee would take over. Will was sure of it. But Lee wasn't in the best of health, either . . .

No time to worry about that. The Yankees wouldn't care that some of the South's best military commanders were sick. There was nothing fair about war.

At Roman's urging, Will found a log and sat down. He hadn't thought all day about the injuries he had suffered at Gettysburg. He felt fine, truly fine. He was as strong as an ox, and when Roman asked him how he felt, he said so.

"I don't know, Cap'n," Roman said. "You got a look about you. Your face is a mite pale."

Will laughed. "How can you tell with blood all over it?"

"I can tell. Maybe you ought to find you a place where you can stretch out for a spell."

Will shook his head. "No. The men may need me."

But Dorothy needed you, and you drove her away.

Will frowned and gave another shake of his head, not signaling a negative this time but instead trying to get that troubling thought out of his brain. He didn't need to be dwelling right now on what he might have had with Dorothy. Maybe after the war he would go to Richmond and find her, see if she still had any feelings for him.

He didn't have to wonder how he would feel about her when the war was over. He knew he would love Dorothy Chamberlain for the rest of his life.

⌾ⲙⲙⲙ⌾

DESPITE HIS intentions, he dozed off while he was sitting on the log. He didn't sleep very long, though, because a short time later the Yankees attacked again. He bolted upright and looked around wildly for a second as he tried to remember where he was and what was going on. Then his instincts took over. He drew his pistol and saber and strode forward, toward the spot where the Federals were attacking.

They came charging through the woods and along the turnpike, but their pace was more of a stumble than a run. Crude breastworks had been thrown up across the road, and off the road, the Wilderness itself served to slow down the Union attack. Gen. Edward Johnson's division, including the Stonewall Brigade, was spread out to the north of the turnpike, while the division under the command of Gen. Robert Rodes formed a defensive line stretching south from the turnpike. Will knew that the Confederates were positioned well.

He came up behind three of his men crouching behind a log and firing into the oncoming Yankees. Will called to them, "Stay low, boys," and emptied his pistol over their heads. He could see the blue line coming through the trees, but the thick growth made everything vague and fragmented, almost as if Will was viewing the attack through a prism. He jammed his empty pistol back in its holster and waved the sword in his other hand toward the Yankees. "We'll stop them then take the fight to them!"

That was what happened over the next few minutes. Blunted by the terrain and by the stiff opposition of the Confederates, the Federal attack fell apart. The Yankees retreated. As they turned to run, Rebel yells welled from the soldiers along the defensive line. They scrambled out from behind trees and bushes and gave chase, firing as they ran through the woods.

The same thing that had worked against the success of the Union attack, however, also affected the Confederate counterattack. Once again Will had to struggle through the brush and exhaust himself before he could get close enough to the Yankees to fight them. All up and down the front lines, which stretched for more than a mile through the woods, the situation was the same. Men had to do battle not only with the enemy but also with the Wilderness itself.

And the Wilderness seemed to be winning.

The Yankees regrouped and came back, stopping the Confederate advance. Will leaned against a tree trunk to catch his breath and reached into the pocket of his jacket to bring out one of the spare cylinders for his revolver. He broke the gun open, replaced the empty cylinder with the loaded one, and snapped the gun closed. He dropped the empty cylinder in his pocket then leaned out to take aim at the Yankees, who seemed to be trying to mount yet another charge.

It was more difficult than ever to see anything clearly now. In addition to the thick woods and undergrowth, smoke from the fires and from the barrels of countless rifles and pistols rolled through the Wilderness. The wood smoke was gray, the powder smoke white, and both blended together to form clouds of what seemed like ground mist, as if the hour were early morning rather than late afternoon. Men charged and countercharged through the smoke, appearing and disappearing like phantoms. Sometimes only parts of their bodies were visible. Will saw a pair of legs run past, but the man's torso and head were cloaked in the smoke. The image seemed grotesque to him, as if the disembodied legs were running on their own.

Footsteps pounded close beside him. He glanced over and saw a Union officer running by the tree. Will could have lifted his pistol and shot the man down. For some reason, he didn't.

Instinct must have warned the Yankee of the danger he was in. He stopped short and twisted his head to peer over his shoulder. His eyes widened as he saw Will leaning there against the tree, arm hanging at his side, pistol in hand. The Union officer could have raised his own revolver and fired, but instead he turned slowly to face Will. All around them, men screamed and cursed. Tree branches cracked as bullets broke them. A constant popping heralded the lead flying through the brush. For a long moment, the two men stood there, their gazes locked. Finally the Yankee nodded. It wasn't a gesture of agreement, just an acknowledgment of Will's presence. Will nodded in return.

Then the Yankee turned and plunged off into the brush. A moment later, muskets rattled nearby and a man screamed. Will supposed the Union officer had run into several Confederates and gotten the guts blown out of him. Will wasn't sure if he was happy about that or not. All he knew was that he was glad he hadn't been the one to kill the Yankee.

Suddenly he was tired, damned exhausted. Weakness spread through his body, and he couldn't seem to get his breath. His throat was parched from the acrid smoke. He wanted a drink. With his back against the trunk, he slid down to the ground and sat there, struggling to get air into his lungs.

After a while, some of his strength came back. He used the tree to brace himself and climbed to his feet. The gloom under the trees was like a physical thing, wrapping around everything and making it more difficult to see than ever. For a moment, Will thought the gathering darkness was a sign he was about to pass out. Then he realized it was dusk. Night was falling. The sounds of gunfire began to die away.

But the crying of wounded men continued. It came from all around and offered no clue of how to get back to the Confederate lines.

"Water! Oh, God, I need some water here!"

The voice came from Will's left. He wasn't sure, but he thought the words were couched in a Northern accent.

"I'm dyin'! Oh, Lord . . . somebody help me! I'm fixin' to go to glory!"

The Southern voice came from Will's right. That was as good a sign as any, he told himself. He stumbled in that direction. The shadows had grown black and impenetrable in what seemed like a matter of seconds. He fell over logs and kicked away vines that clung to his ankles. At least, he hoped they were vines. The horrifying thought came to him that maybe they were the hands of the wounded, reaching out in hopes of finding someone to comfort them as they lay dying.

He was in the open before he even realized it. Halting his shambling progress, he looked around and saw that he was in the field where the Confederate line had been established earlier in the day. Axes rang in the trees on the far side as men erected new breastworks or strengthened existing ones. A few low-voiced commands were called back and forth. No one wanted to speak too loudly, because that might attract Yankee snipers. Those were the Confederate lines, on the west side of the field now, instead of the east. He started striding toward them.

Guns rattled and banged behind him, but he kept going. The field was littered with bodies, both living and dead. Some of the men were hung up in the bramble bushes and struggled feebly against their thorny grip. A few called out for help as Will passed, but he kept going. An invisible hand tugged at his hat, and he knew it was really a bullet passing through the crown. He was too tired to care how close he had come to death.

As he reached the edge of the woods, a voice hissed, "Who's that? Who are you, damn it?"

"A friend," Will said wearily. "Captain Brannon, from the Thirty-third Virginia."

"Ain't none o' your boys 'round here, Cap'n."

"That's all right. I'm sure they're fine, wherever they are."

The picket just stared at him as Will stumbled past.

Will found a place to sit down behind a bush. The bush wouldn't stop a bullet, but at least it would conceal him. He took off his hat and pulled a handkerchief from his pocket to mop away some of the sweat and grime on his face. He fumbled with the canteen attached to his belt, and when he got it loose, he shook it. A little water remained. He unscrewed the cap and tilted it to his mouth. The precious liquid spilled past his parched lips and trickled down his raw throat. But there was too little of it, not enough to give him any real relief. It only made him aware of how miserable he really was.

After a while, he lay on his side, wadded his hat under his head, and went to sleep. There was nothing else to do. A small voice in the back of his head shouted that he was an officer, that he had duties and responsibilities, but at that moment, he just couldn't think straight enough to remember what they were.

⚮

IT WAS still dark when Will awoke. He was stiff and sore all over, and the cuts on his hands and face still stung like fire. He groaned as he pushed himself into a sitting position.

The woods still burned here and there, but he easily spotted a campfire toward the rear of the Confederate lines. As he pushed himself to his feet, he decided he ought to go back there and find out what the situation was. He could hear the crackling of flames and the moans of the wounded, but he also realized that no guns were firing. This lull might not last long, but at this particular moment, no one in the Wilderness was trying to kill anyone else.

An orderly handed him a cup of coffee as he came up to join the circle of officers gathered around the fire. "Here you go, Cap'n," the man said. "That'll make you feel a mite better."

Will was still so thirsty he could hardly stand it. He gulped down the steaming brew, not caring how hot it was, not caring that he blistered his lips and tongue. Almost immediately, he felt the bracing effect of the coffee and wondered if the orderly had added a dollop of whiskey to the cup as well.

His memories of the night before were fuzzy. He recalled making his way through the Wilderness back to the Confederate lines, but his walk across the clearing seemed like something out of a dream, a nightmare, evil and distorted and surely not real. He dragged in a deep breath and forced his attention to the conversation going on among the officers around him.

It was clear from what they said that both columns of the Confederate army had had their hands full the previous day.

Along the Orange Plank Road, Hill's corps had engaged the Yankees in the same sort of furious back-and-forth, ultimately inconclusive fighting that had gone on all day here on the turnpike, several miles north.

"Longstreet should be up soon," one of the men commented. "I heard he was leaving his bivouac around one and planned to be in position by dawn."

Will frowned. Longstreet's corps hadn't joined the fight yet? If that was true, Hill's men must have been battered terribly. But no worse than Ewell's had been, he thought. They had seen their own share of hell here in the Wilderness.

"What are we supposed to do?" he rasped.

"Hold here," one of the officers replied. "And at dawn demonstrate toward the Federals to keep Grant from drawing on the corps in front of us for reinforcements elsewhere."

Will nodded. That was a sound plan, though not a daring one. Once Longstreet arrived, his corps combined with Hill's could press forward and perhaps force the Yankees to pull back to the north. They might even be able to flank the Yankees and roll right up the backside of their army, in which case Ewell's corps could smash forward and pin the Federals between two forces. That was a lot to hope for, but it could happen.

"Do any of you know where the Thirty-third Virginia is regrouping?" he asked.

One man laughed. "They could be anywhere. I don't think any units are still together anywhere out here. We've been scattered to hell and gone."

Another said, "I think some of them are just south of here. Your men, Captain?"

Will nodded. "That's right. I got separated from them during the fighting yesterday afternoon."

"Good luck finding them and regrouping. You want something to eat before you go?"

"No, thanks." Will had no appetite. He wasn't sure if he would ever be hungry again.

The lull in the fighting continued as Will made his way south along the line. It was almost impossible to see anything, but as he passed clumps of men, he asked in a low voice, "Thirty-third Virginia? Anyone here from the Thirty-third?"

His quest was finally rewarded. "Cap'n Brannon? Is that you suh?" The voice belonged to Lloyd Grady. Will recognized it right away.

"It's me, Sergeant," he said. Grady stood up and came toward him, a slender figure in the darkness. Will clapped a hand on his shoulder. "How are you?"

"Tol'able fair, Cap'n. Took a Yank bullet through the calf o' my left leg, but it ain't hamperin' me much to speak of. How about you?"

"I'm all right," Will said. "Where's the rest of the company?"

"Got half a dozen of the boys here with me. There's a few more over yonder, by that deadfall. You probably can't see it now; it's too dark. But I seen 'em there last night when the sun went down, so I reckon they're still there."

"What about Roman? Have you seen him?"

"That darky o' yours?"

Will started to correct Grady and point out that Roman was a freedman, but he didn't suppose it was worth the time and energy right now.

"Haven't seen him since the middle of the day yesterday," Grady went on. "He's probably all right, though. He was stayin' in the rear, wasn't he?"

"He was supposed to," Will said warily. Where the head-strong Roman was concerned, though, such expectations didn't always mean anything.

"You know what we're gonna do today, Cap'n?" Grady asked. "We fixin' to fight the Yanks again?"

"That's right." Will glanced at the sky, what little he could see of it through the overhanging trees. He thought it held a tinge of red, which meant that dawn was approaching. "It'll probably be starting anytime now . . ."

Less than ten minutes later, as he waited with the small group of men from his company, Will heard the roar of artillery as cannonballs and explosive shells were fired, along with the loud rattle of canister rounds. Rifle fire began to pop and crack. A few halfhearted Rebel yells drifted through the woods, but for the most part, the men fought in silence as the second day of battle began.

It was more of the same, the fighting becoming fiercer as the sun rose and its scattered light slanted through the branches of the trees. Will carried four cylinders for his pistol, each already loaded and capped, since reloading was a time-consuming process, especially during the heat of battle. He emptied all four cylinders during the first couple of hours after sunrise, fighting alongside Grady and the other men as they turned back several Federal thrusts. Then, not long after Will had reloaded the cylinders, the order came to move forward. The time had come for the Confederates to go on the attack.

The exultation that Will had experienced during the first clashes the day before was nowhere to be found today. That emotion had been leached out of him by the hard, bloody fighting that had gone on all day and into the night. Now his spirit was numb. His body responded to his brain's commands. Logic and duty dictated that he kill as many of the Yankees as he could. But he took no pleasure in it.

Nor did he take foolhardy chances. The night before, he had walked in the open through the bramble-choked field while bullets flew all around him, and the thought that he might die, probably would die before he reached the other side, had never entered his mind. Today he fought from cover and didn't press attacks that had no chance of succeeding. The victories he and his men won were small but consistent.

Will had no idea how the battle was going elsewhere. He didn't know if Longstreet had arrived to join Hill and Lee along the Orange Plank Road. Some engagements could be followed by watching the movement of the clouds of smoke that always hung over a battlefield, but not this one. Though the front stretched over miles, this was a battle of feet and inches. Two huge armies had collided here in the Wilderness, but the fight was between small groups of desperate men. And as the day wore on, it began to dawn on Will that there might be no clear-cut victory for either side, only survival.

The shooting intensified to the north, and a courier who was hurrying along the line told Will that Brig. Gen. John B. Gordon's Georgians were attacking the far right flank of the Union army. "Keep the Yanks in front of you busy," the courier told Will. "As long as they're hoppin', they can't go to the aid of the boys out on the flank."

Will nodded his understanding. He waved his saber in the air above his head, signaling not only to the men from his company but also to the other Confederate troops in the vicinity. As the only officer here, it was his responsibility to lead all of them, not just the men of the Thirty-third Virginia.

"Forward, boys!" he shouted. "Forward!"

Suddenly the saber leaped out of his hand, and a stunning impact shivered up his arm to his shoulder, numbing the whole arm. He went to one knee but came right back up again. Grady yelled, "Cap'n, are you hit?"

Will saw his saber on the ground a few feet away. He picked it up and saw the nick in the steel on the top edge of the blade, about three inches in front of the pommel. A Yankee bullet had clipped the saber. But it was all right, and so was he. A little nicked up here and there, but still a perfectly good weapon.

He slid the saber back into its scabbard and drew his pistol. "I'm fine, Sergeant," he said. "Let's go."

Left arm still hanging limp and useless, Will broke into a shuffling run toward the haphazard Federal line. He stopped every few yards, lined up a shot, and fired. The ground was rough, and when he glanced down he saw that he wasn't charging over dirt. He was stepping on the bodies of dead men, Union and Confederate alike.

The sounds of an even larger battle continued to the north. Will hoped Gordon's attack was successful. The Confederacy desperately needed a victory. The army would fight on regardless, but the people of the South needed the hope it would bring them if the seemingly unstoppable Grant were whipped.

Nightfall snuck up on Will again. Was it possible he had been fighting all day? He didn't remember eating or drinking anything since that cup of coffee early that morning in the predawn hours. He knew he must have, but he had no memory of it. All he really remembered of the day was the revolver bucking in his hand and the smoke stinging his eyes and mouth and nose. The feeling had come back in his left arm, so he was confident no permanent damage had been done to it. He was still whole. He had lived through another day of battle.

Grady and the other men were still with him. He turned to look at them in the fading light. Their faces were black as charcoal from the powder they had burned all day and the day before. Their arms were black to the elbows. But they were grinning, and Grady summed up the feelings for all of them when he said, "We may not have out-an'-out whipped 'em, Cap'n, but we sure as hell fought the bastards to a standstill."

"We surely did, Sergeant," Will agreed. "We surely did."

Chapter Fifteen

A HAND ON HIS shoulder shook him awake the next morning. Will opened his eyes and saw Roman's anxious face peering down into his.

"Cap'n? Cap'n Will? Are you all right?"

Something was wrong with Roman's voice. It was faint and faraway, even though Roman was leaning right over him. Will frowned and gave a little shake of his head. "Speak up," he said. "I can barely hear you."

"Cap'n, there's somethin' wrong . . ."

Roman's voice faded away completely then, and with it went Will's sight. He was adrift in blackness, floating as if he found himself in a wine-dark sea. It was tempting to just let go, to allow the gentle currents to sweep him off to wherever they wanted. It was quiet where he was, and so peaceful. Men weren't trying to kill each other. A fella could spend the rest of his life here with no problem at all . . .

Then a disturbing clamor rose, and after a moment Will recognized it as voices. Someone was shouting orders. He felt a tugging on his arm, and reluctantly he opened his eyes again and saw Roman.

"My God, Cap'n, you nearly went away from me then!"

Will forced himself to sit up. What was all the commotion about? He saw that he was still in the Wilderness, sitting on the ground beside one of the thousands of fallen trees. Men hurried about, calling to each other. Will got the impression that the soldiers were getting ready to abandon their positions and move out, bound for somewhere unknown.

"I'm all right, Roman," Will said, and his voice sounded perfectly normal to him.

So did Roman's when the young man asked, "Are you sure, Cap'n?"

"Of course I'm sure. I was just having a bit of a hard time waking up."

But he wasn't certain that was all it had been. His heart was pounding as if he had run all night instead of sleeping. He still felt a little lightheaded, and his muscles were weak as he leaned a hand on the log and levered himself to his feet. He had fooled himself at times into believing that he was still the same man he had once been, before Gettysburg, but he knew now it wasn't true. It wasn't true at all.

The war wasn't going to wait for him to recover. He took a deep breath, trying to ignore the pain in his chest, and asked, "What's happened?"

"The scouts say the Yankees got a bunch of ambulances headin' for Fredericksburg."

"Grant's withdrawing? We're not going to fight again today?"

"Ain't nobody fightin' right now."

That was true. Will listened and heard only a few scattered rifle shots. Pickets trading rounds, he imagined, not really caring if they hit anything. Yet battles had developed from such desultory hostilities before, but he had a feeling that wouldn't be the case today.

"What else have you heard?" Will asked. He had fallen asleep the night before without having received any reports on the rest of the battle. All he knew about was the bloody stalemate that had occurred along the Orange Turnpike.

"General Longstreet was hit yesterday."

"My God! Not Old Pete! Is he all right?"

Roman shook his head. "Don't know for sure. The soldiers I heard talkin' about it said everybody thought at first he was dead, so I reckon it must've been pretty bad. He's still alive, though. I've heard that for sure this mornin'. Some folks say it was some of his own boys who shot him by mistake."

Will closed his eyes and sighed. Stonewall Jackson had met his death in the same fashion, shot out of the saddle by Confederate troops who mistook him and his companions for a group of

Yankee cavalry. What was it about these damned woods that made such things happen?

"When there's time, we'll have to pray for the general's recovery," he said as he opened his eyes again. "Right now, however, we'd better try to round up as many members of the company as we can."

"I can do that while you rest, Cap'n."

Will slowly shook his head. "The company is my responsibility, not yours."

Lloyd Grady was nearby with the other men Will had fought beside the day before. Will joined them and told the sergeant to regroup the company as best he could. Will would be engaged in the same task.

"Yes suh," Grady replied. "I've heard tell we'll be makin' a night march this evenin', Cap'n."

"I don't know anything about it yet, Sergeant. I'll find out and let you know."

Will and Roman moved along the line. Whenever they recognized someone from the company, they sent him to join the group gathering around Grady.

A short time later, they reached the headquarters of Gen. Edward Johnson, the division commander. His brigade commanders were present as well—Brig. Gens. James A. Walker, John M. Jones, George H. "Maryland" Steuart, and Leroy A. Stafford—along with their staffs and many of the junior officers. All of them made quite a crowd around Johnson's tent. Will and Roman joined the knot of men, moving up as much as possible so they could hear the discussion.

". . . reports of Federal cavalry to the southeast," Johnson was saying. "That means that the Yankees are preparing to move in that direction, and General Lee is of the opinion—which I share—that their immediate destination is Spotsylvania Court House. General Anderson, who has taken over First Corps in the absence of General Longstreet, will lead the advance to Spotsylvania, followed by Second and Third Corps when it has been positively established that the Federals have withdrawn from before our lines."

One of the brigadiers spoke up. "It's our intention, then, to reach Spotsylvania before the Yankees?"

Johnson, a tired-looking man with bags under his eyes and a bad foot that required him to use a heavy cane, nodded emphatically in response to the question. "That is correct," he declared. His hand tightened as it clutched the head of his cane. "God willing, when Grant gets to Spotsylvania, he will find the Army of Northern Virginia waiting for him."

MAC BRANNON checked his pistols. He felt like a human arsenal, what with one pistol carried in a flapped holster on his hip, another tucked behind his belt, and two more stowed in holsters attached to his saddle. All of them were fully loaded, and Mac positioned them so he could switch from one gun to another practically in the blink of an eye. Fighting from horseback required the extra weapons, because reloading or even switching cylinders was an awkward task to execute on the back of a plunging mount. Mac had accumulated the pistols over the long months of the war, picking them up whenever possible on battlefields after the fighting was finished. The fact that the original owners of the guns were dead bothered him at times, but he told himself that he was putting the weapons to good use—namely, keeping himself alive.

He suspected that before the day was over, he would be using them again.

Gen. Fitzhugh Lee rode alongside him, keen eyes scanning the road ahead. Behind them was Lee's staff, and strung out behind them was Lee's division. For the past few days, ever since word had reached them of the impending battle in the Wilderness, these horsemen had ridden long and hard. Dust from the road coated their uniforms and their sweat-streaked mounts. Many of them wore impatient expressions, and not the least impatient was Lee himself.

"We should have been there, blast it!" he burst out in a low voice that only Mac could hear. "What if something has happened to Beauty?"

"I'm sure General Stuart can take care of himself, General," Mac said. "He always has before."

A faint smile plucked at Lee's wide mouth under his full beard. "Yes, that's true enough. But I still wish we'd been there to lend a hand."

Separated from the rest of Stuart's cavalry as they were, Lee and his men had been unable to take part in the battle, and now they had received news from Stuart that as of the night before, May 7, the Yankees had disengaged and were preparing to march, possibly to the southeast toward Spotsylvania Court House. Stuart's orders were for Lee to proceed to Spotsylvania to counter any forward movements by the Federal cavalry.

"We wouldn't have been able to do much," Mac pointed out. "You remember what it was like at Chancellorsville, sir. And the Wilderness is even worse farther west. It's no place for cavalry."

"Perhaps not, but I'll wager General Stuart managed to get in on some of the action anyway." Lee shook his head. "Well, perhaps it will be our turn next. Phil Sheridan commands the Federal cavalry, and I'd like to get in some licks against him."

Mac suspected they would have that chance, probably sooner rather than later. If Grant really was moving the Union army toward Spotsylvania, no doubt he would send the cavalry ahead first.

They rode steadily southwest along the Fredericksburg Road toward Spotsylvania Court House, the crossroads village where the Virginia Central Railroad and the Richmond, Fredericksburg, and Potomac also intersected. The settlement was a vital link in the supply lines for the Confederate army and would be quite a plum for Grant if he could capture it. Not only that, but the Yankees would be one step closer to Richmond itself.

Right now, Mac thought, Fitz Lee's men might be the only Confederates in Grant's way. They couldn't let the Yankee cavalry ride unopposed into Spotsylvania. If that happened, the battle would be over before it truly began.

The village was not at the crossroads itself but rather a short distance to the west. As Lee's cavalry approached the intersection on the morning of May 8, 1864, rifle and pistol fire crackled in the distance. It seemed to be coming from Spotsylvania Court House itself. Lee reined in and signaled for the riders behind him to halt as well. He leaned forward in his saddle and frowned in thought for a moment then gestured toward the crossroad that ran north and south.

"If the Yankees are already in the village, there'll be more of them coming down that road anytime now," he said. "We'll meet them north of town and drive them back."

He wheeled his horse into the crossroad and put it into a trot. Mac followed on the stallion. The rest of the division came along behind them.

Open fields lined both sides of the road. Vision was unobstructed. So a good distance still separated the two groups when Lee and Mac spotted Federal cavalry approaching up ahead. Lee reined to a halt, stared at the blue-clad enemy for a second, then turned in the saddle to bawl out orders.

"Dismount! Dismount! Horses to the rear! Carbines ready!"

Mac knew that Lee would have preferred to charge the Yankees on horseback, but under the circumstances, establishing a defensive line was the prudent thing to do. They had to block the Federals from coming any farther south along the road. Lee was a daredevil by nature, but he had learned over the years that sometimes he had to curb his reckless impulses.

Mac swung down from the saddle and pulled his carbine from its sheath. He handed the stallion's reins to one of the men charged with getting the horses safely to the rear. Turning back toward the north, he saw that the Yankees were still mounted and coming fast now. Across the road and on both sides of it,

Confederate cavalrymen hurried to find places from which to fight. Fitz Lee strode back and forth, directing the establishment of the line with jabs and slashes of his saber. As Lee's aide, Mac stayed with him, the carbine held ready to fire when the time came.

"General, you'd better get behind some cover," Mac said after a moment. The Yankees were still charging, and Lee was out in the open.

The general nodded reluctantly. "I suppose you're right." He replaced his saber in its scabbard and drew his pistol instead. "Come on, Mac."

The two men crouched behind a stone culvert that spanned the ditch beside the road. Mac leveled his carbine at the onrushing Federal riders. Beside him, Lee waited and let the Yankees get closer and closer. Finally he bellowed, "Fire!"

The volley that rang out from the dismounted troopers ripped through the Union riders and unhorsed several of them. Some of the horses were struck as well, and with high-pitched screams they reeled forward or reared up and toppled to the side or backward. The men atop these mounts were thrown and in some cases crushed by the wounded horses as they fell. Suddenly the road was a confused tangle of billowing dust and thrashing animals. The Yankee charge broke. Men who were still on horseback veered away from the road and circled back through the fields. More of them fell as the Confederates continued to fire, not in volleys now, but each man shooting at his own pace and picking his own targets.

Mac had gotten a good enough look at the Union force to estimate that it was only a single brigade. Though the Confederate brigades were smaller than their Union counterparts, Fitz Lee's force still outnumbered the Yankees. And in this first clash, the Yankees had suffered much greater losses, Mac estimated, so the numerical advantage had become even larger. He felt a surge of confidence. The Federal cavalry would not get past them today.

But that didn't mean the Yankees would give up without a fight. Already the blue-clad troopers were dismounting and looking for cover of their own. Bullets began to whine through the air around the Confederate defensive line. Mac glanced over nervously at Fitz Lee, who had risen up from his crouch to get a better look at what was going on.

"Better get down, General," Mac advised. "You don't want one of those Yankee sharpshooters ruining your hat."

"Or what's in it, eh?" Lee replied with a grin. He dropped down and turned so that he could rest his back against the stone culvert. "They shouldn't have charged us. That was foolish. Still, I suppose their commander thought his only chance of breaking through was with a quick, hard strike."

"You've adopted those tactics in the past yourself, General," Mac pointed out.

Lee's grin widened. "So I have. And they've been successful, too. But they won't be today. I'm sure of it."

"Yes sir," Mac agreed. He finished reloading his carbine and now drew a bead on the Union line. When he saw one of the Yankee troopers dash out from cover, Mac led him a little and squeezed the trigger. The carbine kicked against his shoulder and spewed white smoke. Mac caught a glimpse of the Yankee spinning off his feet, falling, then lying motionless. Mac tried not to think about the fact that he had just killed or badly wounded a fellow human being.

He took a cartridge from the pouch on his belt, tore it open with his teeth, and grimaced at the taste of the powder. It was almost impossible to tear open the cartridges without tasting a few grains of powder. The stuff had a harsh, bitter taste, and it mixed with a man's saliva to leave black streaks around the corners of his mouth. Mac spat and continued reloading.

After an hour of sporadic firing, the barrel of the carbine was so hot it blistered Mac's hand whenever he grasped it to reload. The buildup of burned powder was so thick inside it, despite the fact that he fired a Williams cleaner round every four or five shots, that he was having trouble ramming the bullet and powder charge home each time. His shoulder ached from the pounding of the recoil, his hand stung from the little cuts left by slivers of exploded percussion caps flying off the nipple, and his ears rang from the sound of firing. Those sensations were all too common. Mac experienced them every time he went through a battle like this. If he lived through the war, he would be half-deaf when it was over. He was sure of it.

"We're holding them!" Fitz Lee exclaimed with a bold, triumphant grin. "They're not going to get past us!"

"The cavalry won't," Mac agreed. "But what about when the Federal infantry gets here?"

Lee's grin vanished, replaced by a thoughtful frown. "Yes, there's that to consider. If Grant and Meade are truly coming in this direction, they may be here well before the day is over. I doubt that we have the men or the ammunition to hold off an entire corps of infantry."

But Lee would try to do so if necessary, Mac thought. He had no doubt of that. He had set himself to block this road and hold it against the Yankees, and he would fight to his last breath to do so.

Mac knew he would fight alongside the general for as long as Lee stayed here. They would experience either victory or defeat together, as they had done throughout the war, ever since the early days not long after First Manassas.

A short time later, Mac heard shouts behind him and turned to see what had caused the commotion, thinking that maybe the Yankees were attempting some sort of flank attack. Instead, to his surprise he saw ranks of men in ragged gray and butternut marching up the road toward the cavalry's defensive line. Mac had no idea whose command these men were from, but he knew he was glad to see them.

An officer rode up, dismounted, and saluted Lee. "Colonel John Henagan, sir," he introduced himself, "commanding Kershaw's Brigade of General Kershaw's division of the First Army

Corps. We've been sent by General Anderson, now commanding the corps, to assist you if necessary."

Lee returned the salute then shook hands with the colonel.
"Thank you, sir. So Richard Anderson's now commanding First
Corps?" he stated more than asked. "Has something happened
to General Longstreet?"

"I regret to report that General Longstreet was seriously
wounded two days ago and is under the care of the surgeons."

Lee struck his palm with a fist. "Longstreet wounded! My
God! How serious is it?"

"Quite serious, but from what I hear, it is hoped that the
general will recover. Can you make use of my men, General?"

"Indeed I can," Lee said. "Bring them up to strengthen this
line. We've been fighting for a while. I'd like to pull some of my
boys back and give them a breather."

Henagan nodded. "Of course, sir. We'll be ready."

Mac was watching down the road and listening to the conversation at the same time. Now, as he spotted new activity
along the Union line and watched thousands of fresh troops
surging forward, he said over his shoulder to Lee and Henagan,
"You might want to get ready in a hurry, sirs. Federal infantry is
moving up now."

Lee lifted his field glasses and studied the situation for a few
seconds before grunting his agreement. "So they are. Quick
now, Colonel Henagan."

"Yes sir!"

Mac saw the weariness on the faces of the infantrymen as
they poured forward to reinforce and in some cases replace the
cavalrymen who had fought off the initial Yankee advance.
Those soldiers had come from the Wilderness, and they must
have marched all night to reach Spotsylvania. They had to be
tired, but they were still ready to fight.

"What did you find in the village itself?" Lee asked Henagan.
"We heard firing coming from there earlier, just as we arrived in
the area."

"That was General Rosser's brigade, trying to turn back some Yankee cavalry. They were unable to do so."

"Then the Yankees have beaten us to Spotsylvania and taken it?" Fitz Lee sounded outraged.

Henagan shook his head. "Not anymore. Their occupying force was a small one, and they turned tail and ran when they saw us bearing down on them. Never fear, General, Spotsylvania is ours."

"Good," Lee said with a grim nod. "We'll hold it, starting right here."

Mac thought that Lee might withdraw toward the rear and leave the defense of the road in the hands of Colonel Henagan. He should have known better, he told himself as Lee stayed right where he was. Lee sent the most exhausted of his men to the rear, but he wasn't going anywhere himself. That meant Mac wasn't, either.

From the way the Union infantry charged forward a short time later, their flags fluttering and the men shouting their enthusiasm, Mac suspected that the Yankees were not fully aware of the combined Southern infantry and cavalry force now in the line. The Northerners acted like men on the verge of overrunning a much smaller force.

The volley that roared out to meet the advancing troops was thunderous as well as devastating in its intensity. Men in the front ranks were scythed down ruthlessly, and the charge stalled almost immediately as the pile of bodies hindered the assault.

More volleys erupted from the Confederate line. Stunned at the mass of rifle fire on their ranks, the Yankees still standing quickly wheeled around and tried to flee. Many of them were cut down by relentless Southern volleys. Despite the brave efforts of their officers to rally them, the mass of soldiers fled the field helter-skelter, leaving the road and bordering fields littered with dead and wounded comrades.

Mac lowered his red-hot carbine. He had fired into that wall of blue several times before and after it broke. The next time the

Yankees came, he thought, they wouldn't be so confident. They would be cautious, and they would come in greater numbers.

Despite this ignominious rout, the battle for Spotsylvania had just begun.

✺✺✺

ROMAN HAD found a horse for Will. It was a buckskin whose light-colored hide unfortunately made it a good target for enemy sharpshooters. But any mount was better than none, especially since Will realized that he didn't have the strength to march from the Wilderness to Spotsylvania. He was weary down to his bones. It was all he could do to climb up onto the horse with Roman's help.

"Cap'n, I think it might be a good idea to have one of the surgeons look at you," Roman suggested as he walked alongside Will's horse on the morning of May 8. Second Corps under General Ewell had pulled out of its positions along the Orange Turnpike after midnight and started southeast, joining up with Hill's Third Corps along the way. First Corps, now under Gen. Richard Anderson, was well ahead of them, making a dash to Spotsylvania so as to get there before the Yankees did.

Will shook his head. "I'm fine, just a mite tired. We'll go on."

"Cap'n, I never saw a white man look as gray as you do now."

"I'll rest when we get to Spotsylvania," Will said, and with a wave of his hand silenced the rest of Roman's protests. "We should be there soon."

Indeed, the sounds of battle could be heard in the distance. Anderson and his men were engaging the Yankees. It was possible that Mac was in the middle of that ruckus, too, Will thought. He had heard that Fitz Lee's division had been recalled and was supposed to link up with Stuart to protect the roads into Spotsylvania.

The road Ewell's men were following crossed the Po River then swung almost due east toward Spotsylvania. This route took them around the right flank of the Union army and once more put them between Grant and Richmond. Over the next hour, Will kept his men moving at a brisk pace. Couriers brought word that Confederate cavalry had met the Yankee advance earlier in the day and held it off until the reinforcements under Anderson arrived. Will had a feeling that Mac had been in the thick of that fight. That was where Fitz Lee would be if at all possible, and wherever Lee was, Mac would be there, too. Will hoped his brother had come through the battle unhurt.

I'd like to see old Mac again one more time.

Will frowned. Where the devil had that thought come from? he asked himself. True, he was tired and weak, and his heart seemed to beat erratically in his chest, but he would be all right. He was sure of it. Like he had told Roman, he just needed some rest. Maybe . . . maybe when this campaign was over, he would see about taking medical leave. He could find Dorothy and spend some time with her. If he did that, he vowed that he wouldn't rush to return to duty this time. That was all that was wrong with him—he had tried to come back too soon.

Ewell's corps moved up on Anderson's right flank just in time to meet a new attack by the Federals. Will sent his men forward to take their places behind a hastily thrown up breastwork of logs. As they opened fire on the oncoming Yankees, he dismounted and handed the reins to Roman. "Hang on to this horse," he said. "They're getting scarce."

Roman frowned, and Will knew he had offended the young man. He hadn't meant to sound as if he blamed Roman for the death of his last horse, but that was the way Roman had taken it. No time now to worry about hurt feelings, Will thought. He drew his saber and paced back and forth just behind his men, calling encouragement to them as they fired over the breastworks. After a few minutes, the Yankees began to fall back. Their attack had been disorganized to start with and had had no hope of succeeding, especially against a defensive line now bolstered by the arrival of two more Confederate corps.

"They won't pass," Will muttered. "They will *not* pass."

He tightened his grip on the saber as pain crept through him, spreading out from his chest. The Yankees couldn't whip them, and he was damned if he was going to let a little pain whip him.

"Give 'em hell, boys, give 'em hell!"

Chapter Sixteen

B Y THE END OF the day on May 8, the Confederates arrayed north of Spotsylvania had started to dig in. All during that night and the next morning, they did an even better job of it—digging trenches, erecting breastworks and earthworks, piling everything in front of them they possibly could to shield them from the Yankees' fire. When the Army of the Potomac attacked again, as it was bound to do, Grant would find Spotsylvania a tougher nut to crack than ever.

On the morning of May 9, Fitz Lee was huddled with General Stuart and the other two cavalry divisional commanders: Gens. Wade Hampton and William H. F. "Rooney" Lee, the son of Robert E. Lee and Fitz Lee's cousin. Captured by the Yankees the previous year, Rooney Lee had been exchanged only a couple of months earlier and had reclaimed command of the division that had been led by Gen. John Chambliss while Lee was a "guest" of the Federals.

The commanders discussed possible moves by the Union cavalry and what they would do to counter them. Mac knew he should have been there, but Fitz Lee had insisted that he find Will. Mac hadn't asked that favor; Lee had brought up the matter himself.

So Mac tread carefully along a salient thrust out from the Confederate lines. Rodes and Johnson were up ahead, he was told by the men he passed, beyond a small house that had been shot up badly the day before. Whoever had lived there would have quite a job waiting for them when the war finally moved on. It might be better to level the place and rebuild from the ground up, Mac thought.

He recognized the colors of the Thirty-third Virginia and quickened his pace. From what he had heard, the fighting had been heavy here the day before, especially late in the day when

255

this salient had been pushed into the Yankee lines. Mac hoped that Will had come through the battle all right.

Seeing a familiar face behind one of the log breastworks, Mac called to the man, who wore sergeant's stripes on the threadbare sleeve of his uniform tunic. "Is this Will Brannon's company? The Thirty-third."

"Sure is, Cap'n," the sergeant replied. He was sitting with his back to the logs, whittling on a homemade mouth harp. He got to his feet and gave Mac a casual salute. "I'm Lloyd Grady. Say, I know you, don't I, sir? You're Cap'n Brannon's brother, ain't you?"

"That's right, sergeant," Mac answered. "Do you know where can I find him?"

Grady frowned and used a grimy thumb to point along the line of defenses. "He's over yonder with that darky of his'n. He's feelin' a mite poorly, but I reckon a visit from kinfolks might perk him up. Hope so, anyway, 'cause I reckon the only visitors we'll have later will be wearin' blue."

Mac felt a quick surge of worry. "Will wasn't wounded yesterday, was he?"

"Not to my knowledge, Cap'n. You best go see him for yourself, though."

With anxiety growing inside him, Mac hurried along behind the breastworks. Here and there, a rifle cracked, and from time to time a bullet whined overhead, but Mac didn't pay much attention to those distractions. He was too worried about Will right now.

He spotted his brother sitting on an empty powder-keg stool. He had a chessboard on his knees, and Roman was hunkered on the other side of the board. Neither of them noticed Mac as he came up, until he said, "Aren't the two of you ever going to finish that game?"

Will lifted his head, and Mac felt a moment of shock when he saw how gaunt and haggard he looked. His eyes seemed to be gazing at Mac out of dark pits. But those eyes suddenly sparked with happiness, and a grin spread across Will's face as he exclaimed, "Mac!" He handed the chessboard to Roman and stood up, reaching out to embrace his brother as Mac stepped forward. They slapped each other on the back several times. Mac thought that Will felt fragile somehow, as if he might break if he were handled too roughly.

"How are you?" he asked as he stepped back. His voice was gruff with concern.

"Oh, you know me. I'm fine, never better."

"That ain't true, Cap'n Mac," Roman put in, and Will shot a frown at him. Undaunted, Roman went on, "He's been feelin' mighty bad the past day or two."

"Why don't you go see one of the doctors?" Mac suggested.

Will waved off the suggestion. "I don't need a sawbones. I just need a little rest. I'll be fine once this campaign is over and we've sent Grant packing."

Mac put a hand on his brother's arm. "I don't know. You don't look good to me."

"That's what I've been tellin' him," Roman said.

Will shrugged off Mac's hand and glared at them. "Both of you are worse than old mother hens. Why don't you worry about the blasted Yankees instead of me?"

"I worry about the Yankees," Mac said. "But I can't do anything except fight them when they come, though."

"That's all I'm doing," Will exclaimed. "And I'd like to be left alone to do it!"

Mac looked at Will for a long moment then heaved a sigh. "You always were a stubborn old rascal."

Will's grin came back. "That's right. All the Brannons are, but I'm the oldest and the stubbornest."

"You're forgetting about Ma."

Will laughed. "That's true enough."

They smiled at each other, and then Mac's expression grew more solemn. "You give me your word that you'll get some rest when this campaign is over?"

"Actually, I plan to take medical leave and go to Richmond. I want to see Dorothy again."

Mac felt a sense of relief. He nodded. "I think that would be the best thing in the world for you. Nothing like the medicine of a good woman."

"You're a fine one to talk, you old bachelor."

"Pot calling the kettle black," Mac pointed out.

Will clapped a hand on his shoulder. "Yes, I suppose you're right. Can you stay and visit a while?"

"I think so. General Lee is huddled with Stuart and the other commanders. They're trying to figure out what Sheridan will do next."

Will shook his head. "I don't want to talk about the war. You hear anything from home since we left?"

"Not a thing. I hope they're doing all right. There are Yankees all over that part of the country now. I'm afraid Culpeper is officially behind enemy lines."

"The folks ought to be fine," Will said. "The Yankees shouldn't be down here in the first place, damn their eyes, but I've got to admit that I haven't heard any reports of their mistreating civilians."

"What about Titus and Henry?"

Will shrugged. "I understand that as long as they're not in uniform or bearing arms against the Yankees, then the Yankees ought to leave them be."

Mac nodded. He knew Will was right, but still, it was hard not to worry about the people back home . . .

⟨∞∞⟩

STRANGE VOICES woke Titus from his slumber. He forced his eyes open, wincing as the bright light struck them. Slowly he rolled onto his side. But dust from the straw in which he lay tickled his nose, and he almost sneezed. Some instinct, however, warned him to stifle the impulse. He did so, cupping his hand over his nose and mouth. If he couldn't stop the sneeze, at least he could muffle it.

The tickling sensation passed. He sat up and felt both dizzy and disoriented. He realized now that he was in the hayloft in the big barn across from the farmhouse, but everything was spinning crazily around him. His head felt like it was going to fly off his shoulders. He used both hands to hold on to it to keep that from happening.

Gradually, he gained control of himself. The dizziness faded. He had had too much to drink the night before . . . but why should one night be different from another?

For one thing, he thought, it was harder to get his hands on a bottle of whiskey now that Quinn was out of the picture. He didn't regret Quinn's death, of course. That no-account moonshiner proved to be a murdering son of a bitch who had deserved to die. Quinn had killed Polly, and Titus hoped he was burning in hell. But he had to admit that Quinn had cooked up better whiskey than anybody else in the county. And since the damned Yankees had moved in, the supply of good booze had grown desperately short.

Somebody ought to do something about that, Titus thought. Fighting a war was one thing, but making it hard for a fella to get a drink . . . why, that was downright inhuman.

One more mark on the wall. One more reason that one of these days, he was going to find a way to kill some more Yankees. One of these days, when he got around to it . . .

The voices were still talking out there in the yard in front of the house. Titus crawled on hands and knees over to the hayloft door. It stood open a few inches. He peered carefully through the gap and stiffened when he saw the blue uniforms.

A Federal patrol was down there, sitting their horses in front of the house while Abigail and Henry stood on the porch facing them. Henry was hard-faced and angry, but Abigail looked more conciliatory than usual. She was saying, "I give you my word, Captain, we're not harboring any Confederate spies."

The voice of one of the Yankees, a man wearing an officer's hat, drifted up to Titus. "You're sure about that, ma'am? What about this young fellow here?"

"I can speak for myself," Henry said. "I'm not in the army and never have been. Recently I was the duly appointed sheriff of Culpeper County until you Yankees came in here and took over everything."

"Better keep a civil tongue in your head, young man," the officer shot back at him. "Sheriff, eh? So that'd make you one of the local officials. We've been asking all the civic leaders we can find to take a loyalty oath."

"You'll be wasting your breath with me. I won't take an oath to anything except the Confederate States of America." Henry shook off the warning hand that Abigail placed on his arm. "No, I mean it, Ma! I'm not looking for a fight, but I won't let these Yankees run roughshod over me, either."

From his hayloft perch, Titus noticed the way the Federal troopers stirred at Henry's assertions. None of them liked the way he was talking. Truthfully, Titus was a little surprised by it himself; he wouldn't have thought that his little brother had that much backbone.

But then he recalled how Henry had stood up to him about Polly. The youngster had changed while Titus was gone. Might as well admit that.

Titus thought as well about how easy it would be to pick off some of those blue-belly bastards from up here in the loft. If he had one of those new fifteen-shot Henry repeaters, he would bet that he could empty a lot of saddles before they got him. The thought of blowing the brains out of a dozen or more Yankee skulls put a smile on his face.

But he didn't have a Henry or even his old Sharps. Not even a pistol. He was unarmed, and he couldn't do a damned thing to those Yankees. Not today.

"Take it easy, son," the captain said to Henry. "We're not looking for trouble, either. And I won't ask you to take a loyalty oath today. But I will ask you for your parole that you'll not take up arms against the forces of the Federal government."

"I don't recognize your Federal government," Henry said then added, "but I haven't fought against you so far, and I don't aim to start . . . yet. Not as long as you leave my family and our farm alone."

"No one's going to bother you folks. We have orders to that effect. So I'll accept what you've said. However, the time's coming when you'll have to unbend that stiff neck of yours a mite. You'd better remember that." The captain looked at Abigail again. "Are there any other males of fighting age on your place, ma'am?"

Titus saw her hesitate. She didn't know whether to mention him or not. But the Yankees were liable to search the barn, and if she lied, that might cause trouble for the family.

Of course, he didn't really give a damn anymore. But he was tired and wanted to go back to sleep, and he didn't want a bunch of fuss disturbing his rest. Before Abigail could answer the officer's question, Titus pushed the hayloft door open farther and called, "Hold on there, Cap'n! I'll be right down!"

Several of the troopers swung around and lifted their rifles, ready to fire if Titus represented a threat. He just gave them a big grin and waved at them.

"Hold your fire, men," the captain said in a low voice. He called up to Titus, "Sir, who are you?"

"Just a minute," Titus said, still grinning. "I'll come down."

He went over to the ladder and climbed clumsily to the ground. The Yankees were still tense as he strolled out of the barn, picking straw out of his hair and beard.

"Captain, this is my son Titus," Abigail said from the porch.

"Late of the Army of Northern Virginia," Titus added. "But I ain't a soldier no more, Cap'n. I've done mustered out." That was a lie of sorts. But after what had happened at Fredericksburg, he supposed he was carried on the rolls as missing in action and presumed dead, so it didn't really matter.

The officer frowned at Titus in disapproval. "My word, man, you're intoxicated! And it's not even noon!"

"Lemme guess," Titus said, swaying a little as he spoke. "You're one o' those fellas who don't believe in drinkin'.."

The captain didn't bother to conceal his disgust. He looked over at one of the other Yankees. "I don't think this sorry sot represents any danger."

"No sir," Titus said. "I ain't no danger to nobody, 'ceptin' maybe my own self. I've done give up fightin', and if you want me to swear one o' them oaths, I'll be more'n happy to do it."

He lifted his right hand without waiting for the officer to respond. "I swear not to shoot no Yankees an' to be loyal to the Fed'ral gov'ment, s'help me God."

His voice dripping with scorn, the captain turned to his command. "All right, men, let's move out. There's no reason to worry about these people."

The cavalrymen turned their horses and rode out briskly.

Titus waved a hand over his head and shouted after them, "Y'all come back anytime, hear?"

Before the Yankees had ridden out of sight a hand grabbed Titus's shoulder and jerked him around.

"What's wrong with you, Titus?" Henry shouted, his face darkened with rage. "How could you do that? How could even a miserable excuse for a man like you swear an oath to those . . . those bastards!"

"Henry!" Abigail snapped from the porch.

"I'm sorry, Ma," Henry said over his shoulder. "But I can't believe even Titus would do such a thing."

Titus laughed. "'Even Titus,'" he repeated. "Reckon that says what sort of opinion you have of me, little brother."

"My opinion is that you're a stinking, good-for-nothing drunk. But even so, I didn't think you were a traitor—"

Titus's hand shot out and gripped Henry's upper arm so tightly that Henry gasped. Titus wasn't drunk anymore. In fact, he was stone cold sober.

"Don't you ever call me a traitor," he hissed. "Those Yankees were lookin' for any excuse to cause trouble. But they rode off, didn't they? They don't figure they've got anything to worry about from the Brannons." He gave a curt, humorless laugh. "They'll find out how wrong they are."

"But you swore an oath," Henry said. "You swore to God—"

"You think that means anything to me? A promise to a Yankee don't mean nothin'. I get the chance, I'll put a bullet through that son of a bitch cap'n just as quick as if I'd never said a word to him."

Henry stared at him for a second. "You *are* disgusting."

Titus released his arm and laughed again. "I just don't give a damn what you or anybody else thinks of me, little brother." He turned toward the barn. "Now, if you're through jawin', I got me a nap to finish."

GEN. PHILIP H. "Little Phil" Sheridan was on the move with the Union cavalry. Mac was informed of that by Fitz Lee as soon as he returned to camp. The place was a beehive of activity as men prepared themselves and their horses for a speedy departure.

"Thank God you're back, Mac," Lee went on. "I didn't want to leave you here, but we have to move quickly. Scouts report that Sheridan is already well ahead of us, apparently on his way to Richmond."

"I'm sorry I wasn't here, General."

Lee shook his head. "That's all right. I sent you to see about your brother. How is he, by the way? He wasn't wounded in the fighting yesterday, I trust?"

"No sir. But his health isn't good, I'm afraid. He says that when this campaign is over, he's going to take medical leave."

"I'm sorry to hear that. We need all the fine officers we can muster, and from what I've seen, Will Brannon is a good one indeed. I wish him the best."

"Thank you, sir."

"Now," Lee went on in a more businesslike tone, "you'd best get that stallion of yours saddled. We'll be riding out in a half-hour or less."

Mac was prepared when three brigades of cavalry were ready to ride out. Two of them were commanded by Fitz Lee; the other was under Stuart's personal command. The other three brigades of Stuart's cavalry would remain at Spotsylvania with the bulk of the army, just in case Sheridan's maneuver was a feint and the Federals planned to double back and attack the Confederates from the rear.

Mac didn't believe that was the case; he had studied the map as Fitz had traced the Union cavalry's movement. Sheridan was headed northwest. Judging by the amount of dust raised, it was a formidable group, perhaps as many as ten thousand men. Then the Yankees had turned southwest then southeast on a course that eventually would take them straight into Richmond. Mac didn't know if it was Sheridan's intention to attack the city itself or just to wreak as much havoc as he could to the railroad lines and supply depots in the vicinity. Either was a possibility, and whatever the mission was, the Yankees had to be stopped.

"It'll be our job to nip at Sheridan's heels while General Stuart tries to get ahead of him," Fitz explained as they rode south from Spotsylvania. "There's a large supply depot at Beaver Dam Station, on the Virginia Central. I wouldn't be a bit surprised if that's Sheridan's first objective."

Mac nodded in agreement. With the supply situation as desperate as it was, the destruction of a crucial depot, such as the one at Beaver Dam Station, would be a critical loss for the country as well as the army.

Lee's cavalrymen rode hard, none harder than Fitz Lee himself. By midday, outriders galloped back to report that the rear of the Federal column was in sight. Small groups of horsemen dashed ahead to harry any stragglers, and soon the afternoon air was filled with the sound of sporadic gunfire.

Mac could tell that Lee wanted to ride forward and lead the scattered clashes himself. He had to stay with the main body of troopers, though, and again it galled him to have to place duty and responsibility above his natural inclinations.

Lee was worried about something else, too. "Flora and the children are at Beaver Dam," he said, referring to Stuart's wife and two children. "That's the Fontaine plantation nearby. The station was named for it."

"You don't believe the Federals would do them any harm, do you, General?" Mac asked.

"I'd like to think not. Cavalrymen, North or South, are a breed apart, I've always said. But still, they *are* Yankees. They can't be trusted."

Sheridan's force was too large for Lee to attack directly. Heavily outnumbered, the Confederate cavalry would have been crushed, and that would have been a waste of lives. As nightfall approached, Lee sent couriers to find the bands of raiders who were making quick strikes at Sheridan's rear and recalled them. By the time darkness settled down, the two brigades had made camp.

Fitz smoked his pipe and paced restlessly. "I'm not sure we've done a damned bit of good," he said to Mac. "We should have tried to get in front of Sheridan, too. There's no need to drive him forward. He's already headed for Richmond."

That doubt was as close to a criticism of Stuart that Lee would ever utter, Mac knew. Lee's admiration for his commander knew almost no bounds. But even Stuart could make mistakes.

Mac sat on a stump and smoked as well. He gazed to the south and saw a faint orange tinge in the sky. "Something burning down yonder," he commented.

Lee swung around. "What?"

Mac pointed with the stem of his pipe. "That glow in the sky. That's a pretty big fire."

"My God," Lee breathed. "That's just about where Beaver Dam is."

Mac felt his spirits sink. "Then those Yankee horsemen have fired the depot."

"Or our people saw them coming and set it ablaze themselves, rather than let Sheridan get his hands on it."

"I didn't hear anything like a battle going on."

"Neither did I." Lee shook his head. "The Yankees got there first. There's no doubt."

"What do we do now, sir?"

"Follow our orders," Lee snapped. "Until I hear otherwise, I intend to stay on Sheridan's trail and make life as miserable for him as I can."

By the next morning, those orders had changed. A galloper arrived with word from Stuart. Fitz Lee was to circle to the east and head for Richmond just as fast as he could. Gen. James B. Gordon's brigade, which had been under Stuart's command, would take over the job of harassing the rear of the Federal cavalry column.

"The Yankees got to Beaver Dam Station before we could stop 'em," the courier said, confirming Lee and Mac's speculation. "It all went up in flames—the warehouses, the locomotives, the station itself . . . The Yankees were tearin' up track this mornin', last I heard. But General Stuart's convinced they're really headin' for Richmond."

That seemed a foregone conclusion to Mac, too. He started to saddle his stallion before Lee gave the order to prepare to move out.

That day, May 10, passed as a long dash for the horsemen, with Lee's cavalry swinging first to the east then to the south, trying desperately to get around and ahead of Sheridan's relentless massive force. The Federals were less than twenty miles from Richmond now. Even if Sheridan had as many as ten thousand men, he couldn't hope to capture and hold the capital city. It was heavily fortified and defended. At best, or worst, Sheridan might be able to execute a fast strike into the city, but he would have to withdraw eventually.

But what damage might he do while he was there? One thing was certain: Such a raid would strike terror into the heart of the Confederacy as well as the government.

During the day Lee's horsemen crossed the North Anna River, and by nightfall they were near Hanover Junction. Almost two years ago, Stuart's cavalry had passed through the area during the first ride around the Union army, then under the command of Gen. George B. McClellan and almost within sight of the Confederate capital. So much had changed since then, Mac thought as he studied the familiar landscape, but at the same time, so much was still the same. The war was still going on, and once again the Yankees were again menacing Richmond, albeit from a different direction this time.

Mac felt a great weariness gripping him as the column halted and he unsaddled and cared for his horse. He knew it had little or nothing to do with the long, hard miles he had ridden today. He was tired of war, tired of killing. Tired of both sides contending with each other at gunpoint. In that shadowy dusk, the truth of the matter burst on Mac's brain.

One army or the other would win the war . . . but in this great clash between North and South, neither side would emerge truly triumphant.

A short time after sunset, Stuart rode into Lee's camp with an escort. Fitz Lee greeted the general warmly, pumping his hand enthusiastically.

"Are we ready to strike them yet, General?" he asked.

Stuart took off his plumed hat and ran his fingers through his hair. Mac thought he had never seen the man look so tired or so grim. The general styled himself a cavalier, a bold, laughing knight of old, and his camps always rang with music and laughter. But not tonight. Tonight Stuart looked like a man at the end of his rope, and Mac didn't think anybody in camp was going to feel like singing or laughing.

"The scouts tell me that the Yankees are camped at Ground Squirrel Bridge, on the South Anna," Stuart began. Bitterness tinged his voice. "They are closer to Richmond than we our-selves are. But we shall steal a march on them in the morning. Pass the word, Fitz, that we'll be up and in the saddle early."

"Yes sir."

Stuart slapped his hat idly against his leg. "We can hit the Telegraph Road not far from here. That will enable us to pro-ceed southward at a fast pace. Sheridan will have to come over the Mountain Road. It should be a slower route."

Mac tried to recall the layout of the area. In the days before the war, the Brannons had come to Richmond at least once a year to attend the fairs. Mac had traveled these roads before. He recalled that the Telegraph Road and the Mountain Road merged not many miles north of the city and became the Brook Turnpike, which was the main thoroughfare leading into Rich-mond from the north. With Stuart's coming down one road and Sheridan the other, a collision was inevitable.

"There's an abandoned inn not far down the turnpike from the intersection of those roads," Stuart continued. "I think that is where we shall meet the enemy, gentlemen. The place, if I recall correctly, is known as Yellow Tavern."

Chapter Seventeen

WILL HAD BEEN REJUVENATED by Mac's visit, but the remainder of the day—May 9—proved not to be so pleasant. The Yankees spent the afternoon attacking the Confederate line in waves, especially along the half-mile-wide salient that thrust out from the right side of the line. The attacks were not huge affairs, as if Grant was not trying to overwhelm the defenders but merely to gauge the strength of their positions. Inside the Mule Shoe, as some of the men had started calling the salient, those positions were strong indeed. Earthworks, log breastworks, and trenches gave the Confederates plenty of cover from which riflemen and artillerists ripped into the attacking Federals. In addition, trees were cut down and the trunks were shaped into sharpened points and planted in the earth, facing the Yankees and creating formidable obstacles in front of the trench line.

Captain Brannon prowled the line behind his dug-in company, calling encouragement to the men and from time to time taking a few pistol shots at the enemy. The pain in his chest came and went without warning. Sometimes the agony stabbed through him; other times it was only a dull, ignored ache. Thankfully, Roman had ceased to badger him about withdrawing from the field and seeing one of the surgeons. It was all right to withdraw and even concede defeat during a game of chess, but this was no game. This was war, the real thing, and Will's men needed him. He had been apart from them too much during the past year.

The next day the unseasonably hot weather continued, as did the sporadic attacks on the Confederate line. During the morning, Will took notice of heavy firing coming from the far left end of the line and wondered if the Yankees were trying some sort of flanking attack. After a while, the shooting died down.

Will concluded that whatever the Yankees had been up to, they hadn't succeeded. If it had, the fight would still be going on.

Traverses—smaller trenches that ran at right angles to the main forward trench—led toward the rear of the Southerners' position. Late in the afternoon, Will went back along one of the traverses to meet with the other company commanders and his regimental commander. Their orders were the same as they had been from the first: Hold the line. Don't let the Yankees through. Such councils of war were a waste of time as far as Will was concerned, but the army seemed fond of them. He wondered if the Union army conducted its business in the same way. More than likely, he decided. Some things were common to all armies. He would be glad when the war was over and he could go back to being a civilian. He had adapted to military life better than he had expected, and he liked to think that he had made a pretty good soldier. But once this was finished, he wouldn't ever have the desire to put on a uniform again. He was certain of that. Nor did he want to go back to the sheriff's job in Culpeper. All he desired now was to work the farm and sit on the porch of an evening with his pipe and his wife and children. The children he and Dorothy would have . . .

He stopped momentarily in his tracks and grinned. "You're getting way ahead of yourself, Will Brannon," he said aloud. "*Way* ahead of yourself."

At that moment, a shout caught his attention. He hurried along the traverse and reached the trench then climbed out, using the steps that had been cut into its sides.

"What's going on, Sergeant?" he called to Lloyd Grady. Simultaneously a nearby battery opened fire with canister.

"Yanks are comin', Cap'n!" Grady shouted over the roar of the guns. He waved toward the woods that ended about two hundred yards away to their front.

Will snatched his hat off so that it wouldn't identify him as an officer and stepped up on a stump to get a look. Bullets singed the air, but he had to know what the situation was. The

Yankees were charging in an unusually narrow front, but their ranks were unusually deep as well. Nor were they stopping to fire as they came across the open ground, as they always did. Instead they were running all-out toward the Confederate line, and their bayonets were fixed to the rifles they brandished as they charged.

"Fire!" Will shouted along the line then turned and shouted the order down the other direction. Rifles were already popping and cracking, but the command prompted more of the defenders to join the action. Quite a few of the Yankees fell as the shots raked their front ranks, but those men who survived and those who were behind them came on full-tilt. In what seemed like the blink of an eye, they were immediately in front of Will, only a few yards away from the Confederate defenders.

Will lifted his pistol and fired, saw one of the Union soldiers driven back with a spurt of blood as the ball smashed through his head. Will shifted his aim and fired again. The sharpened tree trunks slowed the Federal charge, but some of the Yankees made it through the barrier and bounded to the top of the log parapet right in front of Will.

He shot one man in the belly, and another was blown off the wall by Grady. One of the Yankees leaped at Will, thrusting at him with his bayonet. Will twisted out of the way and fired. He was so close to the Yankee's chest that the blue jacket caught fire from the burning powder that spewed from the pistol barrel as he discharged the handgun. The bullet knocked the Yankee off his feet. He fell gasping and bleeding inside the trench. A second later he was torn apart as several other bullets ripped through him.

Will looked up and saw a Yankee still trying to clamber over the breastworks, but the man was knocked back, his skull shattered by the stock of a rifle swung like a club. The grimy-faced defenders fired furiously, shooting as fast as they could reload. When that wasn't fast enough, they fought hand to hand with the attackers. Will emptied his pistol, staggered back into a traverse to replace the empty cylinder, and joined the fight again. If his chest hurt, he didn't know it. All of his senses were focused on battling the enemy.

An uproar to the left, noticeable even in the din of combat, caught his attention. Less than a hundred yards away, the Yankees had breached the line and were overrunning a company of Georgians. The line continued to crumble to the left as more and more Yankees made it over the breastworks and into the trench. Will wanted to aid the Georgians, but he couldn't. His men still had their hands full right here with what seemed like thousands of Federals directly in front of them.

Seeing that the bayonet charge had been repulsed along the section of the line held by Will's company, any Yankees who reached the parapets began to take cover there, raise their rifles over their heads, and fire blindly into the trenches. Several of Will's men fell to these blind shots. But the press of more troops charging behind them forced the men who had emptied their rifles to climb the breastworks anyway, so the hand-to-hand fighting continued.

After Will had emptied his pistol a second time, he jammed it in its holster and drew his saber. He thrust and slashed with the blade, striking at anything blue that came within reach. Panting with exertion, he ripped the saber free from one body and whirled to confront another. The tip of a bayonet ripped through the side of his jacket and drew a fiery line across his ribs. Will smashed the hilt of the saber in the man's face then backhanded the blade across his throat. Blood splashed up to his elbow as it fountained from the man's neck. Will shoved him aside.

The Yankees fell back for a second, and that gave Will a chance to glance down the trench. It was full of Federals where the line had collapsed. The men who had been trying to hold on there must have been pushed back to the second line of trenches, about a hundred yards to the rear. The Yankees had to be stopped before they gained any more ground and established a strong breach in the Confederate line.

Will hurried in that direction, shouting, "Pinch 'em off! We've got to stop them! Down here, boys, down here!"

Some of the defenders went with him and others stayed where they were, battling the Yankees who were still trying to overrun their section. Will and the men who followed him fell on the Yankees from the side, taking them by surprise. Will moved like a whirlwind, hacking with his saber until the blade was covered with blood and no sign of steel showed through the crimson coating.

The hour was growing late. Dusk would be upon them soon. The sun would *not* go down on enemy soldiers behind Confederate lines, Will vowed. He fought as fiercely as he ever had, as did the men who stood with him.

Suddenly, the Yankees pulled back. They were no longer fighting to increase their penetration of the Confederate line but rather to escape from it. Will chopped down a Union soldier who ran past him. He shouted, "They've turned tail, boys! Look at 'em run!"

It was true. The assault had almost been successful with its unusually narrow front; the attack had in fact broken through the Confederate line. But the Yankees had been unable to hold the ground they won, and now they were withdrawing—the ones who still could. Hundreds of blue-clad bodies lay sprawled in the trenches or draped over the log breastworks.

With the attack repulsed at last, Will had to see to his men. He turned to go back along the trench and reeled as his balance abruptly deserted him. He had to put a hand against the wall of the trench to steady himself. An eerie weakness began deep inside him and spread outward through his body. With gritty determination, he forced himself upright and moved along the trench toward his company's position. When he got there, he saw Grady sitting with his back against the trench wall, arms folded across his middle, his uniform sodden with blood. Grady's head was tipped back. Will saw the sergeant's Adam's apple bob as he swallowed.

"Sorry I . . . can't get up . . . Cap'n . . . damn Yanks . . . ripped the guts outta me."

Will went to one knee, his own pain forgotten as he put a hand on Grady's shoulder. "That's all right, Sergeant," he said. "You and the men did a fine job here. An outstanding job."

"Thank you . . . sir. Are the Yankees . . . gone?"

"They're pulling back as fast as they can. They won't pass. Not today."

"That's . . . mighty good to know." Grady licked his lips. "When they come back again . . . you give 'em hell for me."

"I will, Sergeant. I surely will."

By then he was making a promise to a dead man. Grady's eyes were open and staring but no longer seeing. With a sigh, Will closed them.

Artillery still roared, shells still burst, rifles still cracked, bullets still whined through the air. Will ignored all the tumult as he slid into a sitting position in the bottom of the trench, put his arms around Grady, and held the man. Grady hadn't been the company sergeant for as long as Darcy Bennett had, but he'd been a good, dependable soldier. Will didn't know much about him, but he figured that somewhere, Grady had people who loved him, people who would have held him if they had been here. So he did it for them, and tears cut streaks in the powder grime on his face.

⌒ⱮⱮⱾↃ

FOR SEVERAL weeks, the weather in Virginia had been quite warm, even hot. That changed on the morning of May 11. A cool wind blew, and judging by the looks of the clouds that moved in to the north, Mac thought it might be raining up at Spotsylvania. Around Yellow Tavern, only a few miles from Richmond itself, the sky was still mostly clear, but that chilly wind was blowing . . .

Mac wondered if Will was getting rained on, but he didn't have much time to spare worrying about his brother. Very early that morning, the cavalry had been on the move, racing down the Telegraph Road. Stuart and his escort accompanied Fitz Lee's two brigades. Mac was unsure how many men they would be facing later in the day, but no matter what the odds, the Yankees had to be stopped. Richmond seemed only a stone's throw away.

Yellow Tavern was an unimposing place. At one time it had been a stagecoach inn, a resting place for travelers. Now it was abandoned, a ramshackle frame building on the verge of ruin. Mac wasn't sure why it had been called Yellow Tavern; as far as he could tell, no coat of paint, yellow or otherwise, had ever adorned its warped boards.

Stuart, Lee, and the two brigade commanders, Gens. Lunsford Lomax and Williams Wickham, sat their horses in the road in front of the tavern and conferred on their strategy. Stuart pointed to the north, where Telegraph Road came in from the northeast and Mountain Road came in from the northwest to form the Brook Turnpike. "Our defensive line will be there, just beyond the intersection," Stuart declared.

"General Wickham, you will deploy your men to the right, straddling Telegraph Road," Lee added. "General Lomax, you will have the left, across the Mountain Road." Both brigadiers nodded their understanding. Lee raised a gauntleted hand and pointed to a small hill at what would be the left end of the line. "Captain Griffin will place the guns of his artillery there, where he can command the field."

"An excellent arrangement," Stuart said. He seemed more himself today, Mac thought. His gloomy mood of the previous evening had vanished for the most part, and he seemed eager for the confrontation. Even his horse was in high spirits, stepping around the road skittishly. "We'll give Sheridan's boys a warm welcome. A most warm welcome indeed."

"Sir, is there any word from General Bragg?" Wickham asked.

The day before, Stuart had sent a message to Braxton Bragg in Richmond. Bragg had commanded the Confederate army in Tennessee that had lost Chattanooga to the Yankees the past

November. Following that defeat, Bragg had been removed from field command and transferred to Richmond, where he now served as army chief of staff and commander of the city's defenses. Stuart's message had asked for any help that Bragg could spare to turn back the Federal cavalry thrust.

Stuart shook his head in reply to the question. "Nothing yet from Bragg, but I trust we will be hearing something soon. Good news, no doubt."

Mac wished he could be that optimistic. But over the next hour, as the dismounted cavalrymen spread out to await the inevitable Yankee assault, he saw just how thin the line was stretched. There was no question that they were going to be outnumbered. The Southerners would have to rely on their spirit and the fact that they would be fighting from defensive positions to offset that disadvantage.

Fitz Lee remained mounted, and so did Mac. Lee would be moving up and down the line during the battle, as would Stuart, monitoring the situation and reacting to any developments. Mac knew that he would spend the day galloping between the two generals, carrying messages for them.

The hour was just past midmorning when the Yankees appeared in the distance. Mac had been watching the cloud of dust that marked their approach, so he wasn't surprised. He could even smell the dust on the cool north wind.

Beside him, Fitz Lee leaned forward in the saddle. "Here they come," he murmured

A full brigade of Federal cavalry came galloping down the Mountain Road toward Lomax's men. The dismounted Confederate troopers opened fire, as did the light artillery battery on top of the hill to the left. Mac watched tensely as the Federal riders came on, seemingly invincible. Firing pistols from horseback, they swept across the field toward the Confederates.

But then the fire from the dismounted troopers began to take a toll, as did the bursts of canister from the guns atop the hill. The Union charge made it almost all the way to the defenders before it broke—but break it did. The Yankees wheeled their horses and retreated.

"That's giving them a taste of fire!" Lee exclaimed as he clenched a fist in excitement. "They thought they could ride right over us. They know better now, by God!"

The battle was only beginning, though. The Yankees charged again and again, but each time they were beaten back. Stuart's men, fighting from behind rocks and in gullies and creek beds, were crack shots with their carbines. Each time the Yankees came thundering toward them, the Southerners picked their targets and fired coolly and calmly. In the face of such withering fire, the Federal cavalrymen had no choice but to break off their attacks and turn back.

Lee rode the entire length of the line several times that morning and into the afternoon. Mac went with him, except when Lee sent him looking for Stuart to deliver reports and ask if there were any new orders.

On one of those occasions, Stuart laughed. "Tell General Lee that I have received a reply from General Bragg. He can muster four thousand men to defend the streets of Richmond, and he's summoned three brigades of General Beauregard's men from the James River! The capital will be safe, regardless of what happens here!"

Mac snapped a salute and wheeled the stallion to carry the news back to Lee. When he found the general and delivered the message, Lee frowned. "Is General Bragg sending any men to help us?" he asked.

"General Stuart didn't say anything about that, sir."

"He must think we can stop Sheridan by ourselves, then." Lee nodded. "So be it."

Mac wasn't sure if that was going to be possible. So far the Yankees had gained little if any ground. The Southern cavalrymen were standing firm, and losses had been heavy on the Federal side. Dead and wounded men and horses covered the ground in front of the Confederate line. The light artillery had been especially effective. Every charge the Yankees mounted ran smack-dab into a deadly hail of canister. But the Federal force was so much larger. Would Sheridan be stubborn enough to keep battering away, spending the lives of his men, until the defenders were finally overrun?

A bit later, it became obvious that Sheridan was employing a new tactic. Firing from the far right flank made both Lee and Mac jerk their heads in that direction. Lee lifted his field glasses and peered for a moment before bursting out, "My God, they've gotten around us! Sheridan's trying for the turnpike, so he can cut off our retreat!" He swung toward Mac and reached over to grasp his arm. "Find General Stuart and warn him we may face danger in our rear."

"Yes sir!"

Mac wheeled the stallion and put the big silver gray horse into a gallop. He and Lee were on the right side of the line, behind Wickham's men. The last time Mac had seen Stuart, the general had been toward the other end of the line. He raced from east to west behind the fighting, leaping the stallion over shell craters and ignoring the explosions around him. The noise of battle was a hellish cacophony, but Mac had no time to worry about such things. He had to find Stuart.

A few minutes later, he spotted a distinctive figure in a plumed hat and silk-lined cape. Mac angled toward him. Beyond Stuart, an especially intense charge was sweeping up the hill toward the artillery emplacements. Sheridan had figured out that a frontal attack was doomed to fail as long as those guns were raking the field, so now he was sending a heavy attack against them. As the gunners atop the hill swung the cannons around to protect themselves, that opened up the area in front of Lomax and Wickham to renewed attacks. More blue-clad horsemen poured across the field toward the Confederate line.

Suddenly, a huge explosion burst close at hand and sent Mac spilling out of the saddle. He flew through the air and crashed to the ground, losing his cap and having the breath knocked out of him. The impact stunned him. After a moment he was able to push himself up on hands and knees, and his first thought was of the stallion. He didn't worry about whether he himself was wounded, but only about what had happened to the sterling mount that had carried him safely through so much danger over the past two years.

The stallion was down, too, thrashing his legs. Mac saw the bright gleam of blood on the animal's sleek flank. "No!" he shouted as he scrambled to his feet and lunged toward the horse.

With a shrill whinny that sounded more outraged than injured, the stallion got his hooves underneath him and heaved upright. He shook his head, the long mane flying.

Mac threw his arms around the horse's neck and hugged him tightly. He was crying and laughing at the same time as he inspected the animal's shoulder and saw several gashes that were bleeding freely but did not appear to be too deep or too serious. With trembling hands, he checked the horse's legs. None of them were broken. The stallion was all right, and so, Mac realized, was he. His ears still rang from the explosion, but other than some bruises from being thrown to the ground, he was unhurt.

He didn't waste time looking for his cap. He gathered the reins and swung up into the saddle. He still had to find Stuart and deliver Lee's message.

Mac swept his gaze over the battlefield. It looked like the left side of the line had collapsed. Lomax's men were retreating. Farther on, the Yankees had gained the top of the hill where the artillery was positioned and seemed to be winning the battle to wrest control of the guns. The whole Confederate line looked to be on the verge of collapse.

Gen. James Ewell Brown Stuart was not the sort of man to give in easily to defeat, however. Mac spotted him racing back and forth along the line, waving his plumed hat and trying to rally his men. The general had left a small band of cavalrymen in reserve, and he signaled them up now as Mac approached.

When the riders thundered up, Stuart bellowed, "Charge, Virginians, and save those brave Marylanders!" He clapped his hat on his head and led the attack himself.

Maryland men manned the guns on the heights, Mac knew. Clearly, Stuart meant to chase the Yankees away from his gunners as well as rally Lomax's men, who stopped their retreat and turned to fight again as they saw Stuart, ever the bold cavalier, leading the charge.

Mac galloped nearer Stuart, determined to make his report as soon as there was a break in the fighting. He was close enough to hear an officer he recognized as Maj. Reid Venable, Stuart's aide, calling to the general to get back from the fighting.

Stuart's laughter pealed out. He was truly himself again now, all doubts forgotten in the heat of battle. "I don't reckon there's any danger!" Stuart called back to Venable. He drew his LeMat revolver and plunged forward.

Again the Yankees had come close to overwhelming their foes, but Stuart's daring action had turned the tide at the last minute. Many Federal horsemen had been knocked off their mounts during the fighting, and instead of meeting the Confederates on foot, they turned and ran or were hefted onto the mounts of friends or comrades, riding double and withdrawing from the fight. The attack crumbled. Maybe now Stuart could turn his attention to the possible threat in the rear, Mac thought as he urged the stallion closer to the general.

Stuart was firing his revolver at the fleeing Yankees. Mac was only a few yards away when he saw one of the Northerners turn and lift a pistol. Smoke bloomed from the muzzle of the gun.

The general's head jerked forward so violently that his hat flew off. He sagged forward in the saddle and pressed a hand to his right side.

Mac came up alongside the general and reached out a hand to steady him. "Are you hit, sir?"

"I am afraid I am," Stuart said. His voice was calm, but a taut edge to it told Mac that he was in considerable pain.

Another officer, a captain named Dorsey, spurred up on Stuart's other side. The general's horse was beginning to panic, so Dorsey wrapped his arms around the wounded Stuart and helped him to the ground.

"Get another horse for the general!" he shouted. "Some of you men help me here!"

Several of Lomax's cavalrymen sprang forward to hold Stuart upright while a more suitable mount was found. The general was still conscious and alert. He looked around and said, "Go and tell General Lee and Dr. Fontaine to come here."

Dorsey looked over at Mac. "Captain Brannon, do you know where General Lee is?"

Mac was already turning the stallion. "I'll tell the general what happened!" he called over his shoulder to Dorsey.

He rode as he had seldom ridden before, taking chances, pushing the stallion as hard as he could. The horse labored valiantly, not letting its injuries slow him any. Mac was halfway across the battlefield when he encountered Fitz Lee coming the other way.

"Mac!" Lee exclaimed. "Did you tell Beauty the Yankees are trying to flank us?"

"General Stuart's wounded, sir!"

Lee's eyes widened in shock. "Dear Lord, no! Is it serious?"

"It looked pretty bad, sir," Mac replied honestly. He was no doctor, but he had seen the rapidly spreading bloodstain on Stuart's uniform. "I'll take you to him!"

But Stuart was no longer where he had been wounded. Seeing a cluster of men under some trees nearby, Mac and Lee raced there and found the bloodied general sitting on the ground with his back braced against a tree, surrounded by some of his officers. Lee was out of the saddle before his horse stopped moving, and Mac was right behind him.

The circle of men parted to let Lee through. He knelt in front of Stuart and said in a broken voice, "Beauty," using the old West Point nickname.

Stuart summoned up a smile and clasped Lee's hand. "The command is yours now," he murmured. "You'd best get to work."

"I can't leave you, General," Lee said.

"Go ahead, Fitz, old fellow. I know you'll do what's right."

Mac saw Stuart squeeze Lee's hand, and Lee seemed to draw strength from his mentor, even though Stuart was the one who was wounded. Lee nodded then released Stuart's hand and stepped back.

Dr. John B. Fontaine hurried up with an ambulance wagon. As gently as possible, Stuart was lifted and placed in the back of the wagon while Fitz and Mac stood by, watching with grim expressions on their faces. Mac had been on the scene when Stonewall Jackson had suffered his mortal wound, and now he feared that he had seen the end of another great leader.

Several Confederate troopers ran past the ambulance, hurrying away from the battlefield. Stuart saw them and raised himself on an elbow.

"Go back! Go back!" he shouted at them. "Do your duty as I have done mine and our country will be safe! Go back!" He settled down a little. "I had rather die than be whipped."

The ambulance rattled off, its driver looking for some safe route away from the battlefield. Mac and Lee watched the wagon go.

"You heard him, Mac," Lee said. "We can't let him down."

"No sir," Mac agreed.

But as he looked to the north he knew that they were still outnumbered by more than three to one. *I had rather die than be whipped.* Those were noble words, a noble sentiment indeed.

But Mac feared that before it was all over, both of those things might come to pass for the Confederate cavalry.

Chapter Eighteen

THE WIND WAS COLDER and stronger now. The sun was gone, hidden behind thick banks of clouds that scudded across the sky. Heavy drops of rain fell from time to time. A late afternoon storm was moving in on this crossroads a few miles north of the Confederate capital.

Mac slumped in utter exhaustion atop the stallion. With his cap lost in the explosion that had unhorsed him earlier in the day, the rain plastered his brown hair to his head. He was too tired to care about being wet, however. Beside him, Fitz Lee was equally despondent.

They were on a small rise to the east of the battlefield around Yellow Tavern. Several hours had passed since General Stuart had been wounded and rushed from the field. During that time, Lee had done his best to rally the men and turn back Sheridan's men, but in the end, the odds simply had been too great. No matter how stubbornly the Southerners fought, the Yankees just kept coming.

Now, before all the men were slaughtered in the command that had fallen to him, Lee had withdrawn, ordering a general regrouping to the east. The Federal cavalry was pouring on toward Richmond, unopposed.

"We failed, Mac," Lee said bitterly. "Failed."

"You did everything possible, General," Mac said. "No man could have done more."

"You are forgetting General Stuart, Captain."

"No sir, I'm not." Mac's tone took on an edge that only his long association with Lee would allow. "General Stuart could have done no more than you yourself did. There were just too many of them."

For several moments, Lee said almost nothing. Finally, his thoughts were enunciated. "Bragg will keep them out of the city, and then tomorrow we'll hit them from the rear. They'll be between us. Sheridan thinks he's won, but he hasn't."

"No sir."

Slowly, Lee turned his horse and rode away. Mac followed.

Rain continued all through the night of May 11. The fierce storm hampered the work of the Confederate scouts in discovering what Sheridan was doing. By the morning, however, it was obvious that he had not attacked Richmond, as everyone had thought he would do. In fact, reports indicated that Sheridan's cavalry was moving rapidly to the east in a withdrawal.

"What can he be up to?" Lee muttered as he paced back and forth in front of his tent. "We thought all along that he was after something in Richmond."

One of the officers gathered around the tent suggested, "Perhaps Sheridan's goal was only to destroy our supplies and draw our cavalry away from the rest of the army."

Lee nodded. "Perhaps." He was angry and melancholy at the same time. Earlier, word had come from Richmond that General Stuart was still clinging to life but was in grave condition, not expected to live through the day. His wife and the children had been summoned, but it was not known if they would arrive in time or not.

Mac sympathized with Lee, knowing how close to Stuart the general had been for many years. From what Mac had heard, Lee might not have made it through West Point without Stuart's help. He didn't blame Lee for being upset.

More scouts rode in, breathless from racing across country. From their reports, it was obvious that Sheridan was heading for the Chickahominy River.

"He wants to put the river between him and us," Lee mused. Under the canvas cover that extended from the front of his tent, he spread out a map and suddenly stabbed a finger at it. "Meadow Bridge—that's where Sheridan will try to cross. Get some men there as fast as possible and burn it. The rest of us will follow and trap them there."

"It'll be hard to set fire to the bridge in this downpour, sir," one man pointed out.

"Do it!" Lee snapped. "We mustn't let Sheridan get away."

A small group of cavalrymen galloped off immediately, bound for the bridge; the rest of the men got ready to ride. Still exhausted from the previous day's battle, both men and horses were slower to move than they might have been otherwise. Soon, though, the cavalry was splashing down muddy roads toward the Chickahominy River.

Mac kept his eyes open for smoke from the burning bridge, and when he didn't spot any during the ride, he was afraid that the men had been unable to set it afire. A short time later, the cavalry came upon a column of gray-clad infantry, soldiers sent out from Richmond by Bragg in an effort to chase down Sheridan before the Yankee cavalry got away.

Lee conferred briefly with the commander of the infantry then rode on toward the river. Mac could hear gunfire up ahead. Some sort of fight was going on. A few minutes later, as the large group of horsemen approached the river, he saw a furious clash unfolding between Federal and Confederate cavalry.

"Those are Gordon's boys!" Fitz Lee called out, recognizing the battle standards. Mac knew he meant the brigade under the commanded by Gen. James B. Gordon, from Rooney Lee's division, which had been harassing Sheridan's rear ever since taking over that task from Fitz Lee's brigades a couple of days earlier. Gordon had followed Sheridan to the river and was making a last-ditch effort to stop him.

With a sweep of his saber, Fitz Lee sent his men charging forward to join in the fight. Carbines and pistols were unreliable in wet weather like this; some firing went on, but steel rang against steel as sabers did most of the work this day.

Mac saw that the bridge over the Chickahominy was partially burned, but the Yankees had managed to repair it and make it usable. Most of them, he saw to his disgust, were already on the other side of the river. Some of Sheridan's men were fighting a rear-guard action. As Mac watched, the last of them made it across the bridge and dashed into the trees on the far side of the river.

Lee called a halt to the attack and went looking for General Gordon. He found the man wounded, lying under a tree and being tended to by a surgeon. Lee talked briefly to the doctor then came back over to Mac, shaking his head.

"The surgeon suspects that General Gordon is mortally wounded," Lee said. "My Lord, how many good men do we have to lose?"

"Are we going after General Sheridan, sir?" Mac asked.

Lee considered for a moment then shook his head. "No, the enemy still outnumbers us greatly, and he's no doubt planning to rendezvous with General Butler's force already encamped along the James. The important thing is that Sheridan no longer poses an immediate threat to Richmond. . . . If he ever did," Lee added bitterly.

"He was after our cavalry all along," Mac said. "He wanted to lure us to our destruction."

"Yes. So it appears. And we almost gave him what he wanted." Lee took a deep breath and squared his shoulders. "We've been licked. No use lying about it. But we're still alive, and we'll fight another day. I just wish . . ."

His voice trailed off and he shook his head. Mac knew exactly what he meant. He wished that Stuart were still there to lead them. For all his excesses, for all his spectacular failures, Stuart had compiled a remarkable record of victories far more marvelous than his recent disappointments.

How many good men had to be lost? Fitz Lee had asked, and Mac hated to think of the answer.

6∞9

WILL SHIVERED in the cold mist. At least the rain had tapered off a bit on the morning of May 12. The day before, a cold front had blown through, bringing wind and heavy rain and even hail. After the narrow thrust at the Mule Shoe late on the afternoon of May 10 was almost successful, Will had expected the Yankees to try the tactic again the next day with even more men. He supposed the bad weather had scotched those plans, if indeed that was what Grant had intended to do.

He tried to rouse himself from his drowsiness as his head nodded forward. The time was not yet dawn. A thick gray darkness, made even more impenetrable by the mist, was suspended over the battlefield.

Roman appeared beside him, hunkering down to press a tin cup into Will's hands. "Have some of this, Cap'n," Roman said. "Maybe it'll help you perk up a mite."

Will lifted the cup to his lips and sipped. He looked sharply over at Roman in surprise and then took another drink. "My God," he whispered. "Is this *real* coffee?"

"Well . . . not entirely. But it's got real coffee in it, to go along with the roasted grain."

"Where in heaven's name did you find it? And it's even *hot.* You're a miracle worker, Roman."

"Naw, I just traded with General Lee's cook for it. I been carvin' a figure of the general on that Traveller horse of his, and the cook took a shine to it."

"I never saw anybody who can work with wood like you can," Will said. "If that don't beat all."

"You drink up, Cap'n. It'll make you feel better."

Will didn't know if that was true, but the hot, potent brew certainly couldn't hurt. He'd been chilled to the bone ever since the nor'easter came through. Sometimes he was so cold he felt as if his heart was going to freeze in his chest.

And maybe that would be best, he thought. If he were frozen, at least he wouldn't have to kill and watch men being killed all around him. He was so utterly tired of death. He had never realized until he was surrounded by thousands of corpses just how boring death could be.

He wanted to see his family again, though, and Dorothy Chamberlain. That hope was what kept him going. It was a false hope, he suspected; he had felt the center of the pain shift inside him, drifting closer and closer to the core of his being. When it reached a certain spot, he would die. He was sure of that. But maybe not yet. Maybe he could hold on long enough to see his loved ones again.

"Maybe we can finish that game today," Roman said.

Will chuckled. "You're assuming the Yankees will give us time to play chess."

"Look around, Cap'n. You really think those Yankees are gonna attack on a cold, wet, miserable day like today?"

"Not if they've got a lick of sense," Will agreed with a grin.

In fact, it was thought by some that the Yankees were through attacking, that Grant had finally come to his senses and realized that he could not overwhelm the Confederate position. Reports had come in that some of the Federal wagons and equipment were shifting to the east, toward Fredericksburg. A few men were even confident enough to gleefully maintain that the campaign was over and the Yankees had been whipped.

Will didn't believe that, and he had worried earlier in the night when some of the Confederate artillery in the salient began to be withdrawn. Getting ready to move fast was all well and good, but it struck Will as foolish to be weakening their defenses when so many Yankees were still out there, only a few hundred yards away in the darkness.

A short time later, the sky grew a little grayer. Dawn was not far off. Heavy clouds of mist and fog cloaked the landscape, however. The sun was in its proper place in the heavens, Will supposed, but it seemed unlikely that anyone in the vicinity of Spotsylvania Court House would see it today.

He was growing drowsy again, the restorative effects of the coffee wearing off, when he heard a sudden shout somewhere nearby. Then another and another. Will lifted his head and murmured sleepily, "What are the boys cheering?"

"That ain't no cheerin', Cap'n Will," Roman announced from beside him.

A mighty roar of gunfire erupted. Will surged to his feet. He grabbed Roman's arm. "Get out of here! Get to the rear!"

"No sir! I ain't goin'!"

There was no time to argue. Will drew his pistol as he saw shapes clambering over the breastworks. Muzzle flashes split the darkness as the defenders opened fire. By the light of the guns, Will glimpsed the blue uniforms of the invaders. Somehow the Yankees had gotten right on top of them.

With his saber in his left hand and his pistol in his right, Will threw himself into the frantic fight. The Yankees may have approached quietly, but they were shrieking and shouting like hellions now as they stormed the Confederate line. Everything was chaos, and Will thought, not for the first time, that this was what hell must be like: the terrible din, the cries of pain and rage, the acrid clouds of powder smoke as bitter and galling as any brimstone . . .

Like a great tidal surge, the Yankees washed over the Confederate defenses, more Yankees than Will had ever seen in his life. He could slaughter them all day and still not come to the end of the killing. He laughed, half-mad with the thought that perhaps he was already dead, that this really *was* hell, and that he would spend eternity hacking and slashing and firing at the enemy, feeling the splatter of blood on his face and smelling the foul gases that burst out when he rammed his saber into their bellies and ripped them open.

He might have gone completely mad had not something smashed into his head and sent him reeling backward into the mud. He was numb, barely conscious, only vaguely aware that someone had grabbed him and was dragging him through the trenches. Mud splashed around him, coated his face, and clogged his nose and mouth so that he coughed and sputtered. His head hurt so much he was sure his skull would fly apart at any second.

Then oblivion took him, and his last thought was one of gratitude that at least he wouldn't hurt anymore.

⟨⟨⟨⟩⟩⟩

THAT WAS wrong, too. When consciousness returned, the pain was worse than ever. He couldn't stop himself from groaning, and as he did so, hands grasped his shoulders.

"Cap'n Will! Cap'n Will! You're alive!"

Will tried to force his eyes open. It was hard to tell which hurt worse, his head or his chest. Then he realized that his left eye was open, but his right would not. Bleary and disoriented, he looked up and saw that Roman loomed over him in the grayness. Moisture fell on Will's face. He could not be sure if it was rain or tears.

"Wha . . . what happened?"

"You got shot in the head, Cap'n," Roman said, his voice shaking. "I grabbed hold of you and pulled you out of there."

"Where . . ." Will's throat closed up for a moment, and he couldn't speak. After a moment, he finished the question. "Where are we now?"

"'Bout a quarter-mile back from the front, by that old house."

Will could see the wall of the house now, rising above them. Roman had dragged and carried him a quarter of a mile, thinking that more than likely he was dead, and had placed him here where at least he would have a little protection from the weather. Somehow, Will wasn't surprised by the young man's actions. Some people would think that Roman was just a devoted servant. Will knew better. Roman was a friend, one of the best friends he'd ever had.

"I can't . . . open this eye."

"They's blood dried all over it, from where that bullet hit you in the head. I see an old bucket over yonder that's got some rainwater caught in it. I'll get that and clean you up, Cap'n."

Will closed his left eye and nodded wearily. The movement made his head hurt even more. A grim smile etched lines on his face. It was amazing just how much pain a human being could stand. After a while it came to be the natural state of things.

While Roman was getting the water, Will listened. He heard the roar of cannons and the crackle of rifle fire and a low rumbling that he recognized as angry, desperate shouts from thousands of fighting men, all blended together. The battle was still going on.

Roman came back with the bucket of rainwater. He tore a strip of cloth off his shirt and soaked it, then began using the wet cloth to wipe away the dried blood on Will's head and face. Though the young man's touch was as gentle as he could make it, Will's head thundered in agony every time Roman dabbed at the blood. Eventually, Will was able to open his right eye, and he was grateful to discover that he could still see. His vision was blurry, but that was better than nothing.

"How does the . . . head wound look?" he asked.

"Not as bad as I feared it would be, when I saw all that blood," Roman said. "Looks like it just clipped you a mite, Cap'n. You got a gash 'bout an inch long on your head." Roman's fingers prodded the area around the wound. "Don't seem like it busted nothin'."

Will gritted his teeth against the renewed pain. "Help me . . . sit up."

"No, Cap'n, you just lay there and rest—"

"Help me . . . up!" Will insisted.

With a sigh, Roman got an arm around his shoulders and raised him. Will scooted back against the foundation of the old house and gazed toward the north. They called the salient the Mule Shoe, and from here Will could see the whole toe of the shoe. What he saw sickened him. It was difficult to make out details because the scene was cloaked in mist and rolling clouds of powder smoke, but it was obvious from the number of blue uniforms he saw that the Yankees had completely overrun the defenders at the tip of the salient. Here and there, knots of gray-clad Confederates were still struggling with the invaders, but they were heavily outnumbered and putting up a losing fight.

"My God," Will murmured. "They've beaten us. What of the company? What of the rest of the brigade?"

Roman shook his head. "I don't know, Cap'n. I heard some of the men who were retreatin' say that nearly everybody up there's been killed or captured. General Johnson was took prisoner by the Federals, and I think General Steuart was, too. But I ain't sure of none of it." He looked around. "We got to get you outta here, Cap'n. Those Yankees'll be comin' up here before much longer."

"Well, I can still fight," Will said angrily. "Where's my pistol, my saber?"

"No sir, you can't." Roman's voice was firm. "If I have to, I'll pick you up and carry you, but you ain't goin' back in that fight. Ain't nothin' you can do to help those boys. You'll just get yourself killed for no good reason."

Fury welled up inside Will. "How dare you tell me what I can't do, you goddamn nig—"

He stopped short at the realization of what he was about to say. Horror washed over him as he saw the stricken look on Roman's face.

After a moment, Roman said, "That's right, Cap'n. I'se just a goddamn nigger. But I still say you ain't goin' back in that fight."

Will struggled to find his voice, to put aside the pain—both physical and spiritual—that threatened to overwhelm him. "I'm sorry, Roman. Lord knows I'm sorry. You're right. Let's get out of here."

Bracing himself against the wall of the house, Will pushed himself to his feet. Roman grasped his arm to help him. They turned and started around the house, Will limped along with Roman supporting him.

On top of everything else, the dampness aggravated his condition even more, making Will's old leg wound hurt like blazes.

They were not alone in heading for the rear. Dozens of retreating Confederate soldiers ran past them. The two of them, however, maintained a slow but steady pace.

Not everyone was retreating, Will saw. Troops were moving in from the west. Will recognized Gen. John B. Gordon as he rallied his men and moved them into position for a counterattack. Will wished he could join them, but he now realized that he was in no shape to fight. Like it or not, he had to admit that. The way his heart was pounding and thumping so erratically, he wasn't sure he was even going to live through the morning.

Another officer rode up, hatless, white hair and beard standing out in the gloom. As the soldiers took notice of him, they called out, "General Lee! General Lee!"

Will and Roman saw Gordon ride over to join Robert E. Lee. "What do you want me to do, General?" Gordon asked.

"I see you are forming for a counterattack," Lee said in his softly accented voice. "Please continue, General."

Gordon snapped a salute and turned to ride away.

Will took in the scene over his shoulder. "Wait," he said to Roman. "By God, I want to see this."

They turned, and Will felt a sense of awe welling up within him as he saw the hatless commander of the army riding slowly toward the center of the line that was forming.

"He's going to lead the charge himself," Will whispered.

Will was not the only one in the field to realize Lee's intentions. The perception began to sweep through the ranks.

In less than a heartbeat, Gordon wheeled his horse and galloped back. "General Lee, sir!" he called out. "You shall not lead my men in a charge. No man can do that, sir. Another is here for that purpose."

Murmurs of agreement began to rise from the surrounding troops. Quickly they escalated to shouts.

"These men behind you are Georgians, Virginians, and Carolinians," Gordon continued. "They have never failed you on any field. They will not fail you here. Will you, boys?!"

A chorus of "No! No!" rose from the soldiers. One man reached out and grabbed the bridle of Lee's horse, Traveller. "General Lee to the rear!" he cried, and the other men took up the shout. "General Lee to the rear!" The troops swarmed around Lee, forcing his horse to turn.

The general didn't resist them. His lined, weathered face was taut with emotion at this display of affection and admiration from the men he was sending into battle. He lifted a hand slightly, as if in benediction, then began to ride slowly toward the rear. The mass of soldiers parted to let him through.

Will swallowed hard. "We'll never see the like of it again," he said. "When this war is over, there will never be another to equal it."

"I sure hope not, Cap'n," Roman said. "I surely do."

They trudged on, and behind them Gordon's men went into battle. A few minutes later, Will and Roman came upon another house, not quite as bullet-pocked as the one they had left in the Mule Shoe. They stopped there to rest.

An old bench sat on the porch of the house. Roman lowered Will onto it. "I'll see if I can find you somethin' to drink, Cap'n."

Will nodded. "Thank you. That would be good." His lips were crusted with dried blood and powder grime. He wanted to lick them but knew the taste would sicken him. He already felt nauseous, probably from his head wound.

He leaned back and realized he had a clear vantage point from which to watch the battle. He saw Gordon's men thrusting forward in their counterattack, saw as well the fighting that erupted on both sides of the salient. It was worse to the west. Those were General Rodes's men over there, Will knew, and they put up a valiant battle. The way men swarmed over the parapets, first in blue, then gray, then blue again, reminded him of ants swarming over an anthill, locked in mortal combat as they tried to wipe each other out. A soft laugh came from Will's lips. They were ants, all right. Tens of thousands of men swarmed over the Virginia countryside, killing and dying, and what they did had just about as much effect on the universe as the ants in an anthill. How could it all be so important and yet so meaningless at the same time? Will's laughter grew louder then choked off in a sob.

Again and again the two sides clashed as Will and Roman watched through the finely falling rain. Even before this day was over, the area around a sharp bend in the Confederate line where the Yankees hit General Rodes's defenders would be called the Bloody Angle. No truer name had ever been coined. The trenches ran with blood. The feet of countless struggling men churned the ground into crimson mud as they fought for their lives. Will saw Yankees perched on top of the log breastworks shooting down into the trenches. Men behind them passed up loaded rifles, so they were able to maintain an almost continuous fire. Inevitably, though, they were knocked off the parapets and other Yankees had to scramble up to take their places, so that gave the embattled Confederates a few seconds to catch their breath before the killing began again.

A part of Will still believed he should have been there among them, dying along with those men and boys who were selling their lives so valiantly. But it wouldn't have altered the outcome one bit, and he knew it.

A short time later, he was horrified when Federal artillery was brought up and fired at point-blank range into the ranks of defenders. So close like that, men were blown apart by the canister rounds. Withering rifle fire dropped the Yankee gunners, though, and after a few minutes the guns were withdrawn.

A surgeon hurrying past the house paused and noticed Will and Roman on the porch. He rested a foot on the bottom step. "Are you injured, Captain?" he asked.

"Head wound," Will said, pointing to the gash on his head, which was still oozing blood.

"Go back to the rear," the surgeon ordered. "A new line is being established eight hundred yards behind the old one. Our field hospitals are behind that new line."

"Yes sir, we'll do that," Roman said. "Soon as the cap'n here feels up to it."

"It had better be soon," the surgeon said with a frown. "I fear we won't hold this salient much longer."

Will knew the man was right. The defenders couldn't hang on to the Mule Shoe. There were too many of the enemy, and the defenders had lost too many men.

For the time being, though, the Confederates still held. They were a good half-mile farther back than they had been that morning, and night was coming on. An entire day had passed in battle. There was no way of knowing how many men had died today, Will thought. Thousands, surely. Corpses were stacked four or five deep on open ground; in the trenches it would be even worse.

Roman tugged at Will's arm. "Come on, Cap'n. You heard what the doctor said. We best get outta here."

Will didn't argue. The pain in his head and chest had receded to dull aches, but he was so weak he could barely rise. Roman had to help him get to his feet and walk. As he shuffled along, Will felt like he was a hundred years old. The war did that. It drained almost everything a man had and left him a near-lifeless husk. And then it took the rest. But it had to be done. The price had to be paid, because some men could not run. These men could not run.

They fought because the Yankees had invaded their homeland. Some yapped of slavery, some yammered about states' rights, some pontificated about tariffs and economic development. The politicians knew nothing of the reality. But Will knew why he was here and why most of the men who had fought alongside him were here. The Yankees had raised an army, shouldered arms, and marched boldly, arrogantly, into Virginia, streaming out from Washington toward Manassas with rich men and beribboned ladies trailing along behind to watch the show. They had believed that the Southerners would turn tail and run at this display of military might. Thirty minutes, a few gunshots—*pop, pop, pop!*—and the war would be over. Truly, that was what they had thought. No more than a thimbleful of blood would be shed.

They should have been here today, Will thought as he and Roman tramped on into the mist. *God help us all, they should have been here.*

Chapter Nineteen

COLD RAIN GAVE WAY to hot, brassy sunshine that dried the roads and raised tendrils of steamy mist from the soggy ground. The opposing armies north of Spotsylvania Court House might have enjoyed the better weather had there been a respite from the fighting. But for the next week following the horrific battle for the Bloody Angle, combat continued along the newly established Confederate line. Though nothing approached the tremendous scale as the attack on May 12, Grant's troops continued probing the Confederate position with a brigade here, a division there, a corps over yonder. Each time, the bitter battle failed to gain much ground. Union losses were tremendous; if Grant persisted, his force might be slaughtered. So it came as no surprise when Grant began to shift his units to the east then filter them southward. Once again, he was trying to maneuver around the right flank of the Army of Northern Virginia, with his eye still on the prize that was Richmond.

Will Brannon had not taken part in any of the fighting that followed the engagement in which he was wounded. A surgeon had dressed the gash on his head and told him that he was lucky; another inch and he would have been a dead man. Will wasn't sure he considered that luck. But he was declared unfit for duty and ordered to remain in the hospital for the time being. It didn't really matter whether he was on the front lines or not, he told himself bitterly.

He no longer had a company to command.

A handful of his men had survived the collapse of the Confederate line on May 12. The others had all been killed or captured. The few survivors had been scattered, dispersed to other companies that had also suffered enormous losses. Will felt adrift, unneeded, as he lay there on a crude pallet in the field hospital, trying to ignore the pain in his head and chest.

He had begun to cough up foul-smelling phlegm and figured he was rotting from the inside out. He was no doctor, but he thought he knew what was wrong. When the bullet had struck him at Gettysburg, it must have fragmented inside his chest, and not all of it had been removed by the surgeons. Even a tiny sliver of lead left within him would be enough to make his internal injuries fester and fail to heal. He was beyond help now. Whatever was wrong with him, whether his theory was correct or not, it was going to kill him.

Roman tried to raise his spirits, but it was an almost impossible task. Will played chess with the young man out of friendship and gratitude for all the times Roman had helped him. What had passed between them when Will lost his temper was forgiven and forgotten. Will was glad of that. He could be at peace with himself regarding that part of his life.

But many other regrets plagued him. He could have been a better son, a better brother. He wished he had a chance to be a good husband to Dorothy, a good father to the children they might have. That wasn't to be, and Will felt the loss keenly. He had Roman write a letter to Dorothy, expressing his regret that what might have been would never be.

"You don't want to be sayin' those things, Cap'n," Roman told him. "You go to thinkin' bad things are gonna happen, they mostly do."

Will smiled tiredly. "But even more often, they happen despite what we think."

"You make it sound like you believe the world to be a bad place, Cap'n."

"Look around you," Will said. "How could anyone with eyes to see believe otherwise?"

It was true that the field hospital was a horrible sight, packed with maimed and mutilated men, most of whom would die from their wounds. Few of those who survived would ever be whole again. The air stank with the smell of festering flesh and was never silent but always filled with groans of agony.

"What you need is to get outta here," Roman said.

"There's only one way out for me."

But the morning came when, to Will's surprise, his head no longer hurt. That injury, unlike the one in his chest, was healing. He was able to stand and walk outside with Roman's help, and the fresh air was like a tonic to him. He breathed deeply of it and felt a little strength seeping back into him.

Roman found him near some trees, their leaves rustling in the wind.

"I heard that we're movin' out, Cap'n," Roman told him.

Will leaned back against the nearest tree. He noted that he was able to stay there without Roman's having to support him.

"Moving where?" he asked.

"Down to the North Anna River. General Lee figures that's where the Yankees are headin', and he wants to get there first."

Will nodded. "Sounds reasonable. Grant's been trying to get around us right from the start."

"The sick and the injured are all bein' sent to Richmond. You'll get to see Missus Chamberlain again, more'n likely."

Will's eyes darted sharply at him. "You sent that letter to her, as I asked?"

"Yes sir, I did."

"Good. Then let those words serve as my farewell to her. I'm not going to Richmond."

"Cap'n—?" Roman looked and sounded shocked.

The pain in Will's head might be gone, but the pain in his chest wasn't. He wasn't going to subject Dorothy to seeing him like this. He wouldn't force her to endure his last days at his side, unable to do anything for him. Better to be here with the army, trying to accomplish something with however much time he had left.

Will straightened up from the tree, standing upright. "I'm going back to the fight."

"Cap'n, the company is gone. Ain't nobody left for you to lead no more."

"I'll join another company, then. I'll fight as a private if I have to. And I'll go as high as General Ewell, if need be, to see to it."

Roman stared at him as if Will had lost his mind. And perhaps he had. He had lost almost everything else. Why not his mind as well?

"Cap'n . . ."

From somewhere a grin appeared on Will's face. "You'd be wasting your time trying to argue with me. You ought to know that by now."

After a moment, Roman said, "Reckon I do. But that don't mean I got to like it."

"Nobody has to like anything. All we're actually required to do in this world is be born and die."

And he was more than halfway there, Will thought.

⌀

THE NORTH Anna River was a beautiful stream running between high, wooded banks. This spring it was full and had a strong current because of the recent rains. Ewell's corps were the first to arrive at nearby Hanover Junction, where they were joined by numerous reinforcements sent by Bragg in Richmond, Breckinridge in the Shenandoah, and Beauregard, who had succeeded in bottling up the Yankees under Butler along the James River south of Richmond. As the rest of the Army of Northern Virginia arrived, Robert E. Lee positioned them along the North Anna, where he planned to make another stand against Grant and the Army of the Potomac. Bridges used by the Confederates to cross the river were destroyed, and in places where the southern bank was higher than the northern, artillery batteries were emplaced. Grant had reinforcements of his own, drawn from reserves around Washington, D.C. He would find a formidable, but still outnumbered Confederate force waiting for him on the south bank of the river.

Will Brannon was among that Confederate force. He hadn't had to go as high up the chain of command as Ewell to get what he wanted. Col. J. H. S. Funk, the regimental commander of the Thirty-third Virginia—that is, what was left of it after Spotsylvania—was glad to place Will in command of one of the reorganized companies.

"You look like hell, Captain," the colonel said bluntly. "If you find the duties of command too strenuous for you in your current condition, I want you to notify me immediately so that you can be replaced. We cannot risk inadequate leadership."

"I give you my word, Colonel, my leadership will be more than adequate," Will vowed.

His company was positioned beside one of the batteries. The riflemen were charged with protecting the battery's gunners. They would keep up a steady covering fire so that Federal sharpshooters would have a more difficult and dangerous time of it if they tried to pick off the artillerymen.

Will strode back and forth beneath the oak trees, hollow-eyed and gaunt-cheeked above his beard. The last time he had seen himself in a mirror, he had barely recognized his own features. Three years of war had aged him decades. His black hair was streaked heavily with gray. But he managed to stand upright whenever a fit of coughing was not upon him.

Roman sat with his back against a tree trunk. "You gonna wear a hole in the ground pacin' like that, Cap'n," he said.

Will grinned at him. "If I do, we'll make a trench out of it for when the Yankees come."

Roman just smiled faintly and shook his head. He had realized the futility of fussing and arguing with Cap'n Will. The captain knew what he wanted to do, and Roman supposed he had a right to do it. White men made up their own minds, even when their decisions were foolish. Roman reminded himself that he had that right now, too, since he had been granted his freedom. He had the right to make just as big a fool of himself as any white man.

There had been fighting the day before, on May 23, but Will and his men had not been involved in it. The Yankees' attempt to thrust a division across the river had been turned back. Will wasn't sure where they would strike next, but he was confident that there would be another attack. Grant wasn't going to give up after all this time. The Federal commander had proven that he was more than willing to spend the lives of his men to try to get what he wanted.

The heat of the past few days had receded again, and now a few fat raindrops were falling. Under the trees, Will, Roman, and the other men stayed relatively dry. Will gazed off to the west. He knew from the reports of the scouts that there were Federals south of the river over there. The Confederate line was V-shaped, pointing north. He and his men were almost at the tip of the point. When firing came from the left around midafternoon, he wasn't surprised. He figured the Yankees would try to come in on that flank while at the same time attacking across the river where he was positioned.

"Steady, men," he called as his troops reacted to the sounds of battle. "Our turn will come soon enough."

He glanced at Roman and went on quietly, "You shouldn't be here. There's no need."

"I'll stay," Roman said, unperturbed. "Cap'n Yancy wanted me to look after you, Cap'n Will, so that's what I been doin'."

"And doing a fine job of it, too," Will murmured. In truth, Roman had saved his life several times. But he would have had to be a skilled physician to have saved Will from the thing that sooner or later would kill him.

Federal artillery across the river opened up, and the Confederate battery returned the fire.

"Watch for the muzzle flashes from the sharpshooters!" Will shouted. That was the most effective way of spotting the Yankee snipers. The men manning the guns had to run the risk of drawing Federal fire. Their only protection was Will's riflemen, who were charged with the task of killing or driving off the Yankees whose job was to pick off the artillerymen. It was a dangerous game for both sides.

As an officer, Will knew that he was a target, too. If he got too far out in the open, one of the Yankees might decide to try for him. But hanging back well behind the front went against the grain for him. He had to be up where he could see what was going on.

Bullets thudded into tree trunks and ricocheted off rocks. Roman urged, "At least get behind a tree, Cap'n!"

Will shook his head and drew his saber. He wanted to blaze away at the opposite bank with his pistol, but he knew the distance was too great. He'd just be wasting powder and lead. So he stalked back and forth behind the line of riflemen, weaving in and out of the trees and bushes. Branches fell around him, blasted loose by the flying bullets. Over at the artillery battery, several men had fallen, but the big guns were still roaring. On the left flank, the sounds of battle were louder. The Federals were pinching in. If they were successful, Will and his men might be cut off, trapped here at the apex of the V. He wasn't going to pull back unless ordered to do so, however, and if the Yankees threatened his flank, he would swing around and deal with them when the time came.

The rain came down harder, thrumming against the oak leaves and dripping through the foliage. The thickening overcast made it hard to see as night approached. Still the fighting continued. Artillery blasts tore orange holes in the gloom as flame gushed from the mouths of the guns. Will felt something pluck at his sleeve and a little later there was a tug on the tail of his coat. He coughed wrackingly, wiped his mouth with the back of his hand, and grinned. It was a race of sorts, he thought. Who was going to be the one who actually killed him, one of those Yankees on the other side of the North Anna, or the son of a bitch who'd shot him at Gettysburg?

As darkness settled over the noisy Virginia countryside, the duel between the big guns gradually ceased. And with the guns falling silent, so did the back-and-forth sniping across the river. On the left flank, the fighting continued until far into the night, but the Confederate line held and once again, for what seemed like the hundredth time since this campaign began back in early May, a Union assault was repulsed. Will finally sat down on the damp ground underneath a tree, leaned his head against the trunk, and closed his eyes. After a long time, the pain within him eased a bit, and he slipped into a troubled sleep, watched over by Roman.

⚬⟫⟫⟫⚬

SOMETIMES MAC felt that he had been born in the saddle. Surely he would die there, too, which meant he would have spent his entire life atop a horse. He was so tired he could almost believe that was true.

The cavalry had rejoined the rest of the Army of Northern Virginia at Hanover Junction days earlier. It seemed a year had passed since the fighting at Yellow Tavern, although in truth it had been only a little more than two weeks. Lee's cavalry had spent that time scouting and skirmishing. Long days in the saddle had been followed by arduous night rides to blunt some advance and harry once again the great beast that was the Federal army.

To make matters worse, these operations had been carried out without having an officer in overall command of the cavalry. Instead of replacing General Stuart, Robert E. Lee had ordered his son Rooney, his nephew Fitz, and Gen. Wade Hampton to retain their divisional commands and report directly to him. This arrangement led to a lack of coordination and uncertainty about the movements of each division.

Stuart had lingered more than a day after being wounded, but he had died on the evening of May 12, while the terrible battle for the Bloody Angle was taking place near Spotsylvania. Adding to the tragedy, Flora and the children had not arrived in time to bid him farewell. Reportedly, Robert E. Lee had said of Stuart, "I can scarcely think of him without weeping."

That was a sentiment shared by nearly every man who had ridden under Stuart.

But there was still business to be taken care of and a war to be fought. The cavalry had been kept so busy that there hadn't been time for Mac to visit Will and see how he was doing. For all Mac knew, Will had been killed or captured at Spotsylvania. He had heard about the collapse of the Confederate line and how Gens. Edward Johnson and George Steuart had been captured. Will's position would have been somewhere near that spot. Mac tried to force the worry to the back of his mind, but it was always there, nagging at him.

Today a new group of cavalrymen rode with Fitz Lee's well-seasoned Virginians. They were from South Carolina and were commanded by Gen. Matthew C. Butler. They had seen no combat so far. Their uniforms were clean and well pressed, their horses frisky and stepping lively. To Mac and to the other veterans, most of these fresh-faced newcomers looked about twelve years old.

They were riding toward a crossroads known as Haw's Shop, not far from the Pamunkey River, which was formed by the joining of the North and South Anna Rivers. Rumor had it that the Yankees were trying to slip across the Pamunkey and circle around toward a crossroads village called Cold Harbor, about fifteen miles east of Richmond. The cavalry was supposed to find out if there was any truth to the speculation.

Personally, Mac didn't doubt it for a second. Grant's objective all along had been Richmond. For nearly a month, he had been maneuvering, swinging his army farther east and south, doing everything in his power to get between Robert E. Lee and Richmond. But every time Grant had sidestepped, Lee was there to meet him. In the Wilderness, at Spotsylvania, and along the North Anna, Lee had countered Grant. At great cost, to be sure, but it was estimated that the Yankees had lost even more men.

Today Fitz Lee had three brigades under his command, Gen. Williams Wickham's in the center, Gen. Thomas Rosser's to the left, and the untried South Carolinians under Butler to the right. Lee himself, along with Mac and the rest of his staff, rode with Wickham's men toward Haw's Shop.

It was not yet midday when the guns began to pop ahead of the column. Lee signaled a halt. "Our outriders have run into the Yankees. General Wickham, are you ready?"

"Of course, sir," Wickham replied.

"Then let's see what all the commotion is about," Lee said with a smile.

Mac tugged his hat down tighter on his head as he urged the stallion into a gallop and joined the wild charge down the road toward Haw's Shop. He never had gotten another campaign cap like the one he'd lost; instead he had taken to wearing a brown hat with a soft brim that dipped down slightly in front. The wind tugged at it as he raced toward the enemy with Fitz.

The countryside bordering the road was heavily wooded; the road itself was the only place suitable for a cavalry charge. Within moments, that was exactly what was taking place, as at least a brigade of Federal cavalry came into sight, thundering toward the onrushing Confederates.

Mac drew his pistol and fired as he rode forward. By the time the gun was empty, the two groups were almost on top of each other, so instead of reaching for one of his other pistols, Mac holstered the empty and pulled his saber.

Dust boiled in the road as the two groups of horsemen collided. Horses screamed and fell. Men shouted angrily and cried out in pain. Mac cut and thrust with the saber for several minutes then wheeled the stallion and pulled back. All around him, the rest of the cavalrymen were doing the same. They broke apart, the Federals withdrawing to the east, the Confederates to the west.

"Dismount! Dismount!" Fitz shouted. "We'll have to fight them on foot!"

That was what Mac had been afraid of. Though the cavalry-men were valiant fighters whether they were mounted or not, going into battle afoot was always more difficult for them. It was unnatural, somehow, for men who spent most of their hours in the saddle.

But in terrain such as this, they had no choice. They swung down, drew their carbines, and formed into battle lines.

Mac stayed on the stallion and rode beside Lee as the general saw to the positioning of the men. Lee put the troopers in Wickham's and Rosser's brigades up front, since they were combat veterans. Minutes later, the Yankees charged again, this time on foot. Smoke soon hung thickly above the woods on both sides of the road as fierce fighting developed.

Fitz Lee dismounted and paced along the edge of the road. "We'd better pull back, sir," Mac suggested. Bullets filled the air uncomfortably close to Lee's position.

Lee took his pipe from his pocket, and for a second Mac thought the general was going to light up and be stubborn about moving. But then Lee replaced the pipe and sighed.

"I suppose you're right," he conceded. "We'll move back to that church just up the road."

They had passed the church a short time earlier as they approached the spot where the two cavalry forces met. Now they cantered back to it and dismounted to wait under the shade of a tree as reports came in from the battleground. Rosser's men were standing firm, denying the Yankees any advance. Wickham's brigade was having more trouble but was hanging on. So far, Butler's newcomers had seen little action.

Lee thought it over then ordered, "Swing Butler's men over and move them up alongside Wickham. We must strengthen that part of the line."

As far as Mac could judge from the reports, that area was where the Federals were concentrating their attack, so he agreed with Lee's decision. Now the South Carolinians would have their baptism of fire.

And a hot one it was, on that afternoon of May 28, as reinforcements arrived on the scene for the Yankees. Hours passed
during which the Confederate troopers fought gallantly but
were eventually forced to give ground. Earlier in the day, the
grizzled Virginia cavalrymen had done plenty of good-natured
ribbing of the newcomers. Now Butler's men proved their
mettle, standing as tough and fighting as hard as any of their Vir-
ginian comrades.

Lee kept track of the battle as best he could by watching
through field glasses. Late that afternoon, he exploded, "The
Yankees have *more* men coming up! My God, is there no end to
them?" He thrust the glasses toward Mac. "Does that look like
infantry to you? I think they've moved up the infantry."

Mac lifted the glasses to his eyes and squinted through them.
It was hard to make out anything through the smoke and the dust
and the trees. But it did look like there were a lot of Yankees
coming up.

"I don't know, sir," he told Lee as he handed the glasses
back. "Do you want me to take a closer look?"

"And get yourself shot?" Lee shook his head. "No, I've had
enough. We've all had enough, Mac. We're withdrawing."

There was defeat in the general's voice, defeat and discour-
agement. Mac had never heard those emotions so plainly from
Lee. Stuart's death still weighed on him.

"We must return to the army and let my uncle know that the
Federals are on this side of the Pamunkey," Lee went on.
"Grant still has his eye on Cold Harbor."

"Yes sir," Mac said softly. "It would appear so."

Lee squared his shoulders. "We'll stop him before he gets
there. And if we don't . . . we'll stop him there. No farther." He
sounded distracted, almost haunted. "The time to make a stand
is coming, if our nation is to live. No farther."

THE DEADLY dance continued. Two days later, on May 30, after shifting to the south and east again, the opposing armies found themselves facing each other across shallow, slow-moving Totopotomoy Creek. To keep Grant from moving farther east, Lee hit the other end of the Federal line with the corps now commanded by Gen. Jubal Early.

Early's predecessor, Richard Ewell, never in the best of health and missing a leg from an injury earlier in the war, had become quite ill following a hard fall from his horse during the battle for the Bloody Angle. He was no longer physically able to command. Early's attack served only as a brief annoyance to the Yankees, who forced the Confederates back across the creek.

Word reached a frustrated Lee that still more Union reinforcements were arriving regularly at White House Landing, downstream on the Pamunkey. That would give Grant an almost overpowering advantage in manpower. Lee had to have reinforcements, too, but Beauregard had refused to send more men from the James River peninsula where he was still contesting with Butler's Federals. It took a telegram to President Davis himself to shake some troops loose from Beauregard, in this case a division of seven thousand men under the command of Gen. Robert Hoke.

May 31 dawned with the eyes of both commanders, Lee and Grant, on Cold Harbor, an intersection where five roads met and an old abandoned inn sat nearly hidden in a grove of trees. No one knew quite why the place had been given its name, since there was no harbor anywhere close by, and it was no colder here than anywhere else in Virginia. Now, with May ending and June about to begin, Cold Harbor was suddenly hot as Hades and getting hotter.

But General Hoke's men were bound for there, and Lee figured that Grant's reinforcements would proceed straight there from White House Landing, too. The race was on again. Whoever reached Cold Harbor first would have an undeniable advantage. If Grant extended his line that far and met up with the reinforcements unopposed, he would have succeeded in reaching his goal at last. He would have turned the corner on Lee and could march straight into Richmond from the east. At least some of the Confederates had to be waiting at Cold Harbor when the Yankees got there.

That job fell to Fitzhugh Lee and his cavalry.

Chapter Twenty

MAC CROUCHED BEHIND THE log breastworks, carbine in hand. He watched for a target, but none presented itself at the moment. The Yankees had pulled back after their fierce charge had failed to reach the Confederate line.

This was a new kind of fighting for Mac and for most of the men in Fitz Lee's command. In recent months the cavalry had fought dismounted, in the manner more typical of the Yankee cavalry. Yet in those instances, Lee's men usually didn't have the luxury of fighting from behind breastworks. Most of the time, whenever they were hurled into a fight, there was no time to prepare such defenses.

But today Lee's troopers had reached Cold Harbor well ahead of the enemy, so while a small group of pickets had guarded the roads north of the deserted settlement, the rest of the division had gone to work felling trees and erecting a line of breastworks. Considering that Lee's orders were to hold Cold Harbor at all costs, such a defense seemed prudent.

The Federal horsemen had shown up around midday and charged toward the crossroads. The Confederate outriders had given them a good fight but had pulled back steadily until they reached the breastworks. Then the men behind the works opened fire, and the Yankees were driven back, surprised by the stiffness of the resistance.

Since then there had been several more charges by the Union cavalrymen, each unsuccessful. The fighting was taking a toll on both sides. Lee's men had been outnumbered to start with, and though things had gone well so far, it was questionable how long they could hold on without reinforcements. General Hoke and his men should have shown up by now, Mac thought as he peered through a small gap in the breastworks, alert for any signs of a new attack.

The same thoughts must have been going through Fitz Lee's mind, because the general came up beside Mac. "Blast it, I figured we'd have some help by now." He glanced toward the lowering sun. "It's getting late in the afternoon."

"Yes sir, it is," Mac agreed. "If the Yankees keep attacking after dark, we won't be able to see them coming."

"They won't be able to see us as well, either," Lee pointed out. Then he shrugged. "But you're right, Mac. That'll be a bigger disadvantage for us than it will for them. Maybe it won't come to that. Maybe we'll drive them off before it gets dark."

But as the sun sank toward the horizon, that seemed less and less likely. It appeared, however, that the Yankees didn't want to wait until dark, either. A few minutes later, they launched another attack, the heaviest one yet, concentrating on the left flank of the Confederate entrenchments as well as the center of the line.

Mac heard the sound of seven-shot Spencer repeaters to the left as he reloaded and fired over the breastworks at the advancing Yankees. The carbines carried by the Confederate troopers were single-shot weapons. If they had had repeaters, it might have made all the difference in the world. *If wishes were horses,* Mac thought as the carbine cracked and kicked against his shoulder. Through the haze of powder smoke, he saw one of the saber-swinging Yankees charging toward the breastworks stumble and fall. The man didn't rise again.

Plenty of his comrades continued the charge, and after a few minutes, it became obvious that this time the Confederates would not be able to turn them back. And with the Yankees pinching in from the left, they would soon be cut off from the rest of the army if they didn't retreat now.

Mac heard the reluctance in Lee's voice as the general ordered, "Fall back to the west! Fall back!" The earthworks were abandoned, and the troopers dashed for their horses.

Mac jammed his carbine in its sheath and swung up onto the stallion's back. Lee was close beside him. They were in the vanguard of the troopers who circled around the Yankees on the left flank and galloped west, toward Richmond. Robert E. Lee was supposed to be moving the rest of the army down to interpose it between Grant and Richmond, but the cavalrymen didn't know exactly how far along that maneuver was. All they could do was hope that they ran into friends and not more of the enemy.

ROBERT E. LEE had succeeded in marching his men to the vicinity west of Cold Harbor, and when General Hoke arrived late in the day on May 31, that bolstered the strength of the Confederate force to the point that it seemed reasonable they might be able to withstand a Federal assault. Grant had captured Cold Harbor itself—or rather, the cavalry under "Little Phil" Sheridan had done so—but with Lee lurking just to the west, it seemed unlikely that Grant would be content to just sit there. Richmond had been his goal all along, and Lee was still between him and the capital city of the Confederacy. To reach Richmond, Grant was going to have to go through Lee.

He wasted little time in trying to do so. The very next day, June 1, 1864, the Union army marched west in a line stretching from Beulah Church in the north to beyond Cold Harbor in the south. The Yankees were opposed by an even longer Confederate defensive line. Hoke's fresh troops were concentrated along and on either side of the main road leading west from Cold Harbor. Farther north, between two stretches of woods, were the corps commanded by Gen. Richard Anderson. Beyond them, with the forest at their backs, were the men of the corps now commanded by Jubal Early, including Gen. John B. Gordon's division. Terry's Brigade of Gordon's division was commanded by Gen. William Terry, and among its members were the survivors from the Stonewall Brigade.

They had themselves a good position, Will thought as he gazed across the open ground in front of them. The Yankees would have to come to them across that ground, where there was little if any cover. His men were just inside the edge of the woods, at the top of a slight rise. They not only had cover but also commanded an excellent field of fire. The Yankees would try to soften them up with artillery, but Will was confident his men would be able to hold. It wasn't like being with his old company in the Thirty-third Virginia, but these were good men, good fighters. They would be fine.

He coughed loudly and rested a hand against a tree trunk to steady himself. Each cough made pain lance through his chest. Roman was beside him, looking worried. Will shook his head, pulled a handkerchief from his pocket, and patted his lips when the coughing finally ceased. The handkerchief came away with small spatters of blood on it.

"Cap'n Will . . ." Roman began.

"No use saying anything, Roman. No use at all. You'd best move on back now. The Yankees may be coming soon."

"No sir." Roman's voice was firm and determined. "May not be any use in it, but I'm gonna say it anyway. You're throwin' your life away, Cap'n. You ought to be in a hospital somewhere. The doctors might still be able to help you."

Will just shook his head.

"And I ain't goin' to the rear," Roman added. "I'm stayin' right here with you."

"You're just about the most insubordinate aide a man ever had . . ."

"That's a whole heap better'n bein' some kind of uppity slave, I reckon."

Will had to chuckle, but then he grew more solemn. "If it gets really bad, Roman, I want you to go back. Really. Get out of here. This isn't your fight. In fact, if you were going to fight at all, most folks might expect that you should be fighting on the other side."

"Most folks don't know me, and they don't know you, Cap'n. I'll stay."

Early in the day, while attempting to get a jump on Grant, Robert E. Lee ordered an attack in the center of the line. The assault was to be led by Anderson's men. Hoke's men would be part of the offensive, too.

From his position, Will saw the attack go forward on his right. It started briskly but fell apart almost immediately when one of the officers leading it was blown off his horse. The fighting was fierce for a time but accomplished nothing.

Then, after the Confederates pulled back and both sides had a bit of a breather, the Yankees launched a counterattack.

"Get ready, boys!" Will called as he saw the blue-clad troops starting across the broad, open field. "Here they come!"

Federal batteries opened fire. Shells burst in the tops of trees, sending millions of splinters flying through the air in a deadly spray. Most of the soldiers, however, were behind good cover, and the damage inflicted by the barrage and the wooden missiles was minimal. While the men had their heads down ducking the blasts, though, the Yankee infantry had a chance to charge partway across the field. Will saw them coming and sprang upright, waving his saber over his head. "Let them have it, boys!" he shouted. "Fire!"

The first volley to ring out from the Confederate line was a little ragged, the next one even more so. But they were effective. Most of the soldiers in the front row of charging Yankees went down, spilled off their feet by bullets ripping through their bodies. Will paced back and forth at the edge of the woods, being careful to stay out of the line of fire of his men. He saw the Yankees falling and yelled more encouragement to his men. A few of the Union infantrymen made it more than halfway across the open field, but that wasn't very many. And those few were cut down before they came close to reaching the woods where Will's men were holed up.

All along the line, the Yankees were meeting with the same lack of success. They outnumbered the men they considered Rebels, had better weapons and provisions, and were convinced they were poised on the brink of striking a deathblow to the Confederacy. But none of that counted for anything on this day. The defenders were in too strong a position and could not be dislodged. By nightfall, after hours of fighting, the Federals hadn't gained an inch.

The clouds of powder smoke that had rolled around him all afternoon had left a layer of grime caked on Will's face. He sat down on a log and let his arms dangle between his knees. His head hung forward in exhaustion. Everything required too much effort, too much energy.

Roman, who had never been far from his side all day, came up to him and pressed a canteen into his hands.

"Here you go, Cap'n. You take a drink. At least a swallow. It'll make you feel better."

"Do the men have water?" Will asked hoarsely as he raised his head and stared at the canteen.

"Yes sir. They's a little creek back in the woods. Ain't nobody goin' thirsty today."

"All right, then." Will took the canteen and tipped it to his lips. The water wasn't cold, but it tasted wonderful as it ran down his parched throat.

His head suddenly spun crazily, and he fell backward off the log. Will was only vaguely aware of hitting the ground. He heard Roman calling his name, but the sound was faint. A series of coughs shook him, and then he turned his head and vomited up the water he had just swallowed.

Roman caught hold of his shoulders and pulled him to a sitting position. "I'll have one of the soldiers fetch a doctor," he said as he wiped Will's face.

"N-no," Will whispered. "The surgeons have . . . real work to do . . . Leave them alone . . . to save the men they can save."

"But, Cap'n—"

"It's all right, Roman." Will summoned up a smile. "The fighting is over for today. I'll just . . . sleep for a while now . . . then I'll be fine."

His eyes closed. Darkness was already all around him. He was incredibly tired. He really did want to sleep. But if he did, would he ever wake up again?

Will had no idea.

⌾∭⌾

HE WAS more than a little surprised when he *did* wake up during the night, still alive. His back was propped against the log he had fallen off of earlier. Roman was nearby, stretched out on the ground, exhausted. The night was quiet except for the groans and cries of the wounded on the battlefield. That sound was always there, every time the guns fell silent.

Steadying himself with a hand on the log, Will pushed himself to his feet. He stepped over to the edge of the woods, lifting a hand and calling softly to the men on guard duty so they would know who he was.

"How you doin', Cap'n?" one of the men asked him. "That darky o' yours said you was feelin' mighty poorly."

"I'm all right," Will said, and while it was a lie, the assessment didn't stretch the truth too far. Resting had helped him, and he felt considerably better now. Prompted by curiosity, since he didn't know these men as well as he had known the members of his old company, he asked, "Where are you from, soldier?"

"Over by Winchester, Cap'n."

"The Shenandoah. Beautiful country."

"Yes sir, it surely is. Cap'n?"

"What is it?"

"You reckon we'll get any more to eat tomorrow? We ain't had hardly any rations lately."

"I know," Will said. Hunger was gnawing away at the vitals of the entire army, himself included. Yesterday morning he had eaten half a strip of bacon and a small piece of cornpone. That was the last meal he'd had. "I reckon once we've sent the Yankees packing, we'll have more time to do a little foraging."

"How long's that gonna be? Ain't them dumb bastards figured out by now we ain't gonna let 'em get to Richmond?"

"I imagine they'll get the idea pretty soon," Will said. He hoped it was so, anyway. For now the line was standing firm, but there was a limit to how much the human body could do. There might even be a limit to the human spirit . . .

But if so, these gallant Southerners hadn't reached it yet, Will told himself. They hadn't even come close.

"Cap'n Will?" Roman called to him. "Cap'n, you best rest some more."

"I'm fine, Roman," Will said as he gazed across the moonlit field toward the Yankee lines. The landscape would have been pretty if not for the thousands of dead and wounded strewn across it. Will reached over and squeezed the shoulder of the man he'd been talking to. "When you get home to the Shenandoah, you think about this old captain from time to time."

"Yes sir. I surely will."

Will hoped the man made it home safely. He hoped all the men who fought beside him would survive. But he knew that was impossible. For some reason unfathomable to him, a debt was still owed to the gods of war. And none of them would go home until it was paid in full.

⌒⟫⟫⟫⟩

ON THE afternoon of June 2 there was a brief battle at the north end of the Confederate line, around Bethesda Church. Several of Early's divisions surged forward, throwing the Yankees back a short distance. Otherwise, the day passed with both sides settling for taking a few long-range potshots at each other and throwing an occasional short artillery barrage. After it started raining heavily that afternoon, even those minor hostilities came to a halt.

During the evening and night, the Confederates were busy. Even though it was raining, they dug their trenches deeper and reinforced their earthworks and log breastworks. A sense of inevitability hung in the air along with the rain. From the Wilderness to Spotsylvania to the North Anna, the Yankees had continued coming and coming, blue-clad wave after blue-clad wave, despite incredible losses. No one doubted that when they attacked again, it would be with everything they had. One huge, final blow that would crush the Confederate army and open the way to Richmond. That was what Grant wanted, and it seemed he was willing to do whatever it took to accomplish that goal, no matter how many men died.

The line was lengthened. Will and his men shifted a short distance north, to the woods beyond the Old Church Road, which ran beside Bethesda Church. They dug in, doing everything in their power to be ready for the Yankees.

Will could feel the weakness growing inside him, but he did his best to ignore it and carry on, supervising the preparations for the inevitable attack. But several times an hour he coughed up blood, concealing it as best he could from Roman so the young man wouldn't worry.

He was leaning against a tree when a familiar voice said behind him, "Taking it easy, I see."

Will turned quickly. In the shadows under the trees, it was difficult to make out many details, but he recognized who was standing there.

"Mac," he rasped. "God, is it really you?"

Mac stepped closer and hugged him, a fierce, hard hug. "I didn't know if you were still alive," Mac said, his voice hoarse with emotion.

"I was worried about you," Will said. "We heard about how Fitz Lee's bunch did all the fighting the first day down here, when Sheridan's cavalry showed up."

"I'm fine. Not a scratch." Mac stepped back. "But you're mighty thin, Will. Not much more than skin and bones."

Will shrugged. "We've all been on short rations."

"Are you sure it's not more than that?"

Will didn't answer. Instead he asked, "Did you come here for a visit, or just to nag at me?"

"Is there any place we can sit and smoke a pipe without worrying about Yankee sharpshooters?"

"Come on." Will motioned to Roman, who was standing nearby. "You, too."

They went to the rear and stood under a large tree. The branches shielded them enough from the dripping rain that they were able to get their pipes going. Will suppressed the urge to cough. He didn't want to waste any precious time hacking while he could visit with Mac.

Quickly, they brought each other up to date on the events of the past few days. Since the opening battle on May 31, Fitz Lee's cavalry had been busy screening the far right of the line, along the Chickahominy River, and turning back some isolated Federal forays in that direction.

"I've got a feeling it's just about over," Mac concluded. "The Yankees can't keep this up forever."

"I wouldn't be so sure about that, little brother. We may stop them for a while, but they'll keep coming."

"You sound like you think we're whipped," Mac protested.

"Maybe not. But if Lincoln is re-elected this fall . . ." Will shrugged. "I've had a feeling for a while that we couldn't beat them, but I hoped we could hold out long enough they'd give it up as a bad job. Lincoln won't back down, though, and neither will Grant."

"You're probably right." Mac's voice was hushed and solemn. "Things could change, though. There's always hope."

"We're still alive and still fighting." Will grinned. "That's worth something, I reckon."

"It's worth a hell of a lot."

Will couldn't argue with that. He was tired of talking about the war, though. He said, "You remember how the house smelled early in the winter when Ma was downstairs cooking breakfast and the rest of us were still in bed?"

"Oh, Lord, yes. That was the most wonderful smell."

"And how the honeysuckle bloomed in the summer and it seemed the whole world smelled like that?"

"Sure. And in the evening we'd sit out on the porch and sing songs and tell stories and watch the lightning bugs."

Will laughed. "Cory used to love to catch them and hold them in his hand and look in to watch them flash."

"Yeah, but then he told Cordelia they'd bite her and he'd chase her with them until Ma made him stop."

"Cory was a caution," Will said. "Wonder where he is now."

Mac shook his head. "No telling. I just hope and pray he's all right. That all of them are."

"They are," Will said. "I feel it in my bones. I'm the oldest. I'd know."

"You can't be sure—"

"Sometimes you can," Will said. He looked off into the darkness. "Sometimes something comes over a man, and it's like he's connected to everything in his life that's precious to him. Almost like he can reach out and lay his hand on all his loved ones and draw them to him, even though they're not really there. And with them comes all the memories, and they wrap around him like a blanket, the warmest, most comfortable blanket there ever was, and he knows it all and feels it all and the thing he knows the most is that it's all right. No matter what happens it's all right because he loved those people and those memories and that won't ever go away, no matter what. That's the feeling that comes over a man sometimes, and I reckon it's on me tonight."

Mac set his pipe aside and put his arms around Will and held him. Roman stood behind them and put a hand on Will's shoulder. Finally, fighting back tears, Mac stepped back and grasped Will's hand. "You're the best man I ever knew," he said.

"And you're the best man I ever knew. Take care of yourself, little brother."

"I'll be praying for you tomorrow."

"Pray for all of us," Will said. "I reckon we can use it."

CRUMO

THE YANKEES came at dawn.

Five corps against three, stretched out in a line over two miles long. Thousands of men on the move through the mist that swirled up from the wet ground. The rain had stopped; the clouds were clearing. The eastern sky was orange, and as the light grew and spread over the fields, the men stepped briskly forward, rifles held across their chests. A cannon roared somewhere behind them, then another and another. The men walked faster. A few broke into a run, then a few more and a few more until the whole front line was charging forward and the early morning air rang with shouts and battle cries. A thousand yards separated them from the Confederate lines. The gap closed steadily as the Federals surged forward. From the looks of it, there wasn't much waiting for them. The trenches were constructed cleverly so that they were not very visible from the perspective of the Yankees. But the Confederates were there, waiting, and when the men running forward, away from the rising sun, were close enough, the waiting men rose up and fired, and death roared across the field. The men in the front ranks fell. Not some, not most, but almost all, save for a few horrified men who realized they were the only ones still on their feet. And mere seconds later, they were cut down as well, falling and being trampled by the second wave of men behind them. Those soldiers rushed on because there was nothing else for them to do. They had seen their fellows slaughtered, and the sight filled them with rage and terror and despair, but they charged on anyway because the massive human wave behind them gave them no choice. And they were cut down as the killing continued. This war, the most brutal of all conflicts, had never seen a sight as brutal as this one. One Confederate general said later, "It was not war; it was murder."

The worst of the fighting was in the south, on the Confederate right. But the battle extended from one end of the line to the other, and in the north, not far from Bethesda Church, Will Brannon strode behind his men as they fired as fast as they could squeeze the trigger and reload. He didn't have to exhort them. They were in the grip of the same killing fever that held tightly to all the other defenders. These men knew they were outnumbered. Their one chance for victory was to kill as many Yankees as they could, as fast as they could. They performed that grisly task in splendid fashion.

But the Yankees weren't giving up. They could have turned tail and run, but they didn't. They kept coming, and in some cases they actually got close to the Confederate line. Will spotted cannons being wheeled up to menace his men and shouted a warning as the big guns began to roar. Canister and explosive shot crashed through the trees, forcing the defenders to duck their heads and hunt some cover for a few moments. From behind a tree Will saw the closest Yankees trying to take advantage of the respite in the deadly Confederate fire. The line of blue-clad men surged forward, no more than fifty yards away.

The barrage was still crashing around Will as he sprang forward, pistol in one hand, saber in the other. Hands caught at him, and he stopped, swinging around to see Roman holding on to his sleeve.

"Cap'n!" Roman cried over the roar of the cannons. "Don't do this!"

"The line has to hold," Will said. "When this is over, you go find Mac and tell him . . ." Will shook his head. "Never mind. He knows. Good-bye, Roman."

Roman would have argued, but there was no more time. Will pulled away from him and turned back toward the enemy.

"Follow me, boys!" he shouted. "We'll meet them head-on!"

He charged out of the woods, leading the counterattack toward the surprised Yankees. Only a handful of men came after him at first, but then more and more poured out of the trees. A shell exploded to Will's right. He ignored it and fired his pistol at the Federal troops. They were right in front of him now, thrusting at him with their bayonets. He slashed a path through them with the saber. A bayonet ripped into his side, but it didn't matter. A split second earlier, he had felt a burst of agony inside his chest and knew the end had come. Death, long delayed since Gettysburg, was upon him at last. Half-blinded by pain, he kept fighting as long as he had the strength to lift his arm and swing the saber. One of the Yankees fired his rifle, the bullet driving deep into Will's chest. *Too late*, he thought. He could not be killed now. He was already a dead man, only his muscles and nerves and a tiny portion of his brain refused to admit it just yet. Through blurred eyes, he saw the Union soldiers who were still on their feet turning to flee. Their attack was broken. And it hadn't been much to begin with, Will realized, only a tiny surge, a few dozen men on each side in the middle of tens of thousands, nothing really. Nothing important at all.

He fell to his knees and leaned forward, propping himself up with the saber. Blood ran from his mouth as he stared at the retreating Yankees. He and his men had won this fight. And that *was* important, he thought. Any time brave men faced overwhelming odds and prevailed, even if only for a time, it meant something. A grin stretched across Will's face.

He was still grinning as he slumped onto his side, on the bloodstained ground. His lips moved as he whispered, "Pa . . . ?"

John Brannon was there, the old familiar smile on his face, merriment twinkling in his blue eyes. He held out his hand. "Son . . ."

William Shakespeare Brannon took his father's hand and knew that he had come home.

⊙⟶ℳ⟵⊙

THAT EVENING, June 3, 1864, Capt. Will Brannon of the Thirty-third Virginia Infantry Regiment was laid to rest in a soldier's grave not far from the battlefield just west of Cold Harbor. His brother, Capt. MacBeth Brannon of the First Virginia Cavalry, and the young man known only as Roman stood beside the mound of earth and wept and prayed.

To the east, in the camps of the enemy, the Federals were trying to come to grips with the crushing defeat they had suffered on this day. At the last, though orders had come for the men to charge yet again, they had declined to do so. They stayed where they were, their refusal to move mute but eloquent testimony to the fact that, finally, enough slaughter was enough. Following the battle, Grant delayed for a time, ordering an artillery barrage kept up for several days, but it was pointless and everyone knew it. For the first time in this war, Grant had gone after something—and failed to get it.

On June 12, the Union army began to withdraw. At last, this campaign was over. For now, the price had been paid.

Chapter Twenty-one

TITUS BOLTED UPRIGHT IN bed, gasping. His heart was tripping along a mile a minute. He was so disoriented by the dream that for a moment he wasn't sure where he was.

But then the low sound of weeping reminded him. He was in a house consumed by grief.

His mother was crying. He could hear her sobs through the thin walls. Even though a glance at the window told Titus it was the middle of the hot summer night, Abigail was awake and grieving for Will.

Word of his death had taken awhile to reach them. The note sent by Mac had made its way to the farm in mid-June, brought out by a rider from Culpeper. There had been no official notification from the Confederate government; Culpeper County was still behind enemy lines, in the hands of the Yankees. But there was no doubt about the truth of the news. Roman had risked his life to retrieve Will's body from the battlefield at Cold Harbor even before a truce was called so that the dead and wounded could be tended to. And Roman and Mac had dug the grave in which Will had been laid to rest.

In the stunned silence that had fallen after Abigail finished reading the message aloud, Titus had said, "Well, at least this time maybe there ain't no mistake."

Henry had come near to punching him for that, either that or going for a gun, but he'd restrained himself. Out of respect for Will's memory, he said, but Titus knew better. Henry was still just a little bit afraid of him. And well he should be, because Titus finally had recovered from all the ills that had gripped him and was now at full strength again, as lean and powerful as a wolf. And about as pitiless as one, too.

But that didn't mean he was without feelings. Will's death had hit him hard, too. He just wasn't going to show it. He'd be damned if he was going to sit around and wring his hands and wail out his sorrow at the top of his lungs, the way his mother and Cordelia had done for a couple of days. Besides, he was willing to bet that they hadn't carried on that much when they thought *he* was dead.

He did his mourning in private, and while he was doing that, he realized he couldn't stay here with the family. It would be a hell of a lot simpler, of course, to remain on the farm and forget about the war. But that wouldn't avenge Will's death, and it wouldn't even the score for everything the Yankees had done to him while he was a prisoner. He had promised himself that if he made it back safely to Virginia, he would kill some more Yankees. A lot more Yankees.

It was time to keep that promise.

So he quit drinking and he got plenty of rest, and now he was strong and ready to kill again. He hadn't quite decided how he would go about it, but he was certain that he would think of something. He had to.

And then the dreams started to intrude on his sleep.

Over these last several months, he'd had plenty of nightmares about Camp Douglas and the hellish tortures he had undergone there. These dreams were different, though. Shockingly different.

Instead of the Yankee prison camp, in these nightmares he was back at Mountain Laurel again, in the days that he and Polly had lived there after their marriage. Back then, he had thought that someday he would be in charge of the plantation. That was why he hadn't put his foot down and insisted that they live on the Brannon farm. And he'd been so happy to be married to Polly—as well as stunned that she had agreed to marry him, he had to admit—that he was willing to go along with anything she or her father wanted. But it had been a mistake. Gradually, Duncan Ebersole had wormed his way between them, throwing up more and more barriers to their happiness, forcing Polly to choose again and again between them. Every time, Polly had wound up going along with Ebersole, just as Titus had gone along with Polly.

Now, as he sat there in the darkness and gasped for breath, he could still hear Ebersole's mocking laughter echoing from the fading dream. Even now the planter's hated face seemed to loom in front of Titus's eyes and ridicule him. This was not the first such dream he'd had, and in each one of them, his memories were clearer. He seemed to view those days through new eyes. In the past his vision of reality had been obscured by first love then hate. Now he saw coldly, impassionedly, and what he saw made his eyes widen in horror. He lifted his hands to his head and ran his fingers through the long dark hair that fell to his shoulders. His movements became more frenzied until finally he clapped both hands over his face and shuddered. He knew now everything he had done wrong, everything he should have understood and hadn't.

It wasn't enough. Seeing the mistakes he'd made in life didn't mean he could go back and repair them. There was no going back. Tragedies could not be undone.

But they could be avenged.

Titus knew now what he had to do.

"I'M LEAVIN'," he announced the next morning as he walked into the kitchen carrying his hat, saddlebags, and weapons. A rifle was tucked under his arm and a holstered pistol belted around his lean waist.

His mother stood at the stove, hollow-eyed and gaunt from lack of sleep. Henry, Cordelia, and Louisa were seated around the table, making a meager breakfast on some boiled potatoes. It had been awhile since they'd had any meat. They all looked at him, not understanding.

"Leaving?" Henry repeated. "You mean you're going to town for a while?"

Titus shook his head. "There's nothin' in Culpeper I want since the Yankees took over the place. No, I'm leavin' the farm. I'm goin' back to the war."

He said it bluntly, matter-of-factly, because he knew no other way to say it.

Abigail took a step toward him. "No!"

"Sorry, Ma. It's somethin' I've got to do."

Louisa stood up and reached a hand toward him. "No, Titus. You're not well enough—"

He batted her hand away before she could touch him. "Damn it, woman, are you blind? It's been more'n six months since you brought me back here. I'm fine. I'm ready to start killin' Yankees again."

"It won't do any good," Cordelia said in a dull voice. "It's too late for that."

"Because Will's already dead, you mean? Or because the Confederacy's whipped?"

"Don't say that!" Abigail exclaimed, as offended by the idea that the Confederacy could be defeated as she was by the profanity, maybe even more so.

"Maybe both," Cordelia said.

Titus looked at her. "I ain't givin' up. And as for Will, I know all of you thought the sun rose and set on him, even you, Ma, and there was a time you kicked him out of the family." He held up a hand to stop her from protesting. "But he's dead and gone, and I'm sorry about it, but there's nothin' I can do to bring him back. All I can do is go kill some more Yankees to try to even the score for him and me both." He grinned at his mother. "After all, the Good Book says for us to take an eye for an eye, don't it?"

"Don't you dare try to quote Scripture at me!" Abigail said. "I don't see how I ever gave birth to such a heathen as you, Titus Brannon!"

"Accidents happen," he replied with a shrug.

"Anyway, I'm not sure I believe in . . . in an eye for an eye. Not anymore."

"The war's taken enough," Henry said. "Will's gone, and who knows if Mac will make it through. As for Cory, we don't even know if he's still alive."

"You don't believe in givin' all for the cause, little brother?"

Henry glared at him. "If you want to leave so bad, you can go right on, as far as I'm concerned. I don't care what happens to you anymore. Not after . . ." His voice trailed off as memories choked him.

"Not after what happened with Polly," Titus finished the sentence, his tone deliberately brutal.

"I don't want you to go off and get killed," Cordelia said. "Neither does Louisa."

"That's right, Titus." Louisa swallowed hard. "If you leave, where will I go? What will I do?"

Cordelia reached over and took Louisa's hand. "You can stay here no matter what Titus does. Can't she, Ma?"

"Of course," Abigail answered without hesitation. Her world had been rocked and nearly shattered time and again these past years, but the ingrained Southern hospitality was still intact. "This is your home now, Louisa, for as long as you want it to be."

Tears ran down Louisa's cheeks as she turned to look at them. "Thank you. I can't tell you . . . I just can't tell you how much that means to me."

"Well, this is touchin' as all get-out," Titus said into the brief silence that followed, "but I got to be goin'." He put on his hat.

Louisa came closer to him again. "Titus, I'm begging you—"

"Don't waste your breath." He stepped past her, heading for the front of the house.

He heard crying behind him. He wasn't sure which of the women the sound came from. Maybe all of them. Sure as hell not Henry, though. Henry would be happy to see him go off to maybe get himself killed.

But the heavy footsteps that followed him onto the front porch did belong to Henry. So did the hand that fell on Titus's shoulder. "Hold on a minute."

Titus whirled around and knocked Henry's arm aside. "Don't you ever lay hands on me again," he said, his lips drawing back into a snarl. "You had your chance to save her, and you messed up just as bad as I did, boy."

"What?" Henry asked, frowning in confusion. "What in blazes are you talking about?"

Titus drew a deep breath. He had almost let his anger get away from him there, almost said some things he didn't want to say to anyone. Things he wanted to keep inside, to be shared with only one other.

"Never you mind," he snapped. "Just don't go around grabbin' me."

"After today, I don't care if I ever see you again. I never really thought you'd change, Titus, but after what I just watched you do to Ma and Cordelia and Louisa, I *know* you won't. You'll always be the same sorry bastard you've been ever since you came back from that prison camp."

"Then why are you out here jawin' at me?"

"Because *they* care." Henry jerked a thumb over his shoulder toward the women in the house. "I reckon they've all got their own reasons, but none of them want you to go off and get yourself killed. I'm asking you, for them, not to do this. Not to put them through this all over again."

Titus laughed coldly. "Well, ain't you the noble one?"

"No, I just love my family. But I don't reckon you can understand that."

For a long moment, Titus didn't say anything. Then he grated out, "I don't love anybody no more. The only thing I love is killin' Yankees, so that's what I'm gonna do. And you ain't gonna stop me, little brother."

Henry stepped back, spreading his hands. "I'm not even going to try anymore. I've said my piece. Go on, Titus, get out of here if that's what you want to do. Go to hell."

Titus stepped down off the porch and started toward the barn, pausing after he had gone a couple of steps to look back over his shoulder. "Too late," he shouted back at Henry. Then he stalked to the barn, saddled his horse, and rode away.

Titus took his time getting to Mountain Laurel. He was in no hurry; Duncan Ebersole wasn't going anywhere. From what he had heard, Ebersole was afraid to venture off the plantation, afraid that the Yankees would arrest him. After all, he had been a leader of the local militia during the early days of the war. The Federals who had occupied the county might consider that enough of a military position to justify taking Ebersole as a prisoner of war. If they did that, they could ship him off to Camp Douglas or some other hellhole of a prison camp. The thought of Ebersole in a place like that brought a big grin to Titus's face. Yes, that would be mighty satisfying, he thought. But it wouldn't be a fitting punishment for Ebersole's real crime.

The bluebelly scavengers had to have been to the plantation by now, surely. They had been everywhere else in the county, and Mountain Laurel was the finest house around. Titus wondered if Ebersole had cowered in the cellar while the Yankees looted his proud home. He didn't doubt it for a minute. Bastards like Ebersole were all talk and nothing else, except when they were facing somebody who couldn't fight back.

Titus kept a sharp eye out for Yankee patrols as he rode across the countryside, staying off the roads for the most part and following back trails that he knew because he had grown up around here. The Yankees wouldn't know about these. Following the twisted paths made it take longer to get to Mountain Laurel, but Titus put the time to good use. He went over everything in his head again, putting together all the memories and everything that had come to him in his dreams, moving the pieces around until they formed a clear picture. Always it was the same. He was correct in what he had figured out. He was sure of it.

The summer heat was building in midmorning when he rode up to the plantation, following the long drive between the mountain laurel trees to the circle in front of the big house. The house didn't look too bad. The lawn was overgrown and the flowerbeds were full of weeds, unkempt and untended, but that was all. Titus wondered how many of Ebersole's slaves were still on the place. Probably most of them had run off, but a few likely remained. The older ones, who wouldn't know where else to go or what else to do, and the children who didn't have parents. But those weren't enough to keep up a plantation like this. It would fall into ruin quickly enough.

Titus dismounted and tied the reins to the iron ring, which was starting to rust in places. He left his rifle in the sheath on the saddle and went to the front door. It opened under his touch. No point in locking a door. The Yankees would just kick it down if they wanted in. He would have done the same if the door had been locked.

The air inside the house had a hot, foul, musty smell. Titus grimaced and tried not to breathe too deeply. There was no real contagion here, no sickness he could catch, but he still didn't want to suck down too much of the same air Duncan Ebersole had been breathing.

The boards of the floor creaked slightly under his weight as he crossed the foyer and looked into the big sitting room. Everything in the room had a thick layer of dust on it. No one had been in there for a while. Titus had a pretty good idea Ebersole would be in the library, but he glanced in the other rooms as he came to them. No one was in any of them.

When he paused in front of the closed library door, he heard snoring from the other side of the panel. That confirmed what he expected. He reached down, grasped the knob, and turned it slowly. The door opened.

The reek of long-unwashed human flesh hit him as he started into the room, causing him to wrinkle his nose in disgust. Anyway you looked at it, he thought, the master of this house was a pretty damned sorry specimen of humanity, and he wasn't denying that. But there were some that were worse, and he was looking at one of them now.

Ebersole sat behind the desk, his head slumped forward so that it rested on his crossed arms. Titus came farther into the room. It was a shambles. Ebersole had never straightened up after Polly's murder.

Things looked pretty much the same as they had that awful day, right down to the bloodstains on the carpet. Titus gazed at them for a moment. Just some dark brown blotches, he thought. From the looks of them, no one would have guessed that the blood responsible for them once had run through the veins of the prettiest woman in the county, maybe in the whole blasted state. A woman who maybe had loved him. Not the same way he had loved her, no, but she had felt something for him. If he had just done things differently, what was between them might have grown into something real someday.

Titus shoved that thought out of his mind. What-might-have-beens were a waste of time.

"Ebersole," he boomed. "Wake up."

The disheveled man didn't budge from his slumber. He only snored and snorted. Titus could smell the whiskey on him. How long had it been since Ebersole had been sober? No way to tell, he decided, but it had been a long time, that was for sure. He moved closer to the desk and said Ebersole's name again, louder this time. Still no reaction.

Titus didn't want to touch him. He'd have rather petted a rattlesnake. But his natural impatience was building, and so he reached out and grabbed the man's shoulder. He jerked the planter up, shouting "Ebersole! Wake up, damn you!" Titus's open hand cracked sharply across the man's face.

Ebersole gasped and cringed back against the chair in which he sat. "No!" he cried. "Dinna hit me again!"

Titus let go of him and stepped back. "Then wake up, you drunken sot, and stay awake."

He was a fine one to be chastizing somebody else for being drunk, he thought with a flash of grim humor. But he was sober today and had been for more than a week. He had expected to get the shakes and have the usual demons running around inside his head when he gave up the stuff, but that hadn't happened. His blood was cold, his nerves were steady, and he felt like he could stride through the world without its ever touching him. He felt good.

Ebersole bent over in a fit of coughing, and when it subsided he looked up. "T-Titus? Titus Brannon?"

"That's right. I've come to talk to you, Ebersole."

"Talk to me? About what?" Ebersole sounded astonished that anyone would want to converse with him.

"Polly."

Ebersole's eyes jerked toward the portrait over the fireplace, the portrait of his wife, Polly's mother. Titus glanced in that direction, too, unable to stifle the impulse. He saw that the painting was dented and torn a little in the middle, and something had splashed over it, staining the canvas. He realized that the damage must have been done by a liquor bottle being thrown against it. He had no trouble imagining a drunken, raging Ebersole flinging a bottle at the portrait in his madness.

"P-Polly," Ebersole blubbered. "Me poor lil' girl."

"You bastard," Titus said. "After what you did to her, don't you expect anybody to feel sorry for you. Sure as hell not me."

Ebersole blinked. "Wha . . . what I done t' her? What th' devil are ye talkin' about, Brannon?"

"I finally figured it out. My brother Henry wasn't the father of the baby Polly was carryin'. You were."

Ebersole's mouth sagged open loosely, and his red-rimmed eyes filled with tears. "No!" he said. "Never would I do such a . . . a monstrous thing!"

"Yes, you did. I know now why Polly was in your bedroom that time I came back here. She told me you'd switched rooms, but that was a lie. All the times she went to you and said she could calm you down and talk some sense into your head, that wasn't what she was doin' at all, was it, Ebersole?"

He shook his head, his mouth working but no sound coming out. His eyes large with guilt.

"And after I left, you had her all to yourself again, just the way you wanted it." Titus's voice ground on inexorably. "Until she realized she was going to have a baby. I'd been gone too long, dead at Fredericksburg, everybody thought, so she couldn't blame it on me. She'd been flirtin' with my brother, so she went to Henry and laid with him. I don't reckon he ever thought about sayin' no to her. That way, everybody would think he was the father. When the baby came early, nobody would make anything of it." He shook his head. His features were hard and bleak, but regret lurked in his eyes. "I reckon I ought to be mad at her for what she did, takin' advantage of Henry that way, but I can't be. She didn't see no other way out. That's why she married me, you know—to get away from you. But I let her down by goin' along with you when you said we were goin' to live here. That way you could still get at her."

Ebersole's face was flushed brick-red now. His eyes had begun to pop with rage. His hands clenched into fists and shook.

"What I can't figure out," Titus paused, "is why she went along with you in the first place, why she never told you to get the hell away from her."

Ebersole lurched to his feet. "Because she liked it, ye bloody idiot! She liked it!"

Titus's breath caught in his throat. Horror and sickness boiled inside him. "Shut up!" he shouted across the desk at Ebersole. "Shut your lyin', filthy mouth!"

"Nay! 'Tis time ye heard the truth, ye stupid scut! She come to me, after her mother died. She wanted to comfort me, to help me get through it." Ebersole closed his eyes for a moment and swayed back and forth, transported by the memory. "An' she looked so much like her dear departed mother, she did, so beautiful and so much like her, an' . . . an' I knew I'd go mad if I did no' get some comfort to get me through it . . . Oh, Polly, dear, dear Polly . . ."

As Titus listened to the man blather on, he knew what he was hearing were the justifications and rationalizations of a sick, demented mind. Ebersole had told himself so many times over the years that he wasn't really to blame for what had happened, that it had all been Polly's doing, that he believed it even now. But he was wrong. Titus had seen the pain in Polly's eyes; he just hadn't realized what had put it there. If he had, he would have taken her away from this house of evil and never allowed her to set foot in it again.

But he had been blind to it all, and he had failed her, and now it was too late to set things right. Too late for anything except vengeance.

Ebersole looked at him across the desk. "Ye cannot tell anyone, Brannon. Please. I've never begged a man for anything in me life. But ye cannot tell. I couldna live with the shame."

"You won't have to," Titus said. "No one will ever hear about it from me."

Ebersole slumped forward, leaning his hands on the top of the desk. He heaved a sigh of relief.

Titus drew and cocked his revolver. "Ebersole." The bastard had to be looking at him.

The pitiful excuse of a man raised his head, and his eyes widened as he saw the pistol pointing at him. He had time to open his mouth but that was all.

Titus fired.

The bullet smashed into the bridge of Ebersole's nose, right between his eyes, and threw him backward into the chair. His arms fell on the arms of the chair, as if he were sitting there and listening to someone. But his eyes were open and staring, and there was a spray of blood and brain on the back of the chair just above his head, where it had splattered when the bullet burst out the back of his skull. His bowels voided, making the stench in the room even worse.

But it wouldn't stink much longer, Titus thought as he holstered the pistol. There was a litter of papers on the desk. He swept them into the floor, then he stepped over to the fireplace and lifted the painting down from its hooks. He threw it on top of the papers.

Kneeling, he picked up one of the papers then used his free hand to strike a lucifer. He held the flame to the paper until it was burning well, and he dropped it. The other papers quickly caught fire, and the flames spread just as fast to the canvas of the portrait and ignited it. Titus straightened to his feet as the painting was consumed.

He went to the door of the library and turned to stand there for a moment, looking across the room at the corpse of Duncan Ebersole. The fire spread across the floor to the dry, dusty curtains. They went up with a whoosh! of flame.

That was enough, Titus decided. The house was old. It would burn quickly now. If anybody searched through the ashes and rubble later on, they might find Ebersole's skull with bullet holes in front and back, and they would know that he hadn't died in the fire. Titus didn't care. He would be long gone by then, and he didn't intend to ever come back. He figured that before it was all over, he would die at the hands of some son-of-a-bitch Yankee.

But not before he had killed a whole heap of them. He had settled one score; now it was time to get started on the other.

When he rode away from Mountain Laurel a few minutes later, smoke was beginning to billow from the windows. A few flames could be seen in other rooms, but the library was an inferno by now, and the flames consumed the body of the man who had been master of this house. Now it was going to burn to the ground around him.

Titus didn't look back. He hoped that when he died, he wouldn't wind up in the same circle of hell as Duncan Ebersole. It would be tiresome to have to kill him all over again.

Chapter Twenty-two

ARLY ON IN THE great conflict, war had come to the Shenandoah Valley, northwest of the Blue Ridge Mountains.
Clashes at Harpers Ferry had been some of the earliest fighting
in the war. It was in the Shenandoah as well that Stonewall Jackson had confronted the Yankees and defeated them time and
again in 1862, cementing the reputation that had begun to
accrue to him at Manassas as one of the South's greatest warriors.

In the spring of 1864, Federal troops had moved once more
into the valley, which was a major source of food for the Confederate army. An army commanded by Gen. Franz Sigel was
ordered by Grant to move down the valley and capture or destroy
all the vital railroad links that allowed Robert E. Lee to draw supplies from the Shenandoah. Sigel's campaign had gone fairly well
at first, but then he had encountered resistance led by Gen.
John C. Breckinridge, and the Yankees had been soundly
whipped at New Market and forced to retreat.

Though mightily occupied with other matters at the time—
such as the fighting in the Wilderness and at Spotsylvania—
Grant was not yet willing to give up on the conquest of the
Shenandoah. Sigel had failed, so he was replaced by another
commander, the volatile, volcanic Gen. David Hunter, a long-
time veteran sometimes known as "Black Dave" because of his
temper. Hunter renewed the campaign in the valley just as the
two great armies to the southeast were maneuvering to face each
other at Cold Harbor.

Breckinridge had been recalled to join Lee, and left in command of the Confederate forces in the Shenandoah was Gen.
William "Grumble" Jones, an irascible sort who had gotten along
badly with Jackson when his division was part of Stonewall's
corps. He was a good soldier, though, and moved decisively to
confront Hunter.

In the Shenandoah the Yankees had begun to wage a new type of war. During the course of the war, a great deal of damage had been done throughout Virginia to military and civilian targets alike. But neither army had ever gone after civilians the way Hunter's army now did in the valley. Houses and barns were burned down, men were hanged if they were suspected of giving aid to the Confederates (and most in the valley had), and wanton destruction was carried out for the sake of destruction.

It was up to Grumble Jones to put a stop to this, but though he tried, ultimately he failed, his forces being routed at the June 5, 1864, battle of Piedmont. Not only that, but Jones was mortally wounded during the combat, leaving the Confederates in the valley without a commander.

The valley seemed to belong to the Yankees to do with as they pleased.

But Grumble Jones and his men were not the only Confederates opposing the Federals in the valley. A small but fierce group led by John Singleton Mosby had been operating behind enemy lines for more than a year. Peerless riders and fighters, their strategy was to strike hard and fast then fade away before anyone could catch them. Their targets were Federal supply wagons, rail lines being used by the Yankees, patrols, telegraph wires and stations, and outlying Federal command posts. Mosby and his men were so successful at what they set out to do that he was dubbed the Gray Ghost, because he and his partisan rangers were able to slip away like phantoms from any pursuit.

In addition to Mosby's harassing activities, following the slaughter at Cold Harbor, Robert E. Lee decided to employ the tactics that had worked so brilliantly for him at Chancellorsville. He would split his army and send one part in a large arc that placed it in position to menace the enemy's rear. In this case, the corps commanded by Gen. Jubal Early would leave northern Virginia, march to the Shenandoah Valley, then turn northeast, sweeping the Yankees before them and driving on into Maryland, where they would be poised to strike at Washington, D.C., itself. Lee's goal was not to capture the enemy capital; Early's force would not be strong enough to accomplish that. But Lee would be satisfied if the maneuver prompted Grant to send a portion of his army back to defend Washington from the potential threat. That would be enough to give Richmond some breathing room again.

Thus the seemingly tranquil Shenandoah Valley, isolated by the mountains that surrounded it, once again was on the verge of a stretch of dark and dangerous days.

TITUS HEARD the rustle of leaves above his head and knew he had found the trouble he had been looking for. This narrow back road was overhung with branches that intertwined and formed a canopy over the road. It was the perfect place for an ambush. That was one reason he had ridden down it to start with. The men he was looking for were just the sort to lie in wait for their enemies in a place like this.

His heels jabbed into the horse's flanks and sent it leaping forward. The reaction came just a fraction of a second too slow. The man lurking on a tree limb above, out of sight from the road, was already dropping toward him. He crashed into Titus's back and wrapped his arms around him. The impact pulled the rider out of the saddle. Titus kicked his feet free of the stirrups so the horse wouldn't drag him if it bolted. That was all he had time to do before he was driven heavily to the ground.

The hard landing loosened the other man's grip. Titus pulled free and rolled quickly to one side. He ended up on his back. Movement flickered through the shadows. Someone was about to jump on top of him. He yanked his legs up and drove both booted feet into the stomach of the second attacker. The man doubled over and staggered backward.

The first man was on his feet by now, swinging a foot at Titus's head in a vicious kick. Titus twisted out of the way like a snake, grabbed the man's foot, and heaved. With a startled yell, the man went over backward.

Titus rolled again, this time coming up on hands and knees then surging to his feet. More men were coming out of the woods on both sides of the roadway.

Suddenly a firm voice shouted, "Don't kill him! We want him alive!"

That was all right with Titus. He intended to stay alive. When a man came at him, swinging a club of some sort, Titus ducked under the blow and hooked a punch into his assailant's belly. He lifted his other fist in an uppercut that sent the man staggering back.

Someone grabbed him from behind, pinning his arms while another man rushed him from the front. Titus kicked that man in the groin then drove an elbow into the belly of the man holding him. That loosened the man's grip enough for Titus to jerk free, spin around, and knock the man off his feet with a right hook.

He moved into the middle of the road, giving himself more room to maneuver, and grinned at the men surrounding him.

"I ain't even winded yet," he said mockingly. "I can waltz like this all day."

Despite the dim light of the shaded roadway, he could tell that they wore gray and brown and butternut uniforms. They all looked angry, especially one man with a bristling red beard who came at Titus with fists flailing.

Titus parried one punch, shrugged off another that clipped him on the side of the head, and hooked a left then a right into the man's belly. Then he jabbed a left to the heart and brought his right around in a sledging blow that dropped the red-bearded man senseless in the dust of the road.

Footsteps sounded behind him. He tried to turn to meet the attack but was too late. This time two men grabbed him, one on each arm. He struggled but couldn't pull away from them. In front of him, Redbeard climbed slowly to his feet, rubbing his jaw and shaking his head.

"Hold him just like that, boys," he said. "I'll teach the son of a bitch a lesson."

Red rage blazed through Titus's brain. Something inside him snapped, and he was reminded of his ordeals in Camp Douglas, being tormented by the brutal Sergeant McNeil and the other Yankee guards. Back then, he'd been forced to endure the punishment they handed out, but now he fought back. He smashed the heel of his boot into the shin of the man on his right, and as the man howled in pain, Titus was able to pull free and snap a backhanded blow to his nose. Then he pivoted, hooking his left foot behind the right leg of the other man and throwing him backward.

Redbeard still rushed toward him. Without thinking about what he was doing, Titus let his hand dip to the holster on his right hip. The revolver was still there. He brought it up, his thumb pulling back the hammer as the barrel rose. Redbeard lurched to a sudden stop a couple of feet away, eyes widening in horror as he stared down the barrel of the revolver.

Something sharp pricked the side of Titus's neck. "Pull that trigger and I'll cut your throat out," promised the same voice that earlier had ordered him taken alive.

Without moving his head, Titus looked over and saw from the corner of his eye a Confederate officer wearing a plumed hat with one side of the brim pinned up. The man was very slender and only medium height, not physically impressive at all. But his eyes blazed with a discernible fire, and Titus knew that he meant every word of the threat.

Backing down had never come naturally to Titus, though. Without lowering the pistol or easing down the hammer, he said, "You can cut my throat out, but this ginger-bearded ape will still have his brains splattered all over the road."

Despite his fear, Redbeard flushed angrily. "Who you callin' an ape?" he demanded.

The officer chuckled as a smile tugged at his mouth. "Take it easy, Bob," he said. "Our visitor's just trying to rile you. He thinks if he can make you mad enough, you'll jump him again and I won't be able to run him through with my saber. Then he can turn and shoot me. Isn't that right, stranger?"

"Nope," Titus said. "If I'd wanted you dead, Colonel Mosby, I wouldn't have ridden down this country road plain as day, now would I?"

The colonel frowned a little now. "You know who I am?"

"Who the hell doesn't know the Gray Ghost in these parts?"

Mosby withdrew his saber. "Now you've got me curious, mister. Just who are you, and what are you doing here?"

Titus answered the second question first. "Lookin' for you, of course, Colonel. My name's Titus Brannon. I've come to join your rangers."

Silence hung over the road for several long seconds. "Is that so?" Mosby finally said. "What makes you think we're looking for recruits?"

"You can always use a good man who likes to kill Yankees, can't you? I've heard all about how you been raidin' up and down this valley, makin' life hell for that bastard Hunter and his men." Titus lowered the revolver at last, and the man with the red beard heaved a sigh of relief.

Titus turned toward Mosby. "You've seen me fight. You ought to be able to tell that I can handle myself. I'm even better at shootin' than I am at rough-and-tumble. And you won't find nobody better."

"Or more modest," Mosby said, a dry edge to his voice. "Where are you from, Mr. Brannon?"

"Culpeper. A farm outside of Culpeper Court House."

"All my rangers are drawn from Loudoun and Fauquier Counties."

"That's Mosby's Confederacy," one of the other men put in, pride in his tone.

Titus stared at the colonel. "So you don't want a fella who can kill Yankees with the best of 'em, just because he ain't from the right county? What kind of a way is that to fight a war?"

Mosby didn't answer the question directly. "You talk a lot about killing Yankees, Brannon. Is that your life's ambition?"

"Lately it is. Ever since I escaped from one of their prisons up in Illinois."

For the first time, Mosby looked surprised. "Douglas?"

"That's right."

"I've heard it's supposed to be a horrible place."

"That ain't sayin' the half of it, Colonel."

"And you escaped, you say?"

Titus nodded. "And made it all the way back home to Virginia." He didn't add that he'd had help. That was none of Mosby's business.

"Very impressive," Mosby murmured. "Where were you taken prisoner?"

"At Fredericksburg. That was my first battle."

"So you don't have a great deal of military experience?"

"Why would I need it to be a ranger?" All this talk was making Titus frustrated. "From what I've heard, you boys fight your own way, not the army way."

Mosby's voice lashed at him. "This is still a military unit. Serving in it requires military discipline. From what I've seen so far, you seem to be sadly lacking in any sort of discipline, Mr. Brannon, military or otherwise."

With his left hand, Titus rubbed the close-cropped beard that covered his jaws. His right still hung at his side, filled with the butt of the revolver. "Maybe so," he said, "but I got eyes to see with and ears to hear with, and I know there was a Yankee patrol comin' along this road about two miles behind me when I started up it. They ought to be here pretty soon."

Mosby stiffened. "You're sure about that?"

"Pretty sure," Titus drawled. "I reckon if you listen hard, you can hear their hoof beats even now."

The saber in the colonel's hand flashed up, and once again its tip rested against Titus's neck, in the hollow of his throat this time. "If I thought you were a Yankee spy, trying to trap us . . ."

"You know I'm not. If I was, I wouldn't have said anything until the patrol was right on top of you."

Mosby hesitated an instant then whirled away from Titus and sheathed the saber. "To the horses!" he called to his men. "Get ready for a fight!" He glanced back at Titus. "Since you're here, you might as well join us, I reckon. We'll see just how good at killing Yankees you are."

"All I want's a chance," Titus said, holstering his pistol. He hurried down the road to his horse, which had stopped a short distance away from where he had been knocked out of the saddle.

Within moments, the road was deserted. No sign remained of the rangers except for a welter of tracks in the dust. It would have been better if those had been wiped out, but there was no time to take that precaution. The men who now lurked in the woods on either side of the road would just have to trust to luck that the Yankees wouldn't notice the tracks in time.

Silence hung over the trees, broken a minute later by the growing sound of quite a few horses approaching. A large group of riders came around a bend in the road a hundred yards away. They wore the blue uniforms and black campaign caps of Federal cavalry.

From his position in the forest, Titus watched the Yankees ride past. He was leaning forward in the saddle, peering through a small opening in the underbrush. It was all he could do not to yank his pistol from its holster and start blazing away at the blue-clad riders. He had to wait until Mosby gave a signal, however. He had to prove that he could be a valuable member of this group of partisans. He had his left hand over his horse's muzzle, just in case the animal scented the other horses and decided to make some noise.

The Yankees kept riding, seemingly unaware that they were threatened on both flanks. Titus's impatience grew. Was Mosby going to wait until they were completely past? If he did, the Yankees up at the head of the patrol would stand a good chance of getting away.

Titus glanced to his right and left. He couldn't see any other rangers. They had melted into the trees and bushes, utterly vanishing. Yet he knew they were still out there somewhere; probably the closest members of the band were within a dozen feet of him. But when were they going to start the ball?

Without warning or any signal of which Titus was aware, the men concealed in the trees unleashed a deadly volley, ripping into the Yankee patrol. Rifles blasted, pistols cracked, and bullets thudded into human flesh. Some of the Yankees cried out in pain as they were hit. Others died in silence, toppling from the backs of their startled mounts. The officer leading the patrol slumped forward in his saddle but did not fall. He pushed himself upright and started shouting orders to his frightened men, whose animals were milling around in confusion in the middle of the road.

Rebel yells echoed from the trees as the rangers exploded out of the woods all around the trapped Yankees. Titus drew his revolver and urged his horse forward, joining the attack. He broke into the open and found himself facing one of the Federals. The man had a bloodstain on his right arm. He was reaching across his body with his left hand and awkwardly trying to pull his pistol from its holster. Titus shot him, the bullet tearing away the Yankee's throat and knocking him off the horse. Blood pooled around his head where he lay in the road.

Titus wheeled his horse to look for another target and saw one of the Yankees charging him on horseback only a couple of yards away. The trooper had drawn his saber and was swinging it at Titus's head. Titus jerked his arm up and blocked the slashing blow with his pistol. The saber slid off the long barrel, but the Yankee caught his balance and flicked a backhanded swipe at Titus's face. Titus pulled his head back just in time. The tip of the blade passed only a few inches in front of his eyes.

He fired before the Yankee could try anything else fancy. The man sagged in his saddle as the bullet ripped through his body. He dropped the saber but managed to stay mounted.

Hunched over, his face contorted in agony, he looked up at Titus as if to ask for mercy.

If that was what he wanted, Titus thought, then he really was a damned fool. The pistol roared again, and the Yankee was flung to the ground, a bullet through his head.

Steel rang against steel as some of Mosby's rangers matched sabers with the Yankee cavalrymen. That might be more honorable, but as far as Titus was concerned it was foolish. Anybody who came at him with a saber was going to get a bullet in his guts. Titus looked around for another likely candidate.

The fight seemed to be just about over, however. As Titus watched, the last of the Yankees surrendered. More than half of the patrol was sprawled on the road, either lifeless or close to it. Of the ones still on horseback, several were badly wounded. Only a few men didn't carry some sign of the fight they'd just been in. Mosby's men, on the other hand, appeared largely unscathed. The element of surprise had allowed them to hit the Yankees so hard that the Federals hadn't been able to put up much of a struggle.

The rangers forced their prisoners to dismount at gunpoint. The Yankees all looked pale and frightened. From his knowledge of what was going on in the Shenandoah Valley, Titus knew that they had good reason to be scared. The Yankees had been making war on civilians, and Mosby and his men didn't like that one bit.

There wasn't much breeze under the trees, but there was enough to stir the plume on Mosby's hat as he looked over the captives. He let a moment of tense silence go by. "I'd be justified in hanging you men," he said at last. "I'm thinking about doing just that, so that maybe General Hunter will understand that he shouldn't be terrorizing and killing innocent folks."

The prisoners looked even more nervous.

"But I don't reckon I will hang you," Mosby went on. "Perhaps a firing squad would be more appropriate." He looked over at one of his subordinates. "What do you think, Dolly?"

The man addressed was handsome and sported a thin mustache, and to Titus he didn't look like the sort who would answer to Dolly. He took no offense to being addressed that way by Mosby, however. "A firing squad sounds just fine to me, Colonel," he agreed with a nod.

"See to it," Mosby said.

"For God's sake, Colonel!" one of the Yankees burst out. "You can't just execute us! We're prisoners of war!"

Mosby looked at the man coldly. "Have you ever burned down the house of some farmer here in the valley, just because you believed he might have fed us and let us water our horses at his well?"

"But . . . but that sort of thing is what our officers have ordered us to do!"

"Well," Mosby said, "my orders are to see to it that you don't do that anymore." He motioned to the man called Dolly.

Quickly, under Dolly's direction, a firing squad was formed, and the prisoners were herded to the edge of the trees. Each of the Yankees was ordered to stand with his back against a tree trunk. Some of them started to cry, while others accepted their fate more stoically. The Yankee who had protested earlier said angrily to Mosby, "By God, you'll pay for this atrocity, sir!"

"As you are paying for your own," Mosby replied calmly.

Titus watched the preparations for the execution with great interest. He was impressed. He had heard a great deal about Mosby's ability as a fighter, a cavalryman, and a scout, but now he saw for himself how Mosby dealt with the hated Yankees. He liked what he was seeing. He thought about volunteering for the firing squad but restrained himself. He was not one of Mosby's rangers—yet.

When everything was ready, Mosby raised his sword over his head. "Gentleman, make your peace with God!" he instructed the Yankees. He turned to the rangers forming the firing squad as they lined up at the edge of the road, carbines in their hands. "Ready . . . aim . . . *fire!*"

The volley roared out, and Titus looked eagerly toward the trees, expecting to see the Yankees falling to the ground as blood spurted from their riddled bodies. Instead, most of them were still standing there, although a couple had dropped to their knees and were praying loudly into the silence that fell as the echoes of the shots died away. Most of the Federal troopers just stared ahead in astonishment, astounded that they were still alive. Several had dark stains on their trousers.

Titus was astounded, too. As Mosby and the rangers began to laugh, he realized that the riflemen had fired high, sending their bullets into the trees above the heads of the captives.

Mosby moved his horse closer to the edge of the road and said to the prisoners, "Remember how near you came to death today. Remember how it felt to stare your own mortality in the face. And the next time you're 'ordered' to make war on civilians, find some way not to do it. Because if you do, I *will* find you, and you *will* die next time." Mosby jerked the plumed hat off his head and waved it in the air. "Now run, you Yankees! Run like the devil himself is behind you—because I am!"

Some of the prisoners had the presence of mind to bolt away from the trees and start running down the road. Others tugged their more confused companions along with them. But within a matter of seconds, all the survivors of the ambushed patrol were straggling away, the ones in the lead already around the bend in the road.

When the Yankees were out of sight, Titus could restrain himself no longer. "You let them go!"

Mosby walked his horse over to him. "That's right. I'm not a murderer. Though I must admit it was tempting. When I think about what they've been doing here in the Shenandoah . . ." Mosby shook his head and changed the subject. "You handled yourself well during the fight. I reckon if you want to ride with us, we'll take you on, for a while, anyway. That is, if you still want to be a ranger."

"I do," Titus said.

"I'll put you in Dolly Richards's company then." Mosby looked over at the man. "You have any object to taking in this stray lamb, Dolly?"

"No sir, I reckon not, if that's what you want." Richards didn't seem to relish the prospect though.

"Let's go, boys," Mosby called to the other rangers. "We'll be long gone by the time those Yankees run all the way back to their headquarters with their tails between their legs."

Titus didn't doubt that. He fell in with the other men who rode behind Dolly Richards. Mosby took the lead. Titus could see the plume on his hat bouncing as the colonel put his horse into a trot. That hat might be a little silly looking, Titus thought, but Mosby was a fighter, sure enough.

It was just too bad that he was too softhearted or honorable or something. Having those Yankees lined up like that and then not killing them . . . why, that was nothing but a waste of perfectly good gunpowder and lead.

Chapter Twenty-three

DRIVEN BACK BY Jubal Early's army at Lynchburg in early July, David Hunter's Federals withdrew all the way to the Allegheny Mountains of West Virginia. Early's push into the Shenandoah was starting out more successful than anyone could have hoped. On up the valley and across the Potomac into Maryland, Early continued driving toward Washington. He was opposed by a Federal force commanded by Gen. Lew Wallace, who slowed Early's advance but was unable to stop it until the Confederates were on the doorstep of Washington, D.C. Finally stiffening at that point, thanks to reinforcements that had been pouring into the city, the Yankees brought Early's campaign to a halt and turned it back.

Staging a fighting retreat back down the valley, Early contested the Union forces pursuing him, which included those of "Black Dave" Hunter, who had returned to the fray. At Kernstown, the scene of a battle more than two years earlier during Jackson's Valley campaign, the Confederates finally rallied and turned on the Yankees, defeating them soundly. Hunter and the other Union commanders withdrew yet again, leaving the Shenandoah in Confederate hands once more.

Emboldened by this success, Confederate cavalry led by Brig. Gen. John McCausland managed a stunning raid across the Pennsylvania border into the town of Chambersburg and put it to the torch. This destruction was in retaliation for the damage Hunter had done earlier in the summer in the Shenandoah, which included the burning of the Virginia Military Institute at Lexington along with some of the buildings in the town itself. The cadets from VMI already had been called up and had fought alongside Early's men during the beginning of Early's campaign, so the institute was empty at the time of Hunter's action. Still, the wanton destruction of the school at which

Stonewall Jackson had served on the faculty had been a blow to Confederate pride and morale, leading to McCausland's equally wanton destruction of Chambersburg.

Even before the Chambersburg raid, Grant and Lincoln were determined not to allow the Confederates to have free reign in the Shenandoah Valley. Without the valley, food shortages might become critical enough for the Southerners to bring about the end of the war. Thus forcing the Confederates out of the area became a strategic goal for the Yankee leaders. Yet Generals Sigel and Hunter both had failed to accomplish the task. When he pondered the matter, Grant had it in mind to place someone else in charge, someone he was confident could capture the valley.

That man was the head of his cavalry, Gen. Philip H. "Little Phil" Sheridan.

THE SKY to the east was turning pink and orange with the approach of dawn as Titus knelt at the top of the ridge. To his right was Colonel Mosby, and beyond Mosby crouched John Russell, Mosby's most dependable scout. Two more rangers accompanied the small party that had come to see the large Federal wagon train for themselves.

A hundred yards below, at the base of the ridge, the turnpike from Berryville to Winchester ran past the sturdy brick sanctuary of the Buck Marsh Baptist Church. Supply wagons were parked along the road as far as the eye could see in both directions. From where he was, Titus estimated he could see a hundred of the large, canvas-covered vehicles. The wagons were bound for Sheridan's Army of the Shenandoah, which was camped to the south along Cedar Creek, facing Early's Army of the Valley. So far during Sheridan's initial foray into the Shenandoah, there had been no major battles, only a few skirmishes. But that might soon change.

"There they be, Colonel, just like I told you," Russell said. "And them Yankee guards don't look none too wakeful, neither."

That was true enough, Titus thought. He could see several of the pickets dozing as they leaned on their rifles. The idiots had no idea what was lurking near them in the darkness.

"All right," Mosby said. "John, you and Titus gallop back to Captain Chapman and have him bring up the men."

The two men nodded.

Titus had been with the rangers only a little over a month, but during that time, Mosby had come to trust him. Mosby had seen that Titus was every bit the fighter he claimed to be, and for his part, Titus had surprised even himself by how well he fit in with these partisans. Taking orders had always been hard for him, but it was easier when the orders came from men like Mosby and Adolphus "Dolly" Richards and the Chapman brothers, William and Samuel. They were Mosby's captains, his company commanders, and they fought alongside the men they led with as much ferocity and dedication as Mosby himself. As a member of Richards's company, Titus had participated in several raids, each one of which had been a rousing success. They had made life miserable for Hunter, and now they were continuing to harass Sheridan.

Titus and Russell slipped back from the crest of the ridge and found their horses. They led the animals for a short distance before mounting up, so that the galloping hoof beats wouldn't be heard by the sleepy guards at the Federal wagon train.

Streamers of mist swirled around the wagons as the partisans moved into position. Mosby strung out his men so he could strike up and down the length of the column at the same time. The rangers had two cannons in their tiny artillery detachment, and Mosby sent word along the line that the signal for the attack would be a volley from those guns.

Richards's company was to the left. Titus waited among them, impatience growing within him as the sky grew lighter. If Mosby delayed too long, the sun would be up and the Yankees were liable to see them coming. Titus wondered if something had gone wrong with the artillery.

Finally, one of the cannons roared, sending a shell screaming down on the wagon train to burst with a large explosion. Only one round was fired, but as tense as Titus and his companions were, that was enough to spark them into action. Yelling at the top of their lungs, they charged down the slope. The second round from the cannon blasted through the still morning air as they charged.

A few of the guards, startled out of their half-slumber, managed to lift their rifles and get a shot off, but their resistance was feeble. From the looks of their reactions, most of the Yankees were scared out of their wits. They dropped their weapons and turned to run. Only a few of them had the presence of mind to scramble over to a low stone wall at the edge of the churchyard and throw themselves behind it.

Once they reached that cover, however, they began putting up a fight. Titus saw muzzle flashes from the top of the wall as the crouching Yankees opened fire on their attackers. A man to Titus's right grunted and nearly fell off his horse as one of the bullets struck him. Still the man was able to maintain his balance and continue firing.

Titus's revolvers bucked in his hands as he veered his mount toward the stone wall. At a dead run, he put the horse into a leap that sent it soaring over the wall. Gripping the horse with his knees, Titus fired his pistols right and left as he landed among the Yankees. At least one man went down under the slashing hooves of the animal.

One of the Federal officers screamed for his men to retreat. They didn't waste any time doing so, scurrying away from the wagons and taking off across the field behind the church. Rangers who had circled around beyond the turnpike were waiting for them, however, and as the sun rose a short time later, it was a dispirited bunch of prisoners in blue who were herded off from the scene of the raid.

Titus joined happily in looting the wagons, as Mosby's men helped themselves to anything that might come in handy. Several of the vehicles were driven into Berryville and turned over to the townspeople, who greeted this unexpected bounty with shouts of acclaim for Mosby and the rangers. The citizens turned out to cheer again later when the rangers rode through on their way back to Mosby's Confederacy on the other side of the Blue Ridge. In this part of the world, there was no one better loved than the Gray Ghost and his men.

And even though it surprised him a little, Titus found himself proud to be one of them.

⟨🙰⟩

WITH HIS supply train crippled by the Berryville raid and with Early's Confederates dug in atop Fisher's Hill on the other side of Cedar Creek, Philip H. Sheridan took a cold-eyed look at the situation and decided it was time to pull back to Harpers Ferry. Besides, he had reports from his scouts that more Confederate troops were moving up to reinforce Early. The Federal commander was determined to drive the Rebels out of the Shenandoah Valley, but for now, he could afford to bide his time. In retreating, however, he continued the tactic, relatively new for this war, of burning fields and barns and even houses along his path.

Several days later, Titus was riding with a group of rangers along a country lane that meandered through the valley. Bob McCulloch, the red-bearded man Titus had encountered when he joined the rangers, rode beside him. Titus had no real friends among the partisans, keeping to himself as he did, but he was as close to McCulloch as any of them, he supposed. At the moment, he wished he could be farther away, because McCulloch had a fiddle tucked under his chin and was sawing on it with a bow as he rode. The fiddle was one of many confiscated from a Yankee supply wagon a few days earlier, and McCulloch's music reminded Titus of a cat being tortured.

After the racket had gone on for a while, he exclaimed, "Good Lord, Bob, my ears are gonna start bleedin' if you keep that up."

McCulloch grinned over at him. "What's the matter, don't you like music?"

"Not particularly. If I did, I'd haul off and shoot you for the sins you're committin' against it with that damned fiddle."

McCulloch laughed and sawed harder at the strings. Titus rolled his eyes and shook his head.

The riders were approaching a stone bridge. Ever since the raid on the wagon train, Mosby's men had scattered over the countryside, breaking into smaller groups to harass any Yankees they came across. The bunch Titus was with had had several fights with Union patrols over the past couple of days, but nothing serious. None of the men had even been scratched.

Titus knew that run of luck couldn't continue, but he was going to enjoy it as long as it lasted. As far as he was concerned, this was a great life, and he was happier than he had been in months. Most of the time, he could put away thoughts of his captivity at Camp Douglas and all the tragic events that had followed his return to Culpeper County. He hadn't had any nightmares about Ebersole or about Polly's death for several weeks. He was a little worried about Mac, though. Fitz Lee's cavalry had come to the Shenandoah to reinforce Early's army, and Titus had heard that several sharp little battles had taken place between the Union and Confederate cavalries.

As they came up to the bridge, there was a flash of movement and color from the bank of the stream. Titus reacted instinctively, snaking his revolvers from their holsters and pivoting in the saddle to make himself a smaller target. He thumbed back the hammers, ready to fire if this was a Yankee ambush.

"Hold it!" McCulloch shouted. "Don't shoot, Titus! It's just a girl!"

So it was, Titus realized as he struggled to keep his reactions under control. The young woman had started up toward the road but had stopped short as Titus drew his pistol. Now she stood there halfway up the bank, her arms half-lifted to show that she was unarmed. Slowly, a smile began to spread across her face.

"I don't reckon y'all have to shoot me," she said. "I'm not that dangerous."

Titus wasn't so sure about that. The longer he looked at her, the harder his heart pounded.

She was eighteen or nineteen, he judged, and at first glance her resemblance to Polly was enough to make the painful memory stab through him. But when he took a second look at her, he saw that other than having blonde hair, she didn't look anything at all like Polly. And her hair was a much darker shade of blonde, at that. Nor was she as pretty as Polly had been. When she grew older, she would the sort of woman known as handsome rather than beautiful. But she had an undeniable appeal about her. Titus lowered the hammers and slid the weapons back into their holsters.

"What the hell are you doin' out here, girl?" he asked gruffly.

"Why, I live just over yonder," she said, pointing to a farmhouse visible in the distance.

"Ain't you Jed Wiley's girl?" McCulloch asked suddenly.

"That's right." She frowned at him. "I know you. You're the McCulloch boy. Your folks had the farm that's the Cameron place now." The frown disappeared, replaced by a smile that made Titus reconsider a little. Maybe she really was pretty after all. "You used to be sweet on me."

McCulloch turned red, looked down at the ground, and stammered a little. "Did not!"

"Yes, I think you were." She looked at Titus again. "I'm Danetta Wiley."

Titus gave a curt tug on the brim of his hat. "Pleased to meet you, miss. You ain't seen any Yankees hereabouts, have you?"

"Nary a Yankee all day." She waved a hand toward the creek. "Of course, I've been down there fishing. I haven't really been looking for Yankees."

Didn't that beat all? Titus thought. They were in the middle of a war, with patrols from both sides ranging up and down the valley trying to kill each other, and this girl had been calmly fishing on the creekbank.

"You better run along home," he said. "Some of Sheridan's men come along, you're liable to wish they hadn't caught you out here alone."

"I'm not alone."

Titus looked around, not seeing anyone else. "You're not?"

"No." Danetta Wiley reached under the apron she wore over her homespun dress and pulled out an ancient pistol that looked almost half as big as she was. "I've got this old horse pistol for company."

Titus frowned. "Will that thing even shoot?"

"Oh, it'll shoot, all right," Danetta said.

"But can you hit anything with it?"

"Don't ask her that," McCulloch said quickly. "Even when she was a kid, she could shoot rings around me."

"Is that so?" Titus regarded the girl coolly.

"You come over to my house sometime," Danetta said. "I'll show you how I can shoot, Mr. . . . . What is your name, anyway?"

"Brannon. Titus Brannon."

"You come calling on me, then, Mr. Titus Brannon."

"Well, you're mighty forward, ain't you?"

"I figured we'd be shooting, not sparking."

Titus couldn't stop the laugh that burst out of him. It felt strange. It had been a long time since he'd laughed like that.

"All right, Miss Wiley. If I can, I'll take you up on that invite. For shootin', not sparkin'."

She nodded. "All right, then. Now, if you boys would just ride on, I'd be obliged. You're scaring the fish."

Grinning and chuckling, the rangers rode on over the bridge and down the lane. Titus hipped around in the saddle to look back toward the creek.

"Is that girl touched in the head?" he asked McCulloch. "She acted mighty strange."

"That's just the way Danetta is. You'll figure that out if you're around her long enough."

"I don't plan on it," Titus said.

And yet the idea of spending more time with Danetta Wiley and getting to know her didn't sound bad to him. Not half bad at all.

A COUPLE of days later, Lt. Col. William Chapman and three companies of rangers—not including Dolly Richards's company—came across a group of Union cavalrymen burning houses in broad daylight. They were members of Brig. Gen. George A. Custer's Michigan cavalry, and Custer had ordered the destruction in response to the shooting a few nights earlier of a sentry.

Chapman and his men swept down on the surprised Yankees as they were about to set fire to the house belonging to a man named Benjamin Morgan. Caught up in the fervor of battle, Chapman shouted, "No quarter! Take no prisoners!" The fighting was swift, furious, and merciless. Within minutes, all of the Federals lay dead except one. The lone survivor feigned death and so was spared when the rangers rode away.

A few days later Titus was sitting under a shade tree with Mosby and a number of other rangers when Chapman came up, his face dark with rage above his beard.

"The Yankees are saying we killed those men at Morgan's place in cold blood! One of them survived, and he claims we took prisoners, lined them up, and executed them!"

"That's not the way you reported the incident to me, Colonel," Mosby said calmly.

"That's not the way it happened. What that Yankee says is a damnable lie!"

Titus wasn't sure why anyone cared. Killing Yankees, whether in the heat of battle or executing them by a firing squad, was all the same to him. The results were dead enemies, and that was all that mattered. But Chapman seemed offended by the whole thing. Even though he had gotten along well so far in the partisans, Titus thought, in some ways he would never completely understand them, would never be fully one of them.

"They'll think we've declared open season on them," Mosby mused. "And chances are, they'll try to strike back in kind." He looked around at his men. "We'd best spread the word, boys. Tell everyone you can find who's ever helped us, on either side of the Blue Ridge, to keep a sharp eye out for the Yankees. They're not to fight if the Federal cavalry comes to their places. They should leave that to us and preserve their lives and the lives of their families."

"But what about the havoc the Yankees are liable to wreak?" Chapman asked.

"We'll pay it back when the time comes," Mosby said. "Every bit of it."

Titus stood up and edged over to Bob McCulloch. He nudged the red-bearded man with his elbow. "What say we volunteer to ride over to the Wiley place and warn them?"

McCulloch snorted. "I should've knowed it. One look at Danetta, and you've swooned over her."

"The hell you say! I'm just tryin' to do what the colonel said we should do."

"Sure, sure," McCulloch said with a grin. "I reckon you figure tonight about dinnertime would be the right time to go?"

Titus couldn't help but return the grin. "Sounds like a good enough plan to me."

CHAPTER

DANETTA WILEY met them in the yard in front of the farmhouse as they rode up.

"Well, Mr. Brannon," she greeted Titus, "have y'all come to see me shoot?"

"Not really," Titus said, "but if you're bound and determined to show off, I reckon I can watch."

"Show off, is it? We'll see about that." Danetta waved a slender hand toward the neat farmhouse behind her. "Come on in. We were about to sit down to supper. But I'll bet you knew that, didn't you, Bob McCulloch?"

The red-bearded McCulloch stumbled over his words and finally gave up. "It was Titus's idea!" he blurted out.

Titus grinned as he swung down from the saddle. "Bob didn't put up much of an argument."

Danetta came up to McCulloch and poked a finger against his ample belly, making the flush on his face deepen. "No, I'll bet he didn't," she said.

"Dadgum it, Danetta—"

"Oh, I'm just fooling with you, Bob." She patted his bearded cheek. "Come on in the house. You're mighty welcome, you and Mr. Brannon both."

"Titus," he said.

"I haven't known you all my life, Mr. Brannon, like I have Bob here."

Titus shrugged. "Whatever you say, Miss Wiley."

She ushered them into the house and introduced them to the rest of her family: her parents, Jed and Lucinda Wiley; two brothers, Aaron and Andrew; and two little sisters, Jessie and Peggy. Danetta was the oldest of the siblings. They all remembered Bob from when he had lived nearby, and although Titus was a stranger, they immediately made him feel welcome.

"Do you come from a large family, Mr. Brannon?" Lucinda Wiley asked him as they sat down to dinner around a long table with an Irish linen cloth on it.

"I have three brothers and a sister," Titus replied. "I had another brother, but he fell a couple of months ago at Cold Harbor. He was the oldest."

"We're mighty sorry to hear that, son," Jed Wiley said. "How about your folks? Are they still livin'?"

"My ma is. My pa passed away several years ago, long before the war."

"If he was a good Southern man, that might've been a blessin'. At least he didn't have to see what a sorry state things have gotten in. Never thought I'd see the day when Yankees would be runnin' roughshod over good honest folks."

"That's one reason we're here, Mr. Wiley," McCulloch put in. "Colonel Mosby sent the rangers spreadin' out all over to warn people that the Yankees may be attackin' civilians again."

Wiley snorted in disgust. "When did they ever stop?"

"It may get worse," Titus said. "They have it in their heads that our boys executed some of them when we caught 'em burnin' down houses. That ain't the way it happened, but you know Yankees. They ain't overly bright."

"We'll keep a sharp eye out for them," Wiley promised. "My old scattergun will give 'em a warm welcome if they try anything around here."

McCulloch shook his head. "No sir, that's exactly what Colonel Mosby don't want. He says it's more important for you folks to save your families. Let the Yankees have their way for now. We'll see to it they pay for whatever they do."

"Pay how? You don't expect me to stand by and do nothin' while some damn Yankee puts the torch to my house, do you?"

Lucinda patted her husband's arm. "Now, don't get all wrought up, Jed. These boys are right. A house can be rebuilt, but once a man goes to his grave, he never comes back. And the same can be said for his children."

"Maybe not, but it don't seem right not to fight."

One of the boys—Titus thought it was Andrew—said, "We'll help you fight them Yankees, Pa."

"You most certainly will not!" Lucinda snapped.

"Maybe we'll just run off and join the army," the other boy said. "Then we can fight Yankees!"

Danetta reached over and slapped the back of his head. "You hush that talk! Nobody's running off to join the army—unless it's me." She looked at Titus. "You think Colonel Mosby would let me be a ranger?"

"Aw, that's crazy!" McCulloch burst out. "Girls can't be rangers!"

"I don't know," Titus said coolly. "I reckon it depends on how good you can shoot."

"If there's still enough light after supper, I'll show you."

The sun was still up, though low to the horizon, when Titus and Danetta walked outside the farmhouse. She led him over to the barn, where she picked up an empty burlap sack. "Let me see your knife," she said.

Titus slid the knife from its sheath on his left hip and handed it to her, hilt first. She took it and with one smooth movement drove the blade into the wall of the barn, pinning the burlap sack to it.

"Come on," she said as she started striding away.

Titus followed her. When she had paced off a good distance, she turned and reached under her apron.

"You carry that hogleg with you all the time?" Titus asked.

"Mostly," Danetta replied as she took out the old pistol. She had to use both hands as she cocked and leveled it, but Titus noted that the barrel was rock-steady. Danetta barely seemed to aim before she pressed the trigger. The old pistol roared and the sack hanging on the barn wall jerked a little as the bullet hit in the middle of it. Without lowering the weapon, Danetta cocked it and fired again. Titus's keen eyes saw that the second hole was practically on top of the first one. She fired twice more, and when she was finished, Titus could have covered all four holes with the palm of his hand.

With a triumphant smile, Danetta turned to him. "What do you think? Pretty good shooting for a girl, isn't it?"

Titus was willing to give credit where credit was due. "Pretty good shooting for anybody," he said. Then he reached down, palmed his revolver from its holster, and fired four shots from the hip, the blasts coming so close together they sounded almost like one long roar. As the echoes died away, cheering came from the front porch of the farmhouse. Titus glanced in that direction and saw that Bob McCulloch and the rest of the Wileys had come outside. The two boys, Aaron and Andrew, were the ones doing the cheering.

The center of the burlap sack was in tatters now, shot to pieces by Titus and Danetta. She gave him a look and said, "Now who's showing off?"

"You're a good shot," Titus said without answering the question, "but you still can't be a ranger. And don't you go tryin' that if the Yankees come here, either. You'll just get yourself killed if you do."

"We just met," Danetta murmured. "Why do you care what happens to me, Mr. Brannon?"

"Damned if I know," he said. "But I do."

His eyes met hers in the fading light, and as Titus looked at her, he felt things stirring inside him that he had thought were dead and gone forever.

In a way, he wished they still were.

Chapter Twenty-four

SHERIDAN HAD PULLED BACK after the Berryville raid, but the respite did not last long. As August turned into September, the Federals advanced into the valley again. Perhaps unwisely, Early had sent some men on a foraging expedition into the Blue Ridge Mountains. When Sheridan got wind of this, he struck quickly, bringing about a fight near the town of Winchester, the third battle in that location. This time, the Confederates were defeated, and Early was forced to withdraw, though without Gen. Robert Rodes, who was mortally wounded. The Army of the Valley didn't go far, setting up another defensive line at Fisher's Hill.

The Yankees continued to press the attack, and once again Early had to retreat. This time the withdrawal turned into a rout as the Confederate lines collapsed and the soldiers fled before waves of Union infantrymen. It was an ignominious defeat and left Sheridan largely in control of the Shenandoah Valley.

This was not the only setback suffered by the Confederates in the Shenandoah in September 1864. Even before the battles at Winchester and Fisher's Hill, John S. Mosby was wounded during a scouting mission in Fairfax County. It was only a minor skirmish between a few men on each side, fought with pistols and quickly over, but Mosby was struck in the groin by a bullet that ricocheted off his pistol. The fact that the bullet had spent most of its force might have saved the colonel's life. But he would be out of action for a time. In his absence, William Chapman was in charge of the rangers, so at least the command was still in good hands.

Early's defeat and withdrawal had little effect on the rangers. All during the campaign, they had operated in the rear of the Federal army, cutting supply lines and disrupting communications. Nothing changed as they continued to raid.

Late in September, during a foray into the valley led by Sam Chapman, the rangers attacked a group of Federal cavalry near Front Royal that turned out to be a larger group than they thought. On the verge of being trapped, the partisans had to fight their way free, which they did with few casualties. During the chaos of battle, a Yankee lieutenant named McMasters, unhorsed and attempting to surrender, was shot and mortally wounded. He survived long enough to accuse the rangers of gunning him down in cold blood. In the meantime, six of the rangers were taken prisoner.

Enraged by the lieutenant's death, the Union cavalry commanders—Gens. George Armstrong Custer, Wesley Merritt, Alfred Torbert, and Charles Russell Lowell—met in Front Royal and decided to make an example of the captured rangers. Four were executed by firing squads in front of the townspeople; one of those four, a young man who lived in the area, was killed in front of his horrified mother, who pleaded for his life to be spared but was herself threatened by a Yankee officer's saber. The other two rangers were hanged, and a sign was placed on the body of one of them as it dangled from the limb of a walnut tree.

It read: This will be the fate of Mosby and all his gang.

⊘)))))⦰

"THAT BASTARD Custer!" Titus raged as he stalked across a clearing in the woods where the rangers had camped the night before. "Somebody ought to string him up by that long yellow hair of his!"

"Take it easy, Titus," Bob McCulloch advised. "We don't know that it was Custer who ordered those killin's."

"He was there!" Titus insisted. "Him and Merritt and Torbert and Lowell. Far as I'm concerned, they're all to blame! Bunch of stinkin' murderers!"

The news of the executions at Front Royal had spread like wildfire on both sides of the Blue Ridge. At the moment, Titus and McCulloch were in the Shenandoah along with a dozen or so other rangers, scouting supply lines in preparation for a raid. A short time earlier, as the rangers were getting ready to depart, a dispatch rider galloped into camp bearing a message from Mosby, who had returned to command a couple of days earlier. The letter briefly detailed the atrocity. Just thinking about it set off an inferno of anger inside Titus.

"Next Yankee I get my hands on, I'm stringin' him up from the closest tree," he vowed.

"You can't do that," McCulloch insisted. "Just 'cause the Yankees are like that don't mean we have to be."

Titus swung around toward him. "You ever see a rattlesnake?"

"Why, sure," McCulloch replied with a confused frown.

"Well, when you see one, do you worry about whether or not you're sinkin' down to his level, or do you just chop the son of a bitch's head off?"

McCulloch shook his head. "It ain't the same thing."

"It sure as hell is."

McCulloch sighed and walked off, seeing that he wasn't going to be heard in this argument. Titus didn't want to continue it, either. He'd had more than his fill of wrangling about honor and such with Nathan Hatcher. And where was Nathan now? Either dead or in a Yankee prison again, which pretty much amounted to the same thing.

Worrying about doing the right thing where the Yankees were concerned was a waste of time. There was only one right thing to do, and that was to kill them—as many of them as possible, in any way possible.

A short time later, the rangers mounted up and rode on. Their route was going to take them near the Wiley farm, and Titus hoped he would have a chance to stop by and see Danetta, even if only for a few minutes. During the past few weeks, he had visited the farm several times, and on each occasion he had managed to spend some time alone with Danetta. She made fun of him for courting her in the middle of a war, and he insisted that he wasn't courting her at all, that the only reason he stopped by the farm was for her mother's cooking. But they both knew that wasn't true, and the last time he'd been there, as the two of them stood on the front porch after supper, Titus had taken her in his arms and kissed her. Danetta had returned the kiss with an ardor that surprised him.

"I need to know more about you, Titus Brannon," she'd whispered when she broke the kiss.

"Ask anything you want." He had told her already that he'd been in a Yankee prison camp and a little about his family. He wasn't sure what else she might want to know.

"Have you ever had a steady girl? I reckon you must have, as handsome as you are."

He'd grinned as he slipped his arms around her waist. "You should've seen me when I got out of that camp. I wasn't too handsome then, let me tell you."

"What about girls, Titus? That's what I asked you."

He knew her well enough by now to know that she wasn't going to be put off when she really wanted something. Growing more solemn, he said, "I was married for a while."

"Was?"

"My wife . . . died."

"Oh." Danetta's voice was hushed and a little regretful, as if she were sorry she had started this conversation. "Do you have any children?"

"No. No children."

"I'm sorry—"

"Don't be," he had told her. "The way everything worked out, I reckon it was better there weren't any kids involved."

"I see. Well, I believe I'll understand if you don't want to talk about it . . ."

"I don't," Titus had said.

"We'll discuss something else then."

And so they had, but Titus knew that Danetta hadn't forgotten about that subject. If she wanted to know all the details of his personal life, that had to mean she was getting serious about him. He wasn't sure if he liked that idea or not. Part of him did, but another part said that he had grown too close to her already. He cared about something again, and he hadn't wanted to do that.

Now, as he rode toward the Wiley farm with the other rangers, he thought about Danetta, and to his surprise he thought about Louisa Abernathy, too. She had been in love with him, or at least she had convinced herself that was the case. That was the only way she could justify to herself everything she had done. She had helped bring about the deaths of several men, and she had abandoned her religion and committed fornication, but it had all been for love.

Titus had never returned that love, had never even pretended to. He had used Louisa to help him escape and later had taken what he wanted from her, but he never had promised her anything in return. And that had never bothered him, either . . . until now. When he thought about what Danetta might think of him if she knew the whole story, he felt uneasy inside, like there were bugs crawling around inside him.

Luckily, Danetta didn't know anything about it. Titus was going to see to it that things stayed that way.

Rumor had it that the Yankees were about to send some supply wagons through this way. Up ahead there was a fold in the hills that would make a good spot for an ambush. Even this small group of rangers could stop a wagon train if it tried to go through the narrow gap. As soon as one of the local farmers had told Titus about the wagons he'd spotted the day before, Titus knew what he was going to do. He and the others had ridden hard to get ahead of the wagon train, and they would be ready when the Yankees got to the gap.

The ridgeline appeared ahead. Beyond that, far to the west, a blue haze on the horizon marked the Allegheny Mountains, which formed the border with the breakaway state of West Virginia. Titus and his companions were deep in enemy-held territory. That fact would have made most men nervous, Titus supposed, but he didn't mind. He seldom felt better than when he was on the lookout for a fight.

Bob McCulloch jogged his horse up alongside Titus's. "I reckon you'll be wantin' to stop by the Wiley place."

Titus thought about it then regretfully shook his head. "Not now. When we're done. We can't afford to take the time, not with that Yankee wagon train somewhere behind us."

"You reckon a couple of the boys ought to drop back and make sure the Yankees are really back there?"

"They're there, all right," Titus said confidently. "I can smell the bastards."

It was true that his instincts never let him down. He could sense trouble before it struck, which was one reason Mosby and the Chapman brothers and Dolly Richards had given him more and more responsibility, until now he was leading his own band of partisans. He could feel the Yankees in his bones, and he knew that before this day was over, he and his friends would strike a hard blow against them.

The rangers rode on, the miles falling behind them. By midmorning, they were at the gap in the hills. The ridge rose almost sheer on its eastern side, but there were trails that led to the top on the western side. All Titus and his men had to do was climb up there where they could pour fire down onto the hapless wagon drivers and guards. The Yankees would never know what hit them.

Titus's lips drew back in a grin as he paused to look at the gap. "Let's get up there and get ready," he said. "I feel like killin' me some Yankees today." He heeled his horse into a trot and rode between the bluffs that loomed on both sides.

He was halfway through the gap when he heard the sudden blast of a gun and the wind-rip of a bullet close beside his head. Behind him, one of the men grunted in pain, and another yelled a curse. "Darby's hit!"

Titus bit back a curse of his own and wheeled his horse around. As he did so, he heard another slug whip past him. More shots roared toward the rangers, echoing in the pass. A horse screamed. Bob McCulloch crowded his mount up beside Titus's. "A trap! It's a trap, Titus!"

So it was, a portion of Titus's mind thought coolly. He looked up and saw puffs of smoke rising from behind rocks and bushes and knew that the Yankees had ambushed him and the other rangers as neatly as he had planned to ambush them. That meant the rumor of the wagon train had been a trick and had either been planted by the Yankees or been told to him as an outright lie by the farmer, who had been paid off or threatened into cooperating. Either way, several of the rangers were wounded already, though still in their saddles, and bullets were still buzzing around them like hornets.

"Get back!" Titus shouted to his companions. "Get out of here!" Only some fast, hard riding would save them now.

But it would help if something distracted the Yankee ambushers a little. As the other men yanked their mounts around and kicked them into a run, Titus drew his revolvers and started blasting away at the slopes above him, twisting in the saddle so that he could throw lead in both directions. He aimed just below the puffs of powder smoke that marked the Yankees' hiding places, and he was willing to bet that he nicked one or two of them. The rate of fire lessened a little, and he knew that the others had been forced to duck for cover.

The hammer clicked on an empty chamber. Titus was operating mostly on instinct now and hadn't realized that he had emptied the pistols. Using his knees to guide the horse, he sent the animal sidling toward the edge of the trail as he reached in his pocket for reloads. He never carried less than three, fully loaded, for each weapon, in addition to the one in the gun that normally had an empty chamber for the hammer to rest on. A bullet burned the horse's shoulder and made it jump while Titus was reloading. He clamped his knees tighter on the horse's flanks and finished switching the cylinders. He snapped the weapon closed and lifted it, ready to fire. For an instant, a memory of Danetta's face seemed to float in front of his eyes, but he forced it away.

"Titus!"

The shout came from Bob McCulloch. "Damn it!" Titus murmured as he looked along the path and saw the red-bearded ranger galloping back toward him. McCulloch had fled with the others at first, but he was returning, probably because he had realized Titus wasn't with them.

Didn't Bob realize that Titus didn't intend to escape? He had led them into this trap with his eyes wide open and his arrogant overconfidence. He could see that now. It was his fault, and he was willing to sell his life dearly to give the others a chance to get away. Now Bob was threatening to ruin everything. Titus waved his gun at him. "Get out of here, you stupid bastard!"

The next instant, McCulloch jerked then sagged forward in the saddle. Without thinking about what he was doing, Titus kicked his horse into a run and raced toward McCulloch. His revolvers slammed more shots at the Yankees as he rode.

McCulloch dropped his reins. Titus emptied one pistol and jammed it in its holster, then veered his horse to the side, slowing down and leaning over to snag the reins of McCulloch's mount as he passed. The horse squealed in pain and fright as its head was jerked around, but it came with him. Titus urged his horse to a run again, leading McCulloch's horse.

He almost dropped the reins when something ripped along his left side, but he managed to hang on. He knew a bullet had grazed him. Wet heat spread on his side. He was bleeding. But he knew the wound wasn't serious, nothing more than a chunk of meat being knocked out. McCulloch was hit harder. In those dizzying moments as he grabbed the horse, he had seen the growing bloodstain on Bob's shirt.

The Yankees were still shooting. Titus saw dirt kicked in the air by the bullets that plowed into the ground ahead of them. But they were out of the gap now and heading back into the open, rolling countryside of the Shenandoah Valley.

"We made it, Bob!" Titus shouted over his shoulder. "Son of a bitch! We made it!"

Then another rifle shot cracked in the distance, and Titus heard the unmistakable thud of the bullet striking flesh. He looked back in horror, thinking that McCulloch had been hit again, but as he twisted in the saddle, McCulloch's horse went down, spilling its rider and jerking the reins out of Titus's hand. The animal rolled over and came to a stop with blood pumping out of its side.

Titus hauled his horse to a stop and dropped to the ground. He ran back to where McCulloch was sprawled facedown, stunned. He bent, got his hands under McCulloch's arms, and lifted. "Come on, damn it! I ain't leavin' you here, Bob!"

McCulloch muttered something incoherent. Ignoring the continued pain of his own wound, Titus dragged the other ranger toward his waiting horse.

"You gotta help me, Bob. You're too big for me to lift up there in the saddle by myself. Come on, Bob!"

"He'p me . . . Titus," McCulloch muttered. "It . . . hurts . . ."

"Grab on . . . Here, get your foot in the stirrup . . . Blast it, Bob, you gotta give me a hand here!"

Titus glanced toward the gap. The Yankee cavalrymen would be galloping out of there in pursuit any minute now. Probably some of Blazer's Scouts, he thought as he struggled to get McCulloch mounted. That was a special Federal cavalry unit whose only job was to go after Mosby's rangers. Titus had heard of them but never encountered them until today. They might not even be scouts, he told himself. Didn't really matter, either. Dead was dead, no matter who killed you.

But now that he was out of the trap, he found that he wanted to live again. He wanted to see Danetta again. If that meant leaving McCulloch behind, so be it. He had wasted enough time wrestling with the wounded man.

"Get up there, you red-bearded ape!"

"Who you callin' . . . a ape?"

With that, McCulloch got his foot in the stirrup, tightened his hold on the saddle, and hauled himself up with Titus's help. Titus vaulted onto the back of the horse behind him and reached around to grab hold of the reins. His heels jabbed into the animal's flanks and sent it leaping forward.

"Hang on, Bob!" Titus called.

The other rangers were out of sight now, scattered to the four winds. The ones who were hurt would drift around to some of the farms where they could get help. As for Titus, he knew where he was headed. The Wiley farm.

But not until he'd lost any Yankees chasing them. He was damned if he was going to lead them to Danetta's door!

SHADOWS OF dusk were settling over the Wiley farm when Titus rode in that evening with Bob McCulloch slumped in the saddle in front of him. He had spent all day dodging first the Yankees who had chased them from the ambush site and later other Federal patrols that were in the area. The wound in his side had stopped bleeding, but he felt weak from the blood he had lost.

A lot more had poured out of the hole in McCulloch, so Lord only knew how *he* felt. Titus was sure Bob was still alive, though; from time to time he heard him muttering. He hadn't been able to understand a word of it, though.

Lamplight glowed yellow through the windows of the farmhouse as Titus reined his horse to a halt. "Hello, the house!" he called. "Men hurt out here!"

A moment later the front door banged open. Titus saw a figure start to dart out, and his heart gave a little jump as he recognized Danetta's shape silhouetted against the light behind her. But her father appeared behind her, grabbed her, and pulled her back.

"Who's out there?" Jed Wiley called out in warning, and Titus heard the pair of ominous clicks as the man eared back the hammers on both barrels of a shotgun. If Wiley thought he detected Yankee accents in the voice that answered, he was liable to fire.

"Titus Brannon! Take it easy, Mr. Wiley. I've got Bob McCulloch with me. We've both been hit."

"Well, why in blazes didn't you say so?" Wiley set the scatter-gun aside and hurried down from the porch, followed by Danetta. She leaped ahead and came up to the horse. Her hand caught hold of Titus's thigh.

"How bad are you hurt?" she asked in a tense voice.

"Just scratched. Bob's hit a lot worse."

Danetta turned her head. "Aaron! Andrew! Get over here and help Bob!"

The boys ran over and reached up for McCulloch. "Careful with him," Lucinda Wiley warned as she came up behind them. "Put him on the divan in the parlor."

"He's pretty bloody, ma'am," Titus warned, thinking of his own mother.

"You think I care about that?" Lucinda snapped. "Easy with him, boys, easy."

Come to think of it, Titus decided, Abigail Brannon proba-bly would have reacted the same way.

He waited until the Wiley boys had McCulloch off the horse and were half-leading, half-carrying him into the house. Then he swung a leg over the saddle and slid down. A wave of weak-ness and dizziness hit him as he did so, and he had to reach out and grasp the stirrup to steady himself.

Instantly, Danetta's arm was around him.

"I thought you said you weren't hurt bad," she accused.

"I ain't. It's just that I been dodgin' Yankees all day, and I'm a mite tired."

"Let's get you inside, too. Put your arm over my shoulders while I hold on to your waist."

"Sounds good to me," Titus said with a chuckle.

"Hush!"

She helped him into the house. McCulloch was stretched out on the divan already, and Lucinda was cutting away his shirt to expose the wound. Her face was grim but calm. Like most Shenandoah women, she had dealt with trouble in her life and knew that wailing and wringing her hands wasn't going to do any good. She would patch up the wounded man to the best of her ability and trust in the Lord to take care of the rest.

Danetta took Titus to the kitchen. Aaron and Andrew and the two little girls hovered around them, asking questions, wanting to know what had happened.

"Titus doesn't feel like talking now," Danetta told them as she lowered him into one of the chairs by the table. "Y'all go on and get out of here."

"Aw, Danetta . . ." one of the boys protested.

"You heard me. Scoot!"

The youngsters left reluctantly. Danetta turned to Titus as she ripped a linen towel to make some bandages. "Better get that shirt off so I can see how bad you're hit."

"Yes ma'am," Titus said. He was starting to feel a little light-headed. Maybe he would pass out right here, he thought. Maybe he was hurt worse than he thought and was going to die. That thought sobered him, and he reached over to take hold of one of Danetta's hands.

"Danetta," he began, "I ain't never told you how I feel—"

"And right now, I'm not interested," she interrupted. "There'll be time for you to moon over me later, Titus Brannon. Right now I want to make sure you're not about to die on me."

"If a fella's got to go, that'd be a damned good place," he muttered.

"Hush," she said again, this time in a whisper. She turned her hand in his so that their fingers interlaced and squeezed hard for a second. With her other hand, she touched his face and looked down into his eyes. Then she swallowed and said in a more brisk, businesslike tone, "Take your shirt off."

"Yes ma'am."

Twenty minutes later, he was sitting there at the table with bandages around his ribs, a clean shirt draped over his shoulders, and a cup of coffee in his hands.

Jed Wiley had poured a dollop of brandy into the coffee, and that bracer had given Titus back most of his strength. Wiley sat on the other side of the table and listened as Titus explained what had happened. Danetta stood to one side, listening as well.

"You shouldn't ought to blame yourself, son," Wiley said. "You couldn't have known those blasted Yankees were waitin' up there."

"That's just it," Titus said. "I should have known. The Yankees just did to me what I planned to do to them."

Wiley shook his head. "You saved those boys, pure and simple. Saved Bob, too, if he pulls through."

"How's he doing?"

"I'll find out," Danetta said. She left the kitchen and went up the hall to the parlor. She was back a few moments later. Titus looked at her, his breath catching a little in his throat.

"He's alive," she said. "Ma says he's lost a lot of blood and she doesn't know how badly that bullet tore him up inside, but if he doesn't take the blood poisoning, she thinks maybe he'll make it."

Titus heaved a sigh of relief. "Thank God."

Now where had *that* come from, he wondered? He hadn't thanked God for anything in a long time, longer than he could remember. The past couple of years, during all the ordeals he had endured, if anybody had asked him, he would have said that God didn't exist, that the old boy was just a story that somebody made up.

The devil—now, the devil was real. Titus knew that for a fact, because he had met the son of a bitch more than once, usually wearing Yankee blue.

But once in the clothes of a rich plantation owner . . . He took a deep breath and forced memories of Ebersole and Polly out of his head.

"You see," Jed said. "You did save Bob's life, Titus. You're a hero, that's what you are."

Titus started to argue, then said silently to hell with it. They could think whatever they wanted to. He hadn't told Wiley and Danetta anything about how he'd been ready to abandon McCulloch and save himself. He would have done it if McCulloch hadn't come around enough just then to cooperate. As for staying behind in the gap to cover the retreat of the other rangers, there was nothing heroic about that. He'd just been trying to kill Yankees. It wasn't often he had so many willing targets.

So he didn't say anything. He just sat there and sipped the brandy-laced grain coffee and enjoyed the touch of Danetta's hands when she stood behind him and laid them on his shoulders. Her fingers were warm, and they squeezed his tired muscles just right.

The Yankees had gotten the best of him today . . . but there would be other days.

Chapter Twenty-five

THE EXECUTIONS OF THE six rangers captured at Front Royal and the hanging of another man captured later rankled Mosby to the point that, for the first time, he ordered a retaliation in kind. A few weeks after the atrocity, seven Federal prisoners were chosen by lot from a group of twenty-seven then taken to a spot close to Sheridan's headquarters. The seven were from the commands of Custer and Col. William Powell, whom Mosby blamed for the callous execution of his men. Four were to be shot, the other three hanged. Two of the men, however, escaped into the woods before they could be executed, and the other two were only wounded by the firing squad that was supposed to end their lives. The three fated to be hanged, though, all died with nooses around their necks. Their bodies were left dangling so that they would be sure to be found by the Yankees.

No messages were left on the bodies, but Mosby did write a letter to Sheridan, explaining why the seven prisoners had been put to death. It was clear that Mosby had finally had enough. He concluded with a warning: "Hereafter, any prisoners falling into my hands will be treated with the kindness due to their condition, unless some new act of barbarity shall compel me, reluctantly, to adopt a line of policy repugnant to humanity."

Mosby's message was sincere. He hoped there would be no more atrocities on either side during this conflict.

But as for new acts of barbarity by Sheridan . . . the Gray Ghost had not seen the end of those, nor had the people of the Shenandoah Valley.

◠ↀↀↀ◡

BOB MCCULLOCH swayed in a rocking chair on the front porch of the Wiley house as he tucked his well-worn fiddle under his chin with a flourish.

"If you go to playin' that thing, I'm leavin'," Titus warned from his perch on the steps, where he was sitting with Danetta.

She punched him lightly on the arm. "You hush, Titus Brannon. I like to listen to Bob play."

"But those noises don't even sound like music!"

"They do so!" Danetta smiled at McCulloch. "Bob, play 'Jeannie with the Light Brown Hair.' I love that one."

"Sure, Danetta," McCulloch said with a grin. He started sawing on the fiddle as Titus rolled his eyes and shook his head.

Despite the fact that McCulloch really was a terrible fiddle player, Titus was enjoying himself. He and a group of rangers had ridden in at midday, and Lucinda Wiley had offered to feed them. The other rangers were sitting around the yard or tending to their horses or dozing in the shade of the trees, well content for the moment after the big meal. Despite all the destruction carried out by the Yankees in the valley, some of the crops had been good, and compared to the situation in the eastern half of Virginia, food was much more plentiful here.

Titus was pleased, too, to see that Bob was doing better. For a while there, it had been uncertain whether he would survive his wound. But after a few weeks of care by the Wileys, the color had come back into his face and his strength had started to return. He was still a long way from being ready to ride again, but at least now he was strong enough to be up and around a little. He had eaten dinner with his friends then come out here on the porch to continue the camaraderie.

When McCulloch got to the end of the song, he lowered the fiddle and asked, "Want to hear another?"

"Maybe later, Bob," Danetta told him. "Right now I want to find out what's happening with the war." She looked at Titus.

"You're probably askin' the wrong person," he told her. "I don't know much more than what's happenin' right in front of me. I've heard, though, that General Early is waitin' for a new cavalry commander before he makes another move against the Yankees. Fitz Lee got himself wounded."

Danetta frowned. "Isn't your brother with General Lee?"

"That's right. Wherever Lee is, Mac usually ain't far away. He can take care of himself, though."

"He's your brother. Aren't you worried about him?"

"Sure I'm worried about him," Titus said with a shrug. Not only because Mac was his brother, but also because it had been Mac, along with Will, who had helped figure out that Israel Quinn was responsible for Polly's murder. But before that, Mac had been as quick as anyone else to jump to the conclusion that Titus was guilty. That knowledge tempered Titus's feelings of gratitude somewhat. Still, it would be nice to know that Mac was all right. Losing one brother was enough.

That would have to wait, though. Titus had work of his own to do. He couldn't go gallivanting off across Virginia in search of Mac just to check up on him.

"There's nothing I can do right now except hope for the best," he continued. "I figure there'll be another big fight between Early and Sheridan sooner or later. Maybe the rangers can get in on it. Until then, we're just going to keep on doin' what we can to make life miserable for Little Phil, that son of a—"

Danetta laughed as Titus stopped his sentence short. "I share the sentiment. I'm just too ladylike to express it in such bold terms."

Maybe so, but she wasn't too ladylike to be bold in other ways, Titus thought as he remembered the times they had strolled out in the moonlight during earlier visits. So far he hadn't done anything except hold her and kiss her, but that was enough to enflame his blood if he thought about it too much. He wasn't the sort of man to be patient about these things; he wanted what he wanted when he wanted it. He could force himself to wait if he had to . . . but there was a limit to how long he could do that.

"How about 'Turkey in the Straw'?" McCulloch suggested.

Danetta smiled at him. "Why sure, Bob. You go right ahead and play."

Titus tried not to groan.

An hour or so later, the rangers rode out, men and horses both well fed and well rested. Titus turned in the saddle to wave back at the Wileys and McCulloch, then took the lead. He didn't have anything in particular in mind; he and his small band were just going to drift up the valley today and take whatever Federal targets presented themselves.

A short time after leaving the farm, Titus caught a glimpse of the sun reflecting off something on top of a thickly wooded hill in the distance. He signaled a halt and took his field glasses from his saddlebags. Training them on the hilltop, his keen eyes made out a few figures moving around on the hill. They wore blue uniforms.

"Son of a bitch," Titus muttered as he lowered the glasses. "The Yankees are settin' up a signal post up there. They're puttin' up a tower and mirrors and everything."

"We goin' after them, Titus?" one of the other men asked.

Titus nodded. "Damn right." He turned and looked at the rangers. "We ain't takin' no prisoners, neither."

The men returned grim nods. Mosby's orders were plain on the subject: As long as the Yankees didn't execute any more prisoners, neither would the rangers. It was acceptable, however, to kill the enemy in battle. And if any Yankees should try to surrender, Titus planned not to notice.

He gestured toward a line of trees to the left, knowing that they marked the course of a nearby creek.

"We'll move up along the creek so they won't see us comin'," he instructed. "They've probably got pickets set out at the bottom of the hill, so we'll have to dispose of them first. Then we'll climb the hill and take the others by surprise."

It was a simple plan, but if they carried it out properly, it would be successful. Titus led the men over to the stream. They rode among the trees, moving slowly and carefully. As the creek curved toward the base of the hill where the Yankees were setting up their signal post, Titus silently gestured for the others to halt and dismount. They left their rifles on their horses. This would be close work, which meant knives first then revolvers, when stealth no longer mattered.

Titus remembered Will and Mac both reading books by that fella Fenimore Cooper, about early frontiersmen fighting Indians up in New York and places like that. Titus had never been much of a reader, but Will and Mac had told him all about the stories. As he slipped through the brush today, he figured that he was sneaking up on the Yankee pickets just like those Indians had gone after the early-day pioneers. A grin tugged at his mouth. Maybe he ought to scalp a few of them, just for good measure.

He put that thought out of his head. This was serious business. A moment later he halted, motioning for the men behind him to do so as well, and crouched behind a bush, silent and unmoving. His instincts told him that the pickets were close by. Ever since the day of the ambush, he had been less inclined to trust blindly in what his gut told him, but he knew not to ignore it completely, either.

After a few moments, Titus heard a cough and a rustle in the brush off to his right. He turned his head and gestured for some men to slip off in that direction. A few minutes after that, a gust of wind brought the smell of tobacco smoke to him from the left. One of the Union pickets had lit up a pipe. That might get him in trouble with his commanding officer—or at least it would have if the Yankee survived. Titus didn't intend for that to happen. He sent more men off to the left.

If there were Yankees to the right and left, that meant more than likely they were straight ahead, too. Titus took the remaining men and started forward again. After a moment, he parted some brush an inch or two and looked through the gap to see two Union soldiers lounging against tree trunks, holding the barrels of their rifles while the butts of the weapons rested on the ground at their feet.

Titus slipped his knife from its sheath and used his other hand to pick up a small rock from the ground. He flicked it over the heads of the pickets so that it landed in the woods behind them. The noise it made was slight but loud enough so that both Yankees heard it. They jerked upright.

"What the hell was that?" one asked.

"I don't know," the other man replied, "but we'd better find out. The colonel will have our hides if we let any of them damned Rebs sneak up here."

Too late, boys, Titus thought as the Yankees turned away. *We're already here.*

He exploded out of the brush, covering the distance between himself and the Yankees before the Union soldiers could even start to turn around. Another ranger was right on Titus's heels. Titus went for the Yankee on the right. His left arm looped around the man's neck and jerked back and up. The blade in his right hand flashed across the man's tightly drawn throat, cutting deep, almost to the bone. The only sound the Yankee made was a bubbling gurgle as he died, hot blood gushing over Titus's hand and wrist. A few feet away, the other picket jerked and spasmed in the grip of the second ranger.

Titus lowered the body to the ground. The other ranger gathered up the fallen rifles and passed them back to the others. They would be taken back and given to the man who was holding the horses. Good weapons always came in handy. Then Titus and the men with him began climbing the hill. Slowly, the other members of the band filtered in from left and right, and from the bloodstains they bore, Titus knew they had been successful in their mission to dispose of the other pickets.

The rangers were all together as they approached the top of the hill. Titus had eight men, not counting himself. He didn't know how many Yankees were up there, but he and his companions probably would be outnumbered. He was willing to take that chance, knowing that the rangers were fighting devils, each man worth several of the enemy.

At the beginning of the war, that had been the common belief throughout the South, that sheer numbers didn't matter as much as the courage and honor and fighting spirit of the Confederate soldiers. Three years of brutal combat had proven that idea to be false, at least most of the time.

But not always. In some cases, what was in the hearts of the men was still more important than how many of them there were. Titus knew that to be true of the rangers.

He heard the Yankees talking, officers calling orders, enlisted men complaining under their breath. Following Titus's hand-signaled commands, the rangers spread out so that they could attack in a line. Crouching, Titus drew his pistol, looked at the men on his left and right and nodded. With his legs driving powerfully, he surged up the last few feet of the slope and charged out onto the relatively level hilltop. His Rebel yell split the air.

His eyes took in the scene instantly, noting the positions of the Yankees. Several were directly in front of him. Startled, they wasted precious seconds by whirling around to gape at him. He put a bullet right through the open mouth of one of the men.

The Yankees began to grab for their weapons as Titus triggered his revolvers. Two more men went down. All around the hilltop, guns blazed and men in blue crumpled under the withering fire of the rangers. Titus's momentum carried him among the Yankees. One of his pistols was empty now. He flipped it around and struck with the butt, caving in the skull of one man. His other gun still had a couple of rounds. He shot a hole in the chest of a shocked soldier and shouldered the dying man aside. A gun blasted close beside Titus's ear, deafening him for a moment as he whirled around and fired into the face of the Yankee behind him. He kicked another man in the groin then pulled out his knife and stabbed him as he doubled over in pain. Titus was a whirlwind of deadly motion, and all across the hilltop, the other rangers were attacking with an almost equal ferocity.

Titus was the only one, however, who laughed in delight as he fought.

The fight lasted only a few minutes. When it was over, all the Yankees were dead, just as Titus intended. One of the rangers had been killed, and a couple were wounded. Titus thought the wounded men would be all right. Some of the men began patching up their injured comrades while two others carried the dead man down the hill to the horses.

Titus studied the partially erected signal tower, thinking of the best way to destroy it. He had about decided to burn it down when one of the men called sharply, "Titus! Look over yonder!"

He turned and strode to the edge of the hill. As he peered through the clear October air, his pulse began to hammer. Columns of smoke rose from one side of the valley to the other, as far as the eye could see. Short distances separated some of the columns, but others were so close together that they took on the appearance of a solid wall of smoke.

"My God," one of the rangers breathed. "The whole valley's on fire."

That was what it looked like, all right. But what really horrified Titus, what made him stare across the familiar countryside in a mixture of fear and disbelief, was that one of the black columns was climbing into the sky over the Wiley farm.

After being frozen there for a couple of seconds that seemed much longer, Titus exploded into motion with a choked cry of "Danetta!" He started bounding down the slope, heedless of the brush that ripped and clawed and tore at him, the tree limbs that smacked into him. He was blind with fear, knowing only that he had to get to the horses and back to the farm as fast as he could. The other rangers followed him, but he wasn't aware of them.

He threw himself in the saddle, ripped the reins from the hand of the man holding them, and kicked his horse into a run. His heels jabbed the animal's flanks mercilessly, and he slashed its shoulders with the trailing end of the reins, trying to get more speed out of it. After a few minutes, horse and rider reached a narrow lane that led toward the Wileys. He urged the animal on.

If Danetta was hurt . . . But she couldn't be. He wouldn't allow himself to believe it or even consider it. She would be all right. Mosby had made it plain to the citizens of the valley. They were to let the rangers do the fighting and not try to stop the Yankees themselves.

But that was hard to enforce where proud men like Jed Wiley were involved. Wiley had spent years taking care of his family and his land. He wasn't the sort of man to stand by while either of those things was threatened.

Titus had been so careful not to lead the Yankees to the Wiley farm when he and Bob McCulloch were wounded in the ambush. He knew they sometimes targeted the places belonging to people who gave aid to the rangers. But today was different. From what he had seen up there on the hill, the Yankees were sweeping through the entire valley in an orgy of flame and destruction. It didn't matter whether their victims had ever lifted a finger to help the rangers. The Yankees were raining down hell on them anyway, Titus thought as the wind brought tears to his eyes.

He flung the horse around bends in the road, and finally, the farm came into sight. The fields were burning, as were the barns and the blacksmith shop and the smokehouse. But the farmhouse still stood, and at the sight of it, Titus's heart leaped with hope. Maybe Danetta and the others were inside. Maybe the Yankees were going to spare them.

Then, while he was still a couple of hundred yards away, he saw a blue-clad figure running toward the house with a blazing torch in his hand. Titus hauled his horse to a stop and yanked his rifle from its sheath. He could never get within revolver range in time. He had to make the shot with the rifle.

Well-trained nerves and muscles took over. Titus snugged the butt of the rifle against his shoulder and laid his cheek against the smooth wood of the stock as he cocked the weapon. The rifle was a carbine from the Richmond Armory, a good gun but not the equal of Titus's old Sharps. He would have to have a little bit of luck on his side . . .

He squeezed the trigger. The rifle bucked against his shoulder. Through the cloud of smoke that billowed from the muzzle, he saw the Yankee stumble and fall, dropping the burning brand. A fierce exultation shot through Titus.

Suddenly, there were more Yankees in the yard between the house and the burning barn, and one of them scooped up the fallen torch and flung it as the others opened fire on the house. Titus cried out in futile anger as he saw Jed Wiley step out onto the porch and fire his shotgun at the invaders. One of the Yankees fell, but Wiley was thrown back against the wall of the house as bullets ripped through him.

The torch landed on the roof and quickly set it ablaze, flames shooting up. The house was doomed, and so were the people inside unless they got out. If they fled, the Yankees might shoot them down as they emerged. Titus couldn't let that happen. He had to give the Yankees something else to think about.

He jammed his heels into the horse's flanks and galloped between burning fields toward the house. A long, high-pitched Rebel yell came from his throat. At the same time, he drew his gun and switched cylinders.

The Yankees turned and opened fire on him. Bullets sliced the air around his head. He ignored them and started shooting, picking his targets and squeezing off his shots calmly and deliberately. Several of the Yankees were knocked off their feet by his lead. But Titus realized that he would be among them in mere seconds, and his gun would be empty by then. He wouldn't mind dying, though, if it meant that Danetta and the rest of the family got away safely.

Then more yells sounded behind him, and before his amazed eyes, the Yankees turned to run. Titus glanced over his shoulder. The rest of the rangers had caught up to him. Even the men who were wounded were riding to battle like avenging angels—or in this case devils, Titus thought, because with the fields burning all around them, they looked like they were charging straight out of hell.

They swept up to the farm and cut down the rest of the marauders. Smoke was everywhere now. Titus coughed wrackingly as he threw himself out of the saddle and stumbled toward the burning house. Figures loomed up in front of him. He recognized the two boys, Aaron and Andrew, and the two little girls.

Titus grabbed the girls and shoved them toward the rangers, shouting to his men, "Get the kids out of here!" He caught hold of Aaron's sleeve as the coughing, crying boy staggered past him. "Where's Danetta!"

Aaron waved a hand vaguely toward the house. Titus cursed and pushed him toward the rangers.

The roof over the porch was on fire, and flames leaped from the windows of the house. Titus bounded up onto the porch and saw Lucinda Wiley bent over the body of her husband, sobbing. There was so much blood on Wiley that Titus knew he must have been hit a dozen times. He had to be dead. Lucinda would be, too, if Titus didn't get her out of here in a hurry.

He bent and took hold of her arm and tried to drag her away. "Mrs. Wiley!" he shouted. "Come on! You've got to go!"

Desperately, she clung to her husband's body. "No! I can't go without Jed!"

"You can't help him now!"

But she wasn't listening. Titus picked her up bodily and swung her away toward the edge of the porch. She kicked and fought to get loose from him so that she could go back to her husband's side. One of the rangers was there. Titus thrust the hysterical woman into his arms and snapped, "Go!"

The man stumbled away into the coils of smoke, taking her with him. That left Danetta and Bob. Titus didn't know where they were, but since they weren't on the porch he knew he was going to have to venture into the house to look for them. Waves of scaring heat beat at him as he approached the open front door. He shielded his face as best he could with his left arm.

He didn't have to go far. McCulloch lay face down just inside the door, unmoving. A huge bloodstain covered the back of his shirt. Danetta knelt beside him, pulling at his shoulder, crying, "Bob! Bob, you've got to get up!"

McCulloch was never going to get up again, Titus knew. He counted three separate bullet holes in the back of the big man's shirt. He took Danetta's arm.

"He's dead!" Titus said, deliberately brutal about it so that he could get through to her. "You can't help him! Come on!"

She looked up at him, her face streaked with smoke and tears. "T-Titus?"

She came into his arms and he held her tightly for a moment, feeling her tremble in his embrace. Then he turned toward the edge of the porch, taking her with him. She started to struggle, saying, "We've got to help Bob!"

Titus heard timbers cracking. He held on to Danetta as he lunged to the edge of the porch and crashed through the railing, sending both of them flying through the air as the porch roof collapsed in an inferno of falling beams and bursting flames and swirling columns of smoke and sparks. Titus never let go of her as he rolled over and over, getting them as far away from the blaze as he could.

Then more of the rangers were there, grabbing them and helping them both up and guiding them to horses. Danetta came along without struggling now, her smudged face dull with the emotional numbness that must have had her in its grip.

Titus got her on the back of his horse and swung up behind her. With the rest of the rangers, they rode away from this corner of Hades.

But on this day, no matter where they went in the Shenandoah Valley, more flames awaited them. The whole valley was ablaze. Not a farm was untouched.

Phil Sheridan had had his revenge.

⚬〰〰〰⚬

"HE WAS playing 'My Old Kentucky Home' when the Yankees galloped up," Danetta said. "He was just sawing away on that fiddle and having the best time. And then he saw them coming and got up to run inside and warn us, and they shot him in the back just as he came in the door. Just shot him down like a dog."

Titus bent down and picked up the fiddle that lay in the rubble at the edge of what had been the Wiley farmhouse. The instrument was scorched but intact.

With an inarticulate cry, Titus smashed the remains of the fiddle over his knee.

"That won't bring him back," Danetta said, an accusatory tone in her voice. She waved a hand at the ruins of her home, still smoking the next day after the Yankee raid that people in the valley were already calling "The Burning." Danetta went on, "Nothing will bring any of it back. Not Bob, and not my father, and not our home or anybody else's home."

Titus swallowed, uncomfortable at the pain he heard in her voice. He wanted to do something to make it go away. "We'll make Sheridan and the Yankees pay for this," he said. "By God—"

"Pay?" Danetta cried out in a half-shriek as she turned toward him. "How can you make anybody *pay* for this? How can you put a price on what's happened to us?"

"I wasn't talking about money."

"Neither was I. Not even blood can pay for this. Not even rivers of blood." Danetta turned away from him and put her hands over her face. Her shoulders shook as she began to cry.

He reached out to her, touched her. "Danetta . . ."

She flinched away from his hand. "Go on," she told him bitterly. "Go fight the Yankees some more. You can raid them, they'll raid you, and it'll all go on until everything's dead and burned. Everything."

Titus stared at her unflinching back for a moment, knowing that never again would things be the same between them. He threw his hands in the air and tilted his head up to rage at the heavens. "Goddamn them! Goddamn them all!"

"But don't you see?" Danetta whispered. "They feel the same way about us."

〇⚏⚏⚏〇

AFTER THE Union victories at Winchester, Fisher's Hill, and later in October at Tom's Brook, it seemed that Sheridan was assured of victory in the Shenandoah Valley. So confident was he that he started back to Washington to confer with Secretary of War Edwin H. Stanton and army chief of staff Henry W. Halleck about his next move.

Jubal Early, hearing of Sheridan's departure, struck quickly on October 19, attacking the Union troops camped along Cedar Creek. This bold move was successful at first, as the Federals were forced to retreat. They pulled back to a defensive line north of the village of Middletown. There Sheridan, hearing news of the battle, rejoined his troops after racing back from the vicinity of Winchester. Rallying his men, he launched massive cavalry attacks that turned the tide of battle and sent Early's men scrambling backward. The Confederate withdrawal soon became a rout that did not end until it was well south of the original line of battle along Cedar Creek. Early had delayed long enough while the Yankees were on the defensive for Sheridan to have a chance to get back in the fight, and when Little Phil was on the field of battle once more, the Yankees had attacked and never looked back.

Now the Shenandoah Valley campaign really was over at last.

And a bloodied, starving Confederacy was left to wonder just how much more the fledgling country could withstand.